Phoenix Project
Murder By Stem Cells

Joe Bowden

To Wendy -
Joe Bowden
September 28, 2018

Published by Take Me Away Books, a Division
Of Winged Publications.

PHOENIX PROJECT – A CONSPIRACRY OF SILENCE

Copyright © 2018 by Joe Bowden

Editor: Cynthia Hickey

ISBN-13: 978-1-947523-04-3
ISBN-10: 1-947523-04-X

DEDICATION

To my wife, Elaine, the love of my life, for her patient understanding of periods of talking to myself and my voice to text program. Thank you for helping me accomplish my dreams!

To our Children, Shelley, and Bryce whose love of reading encouraged me to write stories they would enjoy reading.

Above all, for the glory of my Lord and Savior Jesus Christ.

AUTHOR'S NOTE

This work of science-based fiction uses the transformational nature of adult human stem cells to adapt to many different organs and tissues. Current research and medical practices are successful in using these adult stem cells in a multitude of applications.

These cells are different from embryonic stem cells, which are derived from humans before birth, a procedure that most often costs a life. It is the author's scientific belief that the use of adult stem cells are so beneficial as to not venture into the controversy of human embryonic tissue donors.

SCRIPTURE

"Greater love has no one than this,
that one lay down his life for his friends." **John 15:13 (NAS)**

Chapter One

Anguish swept over Stephanie Anna Steffen-Huffman as she read Harry's curt text. "Have the background for the next *Channel 7's Eye on Science* interview COMPLETE by Thursday's production meeting." As the newest investigative reporter, it fell to Steff to tie up loose ends from two weeks of intense research. She had tried three times to finish digging into the background of the Rosch Clinic, and its two top scientists, Michael Lancaster and Peter Hayes. Each attempt was stopped by her increasing anger over a recent discovery of information suggesting the death of her best friend and sorority sister Max at the clinic was not natural. *How can I help Harry promote the clinic when they killed Max. Come on, Steff, you're worked through anger before; get this done or Harry will fire you.* Steff picked up the bulky Phoenix Project reference file, uttered a sigh of resignation, and headed for the clinic's downtown research library.

A short taxi ride brought Steff's to the research library of the world-renowned Rosch Clinic's downtown Denver campus. The library's stark-white on black anteroom presented a feeling of forced order. The lack of visible book stacks further suggested guarding its secrets was important. Leaning over the counter Steff held her press card in front of the young woman behind the desk labeled *Research.*

Turning toward Steff she closed her tablet "May I help you?"

"Yes, where can I find current information on the *Phoenix Project?*"

Opening a well-ordered file drawer she extracted three booklets, closed the file stood up and pushed them across the counter. "These are our current publications. A brochure outlining the technical goals of the project. A detailed press packet about our Stem Cell research team and a short history of the Clinic." This well-rehearsed cadence continued. "Should you require additional information, the Clinic offers a public study room down the hall, first door on your left. In there you will find an extensive collection of publicly available reprints and technical information. They may be copied, but can't be checked out. The rest of the library is off limits without an escort from the Clinic."

I wonder what they're trying to hide? - "Thank you. Do you have Wi-Fi?"

She pointed to a small sign at the corner of her desk. *Public unsecured WiFi available: user clinic – password firebird.* "Also, there is a page charge for on-site printing and photocopying."

Steff jotted down the user and password, picked up the three packets and walked to the study room. On the way, she passed a half-glass door, on the right, with a bold sign *No Admittance.* Peeking through the glass, she saw rows of book-filled shelves along one wall and well-stocked computer cubicles along the other. A quick look up determined no visible cameras, so Steff tested the door and no audible alarms went off. After a longer look around Steff quietly closed the door and made a mental note to check out this room, at a later visit.

The narrow study room, with its floor to ceiling bookshelves, seemed to close in around a small oak table nestled below the room's only window. Steff sat in one of the two institutional chairs facing the window and spread out the clinic's printed material. *Let's see what the PR boys have to say. Hmm --* Opening the glossy PR booklet Steff began underlining bits of text. "...was named Phoenix for a recently developed line of adult stem cells which is able to promote healing of damaged or dying organs. -- life from death... *Must be like the mythical Phoenix bird.* ...new organs from damaged or dying organs with a safe and simple six-month stem cell treatment. *Hmm – this I gotta see...*

The Phoenix stem cell line donor was on death row.

Steff turned on her cell phone microphone and began recording notes to herself. "Do stem cells carry criminal genes?" Steff continued to jot notes along the margin. *Only works when serum testosterone levels are low. Must ask the docs how they found that out.*" More pages and more notes later. ... seems to work best for women and older men after male menopause ... additional Clinical Trials are scheduled ... "Ask Manny to find out what's a clinical trial? "... Stem Cells move into diseased organs and replace damaged cells ... its first successful application was treating diabetics. Steff turned over to the back page and began reading bios of the docs who developed the cell line. First listed was Michael Lancaster, followed by Peter Hayes. As Steff began to underline she realized Harry is interviewing the docs who killed Max. Bolting to her feet, she knocked her chair backward. "Why those dirty snakes... why I'll ...!"

Steff banged closed the booklets, stuffed everything into her backpack, and headed for the exit, pausing momentarily at the No Admittance door, then took a step towards the exit. Wheeling on her heel opened the door and went in. Moving towards the closest bookshelf Steff began to read the book spines. *These are all marked as FDA exhibits.* Moving to the next bookshelf found the same type of books. *This must be all of the stuff that FDS requires for approval.* "I know you're hiding something, but where."

As Steff turned toward the other side of the room a stern faced woman entered the room. "May I see your pass? I don't recognize you from our approved visitor list."

"I'm here to meet Dr. Lancaster, but I can't find him." Hoping to gain some advantage and not get arrested.

"You are not to be in here, please wait for Dr. Lancaster in the lobby. I will give him a call and see when he will arrive."

Before she could call Steff thanked her and headed for the exit. Hurrying down the steps, Steff flagged a passing taxi. She closed the door, gave the driver the News 7 address, leaned back and closed her eyes. *That was too close; I've got to get to the bottom of this. The docs must be the answer -- it's the least I can do for Max.*

The afternoon seemed to drag, between trying to look up more information on the docs, and still deal with station business until Harry tapped on her office window and opened the door. "Steff, have you finished the preliminary profile on the clinic's Phoenix Project? The interview is still on the sheet for this weekend."

"Yes, - ah yes, I still have a couple of references to check." She knew only a small part of her answer was truthful. She spun her chair toward the door and jumped toward Harry, making him take a defensive step backward.

"Oh, sorry about that. I was just thinking about the two docs who developed their magic juice." Steff looked Harry straight in the eye. "Harry, would you consider letting me do this interview?

"You've only been with us for a short while."

"I know, and I don't deserve a solo gig, but I really want to confront these two. I have some history with their clinic."

"I've done the past three and promised to help them defend the trumped-up charges recently leveled against them and the clinic. Now help me out here. Why should I break the pattern and let you..."

"I know, but I have done all the background. I know those charges are entirely unfounded." Steff hoped her research would confirm her hunch. "I would like to ask them about a serious discrepancy in the public record."

"What do you mean?"

"Well, for one, the Phoenix Project PR guys state that none of the patients treated with this wonderful line of adult stem cells had a serious adverse reaction, when I know for a fact, at least, one died."

"How do you know that?"

"I was in the room when one of the patients died."

Harry began pumped his hand in a give-it-to-me motion. "More?"

With all of her composure mustered, Steff related how her friend Max was at the clinic receiving her fifth of six treatments when she began acting all strange, and suddenly passed out. The medical staff did all they could, but Max was dead in just a few minutes. There was supposed to be an autopsy, but the clinic told me she had recently signed a medical request that, in keeping with her religion, she was not to be cut, and her remains were to be cremated within twenty-four hours of her death. I told them it wasn't true, but they showed me a form with Max's signature notarized. I was still in a daze, so I just left it alone and went to call her parents.

"Harry, I tell you Max was a dyed-in-the-wool Christian, who made me promise to oversee the donation of her organs and her well-planned funeral, open casket and all. By the time I got back to the clinic that afternoon, she had already been cremated."

"Could she have changed her mind?"

"Not in less than a week. A couple of months after I moved here, I went with Max to her lawyer's office and signed a power of attorney and a bunch of stuff in case the treatment she'd been on for the past months didn't work, and things went to pot. I received my notarized copies of Max's papers the day before she died."

"Hmm." Harry twisted the end of his small handlebar his mustache. "You think there is foul play?"

"I don't know, but when I went to the clinic to get copies of her papers there was a small sticky note on the back of one of the forms with '**Their lying, she shouldn't be dead**' written with a green marker. When I got home and found the note I remembered the secretary next to the door waving a green marker at me as I walked by her desk. I called the Clinic's legal office to talk with her and was told she won a large scratch lottery and quit the company that very afternoon. It seemed odd at the time, but now I think that Max did not die of natural causes and the secretary was trying to tell there is a cover up. Harry, I would like the opportunity to ask the question. Besides, you owe me one for those gems I dug up for your interview with the city inspector."

"Yes, you did give the station a good point jump in the ratings that week. Okay. It's yours, I will notify production. Stop by my office and pick up our master file on the clinic. Good hunting." Harry then turned on his heel and walked out, closing the door behind him.

Steff pushed her clinched fists up over her head and shouted, "Okay! Max, this one's for you." Steff fell back into her chair trembling and dripping with sweat, "What have I done? I can't stop now."

It took all of five minutes to stop shaking. Taking deep breath, followed by a long sigh, Steff picked up the phone and dialed the front desk. "Hi Sue, I am out doing research for the rest of the day. If Anne Hamilton calls, tell her I will still meet her tomorrow for lunch... yes, please tell her the usual bistro. Also, please do me a favor and call production and let them know I'll have the script questions and notes ready day after tomorrow ... Thanks."

Chapter Two

Abit weak in her knees, and too tired to walk, Steff flagged a taxi. A long exhale, and she fell back into the faux-leather seat, not noticing the over-used lumpy cushion. What seemed like seconds found Steff standing in front of her apartment. A few steps later and still in a daze, Steff opened her apartment door, dropped her keys on the side table and dropped into her couch. *Must call Anne and confirm lunch before I forget.*

Steff was glad for speed dial. After four rings an answering machine picked up, "Hi, you have not reached Anne. I am not going to answer your call until I am ready. Here comes the beep, so speak or forever hold your peace."

"Anne, this is Steff. Just calling to make sure we are on for tomorrow. By the way, I still don't like your new message. See ya later."

Steff opened a can of soup and nuked it in a bright red ceramic bowl. After picking up a tube of crackers, Steff curled up in her writing chair to go over her research notes and compose questions and script for the interview with the docs. After reviewing highlighted sections from Harry's thick research folder, Steff began working on the script questions.

Banging her laptop's keys betrayed her emotion and continuing anger with the clinic and the docs. Reading back the first few questions startled Steff. The tone was angry and confrontational. *Cool it, Steff; remember what dad taught you about interviews. Get the docs comfortable then spring the 'Max question.' Hmm, how about meeting them first to throw them off guard? Ya, ... the*

7

calm before the storm. They may clam up if I am too abrupt too soon.

To break the growing tension, Steff closed her laptop and Harry's notebook, and turned on the TV. As the news droned on and on, Steff had crawled onto the couch and was now sound asleep. The melody playing from her cell phone woke her hours later. The caller ID read "News 7 production."

"Oh pot! What time is it? Hello... yes, this is Steff, what?... yes, I know it's after nine. I'm not due back to the station until after lunch. ... Thanks for the heads up. Yes, I'll keep my script to less than 20 minutes. ... Yes, I'll email it to you, and yes I will bring a thumb drive backup. ... Yes, I know this is my first interview with you guys, and again, I do appreciate the heads up, bye." Steff turned off the TV, steeped a cup of Earl Grey and nuked an almost forgotten slice of pepperoni pizza. *Not the best breakfast, but today I need the extra time.*

Steff opened her laptop and Harry's reference notebook. With a sigh, she began to draft more civil questions for the docs.

Chapter Three

A nne Hamilton's week started out like the previous week and like a hundred before. Check Facebook for posts. Quick shower. Feed Felix before she snagged a hole in another pair of pantyhose. Gulp down a can of weight control. Sonic her teeth, then makeup and off to catch the # 24 bus to her office in downtown Denver.

A friendly voice from behind the cluttered Durango Joe's Gourmet Coffee Kiosk broke into her consistent routine. "Good morning Anne. Would you like to try today's special? It's half price for coffee club members?"

"Sure, why not, but please don't forget non-fat milk." Anne scanned her bright red coffee club card and stepped towards the pickup station. Her thoughts were not the usual mental check-list of today's activities, just Brad. She hoped he would not forget how important today had become. A small hand soon held up the large logo covered cup.

"Here you are, a double cinnamon-caramel latte, with non-fat organic milk."

"Thanks, Sheri, you're a gem." A few quick sips assured Sheri's concoction was drinkable, then off to the south bank of express elevators. Anne hoped she had arrived early enough to use the elevator before Boris. Not his real name, just her nickname for the assistant comptroller who loved to stand too close and enjoyed garlic-tainted curries. A wisp of fresh pine assured its occupants that Boris had not yet used this elevator and the path to her office could be transversed without an unwanted olfactory encounter.

Once inside her office, Anne set about the completion of the day's scheduled activities. First on the list was research for an upcoming project, which meant a couple of hours in the basement file room before lunch with Steff. Picking up her tablet, and Sheri's special coffee Anne hoped she could again find an odor-free elevator. The door opened, and there stood Brad all alone. The problem of any odor disappeared as the door closed behind Anne.

A quick kiss on Anne's blushing cheek dispelled her apprehension. A whispered "Hi Scoots," assured Anne he had remembered."

Her "Si Hoots, to you." Precipitated a round of laughter and small talk until the elevator opened and Brad stepped out. "Wish me luck." He blew a kiss, turned and disappeared around the corner. The elevator felt warmer even as its doors opened in the chilly basement.

Chapter Four

L unch with Anne was usually a fun time filled with all kinds of meaningful conversation and some giggling nonsense, the kind of chatter longtime friends and college sorority sisters relish and enjoy. However, today the table in the corner of a quaint little bistro across from Anne Rice's office complex was somber. Steff leaned across the table, gently picked up Anne's almost limp hand. "You look terrible, what's up?"

Anne stared at her cup, slowly stirring its dark essence. The awkward silence soon broke.

"Steff, I'm not going crazy, but I think my boss is not himself. What I mean is ... aah ... what I really mean is my boss is someone else who looks like Brad, sounds a lot like Brad and even smells like Brad, but he's not Brad. Either he's a fraud or ..."

"Slow down! You've known Brad since college. How long have you worked for him -- more than ten years – right? Then how can you say it's not him? Is he a ..."

"Steff, give me time to finish. You know how it is when you have known someone for a long time and are asked to describe them. You can't because your mental picture is years old. You don't notice those small daily changes. Soon you realize you don't think how he looks; he's just familiar."

"Anne, what are you saying? Are you telling me, Brad...?"

"Steff! I tell you Brad is not Brad anymore. At least, I'm sure he was Brad at 8:30 this morning, but by 11:30 Brad was not Brad.

"Are you sure, I mean, really sure?"

"Here's the scary part. I met my Brad in the elevator this morning. We talked about that dumb thing we did in college fifteen years ago today and had a good laugh. He told me he was off to the clinic for his final physical exam, after finishing his recent stem cell treatment. He squeezed my hand and said, 'Wish me luck' and got off in the lobby and I went on down to file storage."

"Is that it?"

"Oh no, I was in the file room for about three hours and on the way back up the guy I thought was Brad got on the elevator and cheerfully said, 'Hi Scoots, how is your day going?' like this was the first time he had seen me all day."

"Well?"

"Only Brad and a couple of college pals know my old nickname. For more than a dozen years Brad and I have this funny way of saying hello when there is no one around. He says, 'Hi Scoots' and nothing else. I then reply, 'Si Hoots' to make light of his dyslexia, which by the way he hides from his colleagues very well."

"And what is wrong with that?"

"Brad and I did our Scoots – Hoots thing in the elevator earlier this morning. But when I kidded this imposter about doing it earlier this morning the fake Brad got all flustered and sputtered out something about receiving an antibiotic booster by IV injection containing something which blocks short-term memory. Scopolamine, or something like."

"That's true, it does."

"I've seen my Brad after all of his previous treatments, and he was normal, so why is he different after this booster?"

"Maybe he was reacting to the shot or something? Did you think of that?"

"Yes, but when I saw the tape on his arm I asked about it, and this guy answered, 'that's where they drew blood for my final tests. Remember they take blood every time'. But Steff, Brad is super allergic to regular white tape and would have had at the very least a huge welt. He has to use that pink colored bio-tape or have hives for days. There was no sign of any redness, no nothing, just what looks like Brad's dark skin and a strip of plain white tape."

Steff leaned towards Anne. "Did you ask the guy about it?"

"No way, by this time I was flat freaking out. The guy looked at me funny and made some comment about our college anniversary, which was out of left field, so I got off at the next floor."

"Then...?"

"When I got back to my office, I felt a bit foolish and called Brad. His secretary said he was out for the rest of the day and would be out of town until next week and was not taking any calls. Steff, Brad asked me to dinner in the elevator this morning to celebrate our college thing. He has not missed an anniversary in years."

"Anne, I will see what I can find out. Now go home, call in sick, and I'll call you at home later and let you know what I've found out."

"Thanks Steff, you're a saint." Taking her water glass, Anne lifted it, and in toast fashion said, "To Steff, Queen of Query." Without eating a single bite, Anne put on her jacket, walked to the door, turned and blew Steff a kiss, and stepped into the shadow and then out of sight.

Steff just sat there a bit bewildered as one phrase from Anne's plea rang back and forth inside her head: "...*for his final stem cell treatment.*" Steff quickly jotted it down in her notebook along with Brad's name and where he worked.

Strange? In all these years Anne never told me anything substantial about Brad's work, just that it was about world banking procedures. I must find out more about the real Brad. Gathering up her things, she paid the check and decided to walk back to the studio even though it looked like it might rain.

Chapter Five

T he rest of the afternoon crept by painfully. Every time Steff tried to look up information on Brad, work got in the way. After a couple of meaningless meetings, she'd had it. After activating call forwarding, she called Sue to sign out and beat it down the back stairs before another meeting snared her. Too tired to walk home, Steff flagged a taxi. She leaned forward and mumbled her address in the general direction of the driver. A puzzled look from the driver told her he did not understand her address. She leaned close to one of the small holes drilled in the plastic shield separating her world from his and repeated, this time using slow, separated syllables. The trip was short and uneventful. *Must call Anne before I forget.* Steff grew impatience as Anne's phone rang four times. Steff endured Anne's cryptic answer message until the beep. "Anne, just a quick call. I ran out of time today, but I will get you the info later tomorrow. I hope you called in sick. Give me a call when you can. I need some time to figure out what is going on. I will call my contact in Washington DC, and for the umpteenth time, I still don't like this message. See ya later."

Steff sequestered leftovers onto a plate and nuked them. After a couple of hours of pouring over Harry's file and her notes, Steff began to polish her script questions for the interview. *These look better than my first bunch. Oh-oh must call Manny.* A couple of clicks and four rings, then the voice message beep. "Hi Manny, it's me, Richard's little troublemaker. Please give me a call as soon as you get this even if it's in the middle of the night-- thanks a bunch, you're a doll -- Hugs and kisses."

Typing on her laptop was more comfortable on the well-worn couch. Its downside was its comfort and without knowing when Steff was sound asleep. The melody playing from her cell phone woke her hours later. The caller ID read "Manny."

"Hi Manny, yes this is me ... Yes, I was asleep, I know its past two-o-clock, but it's okay ... Manny, I have a job for your unique skills ... Don't laugh; I'm serious ... I emailed you a list of things I need to find out for a friend ... Yes, it must be done quietly, no one can know we're looking ... I know, I know, yes, the standard fee, but Manny this ones on me, not News 7. Thanks, you are a doll, an ugly doll, but a doll none the less ... Don't get fresh Manny, later ... Bye." Steff leaned back on the couch and was asleep again. After what felt like only a few minutes, the cell phone rang again. This time, the caller ID read "News 7."

"Oh pot! What time is it? Hello ... yes, this is Steff ... what?... yes, I know it's after nine; I am just finishing the questions. Yes, I'll be there in time for the production meeting ... yes, I'm ready... yes, I know I need to bring the light-colored suit." A polygraph would have lit up the room.

Steff was glad her apartment was a brisk thirty-minute walk from the station. She could use the draft questions she prepared last night to keep production happy. A quick shower and change into jeans, a cotton shirt, and her favorite brown leather vest made Steff felt like a new person. Grabbing her garment bag and blue backpack, Steff almost ran to the station and up the back stairs to her office. Steff assembled her wits and her material. A few minutes and the thumb drive with her script questions was ready. Up the stairs and Steff calmly walked into production's green room just before the meeting began. *The docs will be here soon. Must keep calm - can't let on I am going to ambush the docs.* A bit sheepish Steff realized she was shaking her head up and down in agreement with herself.

The studio director poked her head around the door, "Steff, we need to load the teleprompter."

"Here you are, but I have one or two questions I may slip in if the docs try to dodge my third question about their *Phoenix Project.*"

"Okay, but remember all we have is no more than twenty

minutes for the segment and five for the wrap-up."

"Right, but if you see me pull out a yellow card, you'll know I am going off script to jump the docs."

"Do you have an agenda here? The station is not keen on setting an ambush."

"It's not an ambush. I just don't want them to dodge the question, but if they do, I go off script, and you guys can cut the tape to fit the time later, and I will dub the wrap-up later."

"Steff, you're making this sound like *Sixty Minutes*. Remember; these guys are friends of Harry, and he is going out on a limb to give you this gig. Don't blow your first solo. We are starting in less than an hour."

"Thanks coach." Steff hurried out of the studio and down to her office. Her tendency to be late had allowed Steff time for some last minute online checking of recent quotes. A few more quick searches to verify what she had found out last night and Steff leaned back to take a two-minute break before the docs arrived.

Sue's call broke into Steff's silence, cutting her much-needed break at less than a minute. "This is Steff... What do you mean, just one doc?...

Chapter Six

M ost life-altering days start out like many others, often mundane and predictable. Such was the case for Michael Lancaster Ph.D. this late summer morning.

Mike rolled over, further crumpling his orange and blue Broncos' bedspread. Nimble fingers silenced the mournful alarm clock and captured a thin black object from the messy nightstand. "Well, magic tablet, what do you have for me today?" Rubbing his sleep-swollen eyes seemed to help focus on the now bright screen. A tap and gentle brush across the smooth glass activated the dormant email app. Soldiers of email boxes marched up the screen flashing a sleep-wrinkled face. Adjusting his collection of pillows Mike sat up and again touched the reflective black glass.

Another touch revealed …

Hey Mike, cover the Channel 7 interview, can't be there, it's the Bell's Palsy thing again -- thanks, you're a real prince - Peter.

Peter Hayes Ph.D.
Director of Stem Cell Research Programs Rosch Memorial Clinic …

Not this interview. The snooze alarm kicked in for its final brazen attempt to wake the entire world. A quick swat silenced its mournful buzz. *Take a deep breath; it's okay. With Peter, these outbreaks are always unexpected.* Tossing down his tablet, Mike rolled out of bed.

The morning marched on much like many in the recent past - a quick shower, a bloodless shave, followed by the predictable protein powder fortified fruit smoothie. Mike muttered as he sat the dirty glass in the already cluttered sink, "I'll have to get these washed or buy new ones." He chuckled in a vain attempt to turn his darkening mood to a lighter shade of gray.

Before Mike could despair any longer, the hall clock began chiming 9:00 AM. Mike drew a deep breath of resignation and exhaled. "Oh well." Mike put his tablet in his shoulder case next to a blue laptop and methodically closed its worn flap. Mike hesitated, then opened the hall door and stepped out, leaving his apartment in total disarray.

Come on; it's only an interview, not the end of the world. Mike slammed the hall door shut, turned and made his way down the back stairs to the waiting limo. Today's shuffle was not his usual quick gait, but more like dead-man-walking.

A kaleidoscope of distant events flashed on and off as Mike's thoughts began to wander. It seemed like decades ago, not four brief, but intense years since he and Peter had won the Award. Now, with the investigation of the clinic by a radical group, he felt like Icarus. *I've flown too high, and now the heat's on. What went wrong? All I ever wanted to do was help sick people.*

The limo driver opened the rear door and with a slight tip of his hat broke into Mike's churning thought world. "On behalf of Channel 7 News, Welcome aboard Dr. Lancaster. I hope you enjoy your ride downtown."

The drive to the TV studio was thankfully uneventful but too short. Mike leaned back in the plush leather seat. His mind continued whirling. *Why do I dread this interview? I've survived tough interviews without Peter. I can defend our research. Peter, why --, why crap out today, of all days?*

The limo's undulating reflection, moving along the massive windows of downtown Denver, became almost hypnotic. Behind Mike's glassine stare, his mind churned through frontal lobe video clips of the past four years at the Clinic ...

– old Doc Uberholtzer announcing he and Peter were awarded the SK Benedict Award for Innovative Research in the Emerging Field of Adult Stem Cell Research.

– Peter's usual rush to be first to the microphone and its

18

accompanying spotlight.

– Peter's words lost in the deafening applause.

– I still wish I knew what he said.

– Peter dancing and crying at the same time.

– Doc Uberholtzer holding up the large cardboard $50,000,000 check

– Me fainting.

– I guess I always knew Peter liked the adulation a bit more than the money. A familiar speed bump signaled their arrival at the studio and reset Mike to the present

The street air, after last night's downpour, had a sweet fragrance, not the usual city oily-smell. The ride up the escalator to the 7 News Studio felt more like a trip to the principal's office rather than this month's informational interview. Sue's familiar face behind the receptionist's desk provided Mike a little comfortable.

"Good Morning Dr. Lancaster. Dr. Hayes emailed and asked me to tell you he will fill you in later, and again to say 'Sorry.' Let me tell Huff you're here. Would you like coffee? You look like a large cup could help - as I remember two lumps, real cream, and no fake cups."

"Yes, thanks." Trying to hide his irritation with Peter, Mike asked. "Who is Huff? I thought the interview was with Harry."

"Harry passed the interview to Huff as some kind of favor. Peter knew, didn't he tell you?"

Mike tried to hide his growing annoyance with Peter and now Harry. "Sue, help me out here. Just who is this Huff guy?"

"She's our new investigative reporter, from the Midwest somewhere."

"Oh, a she is she."

"Yes, Huff is the nickname we underlings gave her. She seems to be always in a huff about something."

"Sort of a Ms. Huff and Puff." Mike's grin almost made it to fruition, but his growing funk dispelled its chance.

"Yep, her full name is Stephanie Anna Steffen-Huffman. She likes to be called Steff, and she never-ever uses the last half of her name."

"Steff with one 'f' or two?"

"Two, her Dad gave her the nickname in junior high." Sue

turned her attention to the phone, pushed a speed dial button, and paused. "Ms. Steffen, Dr. Lancaster is in reception ... Yes, he is alone. Dr. Hayes had to leave Denver to wait out an outbreak of Bell's Palsy. ... If you need more info, ask Dr. Lancaster. ... Okay." Sue replaced the phone and retrieved Mike's coffee.

"Huff, I mean Ms. Steffen, will be down in about fifteen minutes. She asked if you would wait in Studio D, just down the hall, second door to your left.

"Thank you." His footsteps echoed down the marble entryway. Through the double doors and down the corridor was just enough time to rehash his irritation with his friend Harry. *Harry, why now? You know how important this interview is to the Clinic. I was hoping your verbal skills would help clear up all this confusion. Thanks for throwing me to the second team.*

Studio D was quiet and uncomfortably cold. All Mike could see was darkness and a few shadows. A motion sensor turned on an overhead light. The circle of cool white light highlighted a cheap plastic folding chair and a round white plastic table a few steps to his left. The chair was as cold as the light. A chill ran up his spine as cold quickly seeped through his polyester blazer and color matched shirt.

A grin softened tightly closed lips. *I forgot they keep these studios cold, so we don't sweat during interviews. Those hot studio lights will warm me up soon enough.* A brief video game on his tablet did not provide the hoped-for distraction from the impending second team interview. Mike realized he did not know a thing about Ms. Stiff or, as Sue calls her, Huff. A few quick taps on the blue laptop and Stephanie Anna Steffen-Huffman's Google profile appeared.

Mike sipped his coffee as he read lines of citations. *Hmm... hazelnut and hot. Well, let's see who you really are Ms. Huffy Stiff. Wow, over 1200 hits. Hmm – let-a-me-see, here's an interesting one. Well, Ms. Stiff, I see you went to college. Hmm ... a degree in Broadcast Journalism from Bradley College. A Masters in Criminal Psychology from Stanford, and hmm...* Mike continued to read Steff's AP bio. *Both degrees Summa Cum Laude and what do we have here? A Phi Beta Kappa key. Well, Ms. Stiff, you are for sure no dummy.* Contemplation interlaced with sips of coffee filled the minutes before the door burst open and in rushed Steff, clutching a bulging file folder. ...

Chapter Seven

Mike's clean-cut appearance caught Steff off guard as evidenced by a blank stare. Her vision of Mike, from a recent Facebook posting, had been a wild-eyed man with long hair, a full beard and wearing a crumpled lab coat.

Without thinking, Mike stood up. His father had always reminded him it was proper to stand when a woman entered the room. A look of concern crossed his face. "Your lips are moving, but I can't hear a sound. Are you trying to say something?" Before Steff could answer, Mike continued, "You're nothing like I expected. To be honest, I didn't know what to expect, other than you don't look a bit like Harry."

A dimpled smirk broke across Steff's blushing face as she tried to keep her professional detachment. "You, at least, have that right. No, I was not expecting, ah, ua, ah, well someone like you. ... uh, a - I thought you had a beard and uh ..."

"Oh, you must have seen the worst picture of me ever taken. I was a week short of winning a bet with the lab staff that I wouldn't shave or cut my hair for three months when one of the staff posted that scary picture on Facebook. They captured the wild-eyed Einstein-like look, complete with wiry beard and shaggy brown hair."

Steff took a step toward Mike and held out her hand. "Please call me Steff. I'm told you do not like to be called Michael, so may I call you Mike?"

Mike noted her hand was small and smooth to the touch, but cool in his. A hint of Jasmine perfume filled the space between them. "Yes, Stiff, uh-a, Huff, umm. Let me start over. I was ticked off Harry was not doing this interview, and without knowing a thing about you, I started thinking about you as 'Ms. Stiff' or 'Ms. Huff.' After I read your credentials, oh, I hope you don't mind I Googled you. I knew you had to be at least fifty years old, have your hair in a bun, lace-up shoes, and a dark dress that went down to at least your ankles. But you totally destroyed that image when I saw you in the doorway. I would love to address you as Steff."

Mike realized he and Steff were holding hands more than just shaking hands. And to make things worse, they were both staring into each other's eyes. After an awkward moment both glanced down, and as if they had been shocked, quickly pulled back their now warm hands.

"I guess we should get to it," said Steff, again trying to regain the upper hand.

An aide entered the room and motioned. Steff moved across to the aide so gracefully Mike thought she was not stepping, just gliding without sound.

Mike's mind faced a conundrum. The scientist in him wanted to get on with the interview so he could silence the fringe hecklers and get back to his research. However, the shy human part of him was smitten by Steff's calm beauty, hazel green eyes, and graceful lines.

Before Mike could finish trying to put his reeling feelings into words, Steff glided back across the room and, with a short sweep of her hand, motioned toward the door. "Studio B is ready, shall we go?" Without waiting for an answer, Steff, and the aide left the room. Mike followed like a puppy on a leash, warm, bright-eyed, and almost panting.

Chapter Eight

Racks of studio lights revealed a small semi-circular stage surrounded by TV cameras and teleprompters. Serpentine black cords crawled across the cold tile floor, disappearing into the darkness beyond the hot white circle of concentrated light. On one side sat Steff's chair. To its left a small table holding two tall clear glasses of fresh water and a garish spray of tall yellow gladiolas in a tall, pale blue vase. Bits of fern-like greenery failed to moderate the gaudy bouquet. Just outside the hot circle stood Mike, a sandy-haired biochemist nervously straightening his jacket, wishing the interview was over. Background chatter died down as the producer held up five fingers. "Five minutes to camera checks. Let's start cutting the chatter and do our jobs, please."

Mike had now relaxed a bit since first meeting Steff but was still dreading the interview. He took a deep breath. *She's beautiful, and I think she has a delightful sense of humor. This shouldn't be too bad.* Mike took a deep breath, exhaled slowly, straightened his tie and stepped up onto the stage and into a new future.

Mike noted Studio B was no warmer than Room D and began to shiver. *I wish I had worn a real jacket. Here's the powder puff girl. Oh, I hate makeup; I itch the rest of the day.*

The technicians finished with Mike's wireless microphone, set their light meters, and posed him for the usual camera checks. The tall blond studio tech stepped forward and looked Mike in the eye. "Remember; try not to look at the monitor, just at Steff. Just like

24

last time, we are recording, so if you flub an answer, we will just mark the timeline and when you see me point you can start your answer over. Now is a good time to take a quick bathroom break."

When Mike returned, Steff was already in her chair. The selection of harsh studio lights accented a reddish tint in her light brown hair. The studio's backlight system projected an iridescent halo which shimmered when Steff moved. Her transformation from jeans, a western vest, and hair clips into this stunning figure made Mike stop and stare.

That can't be Steff. She was gone only a few minutes. Mike carefully took a deep breath and, against all of his desire to ask her out, moved across the stage to his chair.

"Well, you scrub up pretty well for a reporter."

"An investigative reporter. Remember Dr. Lancaster, an investigative reporter."

"I won't forget." Mike's first genuine smile of the day broke across his now relaxed face.

"Ready?" Steff's voice became business-like. "You have seen the question list. Where shall we begin? And with a wink said. "How about question number one?" Before Mike could answer, Steff looked over at the producer who was holding up one finger signaling one minute to start. After straightening her jacket and microphone, she looked at Mike. Her professional smile slowly changed into a strange half-smile breaking across her dimpled cheeks. Steff put her finger to her now pensive lips. "Shhh, it's your time now."

Chapter Nine

S teff turned to the looming camera. "Good evening, this is Stephanie Huffman bringing you the fifth installment in Channel 7's Eye on Science series. Tonight's special guest is Dr. Michael Lancaster, of Denver's own world-famous Rosch Clinic." A slight tilt of Steff's head focused her full attention on Mike. "Dr. Lancaster Welcome to Channel 7's Eye On Science.

Thank you, I'm pleased to be here Ms. Steffen.

Dr. Lancaster, please tell us about your recent developments in curing diabetes with stem cells, and please call me Steff."

"Stop!" The director emerged from the darkness behind the camera. "Steff, you went off script and blew your intro. You also skipped the first question and messed up the second. Dr. Lancaster works with liver disease, not diabetes." Two quick steps brought her up on the stage. Her warm hand rested on Steff's shoulder. "Steff, please don't fuss with your cue cards. It distracts from your professionalism and unwind your legs. You look like a snake ready to strike. I know this is not your first dance ... just relax." She then turned towards the darkness and stepped off the stage and out of the circle of light. "Okay guys, ... ready? – Okay, stand by for Steff's intro - in – five, four, three, cue Steff - now

Color drained from Steff's face. Her stage makeup no longer hid her growing pallor. White-knuckled fingers dug into the arms of her chair. Short breaths, sucked between clenched teeth, betrayed her crumbling façade. A nearly inaudible *Keep calm, you want this,* hung in the enclosed circle of hot white light. Darkened eyes. Quivering lip. Hissing exhale. Just as the producer signaled now, Stephanie's eyes narrowed their focus on Michael. Without loss of eye contact, she stood and quickly advanced on her prey.

Mike sprang to his feet. "You okay?"

Now rigid and eye-to-eye Stephanie shouted, high-pitched, raspy and hostile. "Why did you let Max die - - WHY?"

"What?"

"You know," Tears blurred her approach as Michael's shoulder became both a crying towel and punching bag. "I have to know. After you injected those stem cells, Max just passed out and died. WHY! ... why?" Hot tears now streamed down her cheeks.

Michael stumbled backward as Stephanie's final grab at his coat lapels propelled him back down into his chair. His foot flew up as the chair spun, kicking the small studio table. Its tall blue vase of yellow gladiolas, along with two innocent glasses of water, were now airborne. The man-made storm spilled water in all directions. Some doused the front of Mike's polyester jacket. The balance along with the vase and glasses skimmed across the stage, leaving a trail of water and flowers, before bouncing off the floor to an early death.

Stephanie rushed off the stage. A primal scream resounded through the studio. Her bee-line escape spun a teleprompter and knocked over the producer's chair, scattering script sheets across the field of interlaced black cords. All was still for a few seconds then a loud slam, then silence.

"What did I do?" Cut into the stunned silence. An intern rushed to the stage and began sponging Michael's dripping jacket.

The studio producer broke into Michael's befuddled thoughts. "Well, I, uh - ah, don't know what that's all about. Please accept our apologies. I'll have Harry call you after we get to the bottom of this outrage. I know Harry will want to reschedule. Let me call the limo so you can get home for some dry clothing. I guess -ah – ah we'll get back to you soon." His voice trailed off as he disappeared back into the darkness beyond the circle of hot lights.

"Okay." Wet fumbling fingers peeled off the lapel microphone and belt transmitter. Michael dropped the microphone system on the disarrayed chair, turned on his heel and stepped off the stage. Slipping his computer bag over his shoulder, Michael hurried toward the faint red glow of the exit sign over the parking lot door, hoping for some sense of order.

Chapter Ten

Steff slammed the studio door behind her and raced across the street to a small park behind the Channel 7 building. *I can't believe I just did that – what was I thinking. I just blew any chance to be able to talk to Mike about Max.* A nearby park bench allowed Steff the opportunity to rethink the last ten minutes. *I didn't realize how much anger I had been suppressing. I guess I need to meet with Harry and see if I can salvage my job and maybe this interview.*

A childhood admonition from her father spurred Steff into action. *Dad always said the quicker you try to fix a mistake; the better your chances are to get a positive resolution. I think the first best step is to go back to the office and give Mike a call and see if I have even a ghost of a chance to fix this.* Steff slowly got up, straightened her jacket, and started trudging across the park and back to the studio. The sky had turned slate gray, and a cold wind began swirling a fine rain mist around the buildings. The damp chill of the impending rainstorm reminded Steff of a day just three weeks ago when she received a call from Maxine Rice.

"Steff, if you have time, can you come-go-with to the Clinic for my last stem cell treatment? I would love you to be there when they tell me my diabetes is cured. You have been an absolute doll these past months."

"Max, you are my oldest and dearest friend; I would love to go-with. By the way, you know you still owe me for all those trips when you were down in bed after your early treatments."

"Don't give me any of that poor-ole-me crap. You jumped at

29

the chance to get away from your dead-end job. Also, I know for a fact you set up your interview with Channel 7 while you were here. Right?!"

"But of course, oh great and wise Max, knower of all things. See-ya noonish."

A gust of wind from a passing bus snapped Steff's thoughts to the present. *Watch where you are going, or you will join Max.* Tears clouded her eyes. *Max -- Max what went wrong? They took you into the treatment room just like in the past and ...*

Steff was glad to be at the studio's back door and out of public view. A quick pass of her key card opened the door. She only made it a few steps inside before she turned her back to the cool wall and began sobbing. Her backpack slipped to her hand, then to the floor. Steff slid down its smooth surface into a heap and buried her head in her folded arms. Warm tears soaked into her sleeve. For the first time since Max's death, Steff allowed her pent-up sorrow to surface. The cool, quiet stairwell became a chapel with God in attendance. Her tears now flowed freely and without the sting of shame. *Max, oh Max, I miss you. You were too young. Too full of life.* Tears began shrinking the painful hole in her heart.

A crack of thunder ringing down the streets pulled Steff back to the present. Her head now felt lighter. She struggled up, grabbed her backpack, adjusted her clothes, and dried her eyes. Steff was glad no one saw her enter her office. She closed the door, fell back into her chair, and turned its back to the door. A couple of eye drops took out the redness but stung a bit. *Am I glad there was no mascara in today's makeup, or I would look like one of those rock band singers, with black eyes and streaks down my face?*

Steff opened up her computer and found Mike's cell phone number from the studio's database. It took a couple of minutes to get up enough chutzpah to call Mike.

Chapter Eleven

T he events of the last few minutes were puzzling Mike. *I haven't a clue just what happened. This sweet petite girl smiled at me one minute and the next ... My shoulder still hurts. She must be a full contact boxer in her other life.* The rest of the limo ride to the clinic was a blur of people, cars, and buildings. A cheerful "We are here" spurred Mike into action. Grabbing his computer bag, Mike opened the door before the driver could get around the limo.

"Thanks again Dr. Lancaster, have a good day."

Mike muttered as he turned, "Mine sure went down the tube, and to make it worse is looks like rain again."

Soon Mike was at his lab suite entrance. Just as he passed his holographic imprinted ID card in front of the door lock console, his cell phone began ringing. After what seemed like forever, the door clicked open, and Mike put down his computer bag and retrieved his cell phone from its bottom. "Hello, this is Dr. Lancaster."

The almost inaudible voice on the other end was quivering. "This is Steff. I believe I owe you an explanation of my actions this morning."

"Yes, you do."

"Can you meet me for a late lunch or a cup of coffee ... ah say at the coffee shop across from the clinic? My treat. "

"Yes, I think we should," Mike's heart skipped a beat. "There's a lot unsaid which needs to be said."

"How about 1:30 pm, after the crowd thins out?"

"Wonderful, see you then. Bye." Mike was almost trembling with no clue why. He removed the nearly dry jacket and donned a crisp, clean lab coat. Sitting down, Mike picked up the day's staff notes on the current cell replacement experiments running in his lab. Mike soon realized he was just counting the pages and not reading a single word. Getting up, Mike put on his UV blocking glasses for a quick look at the cultures. At the door to the central lab, Mike again scanned his ID card and put his index finger into the scan port.

"Recognizing Michael Lancaster, please enter your personal code," droned the synthesized voice. Six clicks later the lock snapped open, and the door swung open and familiar invigorating lab smells filled Mike's nose. *At least, I have a running chance in here. Man, I just don't understand girls, much less passionate ones.* At the large blue incubator suite, Mike inserted his magnetic key card in the door console and keyed in his code.

Stepping through the door Mike moved towards the module with the "Do Not Open, Test in Progress" sign, Mike turned on the three-axis camera system and entered Test Number 4566. Inside the glass-walled chamber, the camera-mounted microscope moved quickly to Test Chamber Number 4566 and locked its laser positioning beam on the reference bar. The tissue slice quickly came into focus. "Let's see, yes, things are going very well. Looks like the damaged hepatocytes are almost entirely replaced." Mike pushed the scan key, and the system moved back and forth across the liver slice generating a picture of today's image superimposed over yesterday's. The scan indicated the treated stem cells had replaced nearly half of the damaged liver cells in fewer than five days.

Mike glanced at his watch. That *was a quick forty-five minutes*. Retracing his steps, Mike arrived at the front door of the clinic just in time to see Steff get out of a cab and walk into the coffee shop. Mike was still amazed by how she walked, almost like sliding on ice, moving but nothing moving. The feeling in the pit of Mike's gut was just like the night of his first prom: juiced but almost sick, flushed face and cold hands.

The delivery truck blared its horn as Mike dashed against the "Do Not Walk" signal. *Why on earth did I do that? The walk light was only a few seconds away."* Gaining his composure, Mike walked in the door, scanned the room, and saw Steff sitting in a quiet booth near the back. As Mike neared the booth, he could see she was crying. "Hi." Mike slid in across from Steff. The well-worn red plastic cushion had a familiar feel, reminiscent of his high school hangout.

"I am really -- really embarrassed. I don't ever lose my composure, much less beat up a guest." Drying her face, Steff, tried to not to make eye contact. "Can I have a second chance?"

Chapter Twelve

Mike leaned across the table. "Steff, I know I don't understand women very well, but what little I do know is what you did at the studio has me baffled. What on earth was it all about? First, you were all smiles then you exploded in my face. I have no idea who you're talking about when you yelling, Max. I'm assuming she was a friend, but I don't know how she connects to the clinic."

"Mike, I'm sorry. I didn't yet... well ...yes, I did want to jump you, and yes, I wanted to catch you off guard on camera. I still want to punish you for what you and Dr. Hayes did to Max."

"I still don't have a clue what you are talking about."

"All I know is when the nurses set Max up for her last stem cell infusion everything was okay until about five minutes after they finished. Max said her throat felt tight, and she had a hard time breathing. Then she made a strange gurgling noise and reached out to grab my arm and fell out of bed. By the time the nurse got around to see what was going on Max had no heartbeat. The nurse yelled for the crash cart, and they worked on Max for what seemed like forever. Finally, the Doc looked up and said, 'I'm sorry, but we lost her. Is there anything we can do or anyone we should notify?' Mike, all I could do was just sit there on my butt and stare at Max."

"I don't know what to say. - Go on ... please finish."

Steff dried a tear. "The chaplain came in and helped me up off the floor. We walked down the coldest hallway in the world to the chapel. All I could think about was why did Max's God let her die. He must be small. After a few minutes, I realized I wasn't hearing a word the chaplain was saying. I thanked him and left to call her parents, back in Minneapolis."

"I am very sorry Steff, but I still don't know who Max is."

"Maxine Rice is, uh . . . or was my dearest and longest friend. I first met her in the second grade. We were almost inseparable all the way through college. We were sorority sisters who remained as close as sisters even after we both graduated and went our separate ways. When Max was diagnosed with Type II Diabetes, her doctor at the Midwest Clinic suggested she look into a new experimental procedure which had been developed here in Denver at the Rosch Clinic. At the time, I did not know this was you and Dr. Hayes' pet project. Max came out here about eight months ago to see if she qualified for this experimental procedure. After a series of blood and tissue tests, the Clinic put her on the treatment waitlist. About two weeks after she completed her two-day orientation program she received a call to come in and start the treatment. Max packed up her things and moved here to Denver so she could begin the infusions since they suggested air travel and the procedures were sometimes incompatible."

"That's correct. We discovered some patients who receive the stem cell treatment sometimes experience vertigo and are prone to air sickness."

"The staff at the Clinic told her she would be receiving a series of six stem cell treatments which were developed to replace damaged pancreatic cells. If the procedure were successful, Max could stop using insulin. Max called me that night telling me all about how they installed her pancreatic infusion line and gave her the first of her six treatments."

"Well, so far what you're telling me is the way we set up the protocol for treatment of Max's type of diabetes. The stem cells need to be placed inside the pancreas so they can attach and replace the injured cells, which produce insulin. This Clinical Trial Protocol has been approved by the FDA and by both our in-house medical and ethics boards. Each prospective patient has to undergo an intensive two-day orientation and testing program so they can make an informed decision if they want to proceed with the protocol."

"You're right. Max spent almost an hour on the phone telling me all the details. After all, I am an investigative reporter, and Max knew I would ask a dozen questions. The first treatment went without incident. However; Max had to spend a lot of time in bed after each of the next four treatments. That's when I came down and became her caregiver for a week or so after each infusion. And, like I said everything was okay until the last treatment. Mike, all I want is to understand what happened to Max. The clinic's protocol indicated this was a safe procedure with only a small risk of side effects. Just before Max's fourth treatment, I was offered a job as an investigative reporter for Channel 7 here in Denver. And as Max would have told you I couldn't leave my old job fast enough. I packed up my stuff and moved her to Denver to take care of Max. The day before the last treatment she called and insisted I come and sit with her. She was so excited. The laboratory tests indicated her insulin output was almost back to normal and in fact, she had been reducing her insulin injections."

"That sounds about right. In the first round of clinical trials we, rather I should say Dr. Hayes, since it was his project, found seventy-five percent of damaged pancreatic cells were replaced in about four months, and by the last injection at six months we would expect a ninety-plus percent recovery of insulin production. In the initial clinical trials, we were only using five doses. When we rewrote the second-tier protocols, we added a sixth infusion to make sure the rehabilitated pancreas had additional stem cells for future repair."

"Like I keep asking, Why did Max die so quickly and why all of the cover up as soon as she died?"

"I still don't get the connection."

"Here, look at this note."

"What am I looking at?"

"A couple of days after Max passed I got enough self-control to look through the paperwork I was given at the clinic. Stuck to the bottom of her cremation certificate, I found that note."

Mike read the note – **They're lying, she shouldn't be dead** -- and headed it back to Steff. "What you think it means?"

"When I first saw it. It didn't make any sense until I remembered the secretary, who gave me the folder with all of Max's papers, waved goodbye to me with a green marker in her hand. She was not just holding the pen; she was pointing the green end at me. Also, her face was tense."

"Is there any way you can verify this note is real?"

"As soon as I made the connection. I called the clinic's legal office and asked to talk to the secretary in the corner office next to the door. The person on the phone then told me she had just won a $100,000 lottery scratch ticket, turned in her resignation, emptied her desk, and left."

"That does seem odd. What did you do next?"

"I asked if I could get her phone number, but was told that information is confidential, which makes sense."

"When I get back to the clinic. I will call personnel for her number and see if they have any forwarding information. What else made you think the clinic was covering up Max's death?"

"Mike, she was a registered organ donor and in her unique way of doing things she had her funeral all planned out in case something went wrong. The day before she died I received notarized copies of her living will, Durable Power of Attorney, specific health directives, and instructions and how she wanted her organs donated. She even had picked out songs and her pallbearers. When I got back to my apartment the afternoon she died, I gathered up all the paperwork and went back to the clinic to take care of her last wishes. I was ushered into an official-looking conference room with a long pecan-colored table with two middle-aged gentlemen sitting on one side. The taller of the two gestured towards the chair opposite them. After giving me their crisp business cards, they identified themselves as contract attorneys for the clinic. On one corner of the table was an ornate jar about a foot tall."

Mike held up his right hand, "Whoa, the clinic has an in-house team of attorneys, and to my knowledge, they do not contract out legal stuff. Now you have my full attention. Please continue."

"They assured me that in keeping with Ms. Rice's religious beliefs, spelled out in her health directive, she was not to be cut on or have an autopsy performed, and she was to be cremated as soon as possible after her death and no later than twenty-four hours. I knew something was phony when they gestured towards the jar and told me she was already cremated. Mike, I know for a fact five hours is not enough time to get all that done and have an urn full of cold ashes. They also said that at Ms. Rice's specific health directive an autopsy had not been performed, and she was cremated at the clinic's registered facility. They stood up and coldly expressed their condolences, extended limp and cold handshakes and ushered me out of the room with a curt, 'We have notified her parents to claim her ashes ... and that's the end of it'. Even before the conference room door was closed a tense-looking secretary handed me a brown bag with Max's belongings and a file folder of papers."

"Are you saying the clinic lied to you?"

"Yep!"

"Wait just a minute, I helped write those treatment protocols, and I remember reading, and approving a memo indicating Max's treatment protocol file was complete, and in the clinic's FDA file."Steff continued, "The secretary also made sure I signed a release form for her belongings and that I received a copy of Max's living will and death directives. Mike, they had to be phony. Max was a very religious person and had often talked about how she hoped her organs would be able to save another person's life. Mike, I tell you she would not have changed her mind the day she had her last treatment. She called that morning and made one of her left-handed jokes about making sure her organs were treated with respect. So I don't think Max changed her mind in three hours and had time to have all those complicated papers drawn up and notarized before her last treatment. The lawyers told me she had changed her mind the day after I received the certified copies, which could not have happened."

"I'm not sure what you mean?"

Steff stood up and leaned toward Mike, "As I understand it, Max would have to have signed papers at the clinic, right?"

"Yes, that's standard protocol so our clinical staff would be able to make sure Max understood everything she was signing, and to be sure there's a two day waiting period before any treatment can begin."

"Well, that would be impossible, since at the time the clinic's slick lawyers say she signed these papers, she was out of town. Max was attending a conference down in Durango."

"Steff, what you telling me makes no sense at all. The

approved protocol has to have a Notary and, at least, two witnesses for any changes. So are you telling me the witnesses also lied? What about the Notary?"

"Mike, what I'm telling you is the file I was given at the clinic has to be carefully executed forgery. One of the so-called-lawyers even signed as a Notary. When I asked the clinic's legal office if I could speak with one of the two witnesses, I was told both were out of the area at a month-long research exchange program with a large Eastern University. When I asked which university, they said they were not at liberty to provide that information due to secrecy constraints. Later on, when I got my senses all straightened out, I tried calling the telephone numbers listed below the two witnesses' signatures. Both of their phone numbers had been disconnected, and there was no forwarding number on file. The Secretary of State had no record of the lawyer being a Notary. When Manny checked their mail forwarding addresses, he could find no forwarding addresses available."

"Who is Manny?"

"Oh, he's my Godfather. His name is Maryon Alexander, but don't call him that. He only answers to Manny."

"I'll keep it in mind if I ever meet him. What does he have to do with this?"

"He works for the NSA as an analyst of some sort or another. He is posted to the Pentagon and lives in DC. He and my father have been friends long before I was born. From time-to-time, he helps me dig up information for my various investigative projects."

"Can he do that, I mean to get information whenever you need it?"

"Sure it's all public record. All Manny does, is to put it together in a way I can understand. He is one of those super geeks you hear about on those CSI programs."

"What did Manny tell you about these two gals?"

"They disappeared the day after they were supposed to have signed the protocol changes. Hmm, that would have been four days before Max was killed. He was unable to find any information about where they could have gone or why. They also closed out their local checking and savings accounts and vacated their apartment without even a day's notice. Oh, by the way, they were also roommates. I also checked around to see if any of their friends knew where they had gone. I also talked to some of their neighbors, and all I got was they were here one day and gone the next. One of their neighbors did tell me they were going to work on a clinic project somewhere in Mexico, not at an Eastern University like the lawyers told me. So to make a long story short, Manny and I both struck out. It's like those two gals have fallen off the face of the earth."

Chapter Thirteen

Maryon Alexander was dead tired. The red-eye from London to DC was packed, hot, and rough. Separating his dirty clothes from his less dirty clothes was a familiar chore. The next item on a blurry mental checklist was to punch the playback key on his landline answering machine. The first three messages blurted out just to be deleted. When the fourth message appeared, the voice rang a familiar tone. "Hi Manny, it's me, Richard's little troublemaker. Please check your email and give me a call as soon as you get this, even if it's in the middle of the night-- thanks a bunch, you're a doll -- Hugs and kisses, Steff."

Well, I'll be. I haven't heard that voice since she moved to Denver. Manny rummaged through his i-phone contacts list until Steff appeared. A quick tap and her contact page opened up. A second tap and Steff's phone rang. Shortly after the fourth ring Steff answered, "Hi, Manny, thanks for calling back."

"Good morning darlin' time to wake up."

"I am awake; at least I think I am."

"Well sorry about that, it must be a bit past two in Denver. But you did ask me to call you as soon as I got your message. I just got back from a conference in London."

"Was it good?"

"Yes, it was good, and I learned a lot --- but talked too much. Well so much for the small talk. What do you need?"

"I'm doing a favor for a friend and need to know what you can find out. There's more information in my email. I hope you have time."

"Ya, I'll be happy to do."

"What's it going to cost me this time?"

"The usual fee, but, this time, it might take two lunches to square my bill. You still owe me for talking you through Max's strange death. Yeah, I'll get on it as soon as I get unpacked. Have a good rest of the night. I'll get back to you soon as I can."

"Uncle Manny, I love you bunches and bunches."

"Yeah –yeah—yeah ... hugs and kisses back at ya."

Manny turned on his computer and searched for Steff's e-mail. It was found buried about halfway down a list of over a hundred e-mails. After a quick read, he knew there was no more to do tonight. Propping up his feet on the well-worn corner of his roll-top desk Manny wondered what Steff was into now. Leaning back in his plush chair Manny closed his eyes for a few minutes, which became four hours.

The morning again came too quickly, which was not uncommon. Manny was always on a plane going somewhere. A quick cleanup, a peaceful ride on the Metro, an unusually quick passage through security and a brisk ten-minute walk brought Manny to his office deep in the bowels of the Pentagon. The debriefing for the London trip seemed like it took forever. Soon he was alone in his office. A few quick keystrokes and Steff's e-mail popped open revealing her request for information about a Brad Smith. *There has to be a million Brad Smith's ... Well, look at that! He popped up on the first page.* Manny spent the next quarter of an hour sifting through a myriad of data packages on Denver's Brad Smith. Finally, Manny had gleaned all he could from the cloud. What he found was a bit troubling. Regular office activities broke into his concentration, and his search for more information on Brad had to wait until late that afternoon.

Manny opened up his contacts list and put in a call to his friend in the international banking section of the NSA. Double-click and the phone rang. "Hi, Phil this is Manny. I need to pick your brain; got a minute? What do you know about Brad Smith? Oh ... I didn't realize he used to be on your college golf team. Yes, I know he is the Secretary to our G8 guy... Ya, I know he has been in the banking group for a long time. Well, let me ask a favor. Can you bundle up his file and send it over by secure courier? ... ASAP ...

Yes, that will be good. Thanks for the offer but you know I barely know a three wood from a putter."

Chapter Fourteen

Mike slowly stroked his chin. "I'm not sure what to make of all of this Steff, but it sure does seem like some things are not what they appear to be. If what you're telling me is true, then someone from inside the clinic is manipulating paperwork to cover up what may have been a medical accident."

"Do you mean malpractice?"

"We don't like to use that term here at the clinic. Speak it out loud in some places, and the room gets quiet. I'm not quite sure what I should do now, but at the very least I need to go back to the clinic and take a look at Max's paperwork. I need to see if I can make any sense of what you just told me."

"Not to be too pushy, but I'll gladly pay for a taxi if we go right now."

"Thanks, but I belong to the old school. You know, open doors, stand up when a lady stands, and all stuff, so please let me pay for the taxi."

As Mike and Steff left the little bistro, a gentle rain began to fall. Steff reached into her backpack and pulled out a small umbrella, and the two of them snuggled underneath it. Even the rain could not quench the occasional whiff of Jasmine Mike sensed in this forced closeness.

The taxi ride to the clinic was uneventful, a backseat full of small talk. The afternoon drizzle had stopped by the time they reached the clinic. Mike checked in at the security desk and obtained a visitor's pass for Steff. As the guard bussed them through the gate, Steff conjured up a half smile.

"I did not realize a simple clinic would have such high security. Do you guys have a hidden Meth Lab downstairs to help cover your overhead?"

"It may be best if I show you rather than trying to explain things to you, and no, we do not have a Meth lab, at least not in the basement." Contagious laughter shortened the time to get to the elevator.

"Hey, remember I am an investigative reporter. Not your average fifth-grade science dropout. You can use longer words, but don't let it go to your head."

The trip up the elevator to Mike's laboratory suite was quiet, as was the short trip down the corridor to Mike's office. Mike paused at a small diamond shaped keypad. A wave of his bright red magnetic keycard clicked open the tall glass doors. Through two more keycard activated doors and they were in Mike's office, which looked more like an unkempt file room than the Director of R & D. "Excuse the mess; I use the vertical filing system. Grab a chair if you can find one ... oh, just a second let me clear one off. There, now you can sit. Give me a minute to sign into the server, and we will see what's up with Max's paperwork."

Steff tried to hide her anticipation and begin fidgeting with a large manila envelope. She extracted from her backpack. Leaning a bit towards Mike, "Would you like Max's case number? I have it here in my notes."

"That would be very helpful. Our cases are filed according to the unique number, so the patient's name doesn't show up. It's all part of HIPA. You know patient's records are confidential ... Hum – That's odd, it says here we have no patients with that case number."

"Well, that would surely be in keeping with what Manny told me shortly after Max died. He thought everything seemed suspicious and wouldn't be surprised if the real records for Max no longer existed."

"How can Manny know that?" ... *Just what kind of analyst is he anyway?*

Chapter Fifteen

D r. Peter Franklin Hayes was about as different from Mike as day is from night. Mike was tall and sandy blond where Peter was short and dark-haired. Mike tended to be reserved and spoke with a slight southern accent. On the other hand, Peter was gregarious and outgoing and spoke with a slight New England accent. Peter and Mike had been in school together since kindergarten. Sometime during the third grade, both boys discovered science, Mike more as a thinker and Peter as a get-things-done person. In their first science fair project, Mike thought up the idea, and Peter made it happen. Their project came in third out of ninety-six projects. They were both disappointed and vowed never to be third again. In years to come, this became a self-fulfilling prophecy. Mike and Peter won first place in about everything they did. Their biology project placed first in the state and first at the international science fair winning the dynamic duo full-ride scholarships to the college of their choice for a full four years plus a second award of $25,000 to fund undergraduate research projects. Peter and Mike both chose the University of Colorado, both graduating summa cum laude just three years later.

After graduation, Mike and Peter were offered full-ride pre-doctoral fellowships at the Johns Hopkins School of Medicine. Both begin working with adult stem cells in earnest. In four years, they published multiple peer-reviewed manuscripts associated with stem cells. During their last year, they completed their dissertations, stood for their oral exams, graduated a year ahead of their peers and were both awarded three-year post-doctoral research fellowships.

During this time, they begin working with a donated stem cell line from a prisoner who years ago was chemically castrated years ago as a plea deal for rape. As part of his prison rehabilitation, he began to donate both blood and bone marrow. One bone marrow donation was cryo-frozen when the prospective recipient unexpectedly died of complications, not associated with her cancer.

When Mike and Peter heard about this untapped reservoir of stem cells, they secured the frozen sample and began growing adult stem cell cultures derived from this individual. As part of their screening process, they tested the effect of this line of stem cells on human tissue biopsy samples, with various degrees of cellular damage. To their surprise and great excitement, several of the damaged tissue samples were repaired by co-mingling with stem cells from this prisoner.

They next added the stem cells to diagnostic liver biopsy cultures taken from humans with various types of liver failure. Again to their amazement stem cells from this prisoner infiltrated into the damaged liver tissue and replaced damaged or destroyed cells with newly regenerated liver cells. With this information in hand, Peter and Mike divided their attention for the first time in their academic and research life. Mike continued to work with liver cells while Peter began to work with pancreatic cells derived from diabetic patients. Both lines of research proved fruitful beyond their wildest expectations.

Soon both were able to demonstrate this particular line of stem cells was able to repair a wide variety of liver damage and damage to pancreatic cells and, in particular, the Islets of Langerhans which are responsible for the synthesis of insulin. As their postdoctoral research programs came to an end, the Rosch Clinic in Denver Colorado offered them staff research posts in their newly established Center for Adult Stem Cell Research. This move was a natural transition for both Mike and Peter. Each was given large research labs, complete with technicians, equipment, and broad-based funding.

Both Mike and Peter continued to pursue their individual lines of investigation. The only commonality was they both used the same prisoner derived stem cell line. One of the unique things Peter discovered in his early insulin research was the stem cells were more active with tissue obtained from females and males with low testosterone levels, such as post-menopausal males.

Using the medical staff of the clinical wing of the Rosch clinic Mike and Peter were able to obtain FDA approval for limited clinical trials in six human volunteers. Three vvolunteers with liver damage and three with diabetes were given small amounts of stem cells infused directly into the damaged organs. Extensive testing on these volunteers revealed significant organ repair in the areas adjacent to the stem cell infusions. An additional FDA approval expanded round of clinical trials was approved. This initial test group of six volunteers and a second test group of ten volunteers were given treatments with higher numbers of stem cells. Over a period of an additional three months of regular infusions of stem cells, all individuals demonstrated significant and organ-wide improvement. Besides the majority of both sets of test subjects experienced a near complete rebuilding of the damaged organ. Also, the first volunteers experienced healing of unrelated tissues.

In their third clinical study of twenty male and twenty female volunteers, all over the age of fifty, verified Peter's initial observation that this line of stem cells was most effective in volunteers who had low levels of testosterone was verified. The third study determined those male test subjects who exhibited normal testosterone levels were significantly less responsive as measured by organ repair. A subset of the male test group, which exhibited normal or high testosterone levels, also exhibited little or no repair of their damaged organs. As per FDA protocols, these test subjects were dropped from the program and were no longer eligible for additional stem cell treatments with this particular line of stem cells.

With the publication of their clinical trials, Peter and Mike became overnight sensations in the stem cell research world. They were invited to speak at numerous symposiums and research conferences. This notoriety led to their being awarded the S.K. Benedict Award for **Innovative Research in the Emerging Field of Adult Stem Cells.** This award came with a $50,000,000 five-year research stipend. This exploding notoriety made Mike both nervous and cautious while Peter became more egocentric and more aggressive in his research and clinical trials.

Chapter Sixteen

I t was during the first year of the Benedict award that Peter had his first outbreak of Bell's Palsy. Bell's Palsy is a nonlethal disease wherein the patient loses the ability to move specific facial muscles. This loss of nerve function in Peter's case was caused by a dormant herpes simplex virus triggered by an allergic reaction to tree pollen.

Because of Peter's vain nature, he took a leave of absence and went to central Mexico for treatment at a clinic which specialized in a multi-pronged attack to Bell's Palsy. Their approach was to use a combination of physical therapy, vitamins, biofeedback, and electrical stimulation. Peter was back to his old self in about four weeks and returned to the clinic. Peter's first outbreak was a mild case, and with his aggressive treatment, there was no permanent damage to the facial nerves on the left side of his face.

His second outbreak came about one year later. This time, the treatment took six weeks before Peter's face was back to normal. It is Peter's third outbreak which is currently giving Mike trouble. Mike thought it odd the third outbreak came after only six months, and it coincided with the scheduled news story on Channel 7. Mike thought Peter had an allergic reaction to something different.

During his second outbreak, Peter had begun to gamble, first at a small local casino, but then quickly moved on to a larger casino operated by local drug lords. Peter's luck at gambling seemed unreasonably good at first. At one time he was almost a quarter of a million dollars ahead. He later figured out he was baited by what appeared to be a string of good luck. It wasn't just a string of good luck followed by some rotten luck, but a systematic program of cheating and drugs designed to guide him to overextend his line of credit. Peter soon had run up $75,000 in personal IOUs and had maxed out his two credit cards. When Peter returned to Denver, he was meticulous to hide his financial troubles from Mike.

Chapter Seventeen

R eginald James Horn, or Reg for short, began his lackluster scientific career as a promising lab tech. Reg graduated from an Ivy League school with high marks in chemistry, biology, and physics. He entered graduate school and gave it a try for one year, during which he discovered his scientific strength was in the laboratory. Reg was a good follower, but not much of an innovator. Whatever his research advisor planned in the laboratory, Reg was able to accomplish with flying colors. But when it came to designing his experiments, Reg just didn't have the drive. During the next ten years, Reg worked at several biochemical research laboratories, as he worked his way from the East Coast to Denver.

Shortly after the announcement of the stem cell award, Peter and Mike began assembling their research teams. At one of his routine blood, donation appointments Peter met Reg. After several minutes of chitchat, Peter realized Reg was one of those diamonds-in-the-rough technicians. After a quick telephone call to the clinic's human resources office, Peter offered Reg a position on his research team, much to Rag's great delight.

Over the next two years, Reg proved his worth to Peter's research team. Time and again he was able to figure out technical problems associated with Peter's ideas. In short, all Peter had to do was to explain to Reg what he wanted to find out in a particular experiment and turn him loose in the lab. Towards the end of the second year of the project, Peter noticed Reg was a bit distracted after returning from a vacation in Mexico. Rag's distraction lasted almost a month during which time he repeatedly told Peter, "I'm just not sleeping very well, but not to worry." Peter was genuinely surprised when one day Reg came bouncing in the lab just like his old self and announced he had gotten the best night's sleep in months, and everything would be okay.

The next few months Reg begins to show a keen interest in Peter's work, asking all sorts of questions about where Peter was taking his research and why certain pieces of data were more important than others. Peter perceived this as a welcome change in Rag's attitude toward research and felt he had a research colleague more than just a competent technician.

It wasn't long after Peter returned from his second trip to Mexico that his countenance and mood changed dramatically. For example, when Mike asked him if his treatment at the holistic clinic was worth the trip, Peter just mumbled, 'Yeah, I guess so' and abruptly turned and walked away. During the next couple of weeks, Peter seemed worried all the time and was jumpy every time his cell phone rang. One particular morning Peter seemed upset with everyone in the lab. It was in this atmosphere that Reg motioned Peter to follow him into the supply room at the back of the laboratory.

"Dr. Hayes, I talked with my other boss this morning. He wants to know how your stem cell line works. Not the PR stuff you hear about but really, how does it work?"

"What do you mean your other boss? I'm your boss."

"Dr. Hayes I'm afraid I have some disturbing news for you. I have been working in your laboratory for months under less than honorable conditions. My other boss is a man who has his fingers in more than one pie."

"I'm not sure what you're talking about Reg, but it doesn't sound very ethical."

"Being ethical has nothing to do with the dilemma you're in. For example, my other boss knows you have a pile of IOUs which are coming due at the end of this week. He also knows when you cash your paycheck on Friday you are still almost ninety-five thousand dollars short. He would like to help you out of your dilemma, and all he wants in exchange is information which you've been able to verify in the laboratory, but have not yet published."

"Hypothetically speaking, if I can give you that kind of information how is it going to benefit me in the long run?"

"My boss will be happy to pay off your IOUs, your credit cards and stake you to a $200,000 offshore bank account. He's not asking for your firstborn or your right hand, but I can tell you if you don't pay off those IOUs when they come due next Friday - well let's say it might cost you your right hand. The people who you owe money to are part of a giant drug cartel which also suckered me into what looked like a couple of really lucky nights at the casino. But before I knew it, I had lost my shirt, and in a drugged stupor, I signed a couple of big IOUs.

Peter pushed his left hand deep into his lab coat pocket. "What does have to do with anything?"

"Much like I am talking to you right now my other boss approached me with a similar deal to pay off my debts. All I had to do was to send him highlights of you and Mike's stem cell projects. At first, I was a bit skeptical but like you, my IOUs were coming due, and I had no money to pay them. So I started sending him a brief overview of each week's work. He paid off my IOUs and after he receives my weekly updates a healthy chunk of change lands in my offshore account."

Peter now was clenching his hidden hand into a tight fist. "How long have you been spying on Mike and me?"

"Remember when I started taking an active interest in how and why you were setting up your experiments?"

"Yes, I was pleasantly surprised by your change in attitude. At the time, I thought you had just caught the research bug."

"In this sense I did. If you think back, I started off by first asking simple questions, then more detailed questions, and finally, you gave me the password to the lab's database and told me to look it up myself."

Peter began to lose his composure as he leaned toward Reg face. "Have you sold out every one of my secrets?" Peter now grabbed Rag's lab coat and pushed him against the storeroom wall. "What about Mike's work?" Peter was now face-to-face with Reg and yelling. "He has nothing to do with my debt! Leave him out of this, or we are through right now."

"Okay. Turn loose and back off -- please. I was having a hard enough time understanding your work. It wasn't until last week that I was able to start looking at Dr. Lancaster's work in the database. By the way, his notes are a lot easier to follow than yours."

Peter backed up, and let his hands relax, "Again, what does have to do with anything? I don't like the idea of anyone stealing Mike's work."

"Dr. Hayes, my boss is not interested in stealing or publishing you and Dr. Lancaster's work. You will always be free to publish your work, attend seminars and give lectures without any interference from my boss."

"Are you telling me this is not some kind of corporate espionage, just a bizarre philanthropist who is interested in stem cell research?"

"I don't think it's quite that simple, but to be honest, I'm not sure what he's doing with it other than the fact that he has set up a laboratory parallel to yours."

"Wait a minute; now you expect me to believe this philanthropist is taking my research and my unpublished data and using it to build some kind of a clone lab?"

"Dr. Hayes, I don't have an answer to that question because my boss has never told me specific details, and I've never seen the lab. I think it started up early last year when he began to ask for model numbers of the Clinic's lab equipment. I started off giving him information on the big-ticket items, then information on smaller items like vacuum ovens, microscopes, and the like. Whenever you guys order a piece of new equipment, he orders one the same day."

"Let's get back to the crux of the matter. Just what do I have to do, or I guess what do I get for selling my soul to the devil, and what is it going to cost me to get it back?"

"My boss would be delighted to talk with you, and he said he would try to answer some of your questions, but not all. All it takes is for you to say yes and I will dial a number on the burner phone I have in my pocket. Don't try to trace the number since I'm just calling another burner phone. Well, what's it going to be doc, a new job or no right hand ... ?"

Chapter Eighteen

C live Andrew Burke III is a person of a singular mind. When he takes on a task, his level of concentration approaches devotion; he thinks of little else until it is complete. During times between straight arrow thinking, he indulges his unique passion, Fedora hats. His keeps his collection in an elaborate climate-controlled wardrobe off his modest bedroom. Within this camera guarded room, select hats garner special recognition based on what Mr. Burke was doing at the time he wore a specific hat. For example, a particular dark brown fedora with a thin twisted red and dark green band was being worn the day Clive leveraged his first small bank buyout. This rather insignificant financial transaction marked Clive's first transgression against his internal moral compass on his downward spiral to becoming an evil financial rogue.

Clive can best be described as a product of rural English upbringing. His father was an underpaid bookkeeper at his village's local bank, a branch of the much larger Bank of Scotland. Clive's father persisted in his desire that Clive has a better life. This desire was fueled by a continuous and unrelenting devotion to the banking industry. Besides his schoolwork, Clive was required to read, digest, understand, and regurgitate banking principles back to his father every Wednesday night. These grueling sessions, described by Clive's father as life's most valuable lessons, only ceased with his matriculation in public school. His father's choice of schools was based solely on the quality of their financial education.

Clive's grades and reputation as a brilliant thinker in public school heralded his admission to Harvard University in the US and his subsequent graduation with high honors from its renowned MBA program. His research concentration resided in the area of financial auditing and corporate structure. His successful completion of this program was a foregone conclusion.

In the summer of his junior year at Harvard, Clive took his first step toward his singular passion for manipulating and controlling large banking systems, and in particular what is termed world banking. This fortuitous step entailed an internship with the British Secretary of the G8 financial group. His tenacity and single-mindedness in the office of the cash Comptroller so impressed the Secretary that he offered Clive a full-time position. The only stipulation on this cherished appointment was for Clive to work two years in the worldwide banking industry at any level to gain a first-hand understanding of financial markets and their inner workings.

His Harvard credentials and a glowing recommendation from the Secretary cemented a position in middle-management of a large Wall Street bank. During his twenty-four-month stint, Clive oversaw the hostile takeover of several mid-size international banking institutions by his employer. Not to be outdone Clive was able to add four fedoras to his collection by vicious leverage buyouts of small family banks outside of his employment, making him a multi-millionaire before he was twenty-five.

His transition into the G8 financial world was both quick and uneventful. Clive quickly realized the real power structure of the G8 was in the hands of its Secretaries. Within eighteen months and two more fedoras, Clive had migrated upward to become the aide-de-camp to the British Secretary. Like Joseph of the Bible Clive was now the second most powerful man in the Secretary's office but, unlike Joseph, his loyalty lay with himself and not the Secretary.

Another twenty-four months of manipulation, back scratching and other questionable corporate antics Clive had managed to cross, without a hint of remorse, the last moral guidepost his father had worked so diligently to plant and nurture during his early development. The notches on his corporate revolver produced another half dozen fedoras, each one uniquely different and appropriately enshrined.

Chapter Nineteen

Mike cleared the screen and retyped Max's patient ID number and hit enter. In the blink of an eye, the display indicated there was not a patient with that ID number. Mike cleared the screen again and entered Max's full name; still the same response: "patient with this name does not exist."

"What does it mean – "name does not exist"- I don't understand. I have copies of all of her records - here look." Steff spread out a sheaf of papers atop the clutter of Mike's desk.

"I'm not sure. Hand me a lab report, and I'll try and come into Max's file using the clinical laboratory's test ID number." With a few quick mouse clicks, Mike was in the laboratory report database. Let's see test report ID 1-7-99-463, a blood glucose test the day you said she died. That's odd; it says 'Report for this test is unavailable,' yet I am holding the certified test report in my hand."

"Here is another test report, this time for a CBC, type and crossmatch in case a blood transfusion is needed during her first stem cell treatment."

Mike typed in the test report ID, but again the same result: 'Report for this test is unavailable.' Three additional lab report ID numbers yielded the same frustrating response. "Steff, in your file of papers do you happen to have her driver's license number?"

"Yes, I have both her old Minnesota and her new Colorado license."

"Let's start with the Colorado number." Mike carefully transcribed the number and touched enter. The flat screen monitor indicated "no file found matching this license number." Mike quickly reentered the number, this time pounding the keys a bit harder, but again to no avail.

"Mike, are you telling me all of these signed reports are not in your system anywhere?" Steff begins stuffing the papers back into her file when Mike held up his finger.

"Let me see her Minnesota license; that would've been the number she would have used in her prescreening before transferring from outpatient admissions into the clinical trials program."

Again, careful but nimble fingers, pounded in the ID number. Mike halfway expected the same result the last half an hour had produced. He had to look a second time when the computer, this time, identified this ID number attached to a pre-clinical evaluation questionnaire. Mike pointed his mouse at the master file tab and clicked. The computer's response did not produce any clarity to their situation. "It says here the questionnaire is complete, but turned in without any identification; therefore, the file was subsequently purged. Hmm, it doesn't say who purged the file, but it did say the file was purged the evening Max died." Scrolling down Mike discovered whoever had purged the file did not know it was attached to Max's Minnesota license number since the default setting was for a Colorado license.

"Do you mean Max actually does exist?"

"So it appears, but only as a Minnesota license number, no other data is available." Mike quickly opened the other available tabs, only to discover any data associated with the Minnesota number came up as "No data available." However, the last tab revealed a ray of hope when the message changed to "You have attempted to open a file previously purged to cloud storage. If you require additional information about this stored file, please contact the System Administrator."

Steff was now standing behind Mike's chair, leaning forward. Her hair brushed his right ear. Mike's mind gridlocked. The science part was ready to grab the phone while the rest focused on the silken touch to his ear and the hint of Jasmine washing across the screen.

Refocus came quickly as Steff almost yelled in his ear. "Well, what are you waiting for—call the Administrator." The sharpness of her voice removed the illusion of warmth from the previous few seconds. Steff's finger pressed on the screen. Small rainbows radiated out from the well-placed digit, covering the link to the clinic's IT administrator.

As Mike reached for the phone, he suddenly realized that at the time of setting up the clinic's master system the IT administrator had given both he and Peter co-administrator status. Looking a bit sheepish Mike turned to Steff, "I am one of the administrators. Let's see what I can find out."

"For a research Ph.D., you sure took a long time to figure that one out."

"I'm not even sure how to get into the administrator files. Let me call our IT department and have them walk me through the procedure." Mike picked up the phone and called IT. "Hi, this is Dr. Michael Lancaster from the research clinic. I need some help in logging onto our system as an administrator. ... Aaah, I need to look at a file which may have been inadvertently purged to the cloud. ... What do you mean I need to fill out a form? I am co-administrator of the system so why do I need to complete a form. ... Okay, I'll wait while you log in. ... What do you mean I'm not listed as an administrator? ... Well, then who are listed as administrators? ... Are we going to do a Catch 22 dance? Somehow, I knew you were going to say I need to be an administrator to answer that question. Let me talk to the director of IT... Oh, you are the director, no surprise there. Don't leave; I'm coming down to your office to get this thing straightened out. Goodbye."

"Did I hear you say you are not an administrator on your own software system?"

"Steff, I haven't got a clue what's going on, but let's get all of Max's papers together and put them in a safe place."

"I have a better idea. Before we leave, let's make two photocopies of everything in this file. You put yours in a safe place, and I'll keep mine."

"What about the other copy?"

"That one, dear boy, I'm going to send by registered mail to my friend Manny, and I want to get it sent to him today."

"There is a print and ship store just around the corner from the clinic on Colorado Boulevard. Until we get some firm answers to who's in charge of the clinic's computer, I think we both will feel better getting the photocopies made outside of the clinic."

"Why not use the one here in your office?"

"One of the things the IT department put in place a couple of months ago is every time we make a photocopy or send a fax on any of the clinic's machines a backup copy is forwarded to a secure storage platform in the cloud."

"Then what you're saying is you don't trust the clinic's IT security programs anymore."

"I've never really had much love for computers for anything other than computational or writing devices. The massive amount of data the clinic stores in the cloud has always bothered me. I guess I just don't trust something I don't understand, and I really don't understand how the cloud works other than every piece of data I generated in my lab is somehow stored in the cloud."

Mike shut down his computer, logged out of his office, returned Steff's pass and then left by way of a side entrance. From there they went down the alley to Colorado Boulevard and over to the print and ship store. After making their copies, Mike insisted they pay cash and not use a traceable credit or debit card.

"Mike, do I sense a growing paranoia in your actions?"

"Yeah, it has to do with the computer. It doesn't feel right, so I'd rather not have a traceable transaction. There's a branch post office about two blocks from here where we can buy a priority letter pack and get your stuff to Manny."

Walking to the post office was actually relaxing. About halfway there Steff hooked her arm through Mike's arm and leaned a little bit towards him causing Mike to almost stumble. His attempt to blame the uneven sidewalk was plausible enough to work.

"Be careful. If you fell, I don't think I could pick you up off the sidewalk." They both chuckled. The hint of Jasmine from Steff's hair was still proving to be a bit disconcerting to Mike's analytical mind.

As he approached the doors of the post office, Mike stepped a bit out in front and opened the door allowing Steff to enter. "I'm still part of the old school. Both my dad and my granddad always insisted we boys always open the door for any woman even if it was just my little sister. "

"I don't mind a little bit of knight-in-shining-armor from time to time. Thank you."

The overnight package to Manny was quickly assembled, addressed, and dispatched, again using only cash. A few steps down to the main door and, this time, Steff beat Mike to the door and pushed it wide open. "I just want to make sure you know I can take care of myself." With a full smile and a quick wink, Mike crossed the threshold and out into the cooling afternoon.

Chapter Twenty

"Mike, I need to call a friend."
"Okay, I'll wait for you." Mike walked a few steps away to wait for Steff.
Anne's phone again rang until her obnoxious greeting began. Steff jammed her phone back into her purse and caught up with Mike. "I don't understand why it keeps going to voicemail. I know Anne is home because she promised to call in sick today. I also made her promise not to answer the door or use her computer until I can hear back from Manny about the odd vibes she got from her second meeting with Brad yesterday."

"Steff, I'm sure she's okay, but if it helps you, I'll be happy to drive you over to her apartment and check in."

"It's a deal only if we can stop by and pick up her favorite pizza. Do you like pineapple and Canadian bacon?"

"If you're asking me is it my favorite pizza, then the answer is no, but I'm hungry enough to eat the box. What's Anne's address? We'll call ahead and pick up the pizza on the way."

"She lives in an apartment complex over on Wadsworth. Here, I'll call her favorite pizza parlor. It's just a couple blocks south of her apartment." Steff's nimble left thumb quickly keyed the number and, using the touch screen, ordered the pizza."

"How many phone numbers do you have memorized?"

"I haven't got a clue. It seems I have a gift. I hear a phone number once or twice, and somehow it gets stored in my gray cell phone book. When I was in grade school, my grandfather played a game. The winner was the one who memorized the most random numbers in one minute using the phone book. He would open the phone book and point to a number, and I would see how many phone numbers below his finger I could memorize before he closed the book. Ever since then phone numbers go in and don't seem to come out. Grandpa told me memorizing numbers was an important skill for a detective. He should know. He worked for the Pinkerton Detective Agency for almost forty years."

"Come on; let's get back to the clinic. I keep my car parked in the secure garage at the back." A few steps outside the print and ship store Mike's hand brushed against Steff's. Much to Mike's great delight Steff reached out and clasped his hand. The walk to the clinic's car garage echoed with small talk about telephone numbers and leaky brains.

Mike waved his ID card across the magnetic pad next to the elevator. After a familiar ding, the door began opening. At the same moment, an electronic voice announced, "Recognizing Michael Lancaster."

"Are all the doors at the clinic this polite or are you just trying to show off?"

"It must be a novelty for you, but to be honest, I don't think I even hear it anymore. I just stand there until the door opens and get on with my business. That's my car one parked over there under the big letter A."

"It sure isn't impressive. I thought the director of research and development would have a big SUV or sedan, not a Volt."

"You can't beat the mileage and besides the clinic pays for the electricity. I can drive around Denver for five or six hours on a single charge. Here get in. I think you find it very comfortable and don't be surprised it doesn't make much noise. Sometimes I sneak up on pedestrians, so I have to be careful when I'm driving, particularly in downtown."

Mike backed out and quietly sped up the exit ramp, made a left turn and headed for Wadsworth. Steff tried calling Anne's apartment but again received her voicemail. The trip to Cedric's Chicago Style Pizza was completed without a single word spoken. Steff just pointed left or right, and Mike blindly followed. They pulled around to the drive-up window, paid for the pizza and a 2 L Dr Pepper and headed to Anne's apartment.

As soon as Mike pulled into Anne's parking lot, they knew something was awry. Almost a dozen white and black police cars and bright red ambulances were milling around the middle of the parking lot. Their blue, red and amber lights were locked in a bizarre game of chase across the brick walls of the apartment complex as they began to leave one-by-one.

A police officer wearing a fluorescent orange vest flagged them down. As Mike rolled down the window, the officer asked for his driver's license and asked what their business was. Mike indicated they were on their way to her friend's apartment with pizza and soda. The officer quickly scanned Mike's ID and closed his tablet. As he handed back the driver's license, he asked who they were visiting and in which apartment.

Leaning across, in front of Mike, Steff told the officer. "We are on our way to visit Anne Hamilton. She lives in apartment twelve in unit nine." The officer then pointed towards a vacant parking place next to one of the flashing patrol cars. "Mr. Lancaster please park your vehicle. I think Detective Foster will want to ask you some questions."

Mike pulled into the parking place and turned off the power switch. Steff looked up and saw a uniformed policeman standing on the deck outside of Anne's apartment window. "I wonder what this is all about?"

Chapter Twenty-one

Eugene James Foster IV, or EJ to his friends, had been a detective since his third year out of the Police Academy. After about ten years he transferred to the Major Crimes Taskforce, where he now worked closely with the CBI forensic unit. EJ's call to Anne Hamilton's apartment was more of a fluke than any knowledge of a possible violent crime by the dispatcher. EJ just happened to be the duty officer on call. On the surface, there was no reason to believe Anne Hamilton's death was anything more than it appeared, an unfortunate fall down a short flight of stairs. EJ ducked under police barrier tape, held up his badge to the officer guarding the door, and made his way to the apartment in question.

EJ kneeled down beside the Assistant from the Coroner's Office and slipped on a pair of black barrier gloves. "Hi John, haven't seen you for a while. Where have you been?"

"I was taking a class on documenting crime scenes."

"Good for you, now let's put it to good use. What do we have here?"

"According to the apartment manager, her name is Anne Hamilton. I'm not the expert, but it looks like she died of a broken neck." He gently lifted the light brunette braided pigtail revealing a small protrusion at the base of her skull indicating a traumatic dislocation of her C1 vertebrae. Injuries of this type are almost always instantly fatal. "I made sure the photo guys had taken several close-ups before they left."

"Good job." EJ then nodded to John. "I'm done here." John then gently covered Anne's body with a clean white sheet and stepped back to give EJ room. After writing a few more notes, EJ closed his notebook just as the body retrieval team from the Coroner's office arrived. They carefully placed her into a jet black, full zippered body bag and gently placed her on the gurney and out they went. EJ turned to one of the officers standing near the bottom of the staircase. "Officer Dean, who discovered the body?"

"The young woman sitting over by the elevator. She comes in twice a week to clean the apartment and tidy up things. She wasn't expecting the victim to be at home this time of the day. She has not given anyone her statement yet. She is still pretty shaken. We called a friend to give her a ride home since she's in no condition to ride the bus."

"Is there anyone else besides her who has seen or heard anything out of the ordinary?"

"The tenant next door saw her come home after lunch, which was unusual. Later she said she could hear muffled voices, and later something bumped against the common wall. She said everything was quiet before and after the bump, except that the victim's telephone rang several times. After a while, she became concerned and knocked on the victim's door. But no one answered. About an hour later she called the resident manager and expressed her concern. A few minutes later she met the manager at the victim's door. The manager knocked several times and after no response opened the door. They entered the apartment where they discovered the body."

"Has anyone taken their statements?"

"Yes sir, I recorded the manager's statement on my tablet and with her consent took her face picture for reference. The cleaning lady was too shook up and said she would come down to the station and give her statement tomorrow. I gave her my card and asked if she needed a ride home. I called her friend, who will be here soon. "

"As soon as you are back at the station please email me a copy. Thank you, Officer Dean; I can handle it from here. On your way out, please ask everyone else to resume their assigned duties.

After several minutes of searching the apartment Officer Dean opened the door.

"Hey boss, there is someone out in the parking lot you need to talk to."

"Who am I talking to?"

"There's a couple parked outside who say they were on their way to the deceased's apartment with pizza. I checked the driver's ID. He is Michael Lancaster, a doc from some downtown clinic. I think you may know the gal with him. She's a reporter for Channel 7, at least, I think she's the one I saw interviewing you while back."

"Go and ask them to meet with me in the lobby."

Chapter Twenty-two

Officer Dean tapped on the window and asked politely," Mr. Lancaster, could you and the lady, please exit the car. Detective Foster would like to speak with you inside." Mike and Steff gave each other a quick 'What's Going On' look. Mike shrugged but fell into step behind Steff and the officer up the steps into the entrance lobby of unit nine.

As they entered the lobby a tall, slender man in his mid-forties approached them with his hand extended. "Hello, I'm Detective Foster. Officer Dean indicated you know Anne Hamilton. If you do, I would like to ask you a few questions."

As Mike begins to shake detective's outstretched hand, a puzzled look crossed Steff's face. "I know you. I interviewed you for a Channel 7 news story a couple of weeks ago. What's going on?"

"Thank you for remembering Ms. Huffman. How well did you know Ms. Hamilton?"

"Anne and I went to undergraduate school together, and after I had moved here, we reconnected and had lunch at least twice or three times a month. What has that got to do with why we are being questioned?"

"I'm afraid I have some bad news. It appears Ms. Hamilton died from an accident in her apartment."

Steff jumped forward. "Are you sure it's Anne? We just had lunch. What happened? —how did it happen? —when did it happen—?"

Detective Foster interrupted. "Please Slow down, I can only answer one question at a time. Yes, we are sure it's Ms. Hamilton. She apparently died from a fall down her stairs a couple of hours ago. The lady who lives next door said she saw her enter her apartment shortly after lunch. She thought it seemed odd for Ms. Hamilton to come home this early in the day. Thinking she might be ill, she knocked on the door about an hour later. When Ms. Hamilton did not answer, and after she heard the telephone ring, and go to voicemail several times, she became concerned."

"That telephone call may have been me. I called Anne about every thirty minutes all afternoon, but she did not answer."

"Thank you, I will need you to give me the exact time of each of your calls. Right after one of your calls. The site manager met her neighbor, and together they entered her apartment and found Ms. Hamilton lying at the bottom of her stairs. It looked like she may have stumbled and fallen to her death."

Steff was now getting a bit weak in the knees and grabbed Mike's arm for support so she could address Detective Foster face to face. In staccato-paced phrases, Steff let Detective Foster know that she did not think that was possible. "Anne was an NCAA gymnastics champion in college and has been a member of a local ballet troupe for years. She had an excellent sense of balance and always knew where her feet were. I don't ever remember her ever falling. Are you sure she fell?"

"Do you know of a reason it may not have been an accident?"

"When we had lunch today, she expressed lots of concern about her friend and was almost in tears. I suggested she go home and call in sick. I was unable to reach her all afternoon."

"Ms. Huffman, would you care to elaborate?"

"Detective Foster, I will be happy to come down to the station tomorrow and give you a full statement. Right now I would like just to go home; I am feeling nauseous."

"I understand." A well-practiced hand provided Steff his card. "Please call this number after ten for an appointment. I want to hear what you have to say in person, and I am not always available. This officer will escort you and your friend back to your car. Drive safely, and I will see you tomorrow."

The drive back to Steff's apartment was somber. Mike's attempt to lighten the atmosphere failed miserably. Steff kept shaking her head and muttering. "It's not an accident – – it can't be an accident – – I can't believe Anne is gone. Mike...uu-aah -- never mind, just get me home." Complete silence became their companion until Mike pulled up to Steff's apartment. "Thanks for the ride I will call you in the morning." Without another word, Steff disappeared into her apartment building.

Mike turned around and headed back to his apartment ignoring the fact his car needed a battery charge. *If she doesn't call in the morning, I'll for sure call her. I need to understand what's going on.*

Chapter Twenty-three

R eg 's polite knock at the door brought Peter to his feet. Three cat-like strides and Peter opened the door to his new destiny. "Come in Reg; I've been expecting you. I'm assuming you have talked to your other boss."

"Yes, he accepts your counter offer for a face-to-face meeting before you make your final decision. He has a car waiting for us at the side door of the clinic. I think it's best you clock out for the rest of the day."

Peter hung up his lab coat, picked up the telephone and informed the front desk he would be gone for the remainder of the day. "No, I will not be available for call forwarding. I will be in a meeting with my cell phone off. If anyone needs to get ahold of me, please have them leave a message or send me a text. Thank you."

Peter and Reg signed out of the laboratory and headed down the stairs to the waiting car. Reg opened the back door and motioned Peter inside. As Peter slid across, Reg bent down his tall, lanky frame and sat beside him. A dark glass separated them from the driver. Peter began to wonder what he was getting into. The car quickly made its way to Interstate 25, then to I 70, finally turning west towards Morrison. Reg handed Peter a black hood. Please cover your head. My boss is not ready to let you know where he lives just yet.

After what seemed like two hours of left turns, right turns, slow-downs, speedups, stops and starts the car turned onto a crunchy gravel road and soon stopped. The driver stepped out and closed the door. Peter could hear feet crunching, what he suspected was loose gravel.

"You can take the hood off now; we're here."

"Do I just sit here or do I get out?"

"We will just sit here until the house guard escorts us around back where you will meet your new boss. He wants me to tell you he would rather have you as a colleague than an employee or someone beholden to him."

After a few minutes, a pleasant looking giant of a man dressed in blue jeans and a stretched T-shirt covering muscles bulging in all directions approached the car. Without a word he opened the door and motioned for them to follow him. The only sound was their feet crunching the fine gravel along the pathway to the side of an unassuming but large house. As they rounded the corner, a mountain vista set behind the large swimming pool greeted them. "Please make yourself comfortable. Lemonade and soft drinks are on the table. Just help yourself. Mr. Burke is on a conference call and will be with you in a few minutes."

"This isn't quite what I expected when you told me I would meet your boss today. I'm not sure what I expected. I certainly wasn't expecting a gentle giant as an escort."

"I must warn you this gentle giant has retired twice. First time as a Navy seal and the second time as a full contact fighter. He's a charming person but will not allow anyone to touch Mr. Burke."

"I'll keep that in mind."

"Would you like some lemonade?"

"I think I'll pass for the time being. I am a little bit too nervous, and the last thing I need now is a sour stomach. How long have you known Mr. Burke?"

"A little over two years. The first eight months I only talked to him on the telephone, and like you one day, I took the black hood drive. I think you will find Mr. Burke is a quick learner, and unfortunately, he is also a stern taskmaster.

"I'm not sure what you mean by, unfortunately."

"Let's just say it's best to do what he asks when he asks. He's very generous with money when he considers a job well done. I have no first-hand experience, but I was told the same thing I'm telling you now, by the person who brought me out here."

"Does Mr. Burke wear a hat? Someone is coming out of the

house wearing a gray fedora with a bright yellow feather in the band."

"Yes, that is indeed Mr. Burke, and it would be good if you complimented him on his hat."

Chapter Twenty-four

Manny's intense concentration on his computer screen was interrupted by a tap on his window. A quick wave of his hand invited the courier into his office. "I have a secure parcel for Manny Alexander."

"That's me, where do I sign?"

"On line 14, and please let me scan your badge after you sign." The exchange of identification technology was both quick and painless. The courier thanked Manny, closed the door and disappeared around the corner of the next cubicle.

Manny logged off his computer and turned his attention to the six-inch thick accordion file sealed with a strip of "eyes only" tape. A quick snip and the file seemed to inhale as it expanded open. Over the next forty-five minutes, Manny skimmed through several hundred pages detailing most of Brad Smith's adult life. A separate file folder titled "Secretary to G8 Representative" seems to be a bit small based on the number of years Brad held this position. Manny spread out the half-dozen sheets of paper and soon realized a large number of pages had been redacted from the file.

Manny signed on to the NSA secure portal. After answering a couple of security questions and scanning his right thumb, he found himself inside the NSA general file site. Three mouse clicks later Manny typed in Brad's file number. After a few seconds, the screen asked for Manny's passcode and soon displayed Brad's file. Manny scrolled down the list of specific files detailed along the left side of the screen until he reached

Brad's G8 file. A double-click revealed the same half-dozen disjointed pages that Manny just read. Upset, Manny scrolled down the screen. *There has to be more.* Near the bottom left side of the screen, Manny found a hotspot labeled "more." Another double-click revealed a pop-up requesting a Delta 2.0 login. That's odd. *What is Brad into that requires this level of secrecy?*

For a few moments, Manny weighed the pros and cons of logging into the Delta system. The last time he logged in it took four hours of meetings, paperwork, and debriefings to satisfy the Delta Operations Team. *Oh well, at least, I know what I'm getting myself into.* Manny uncovered his Webcam and logged into the Delta portal. After entering his Delta passcode and now scanning his right index finger, the screen instructed him to look at the camera and push enter. Manny's image froze on the screen. A metallic computer generated voice requested Manny to enter his badge number followed by the # key. The face recognition software quickly deconstructed Manny's image to a series of triangles. After a few seconds, the security software confirmed his image and opened the Delta portal.

Three mouse clicks and one warning pop-up later Manny typed in Brad's NSA file number. After what seemed like five minutes Brad's file opened up with a pop-up indicating the information in the file is top-secret and Delta-level eyes only. A series of filenames on the left side of the screen was similar to the one he saw in the open system a few minutes ago. Double-Click on the file marked G8 opened up a large file. Manny quickly skimmed down several pages until he came to a section marked Phoenix Project. After a few minutes of reading Manny was not sure whether he was reading classified information about an actual event or a science fiction novel.

Chapter Twenty-five

M ike's alarm clock had just finished its first buzz when his cell phone rang, jolting him into a semi-conscious state. After a few seconds of fumbling and two more rings, he managed to get the phone in the right orientation. "Hello, this is Dr. Lancaster."

"Good morning sleepy head, this is Steff. Are you ready to figure this thing out? I have a couple of ideas I would like to run by you, so can we meet for breakfast? I'm assuming your hesitation means yes. How about meeting me at the pancake house couple of blocks north of the clinic, say in forty-five minutes?"

" Aaaahh …, Yeah. Okay. If you get there before I do, try to get one of those corner booths. They seem to be a lot quieter." Mike made a quick time calculation in his head and determined he had better get ready and leave quickly to get his car to the clinic's parking garage and charging. The short walk to the pancake house should help stir up his appetite. A quick exit down the stairs to his car and on to the clinic's north parking garage was thankfully uneventful. After plugging in the charging unit Mike walked briskly, hoping to beat Steff to the booth, so he could get his thoughts together. But to no avail. Pushing open the glass entrance door he could see Steff waving her hand from the North East corner booth. As Mike started to slide into the booth, Steff patted the cushion next to her. Sit here, you'll be able to see my laptop easier."

There was no argument from Mike. "How did you get here so fast? Your apartment is at thirty-minutes from here."

"I admit I cheated a bit. I've been here since a little before six trying to get enough nerve to call you. After my standoffish behavior last night I was afraid you might not want to see me."

"I didn't get much sleep last night either. I just kept thinking about Anne and Max. To lose two close friends in less than a month can't be easy. Enough of that. What do you have to tell me? You look like you're going to pop with excitement."

"Anne first. I couldn't wait, so I called Detective Foster last night and gave him my statement. He feels confident that the Medical Examiner will say she was murdered. I'll fill you in later. Here, this is more important." Steff opened a file folder and removed two sheets of transparency film and laid them on the table.

Mike took the opportunity to scoot a little closer. "So what's so important about two transparencies?"

"The one on the left is a copy of a power of attorney Max signed in front of me at her lawyer's office a couple of months ago. The one on the right is supposed to be her signature on the new health directives the clinic cited when they had her cremated."

"I'm still not sure what you're getting at?"

"Be patient. I learned a little trick a while back. See what happens when I superimpose the two signatures?" Steff very carefully repositioned the right signature on top of the left signature. "Tell me what you see."

"They look like the same signature."

"Very astute. They are not only looked like the same signature; they are the same signature. No one ever signs their name the same way twice. There's always a small variation. The spacing between the first and second name may be a little bit longer or a little bit shorter, but never identical."

"I see what you mean. How could the clinic get her signature?"

"After Max signed her health directives her attorney sent a notarized copy to the clinic as part of her health directives file. So all they would have to do is to scan her signature, color corrected and paste it into a false document, print the document, have it notarized, and all without a real pen ever touching paper, and poof a new legal-looking health directive was ready to replace the original one."

"I see what you're saying, but I don't follow how they could get a photocopy notarized without the documentation."

"That puzzled me for a long time, until last night. I was going through the documents Manny sent me when I noticed one of those so-called witnesses who conveniently disappeared to Mexico is a notary. Don't you see?"

"I think I know what you're suggesting. Let me see if I can summarize. I'm going to try and think the worst for a few minutes, so bear with me. What I think I hear you saying is one or more nefarious individuals forged all those documents so they could dispose of Max's body before anyone could take blood samples or schedule an autopsy."

"You're on the right track, but I believe all of this happened right after Max was killed. Notice I'm not saying natural causes, I'm saying killed. Why else would anyone try to construct such an elaborate ruse? I think we're fighting a conspiracy of silence within the Phoenix project."

"Let's take a break. I think our waitress is queuing up for the third pass by our table. Let's go ahead and order, and then we can continue." Mike motioned to the waitress who promptly took their order and refilled their coffee cups. Mike continued, "Okay, let me step way out on a limb here and see if this makes sense. You suggested they scanned and copied Max's signature."

"Yes, but I'm not sure where you're going with this."

"While we are waiting, let me take a look at your documents." Mike systematically clicked down through the fourteen documents. Number two was a form letter from the clinic indicating Max's application was complete. Numbers three through nine were internal documents from the staff initially processing the application. Number ten proved a bit more interesting. The top one-fourth of the page started off with a handwritten note started just below a small clinic logo and the words "Pre-admission Summary." This memo was from Peter to the clinic's diabetic program supervisor indicating this candidate should be put on the pre-admit register as a +5 candidate. The balance of the page had been redacted by placing a bright blue sheet of paper over the balance of Peter's memorandum before it was scanned into the system. "I have no idea why this information was blanked out. Normally Peter would have written his general impressions and made notes concerning the potential for a successful outcome, along with specific tests during the pre-admit registration."

"What do you mean the potential for a successful outcome? Also, what does a +5 mean?"

"Since Peter was in charge of the diabetic recovery program he would have the final say for all potential candidates for his stem cell procedure. I would have expected things like "patient is a good or poor candidate" or similar notes all centered on the potential outcome. The +5 just means Max had a greater than a 90% chance of a full recovery from diabetes."

"I would agree with the +5 until fifteen minutes before she died. Max had passed all of the clinical indicators of success. That being said, do you know of any logical reason his notes would've been removed from the permanent record."

"Remember yesterday when we didn't want to use the photocopier in the clinic because every copy is stored in the cloud."

"Are you telling me those copies and who copied them and on which machine may be stored in the cloud? If that's true ... wow, we might be able to see who's behind all of this."

"Here comes our breakfast. Let's eat and then head over to my office and see if I can access our cloud storage locker." There was little small talk as they both wolfed down breakfast.

"Steff, I'll get the check today. If you leave a tip, it'll be your treat next time." Mike had mentally crossed his fingers, hoping there would be a next time.

"Sounds good." Steff packed up her computer, and they made their way back to Mike's office, taking the necessary time to get through the clinic's security labyrinth. Once inside his office, Mike closed the door and the blinds.

"Well, let's us get to it." Mike fired up his computer, and after signing on, he made a couple of calls to the IT department to make sure the clinic's cloud storage was accessible and that his administrator rights had been restored. Soon Mike was able to begin searching for the documents they both hoped to find. Since neither Mike nor Steff had any idea of where to start, Mike set up a simple Boolean search using both Max's name and her patient ID number. Both came back with no data found. Remembering how they used Max's Minnesota driver's license number Mike entered it and waited for the search to return. This time, fourteen documents containing the driver's license number lined up across the top of the computer screen. Mike clicked on the first document which turned out to be a scan of Max's initial application.

Steff pulled out her flip-top notepad and started the list: "Doc 001 – initial application ... everything looks okay''.

Mike turned toward Steff, "Based on our past couple of days I'm going to guess someone wanted to keep Peter's assessment of Max out of her pre-admit file. We already know most if not all of Max's patient records are gone or hidden somewhere. I think these fourteen files were missed because they were all filed under her Minnesota driver's license."

"Let's take a look at the last four files. Maybe there's something else they missed." Mike clicked open file eleven to find it contained four blank pages. The only thing visible was a small clinic logo in the upper left-hand corner followed by the words "Internal Memorandum." There was no way to tell how these pages were blanked out. Much to their anguish, the last three files had suffered the same fate.

Mike reopened file number ten. "Steff, look at how the blue cover sheet is sitting crooked across the page. I'm beginning to think whoever purged these files thought they had covered up Peter's entire memorandum, and somehow the cover paper was askew during this scan. I think if someone were trying to conceal specific information they would have aligned the top of the page in between two lines of handwriting."

"I see what you're saying, but what are you getting at?"

"There's something about the clinic's record-keeping; I forgot to tell you about. Active worksheets are all sequentially numbered in the lower right-hand corner. The office staff would keep track of every worksheet; even if they had coffee spilled on them and were redone. So I think the reason these files are blank is to cover up the sequential number so it cannot be tracked."

"So what you are telling me is somewhere in the clinic there exists a list of who used which numbered form, right?"

"Yeah, I think so. Here, let's try something. The number ten file has a date in the upper right-hand corner. I'm going to log into the master file and search for entries by specific date. Aaaah ... give me a minute. I'm not quite sure how to get there." After several minutes of frustrating search, Mike brought up the master number file. To make sure he didn't miss anything Mike structured his search five days on either side of Peter's assessment memorandum."

"Won't it give you a huge bunch of files?"

"No, remember we only have four or five people in the active clinic at any one time so there should be maybe at most a couple of dozen hits." After a few seconds, the computer populated a list of seventy-five documents. As the cursor crossed a file line, a small pop-up box indicated its sequential number and who signed off on the document. As Mike clicked down the list, everything seemed to be in order until he reached the fourth document logged on the day in question. The fourth document and the three following were all noted as "spoiled and shredded." There was no other information for these four documents.

"What kind of system to you guys have? It seems like everything that might even remotely be related to Max has magically evaporated. I am beginning to develop a real dislike for some computer jockey."

"I can understand. Just give me a minute to think. There has to be something in here about Max after she was approved for the diabetic project. Let's take a moment to summarize just what we have. We have notarized copies of all of Max's real and fake health directives. We have several bits and pieces of information associated with her Minnesota driver's license but no way to internally verify that she even entered the program. Even the documents you received from the clinic's legal team didn't contain any specific information about the diabetic project. Please correct me if I am wrong. All you received was a forged health directive, a questionable copy of her death certificate indicating cardiac arrest as the cause of her death and a form to fill out in case you wanted to see one of the clinic's grief counselors."

"That's it. I read every page in the packet several times and other than the green sticky note I could find absolutely nothing even hinting Max was part of the diabetic project. So on paper,

Max was never here, and I was hallucinating when I reported she died in my arms after receiving what was to be her final stem cell treatment."

"On paper, you are absolutely right, but in my mind, somebody here at the clinic systematically removed every bit of information which leads me to believe Max was either murdered, or the clinic screwed up royally."

"So you agree it was no accident Max died."

"Absolutely. Every patient who made it to their last treatment walked out of the clinic in better condition than when they entered, or so I believed until today. Right now I'm not even sure that is a correct statement since my belief is based totally on the information housed in the clinic's computer and its cloud storage locker."

"Are you suggesting there may be more skeletons in the closet....?"

Chapter Twenty-six

Reg's introduction of Peter to Mr. Burke was cordial. Peter stepped forward and extended his hand. His host leaned slightly back as he gripped Peter's hand. In the past, Peter had met individuals whose handshakes were less than sterling. Some were unimaginative but mostly just limp. This particular handshake was a cross between a warm towel with just enough pressure to indicate life and still be classified as a handshake. Peter wanted to wash his hand but remembered what Reg and told him about his new boss. After cursory comments about the weather and the house, Peter looked Mr. Burke in the eye and asked where he had found such a stunning hat, drawing particular attention to his selection of the broad bright yellow feather.

"Why thank you, Dr. Hayes, it was good of you to notice. Are you a connoisseur of hats?"

"Not really. However, my father always told me a fedora is truly a hat for all seasons." Peter felt a little twinge for telling an outright lie. His father was a baseball cap person. "May I see your hat?"

"Thanks for asking but I'm a little bit particular about who I let touch one of my hats, please don't take this personally,"

"Not at all sir. You referred to your hats in the plural; do you have more than one?"

"You might say I have quite a collection. Perhaps sometime in the future, after I know more about you, I will show you my collection."

"I look forward to that day."

"As do I Dr. Hayes."

"As an aside, I think we've met before. You are the person from the G8 who heads up the co-op stem cell study program with the NSA. We met briefly one afternoon when the NSA team toured the facility a few days before the first patients arrived. You probably don't remember since you shook hands with fifty or sixty people."

"Yes, now that you mention it, I believe I do remember. You are the one who excused himself and left with his technician in tow. Now as I think about it, Reg, you are that technician, are you not?"

"Yes sir, I am. I was there to take pictures so Dr. Hayes could make sure the layout was correct. If I remember correctly, I didn't get to shake your hand. In fact, I don't even recall seeing you, but I did hear your voice. I forgot all about that; it seems like a hundred years ago."

Burke waved his hand to signal Reg to stop talking. Turning towards his new guest, he graciously extended his hand toward the seat to his immediate right. "Dr. Hayes, please have a seat. I'm not a connoisseur of small talk. I tend to get quickly to the point. As you know the point under discussion today is whether you are willing to assist me in learning more about you and Dr. Lancaster's stem cell research. As Reg has mentioned to you, I am particularly interested in the ability of your stem cell line to reverse damage to the liver and other internal organs. Before we go on any further, I need your answer to the proposal Reg outlined to you. In exchange for your help, you will retain all publishing rights to your findings. Would that be acceptable?"

"So far so good."

"It is also my understanding you will not be able to pay off your IOUs to the Mexican cartel this coming Friday."

"Yes sir, you are correct. Not only will I be unable to pay the $75,000 IOU, but I will not even be able to make the $8000 interest payment."

"Thank you for your honesty, Dr. Hayes. By my calculations, you owe a total of $108,000 including $25,000 in credit card debt."

"I'm sad to say you are correct."

"My proposition to you is quite simple and straightforward. In exchange for your helping me understand your stem cell research and providing technical assistance as needed, I will pay off your IOU's, credit cards, and deposit $200,000 in an offshore account in your name. Also, as our relationship grows, there will be regular deposits into your account based upon how quickly you can solve some technical problems my research group has recently encountered."

"Reg did not mention anything about a research group, just that you were acquiring instrumentation similar to what Mike and I have at the clinic."

A half smile was forming on Burke's face, which he quickly dismissed with a wave of his hand towards Dr. Hayes "I'm sorry, a minor oversight on my part. I will fill you in completely as soon as we have an agreement. Dr. Hayes, Before you sign this contract, please understand I have a very low tolerance for insubordination, missed deadlines and withholding any information from me which may impact my project. Are we clear on this point, Dr. Hayes?"

At this point, Peter was beginning to wonder whether he would have better luck dealing with the Mexican cartel, but the thought of losing his right hand was overwhelming. "Yes sir, I completely understand. Do I just sign the contract or do you want me to read it first?"

"Oh, by all means, please read it. I like keeping things simple. As you will see, my standard contract is straightforward, about one-half a page. It briefly outlines what you are to do and how much I will compensate you for your services. What the contract does not have in it is what will happen to you if you fail to hold up your end of the bargain. For the time being, I will leave that to your imagination."

"I understand sir." Peter held out his hand to seal the deal, but Mr. Burke just opened the folder on the table and handed Peter a pen. Peter was surprised by how heavy the pen felt. A quick glance revealed a deep patterned gold inlaid fountain pen. Peter unscrewed the lid as he slowly read the ten-line contract and signed away a considerable chunk of his freedom. Reg then stepped forward, picked up the paper, retrieved the pen and gave it and the original signed contract to Mr. Burke.

Reg closed the folder and handed it to Peter. "Here is your

copy. Much like an IOU it only contains your signature. Understand your new boss takes this stem cell project very, very seriously."

Burke's countenance became more relaxed as if he had anticipated having to persuade Peter to sign the contract. "Thank you, Dr. Hayes, for your quick grasping of the situation. Please take a few minutes to contemplate the importance of your decision. Feel free to walk around the grounds. Enjoy the view. In about half an hour we will all sit down and have a bite of lunch. You will have an opportunity to share the inner-most workings of your project. As a point of reference, I think you will find your interests and my interests follow the same destiny. What you may not know but will come to understand is that your G8 project is nowhere near as secret as you and the NSA think. Suffice it to say that I have been an unseen participant since before the beginning of the project."

"I am guessing there is no point in me denying that I have any knowledge of this project. I sense you may know more about the project than I do."

"Let's reserve that for a chat after lunch. As a matter of common courtesy let me, please apologize for forcing you to wear that awful black hood. Until we know more about each other, I am afraid you will have to put on your hood every time we meet. Hopefully, it will not be long. Welcome aboard Dr. Hayes, I think you will find your future work both scientifically and financially rewarding."

Peter spent the next half an hour wandering around the fenced compound. *What have I gotten myself into? ... Why didn't I stay away from the casino . . . I think it will take all my wits to come out of this alive . . . I'm not even sure I can pull that off ... I need to stay detached until I know how much these guys know about the G8 project.*

Chapter Twenty-seven

Manny reread the troubling information streamed down the screen, line after line of seemingly impossible information. The international banking section of the NSA had entered into a contract with the operations secretary of the G8 economic committee to use some experimental procedure to cure years of wear and tear on each of the G8 Secretaries.

Manny spent the next couple of hours reducing all of the data presented to him to something he can share with Steff and not be declared a traitor for leaking highly sensitive information. Manny felt that sharing some of this information would not violate national security. The most recent e-mail from Steff indicated she and Dr. Lancaster were rapidly becoming friends, and now both were trying to figure out what happened to Max. Dr. Lancaster's work on adult stem cells is the latch pin of this entire G8 project. Manny's logical assumption is that Dr. Lancaster knows more about the G8 project than anyone alive since he is the research and development director of the liver reconstitution project the G8 group contracted.

Manny's gut, a.k.a. Twenty-Three years of operational field experience in the NSA, begin to set things in motion. A quick telephone call to the travel arrangements group provided an E-ticket round-trip to Denver, Colorado, leaving in about three hours, just enough time to pull together necessary files and throw a few things into his well-worn carry-on bag. Manny quickly loaded several files onto his laptop and signed out, His trip to the taxi stand was accomplished as fast as possible without alerting the ever-present security monitors. The all-too-familiar Washington, DC, humidity and its associated aroma almost stopped Manny in his tracks. Regaining his composure, he quickly flagged down a taxi and headed for the airport by way of his apartment. Clearance through DC security had become so familiar as to provide virtually no interruption to Manny's churning thoughts. While waiting to board, he sent Steff a text asking her to meet him at the airport, and, if possible, please bring Dr. Lancaster.

Fortunately, the flight to Denver was smooth since Manny had not eaten since last night and was a bit light-headed. His $7.25 in-flight meal quickly settled his errant G.I. tract. Manny wanted to review the files he had copied but felt uneasy opening them in such a public forum as the middle seat. Instead of rereading, Manny leaned back and began to piece together the bits and pieces of NSA's G8 project. The fatigue of the last several days finally had the upper hand as Manny fell soundly into a dreamless sleep. After what seemed like a few minutes, the flight attendant tapped him on the shoulder and asked him to put his seat into the upright position for landing.

Making his way through the long concourse, Manny felt like a salmon swimming upstream. Down the escalator and a few steps to the right brought him to the open train door. And odd jingle quickly played as the doors closed. A crisp recording of a carefully selected voice filled the speeding car: "Next stop Main Concourse." Manny amused himself by watching the myriad of little propellers which lined sections of the train tunnel. The back-draft spun the propellers as the train sped by. For a brief moment, Manny wondered who came up with the idea, but before he could further explore it, the train entered the Main Concourse.

As Manny exited the train, his iPhone vibrated. His thumb activated the screen. Steff's text message indicated they would meet at the passenger pickup area in front of the terminal. "Look for a small blue Chevrolet Volt." Manny soon found himself outside the terminal. Expecting to breathe in cool Rocky Mountain air, Manny inhaled deeply, just to realize the air outside of DIA smelled more like diesel. Within a few minutes, a small blue car with an arm waving out the window came alongside the pickup zone.

Steff jumped out of the car and threw her arms around Manny. "Uncle Manny it's good to see you. You look terrible."

"I could blame it on my job. Yeah, I will blame it on my job. It's really good to see you kiddo."

"What brings you all way to Denver? You could have simply sent an e-mail. But because you are here, there must be more than just a simple answer to my inquiries."

"As perceptive as always, you are indeed your father's daughter. Always more questions than the world has answers. Is there someplace where we can go that's private? And by private I mean someplace with no Wi-Fi or cameras. What I have to share with you nobody else can know about, just yet."

"Yes, I think I know a good place. Here, let me put your suitcase in the car. I want you to meet a fascinating young man." After Steff had closed the trunk, she motioned Manny into the front seat, and she jumped in the back. "Uncle Manny this is Dr. Michael Lancaster, more commonly known as Mike. He is very curious why you wanted me to make sure he came along."

"Pleased to meet you, Manny. I don't know much about your work but what little Steff has told me suggests you live a pretty hectic life."

Manny's handshake was warm and firm. To emphasize its importance to Mike, Manny placed his left hand on top of the handshake. "I am looking forward to talking further with you. I understand you are involved in some groundbreaking research involving adult stem cells."

Steff put her hand on Manny's shoulder. "We have to move; the security guard is waving at us and pointing towards the exit." Mike merged quickly into the traffic flow and in a few minutes was cruising down Peña Boulevard toward Metro-Denver. Steff and Manny filled the forty-five minute trip to Max's old apartment with a lot of catching up small talk. "I don't think Max would mind us using her apartment. She always complained about the lack of Wi-Fi in the building. She also complained to the manager when she discovered all of the security cameras were just dummies, and besides, I have the key. If we need it more than just today, her lease still has a little over two months left." Mike eased into the parking lot. "You can use Max's assigned parking space parking space over there, number A-15 just beyond the dumpster."

Steff led the guys up the side stairs to Max's apartment. When she inserted the key, it would not go all the way. "That's odd."

"Whats odd?"

"When I came over to empty out her refrigerator I had no trouble getting into the apartment."

"Let me take a look." Manny took a small black case out of the top of his carry-on and kneeled down in front of the door. Unzipping the case revealed an amazing assortment of lock picks. Manny carefully chose one and inserted it into the keyhole. After a couple of tries, he carefully extracted a small piece of metal. "Now try again."

Steff carefully inserted the key in this time the door opened without a hitch. "Okay Manny, was that magic?"

"That bit of metal I removed was the broken tip of a cheap lock pick. Let's open the door carefully and take a look. Somebody had been here before and did not use a key."

Steff stepped back and motioned to Manny. As the door swung inward, it became evident someone had rifled Max's apartment. Things were not torn up just in general disarray: drawers partially open, and cushions ajar. Manny and Mike took a quick look behind all the closed doors and reported all was clear.

Manny opened up his briefcase and placed his laptop on the dining table and after untangling the nest of black wires plugged the transformer into the wall. "Steff put on your detective hat. Is there anything valuable Max could have a hidden? It is obvious this was not a break-in to steal. Her flat screen and the surround sound system appear to all be untouched. When I looked in the bedroom, I did not see any jewelry boxes. Do you know if she had valuable jewelry?"

"I don't think so. Max was a person who liked the natural look, and as far as I know, she didn't have any valuable jewelry. Wait a minute; she did have a small lockbox she kept under her bed. Max gave me a key shortly after her lawyer sent me her power of attorney package."

A quick look under the bed revealed a small rectangular document's safe. Manny picked it up and looked at the lock. "This is a low-security lock, and it was also picked. Do you know what she had in it?"

"A couple of weeks before she ... Aaah - passed away she had me over for supper. Later that evening in her usual micromanaging style she got out the lockbox and spread its contents out on the table. To be honest, I don't remember much of what was there except her passport, a packet of letters from her mom tied with a yellow ribbon and maybe a half a dozen old coins. She said none were particularly valuable; they were from her grandfather. That's all I can remember."

"Now is the time to see how much you do remember." With that, Manny took the key from Steff and opened the lockbox, reached in and took out its paper contents and spread them out on the bed. He held up the box. "Does this look like what you remembered?"

"Yes. The only thing I don't recognize is that small gold ring. The number of coins seems okay." Steff slowly worked through the paper items. When she picked up the bundle of letters, she momentarily clutched them to her chest. "I must not forget to send these back to Max's mother." After a bit more shuffling Steff slowly shook her head. "I'm sorry I can't be more specific, but it looks to me like nothing is missing."

"Back to my original question, is there anything Max could have hidden that someone would need to steal? I'm asking the question again because of your concern about all the information stripped from Max's files."

Mike gently tapped his index finger against his upper lip several times in deep thought. And for the first time since Manny crawled into his car, Mike entered the conversation. "I was just thinking, did Max keep any of her papers from the clinic here in her apartment? Based on what we've seen so far, I think whoever broke in is still trying to remove any association with the clinic. What do you think, Steff?"

"Aaah ... She did keep a lot of her paper files and stuff like that in one of those ugly brown expandable filing things. You know the ones that open up like an accordion. She kept it somewhere in her closet." A frustrating search finally turned up the file sitting on the right-hand side of her upper closet shelf inside a large beach towel. Steff sat down on the corner of the bed and begin rummaging through file sections one at a time. Her puzzled look quickly conveyed what Steff had not found. "There's not a single sheet of paper in here about the clinic or her stem cell treatment. All this paper is just tax stuff, copies of her lease, insurance policies and the like."

Steff gathered up all the papers and stuffed them back into the accordion file and set it on the floor next to the bed. "I will deal with this later. Max's parents have asked me to take what I like, give it to friends or sell it. They don't even want to see the apartment. I think it's still too painful. You guys clean off the table and put the stuff back in the lockbox and put it next to the file. I'm going to make us a pot of hot tea. Max particularly liked English breakfast tea."

Manny and Mike dutifully straightened up Max's papers and put them back in the lockbox along with her passport. Mike relocked the box, placed the key on the table, and returned the lockbox to the bedroom. The guys wandered the apartment straightening out things until they heard the tea kettle whistling in the kitchen.

"The tea will be ready in a minute; I'm afraid all I can offer you is sugar unless you want powdered creamer." Mike indicated no sugar and Manny asked for two spoons full, and both skipped the creamer.

After Steff poured the tea and all were seated, Manny turned on his laptop. After touching several screen tiles, he opened the first of the G8 files he had copied before leaving DC. "Steff, if you don't mind, I would like to ask Dr. Lancaster a few questions first."

"Please call me Mike; Dr. Lancaster sounds way too impersonal."

"Okay Mike, first question. What do you know about the G8 economic group?"

"Not much. Aren't they the group that meets regularly to make recommendations on global finance?"

"Is that all?"

"The way you ask makes me think I should know more. Come to think of it a couple of years back we had someone from the G8 group treated here at the clinic for alcohol-induced liver failure. Beyond that, nothing."

"Tell me about that case. Skip all the technical stuff; just give me the Cliff Notes' version."

"As I recall, this patient was admitted to the clinic as an emergency. Some governmental agency insisted, and I use the term loosely, we were to admit this patient and to keep him alive by all possible means, even if we had to use our stem cells. When I mentioned he was not on the FDA list of approved clinical trial patients, they said that was not a problem and use them if necessary. To determine the extent of damage we did a high-resolution neck to groin MRI. After the radiologist examined the scan, he just shook his head. On the large flat screen monitor, he brought up several sections and pointed out significant liver damage. His kidneys were near failure, his heart was enlarged, and the lower lobes of his lungs were almost opaque due to scar tissue. His advice was to tell the patient to go home and get things in order."

"So what you're telling me is this guy was walking dead, and the clinic could do nothing for him using current medical techniques or procedures."

"Yes sir, that is correct. But as I said we were told to use the stem cell procedure even though this patient could not meet the FDA criteria approved for our clinical trials. We met with the entourage that came with the patient and explained the diagnosis and that traditional methods and procedures would only prolong his life for a short time. The little short guy in the entourage, the one wearing the green and gray herringbone fedora hat, motioned the others and began talking among themselves. Their discussion became quite heated until the short guy held up his hand and all debate stopped.

Our director of clinical services stepped forward and asked, "Is there anything we can do to help their friend feel better." The short guy stepped off to the side and called someone on his cell phone. After a couple of minutes, he walked over and handed the clinical services director the phone. I could see from the expression on his face he did not like what was hearing. He nodded and handed the phone back to the short guy. He then turned to the medical director and indicated this patient was to start my adult stem cell treatment immediately. The medical director protested the next patient scheduled to begin the treatment was already in the hospital. What happened next was a bit of a surprise. Our clinical director said this patient would be receiving his treatment at an off-campus location and under their direct supervision so that the next patient in line could begin their treatment in the morning as scheduled. At this time, a man in his mid-fifties identified himself as an NSA agent and told us any and all information about this patient was now covered by the National Secrets Act. He also explained that the patient also had diplomatic immunity. He then reached into his jacket and handed our director of research a court order asking for all records and test information be turned over forthwith, and he would remain in the building until he was sure that one hundred percent of all information about this patient no longer existed at the clinic. The rest of the entourage left the meeting, and I later learned they secured a private ambulance and took the patient to an undisclosed location. I hope I wasn't too wordy."

"Thank you, Mike, your account is pretty much in line with the documents I found today. Again I need to ask the question, do you know anything else that might be even remotely related to this G8 patient? Also, have you heard any rumors from any of your colleagues about this patient?"

"No sir, except a scrub nurse told me she knew a nurse who was working in a clinic located in a downtown office building. That's all her friend did tell her. She said she was sworn to secrecy and probably shouldn't have told her even that much."

"Steff, in all of your research have you come across any information about the clinic and its possible ties to a group or groups outside of Mike's clinic?"

"I don't recall anything specific. I was more fascinated by the stem cell research and the potential it had to be a real benefit to society. That was until Max died in my arms. That's why I sent you those two e-mails hoping you could find out something I was barred from finding out."

"Mike and Steff, I'm about to tell you something I think you need to know about. In particular, Mike needs to hear this because I believe Max's death and your friend Anne's concern about her boss are all part of a single sophisticated but clandestine project. By the way, I would like to talk to Anne. I need to find out if she knows anything else about her Brad."

"I guess you haven't heard yet. Anne died in what I believe was a staged accident."

"Why do you think it was staged?"

"My contact at the police department, a detective Foster, indicated it happened a couple of hours after Anne told me about her strange encounter with Brad and then later on with the counterfeit Brad. I don't think it was an accident for two reasons. The first is Anne was a collegiate level gymnast and a member of an amateur ballet troupe here in Denver. She always knew where her feet were all the time. She even had a difficult time doing a pratfall in a college play, so falling down the stairs just doesn't make it for me. The second is that Detective Foster told me last night she had blunt force trauma to both the front and back of her skull. I'm not a forensic scientist, but I can't envision how falling down a short flight of stairs going forward could cause both of those fractures. Also, the medical examiner's preliminary findings suggest the blow to the back of her head happened sometime before the blow to her forehead. Also, the medical examiner believes the fracture of her neck at C1 may be the actual cause of death. He is not willing to sign off on a cause of death until all of the forensic data is processed by his office."

"Hmm ..." Manny quickly opened up another file and turned the screen so Mike and Steff could see. "This is part of a file from the NSA's G8 file. I believe this man is the counterfeit Brad Anne told you about. The picture on the left is the real Brad and on the right is the man who will become the counterfeit Brad." Manny then brought up a short video showing eight sequential pictures of the counterfeit Brad through several sophisticated facelift-like surgeries. "As you can see there already was a strong resemblance to Brad. After the surgeries, it would be difficult for an average person not to believe this guy was the real Brad. It appears your friend walked in on something that got her killed. What I'm saying is she was able to determine it was not Brad in less than a minute."

"Let me get this straight – someone killed my friend because an imposter couldn't do his job right."

"I think Anne's death just scratched the surface of a larger scheme, which NSA was unwittingly drawn into."

Steff's eyes focused on Manny. "What do you mean drawn into?"

"The NSA provided their extensive technical expertise in constructing look-a-likes."

Steff stood up and stepped around the table beside Mike. "You're a doctor. Can plastic surgeons really do that? I mean to change someone's face that fast?"

"I'm a Ph.D., not a physician but what I have seen done at the clinic for victims of severe accidents are nothing short of a miracle. Yes, I have no doubt a team of skilled plastic surgeons could pull it off and, with the use of particular types of LED light treatments coupled with growth factors scar tissue and layers of collagen, it could be repaired very quickly."

"LED light, like the flashlight on my keychain?"

"Yes, but a bit more sophisticated. Certain wavelengths of LED light in the far infrared, around 880 nm, can stimulate repair of skin from the bottom up. The process was developed by NASA to treat minor injuries on long-term spaceflights."

Manny broke in, "That's amazing, but I need you and Steff to concentrate on what you're going to see in the next file." A few screen touches later a new file opened up. The first page was labeled "G8 Regeneration Project." A watermark across the middle of the page declared "top secret" and a second line "eyes only." "At this point, I am going to begin trusting you guys with what you're about to see and hear. I'm not too far off since I've already had deep background checks on both of you."

Mike shrugged his shoulders. "The clinic does one of those on all of the senior staff every year, so I'm assuming my skeletons are still well hidden."

Mike's gentle grin seemed to relax Steff, who was now standing, with both hands on the table almost nose-to-nose with Manny. Manny, reflecting Mike's smile said, "Think about it, child, what would you do if you were me? Would you trust a couple of strangers or would you look behind their smoke and mirrors?"

Steff quietly sat back in her chair. "Yeah, I guess I would, but you have known me literally all of my life and still … Yeah, you're right. If everything went south, you have covered your bases with the NSA. Okay, Manny, I guess I'm ready to follow the rabbit down the hole. Let's look at the file."

Chapter Twenty-eight

R eg broke into Peter's introspection. "Dr. Hayes, it's time to get ready for lunch. I think you'll find our host sets out a pretty good spread." As they walked across the vast lawn to the main house, Reg inquired, "Well what you think of him?"

"To be honest, I'm not sure what to think; I just met him a few minutes ago. My first impression is probably not too good since I'm always miss-reading people. This guy gives me goosebumps. I don't know why, he just does."

"That's a little bit how I felt the first time I had lunch here, but over the past year, I found that Mr. Burke can be both a gracious host and a demanding boss. I would suggest trying to concentrate on the former but never - - never forget the latter. Since he is British, this estate is considered British soil by the State Department, and pretty much anything that goes on there is covered by diplomatic immunity. I hope I do not sound too morbid; I would like you not to make the same mistake others have."

"No, you don't sound morbid at all. I think the situation I've gotten myself into does that all by itself. Ahh - what do you mean by the same mistake others have?"

"A few months back someone from Dr. Lancaster's side of the clinic was out here for lunch. He was offered a great deal of cash if he would provide technical information about why the liver cell regeneration project has been so successful. This guy told Mr. Burke he would have no part of selling out Dr. Lancaster's work, and as soon as he got back to the clinic, he was going to blow the whistle."

"I think I'm getting the picture here. He didn't make it back to the clinic, did he?"

"I have no idea what happened, but the next day I read he was run down by a hit and run driver just outside the clinic's back parking lot. You may remember T'sao Wong. He was Dr. Lancaster's chief cell propagator."

"I remember. Mike used to think T'sao was some kind of magician. He could tease viable stem cells out of almost any tissue. Mike said he would be nearly impossible to replace."

"Remember; the police were never able to find the person who ran him down. Suffice it to say T'sao was not the only person around here who has died mysteriously. I tell you this just to keep you on your toes. Just don't give your new boss any hint of disloyalty."

Peter was now convinced he might not get out of this alive. All he could hope for now was to be able to keep Mike out of Burke's crosshairs. Reg pulled open the ten-foot tall doors exposing a large vaulted room lined with tall windows along the south side. This room could effectively function as a ballroom or an elegant dining room. On one end of the hall, a small table had been set next to one of the windows. Mr. Burke rose from his chair at the head of the table and motioned Peter to sit next to him. Reg and the imposing silent bodyguard occupied the other two sides.

After they had all sat, Mr. Burke motioned with his hand and without a sound four waiters dressed in crisp white shirts and large black bowties brought out steaming bowls of New England clam chowder. As lunch progressed, the same four servers repeatedly brought more food and took away empty dishes until Peter thought he could not eat another bite. The last trip by this crisply dressed quartet left a sterling silver tea service complete with cream and sparkling white sugar cubes. The second, third and fourth dish contained a variety of chocolates and other exotic sweets.

Burke motioned with his left hand, "Please, help yourselves. These come from a 300-year-old candy shop on Piccadilly Square. Some say they make the best candy in the world. But I will let you decide for yourselves."

Mr. Burke carefully folded his napkin and placed it to his left. "Dr. Hayes, as I said, I will be happy to answer any of your questions, or rather, I will be able to answer most of your questions, but not all at this time. Before your first question let me tell you what is going on. Remember the patient who was recently brought to your clinic with what we all thought was terminal liver damage?"

"Yes, I remember. Dr. Lancaster was furious when the feds took all of the information, tests, the patient, and left. We were told to pretend like it never happened and to my knowledge, he has not heard anything since."

"You are correct. But what you don't know is that this patient is the Secretary to Britain's Minister for the G8 economic group. Something else most people are unaware of is the secretaries to each of these ministers wield an enormous amount of power in the world of international banking. The last piece of this puzzle is the fact that these Secretaries serve for decades, often serving three or more Ministers and only retire or quit when they are physically no longer able to perform their duties. As I am sure, you are now aware of where this story is going."

"Yes sir, the longer they can stay healthy, the more predictability and continuity there is in the system."

"Very astute Dr. Hayes, but you are thinking way too short term. What I had envisioned is with your and Dr. Lancaster's magic stem cells, the functional lifetime of the Secretaries can be extended, maybe two or maybe three decades. Am I right?"

"There are those of us in this field who believe there is a real possibility, particularly if we can diagnose potentially terminal diseases at a very early stage. This assumes one or more of these diseases are amenable to stem cell reconstitution. Whether it's one or two or, even more, decades is yet to be determined."

"Dr. Hayes, that is the reason I feel you are so important to the G8 and particularly their secretaries. I recently made arrangements with your clinic, on behalf of the G8 Ministers for all of the eight secretaries, to undergo your stem cell treatment to catch early or even prevent a terminal disease from popping up. Please pardon my use of unscientific terms, but I think you get the picture. As the name of your Phoenix Project suggests, like the tale of old, the G8 Secretaries will rise from the ashes of their former lives renewed and, in most cases, probably better than before they became Secretaries."

Before Peter answered, he took a moment to contemplate Rag's repeated warnings about failure. "Yes sir, I believe there's a valid scientific basis for what you are proposing, that is if the secretaries can fulfill the FDA criteria for our Stage II trials."

Burke abruptly stood up, slammed his hand down on the table. "Damn the FDA. If they had their way in the 50's, we would have the most elaborate iron lungs ever created, instead of a polio vaccine. Before I tell you the next part of my plan, I want to remind you of the vocal part of our written contract.

"Yes sir, I believe I fully understand those unwritten phrases. Please go on with my personal assurance that whatever you say stays in this room unless you say otherwise."

Burke set back down and rearranged himself. "Thank you, Dr. Hayes, for your succinct interpretation. Let me go on. This clinic is not too far from your clinic. The NSA and I have set up a, shall we say, a shadow clinic, which has all the modern conveniences and technical staff of your Rosch Clinic, but outside the prying eyes of the FDA. Without your knowledge, Reg was able to give us viable starting cultures of all but one of the stem cell lines which you and Dr. Lancaster so carefully isolated and characterized. These shadow technicians, now armed with your methods and your stem cells, have successfully produced enough of the most potent of your cell lines stem cells to begin medical trials. Dr. Hayes, before I proceed, you need to know this is now a no turning back point for you. Total secrecy from this point on is imperative, or you will not leave here with one cent of the cash we talked about earlier. Your life will then be in the hands of the cartel. Am I clear about this?"

Trying not to show his growing apprehension and fear, Peter reverted to the impertinence of his early career. "It doesn't take a pair of elephant ears to hear what you said. Please pardon my bit of levity, but I do understand the severity of the situation. I'm just a bit nervous."

"I understand. The stem cells produced by our shadow clinic are already used to begin treating the Secretaries. We secured an entire floor in a downtown office building in Denver to house our shadow clinic. One-fourth of the floor was converted into living quarters complete with almost all the amenities of home. Half of the remaining floor is the research laboratory. The rest is a mirror image of your treatment suite at the clinic. There is also space for plastic surgeons."

"I get the setup of the clinic, but why the plastic surgeons? I don't understand. We don't use any plastic surgeons in our treatment protocols."

"That is true. But you do not have to replace highly functional Secretaries for six or more months while they undergo the stem cell treatment. The G8 Ministers authorized me to negotiate with your NSA to provide eight look-alikes who would be trained to carry out routine secretarial duties while the real Secretaries are in the clinic. Part of the look-alike process is the use of plastic surgery and rapid healing techniques. While the look-alikes are undergoing surgery, they are also memorizing everything about the person they are replacing. Once they complete the healing and training process, they step into the Secretaries' real life and the real Secretaries steps into the clinic to begin treatment.

Chapter Twenty-nine

Manny thought this was a good time for a break. He could tell Steff and Mike were showing all the outward signs growing tension. "Before I show you the next file, where is the bathroom?"

"It's off the bedroom next to the closet."

"Also, if you don't mind, I would like some more of that delicious English breakfast tea. Is there anything left here to eat? All I've had to eat the last day and a half is an airplane sandwich and several sodas."

Mike chimed in, "Steff, you know the apartment. I'll fix the tea while you try to find something for Manny to snack on."

Manny closed the bathroom door loud enough to be heard in the kitchen, then set down on the edge of the tub and searched through his text messages. The ninth message was particularly troubling. "M - Brad's file incomplete call ASAP - use S - line ...Phil." For the next few minutes, Manny answered the important messages. *I need to find a secure line. The one over at the Tech Centers ATF office has less chance for an NSA intercept.* He stood up, flushed the toilet, and walked to the kitchen. "Did you guys find anything to eat?"

Mike swept his hand over the small collection of snack items. "Steff was able to find a couple of candy bars, an unopened box of granola bars and, if you want to, we could also microwave popcorn. Name your poison."

"I think I'll stick with the candy bars and a granola bar. They both contain chocolate, so what could go wrong?"

"So vitamin C it is. Here's your tea refill. Now can we see the file or are you going to stall some more? Steff told me Max always kept candy bars in her nightstand drawer. When I went to get them, I could hear you texting."

"Okay, no more stalling. This one e-mail is worth all our waiting." Manny opened his cell phone and handed it to Steff. "What do you think?"

"Intriguing, what is an S-line?"

"That's NSA shorthand for a secure landline. These secure lines use a CRYPTO-like scrambler at both ends. There are several available here in the Denver area. Later on, I would like for you to drive me over to the ATF office in the Federal Tech Center. I have used their line a couple of times. I am pretty sure NSA hasn't tapped their system yet. Now let's get to this file."

Manny opened his laptop and soon had the file in question on the screen. "I just want you to look at the title of the file and read the first paragraph; then I will fill you in on what the file actually contains." Manny then used his cursor to blank out everything except the title and first paragraph. "This way all you will have seen is something which could be found without hacking into secret files. In DC, politicians call this plausible deniability and everything I'm about to tell you is called …"

"Hearsay. Now you have our undivided attention; by all means, let's commit treason together."

"I wouldn't go quite that far, but what I'm about to tell you will put you and Dr. Lancaster potentially in harm's way. What I'm going to tell you about uses the codename 'The Phoenix Project.' Mike, I believe you already know a lot about this project since the clinic uses the same project name for your and Dr. Hayes's stem cell research."

"Yes, I am familiar with the project. The clinic has spent a small fortune on PR material which has been liberally spread out to various funding agencies in a quest for more research dollars. Steff even has some of that information in her backpack."

"Mike, before I go on, I want to tell you I am sorry that you have to hear about your very best friend in this way."

"Do you mean Peter?"

"Yes Mike, I'm afraid so. First, here's the short version. Peter is involved in the administering of your stem cell soup to the G8

Secretaries we talked about earlier today. Not only is he involved, but he has been the technical director of the project for at least fifteen months. The NSA and the G8 ministers have jointly funded this project, but each one for a very different reason. We, I mean the NSA, built and staffed an entire clinic floor, in an office building close to your clinic, in less than four weeks. We built the treatment facility first and began treating the gentleman you described earlier today."

"Are you telling me Peter has been involved in this project for over a year?"

"I'm afraid so."

"If that's true, it would explain his disjointed behavior the last many months. Peter also prided himself on having a peer-reviewed manuscript published every three months. He only finished two manuscripts in the last eighteen months. When I asked about it, he said the aftermath of his last two outbreaks of Bell's Palsy was playing havoc with his sleep patterns, and he had to take naps in the afternoon, to keep his energy up. But I guess you're going to tell me he didn't sleep a wink but spent those hours every afternoon stealing my work."

"Again, I'm afraid so. Not only did he steal your work, but he also stole a couple of your best staff technicians. According to the NSA's internal documents, you lost three key technicians about a year ago. One was killed by a hit and run driver, and the other two told you they were offered once-in-a-lifetime positions with an East Coast startup biotech firm. They told you the East Coast so you would think they were out of the area."

"What does your NSA file say about being sequestered in the name of national security? I'm assuming it must be national security since that's all NSA is supposed to be involved in. Am I right?"

"What the NSA does is very complex and very widespread, and I think there is a better venue for that discussion. Right now we have bigger fish to fry. As soon as we finished building out the new clinic floor, the G8 coordinator, a Mr. Clive Burke, began using your stem cell lines to treat the secretaries to the G8 ministers. He alone chose who was first and second and so forth. Our guy at the clinic said Clive is a real control freak and sometimes is even a bit spooky. I don't know what spooky means in this case, but our guys have been cautious not to rile him up."

Steff interrupted. "So how many of these eight guys have been treated?"

"To date, I think there is one who has finished, two are almost finished, four additional Secretaries are in the pipeline, and the last one is scheduled to start soon. I was able to find a list of the Secretaries from our inside guy. Now, Steff, this is where you got involved. The first Secretary to complete the entire protocol was Annie's friend Brad. What has me concerned now is that the wrong Brad seems to be out in public. I did check out the real Brad's office and was told he has just been given an overseas assignment for the next seven months. A search of his e-mails indicated he exchanged several short notes with your friend Anne, the afternoon she died. I now think Anne was sent these e-mails to convince her the Brad she'd met in the elevator was the real Brad. Steff, I haven't yet figured out the question you asked me in your first e-mail, but I'm going to work on it. I thought I was going to have time to get over to the ATF office to give Phil a call, but I'm going to have to hustle to catch my plane back to DC. I have a 'thou shall not miss' meeting at 0900 in the morning. I would like you guys to quietly see what you can dig up, and I will try to get back here in a few days. Mike don't worry about driving me; I'll call a taxi. They will be able to get me to DIA a lot faster than you could."

Manny quickly extracted two cell phone boxes from his suitcase. He opened both and placed them on the table. He picked up one, looked at its back, keyed in a number, and repeated with the other phone. "Steff and Mike, these are burner phones. Each has only two-speed dial numbers programmed. One to my cell, and the other to its companion. Manny then handed one phone to Steff and the other to Mike. These are out-of-area phones, one from Philadelphia and the other San Diego; so hopefully, there's no way to tie the two of them together. Now, remember kids, be careful. I have drawn you to the edge of the world where most electronic devices are not secure. I have to go."

"Uncle Manny I still owe you, at least, one real lunch for all you've done. Mike and I will dig up everything we can without raising suspicions. How can we best get this information to you?"

"Let me work on it." Manny quickly folded his laptop, stuffed everything in his into his briefcase, and picked up the remaining candy bar along with three granola bars and headed for the door.

"Hey, not so fast. At least, give me a goodbye hug, Steff said."

Manny stepped back, sat down his briefcase and gave Steff a really long hug. With his face way from Mike, he whispered in Steff's ear. "Take care of yourself child and keep your eye on Mike I think he's in for some trouble." Manny stepped back, gave Mike a firm handshake. "You take care of my goddaughter."

"Yes sir, I will." With a quick wink, Manny gathered up his stuff and headed for the elevator. "Later kids."

Chapter Thirty

Mike and Steff were still overwhelmed by the amount of information Manny had just dumped on them. Mike was particularly troubled by what he found out about Peter. "I've known Peter since the third grade. We did school and Boy Scouts together. We even went to the same church. Until an hour ago there was no one on this earth I trusted more than Peter . . . Now I aa-ah ..."

"Mike, I think it's unwise to jump to conclusions. You may not have all the facts. I believe that is what Manny wants us to find out."

"Yeah, you're right. But it still stings. Before I head back to my office. There is one thing I want to re-check." Mike went to the bedroom and returned carrying Max's small lockbox. Placing it on the table, he took out the pile of papers. "Steff, take another look and tell me if there's anything that looks different now that we think Max may have been trying to hide something."

Steff looked through the box again, pushing around the coins. "I still don't see anything out of place."

Mike then poured out the coins on the table and picked up one of the cardboard coin holders containing a Morgan silver dollar. "Take a look at this. Now, do you see anything different?"

Steff held it, turned it over and much to her surprise discovered instead of one-dollar holder there were three. The center holder stuck out a little bit on one side. Steff pulled it out about halfway, and a small key dropped onto the table. "How did you know there was a key in between the two real dollar holders?"

"I didn't know there would be a key; I just knew the dollar holder was too thick. I have been an amateur coin collector since high school, and I have dozens of coins in the same kind of holders. When I first looked into the box something was odd, but I couldn't put my finger on it. After Manny had left, I started thinking where on earth could have Max hid something if she wanted to. Then it dawned on me the coin holder was much thicker than the ones I'm used to seeing. Max was pretty shrewd to think of doing it this way. Do you have any idea what the key may be for?"

"Yes, I have an idea. This key looks just like this one." Steff opened her shoulder bag and pulled out her key ring and showed Mike a similar small brass key. "My apartment complex has a secure storage room next to the mailboxes. You can rent one of these small lockboxes for a month or longer. All you need to get in is your key card and pin number I guess there must be one somewhere downstairs."

"Let's finish up here and see if we can find one." Mike gathered up papers and coins to the lockbox and returned to the bedroom. Steff emptied out the teapot and put the cups in the dishwasher. After a quick look around to make sure they didn't leave any lights on, Steff closed and locked Max's door. They headed to the elevator for a quick trip down to the lobby. After a few minutes, they were able to find several banks of post-office-like boxes. These seem to be as they appeared, just mailboxes. Neither Mike nor Steff was able to find any lockboxes anywhere in the lobby area. "You're the investigative reporter; you have any ideas?"

Steff thought for a moment, "That door we just passed, the one next to the post office boxes, has a lot of wear on the tile in front of it. I'll bet Max's apartment key opens the door." Steff retrieved Max's key card from her purse and inserted it into the slot above a ten-key pad next to the doorknob. The small screen lit up and asked for a pin number.

"I think we are screwed. I don't remember seeing anything which looked like it pin number in her apartment."

"Not to worry, Max's pin number is always 2525, something to do with her mother. She gave it to me when we met with her attorney about my power of attorney. Steff entered 2525, and a metallic click indicated the door had unlatched. As they entered the room, a motion sensor turned on the lights. Two entire walls contained lockboxes of various sizes. The doors were all gray except for a small numbers panel and a small keyhole.

"This may take a while. I don't remember seeing a number on Max's key."

"Don't be a pessimist Mike. You're right, but the size of the key will reduce the number of locks we have to try. The bigger boxes seem to need a thicker one, and the small boxes need a smaller key. If I am right, we only have about twenty boxes to check." Without saying another word, Steff begins trying each lock on the middle-sized boxes. The ninth try produced success. Steff retrieved a large manila envelope from the lockbox. Reaching her hand in she determined there was nothing else present. Steff handed the envelope to Mike as she closed and relocked the box. "Don't just stand there, open it."

Mike reached into his pocket and retrieved a small pocket knife. "I'm going to open the bottom of the envelope just in case we need to get a DNA sample of whoever licked the top. The knife easily opened the envelope. What came out of the envelope was totally unexpected. In between about fifty sheets of paper was an Apple tablet.

Chapter Thirty-one

D etective Foster decided to take advantage of the quiet afternoon to catch up on paperwork. The first two files went quickly, transferring a few notes and filling out a short incident report. The third file proved to be a very different story altogether. The tag indicated "Anne Hamilton Case # ... Opening the file, EJ expected to review the information from the medical examiner and sign off the case and get it off his desk. The first sheet of paper contained a memorandum from the medical examiner, summarizing his report. The first few paragraphs read as expected; however, the last paragraph started with a disturbing revelation. "It is the opinion of this examiner that the cause of one Anne Hamilton's death is ruled death by a person or persons unknown." The disturbing text continued by noting Ms. Hamilton was unconscious for at least thirty minutes prior to her actual death. EJ quickly flipped back in the file to review his notes and take a look at several pictures. An x-ray of the side of her head clearly showed two areas of impact. The one at the back that EJ saw at the scene and a much larger area of trauma to her forehead. What troubled EJ most was an arrow the medical examiner had placed on the x-ray pointing at the junction between her skull and the C1 vertebrae. It was evident her death was caused by a severe rotational disarticulation, commonly known as a broken neck. The damage to the C1 vertebrae indicated she died when someone rapidly twisted her neck. The rest of the paragraph was a technical summary of why this type of disarticulation is not found in falls, even from distances much higher than Ms. Hamilton's half staircase. The last line was the most disturbing; "Injuries of this type are typical of military type activities where the deceased's head is quickly and violently rotated to produce an instantaneous death."

EJ leaned back in his chair and sipped lukewarm coffee from a cardboard cup. *This case now moves into my section.* EJ closed the file and retrieved a rubber stamp from his drawer. Quick pressure revealed the file's new importance; "Major Crimes Taskforce Case Number _____." EJ signed on to his computer and brought up the case file master list and assigned Ms. Hamilton's death the next number. He then transferred the number to the file jacket. EJ now turned his attention back to the file. For the next hour, he carefully read the file. Half of the time he spent going over Stephanie Huffman's interview the evening of the incident. The third time through his interview notes EJ began to believe Ms. Hamilton's death was somehow connected to the odd behavior of Brad Smith that morning. *Smith's actions that morning were very troubling to Ms. Hamilton, even to the point of causing her to share her concerns with Ms. Huffman ... How did she say it - - 'the Brad I went down the elevator with was not the same Brad I went up the elevator with' ... This has to be the key.* EJ closed the file and dialed Mr. Smith's office number.

The friendly voice indicated Mr. Smith was not taking any calls. Furthermore, he was out of the country on business and was not expected back for at least a month and maybe as long as six months. The voice became a bit less cordial when EJ asked for a contact number. The voice indicated she was not authorized to provide any information, about Mr. Smith. When EJ pressed for more, the voice simply terminated the conversation with a curt "thank you for calling."

Mr. Smith being out of the country seemed a bit contrived and convenient. During her interview, Steff pointed out Anne had a copy of Mr. Smith's travel itinerary. According to his itinerary, he was not scheduled to be back in Geneva until the middle of next month. *Hmmm ... I think it's time to give Barry a quick call and find out what I can about this Mr. Smith.*

EJ rummaged through his Rolodex until he isolated Barry's telephone number. A few pokes on his iPhone screen completed the call. After one ring the computer-generated, but pleasant, voice answered, "You have reached the State Department of the United States' Denver regional office. If you know your party's four-digit extension, please dial it now; otherwise, dial zero for the operator. Four quick pokes and two rings later Barry answered his phone. After a minute or so of catching up on small talk, Barry asked. "EJ, the only time you ever call this number is when you need a favor. What can the State Department do for the Denver Police Department today?"

"I'm trying to get some background information on a Brad Smith. Apparently, he is attached to our G8 finance minister." EJ could hear the clicking of an older style computer keyboard.

A few moments later Barry indicated, "We have a Bradley Smith, attached to our G8 Finance Minister's office. Just a minute there's more. Our system indicates he was on medical leave until just a few days ago. Ahaa, sorry, I don't see any data on what his leave was about."

"Is there any information on his current assignment or a contact telephone number?"

"It just says here he was assigned to a posting in Geneva last month. I'm sorry, I don't see any contact number, and that's about all I can get. If you need more information, you probably have to go to somebody with a higher pay grade than mine. Before you ask yes, I have a suggestion. Try calling a Maryon Alexander in DC; he's with the NSA."

"Do you have a number?"

"No, however, I can tell you when Brad's file opened a pop-up indicated if I had any information about Bradley Smith, I was to contact this guy at the NSA's DC office."

"What does that mean, contact NSA?"

"I see these pop-ups every once in a while. Most of the time it's to alert me of an individual on a watch list. Never says anything else, just contact so and so. I will look up this guy's contact information and text you. I'm sorry I can't give you any more information."

"Well, at least, I have someone else to call."

"Are we still on for the Rockies game next Tuesday?"

"Wouldn't miss it."

"I'll pick you up at 5:30... Later."

EJ was a bit more confused than when he first started. *How can Smith be in two places at once? State Department has him located in Geneva, but according to Ms. Huffman, he spoke with Ms. Hamilton in the elevator. Not only did she talk to him, but in three hours he changed into somebody who she said looked like Mr. Smith and spoke like him -- too many indicators – somethings wrong, and now she's dead. Smith is supposed to be in Geneva.* EJ was having one of those detective moments. He sensed something didn't add up between what he just heard, and what he read in Steff's statement. Thumbing back through the file, he found those couple of words which made it all fit together. *Hmm - here it is - Steff said Annie felt sheepish and called Smith's office to apologize, but his office assistant said he didn't feel well after his stem cell treatment so went home to rest. That biddy lied to me. She told me this morning Mr. Smith was out of the country for at least a month. Barry's passport file places Mr. Smith in Geneva.* EJ's thoughts were interrupted by his vibrating cell phone. After a quick touch, the contact information for Mr. Alexander filled the screen. EJ transferred Barry's text into his contacts' list. Glancing at his watch, he realized it was lunchtime in DC.

After a couple of minutes, EJ couldn't wait any longer. He picked up his telephone and punched in the number Barry sent him. After a couple of rings, a crisp voice inquired, "This is Agent Manny Alexander, but before you answer, how did you get this telephone number? It is restricted."

"This is Detective Foster from the Denver Metropolitan Police and to answer your question it was given to me by the State Department."

"Sorry to be so short with you Detective. Things have been a bit hectic the last couple of days. How can I help you?"

"I am doing some background research on a federal employee who may have information about a local murder here. "

"Before we go any further, is this employee a suspect?"

"No, he's a person of interest. It's our understanding this employee is a personal friend of the deceased. We are trying to verify information at this point."

"Okay, who is it?"

"His name is Bradley Smith, and he's attached the office of our G8 Finance Minister."

"Detective Foster, what I am to about ask you may sound strange, but it's imperative you, and I talk. But not this way. I want you to go out to the ATF office in the Denver Tech Center. Take the main floor elevator to the second floor and tell the attendant you need to speak with Elizabeth Peterson. I will call in advance and make arrangements for you and me to talk on a secure line.

"Can you do that?"

"Yes. Can you give me a hint … no, I guess not, come to think of it."

"How long will it take you to get over to the tech center?"

"I could be there in about an hour."

"When you get there, Elizabeth will contact me, and I will call you on her secure line. Will that work for you?"

"I guess we'll be talking in about an hour. Thank you." EJ hung up the phone and wondered, what kind of a mess he had just gotten himself into. EJ called down to the garage and asked for an unmarked car. He gathered up his files, his laptop, and headed down to the garage.

Chapter Thirty-two

A short wave of Burke's hand summoned a fresh pot of tea. "Please renew Dr. Hayes's tea." As quickly as he had come, the crisp white figure faded back into the shadows.

Peter was having a difficult time processing the flood of information he was receiving from his new benefactor including the presence of a stem cell research clinic in Central Mexico. The most challenging part to accept was the fact that a bunch of technicians in Mexico seemed to have duplicated their complicated process. Peter thought he and Mike were the only ones capable of propagating these unique adult stem cell lines. Peter turned to Reg. "I had no idea you developed the technical skills to transfer this technology down to the Mexico clinic. How did you solve the problem of reverse transcription? Neither Mike nor I have published the solution."

Reg started to raise his hand to point at Burke but changed his mind. "Peter, again let me say I'm sorry about the deception, but we are both caught in the same snare. To answer your question, it was straightforward. One day during lunch I set down in your office and read your notes. It's amazing what you can copy these days using just your cell phone. I just photographed all the procedural data and e-mailed it to Burke's office where his staff transcribed everything. Later that same weekend I set down and verified that the transcription matched what you and I had been doing in the laboratory for the last couple of months. So, as you can see, I didn't solve the reverse transcription problem I just borrowed your solution. Remember you and Dr. Lancaster still have the opportunity to publish your solution and will receive full credit from your peers."

At this moment, Peter was drawing little pleasure from that last bit of information. "Tell me, Mr. Burke, how did you set up the protocol for these G8 Secretaries? I'm assuming you either bypassed or jumped over most of the concerns the FDA outlined in our approval of our Stage II clinical trials."

"As I said before the FDA leaves no room for innovative techniques. I know you will not approve of our test methodology but will have to admit it has been very effective."

"Well if all eight of these guys are taking the treatment and are still alive your tests methodologies must be valid." At this point, a chill ran down Peter's spine. The technicians down in Mexico must have tried their interpretation of Mike's technique on volunteers. "I guess you pre-tested these cell lines on human volunteers."

"That is partially correct. We did use humans, but they were not volunteers. They were provided for us by the local prison. Our first half-dozen test subjects didn't tolerate the treatment very well, and we had to delay the start of our project until we found a combination that provided regeneration with the fewest side effects. In our last round of tests, we actually used volunteers. Local health workers were paid the equivalent of ten years of wages to volunteer. We did use your prescreening techniques for our last round of tests, except our volunteers thought we were testing a new flu vaccine. We couldn't afford for that kind information to be out in public."

"Mr. Burke, speaking as a scientist, what were the adverse reactions the first group experienced?"

"To be blunt, they all died. One died after one treatment. The others lived through a couple more treatments, but none lived passed three treatments. We are not sure what happened, but their livers begin to respond, and then the stem cells went wild. There rapid and uncontrolled growth quickly spread into their internal organs. Well, let's say they didn't die quickly."

Peter felt like he was going to vomit but determined to keep his composure even though he was now sure his new boss was some kind of a mental case. In his best scientific voice, Peter suggested the first group died because of high testosterone levels. "Mike and

I determined fairly early that individuals with high testosterone levels were not viable candidates for the treatment. My first assumption was that your first test subjects were individuals living in conditions where they probably had above-average testosterone levels. I would have no idea what would happen to this line of stem cells in the presence of very high levels of testosterone. I guess your group two subjects did okay because you used our screening procedure and chose only candidates with lower testosterone levels."

"Very astute Dr. Hayes. Our team came to the same conclusion. We started off on the wrong track because we started using information from the middle of your project after you solved the testosterone problem. Reg had to dig back to the archives to find out what was self-evident to you and Dr. Lancaster but in our haste, we skipped over it, but that's behind us now, everything is working as well or even a bit better than what you have reported in the literature."

Peter's stomach was feeling a little less turbulent, but he decided to forgo any more of Mr. Burke's chocolate delights. Deciding he had nothing to lose, Peter went right to the core of the project. "While we have been talking I think I have put two and two together. You are the one involved with the NSA project I'm working on just down the street from the clinic."

"Again Dr. Hayes, very astute. How did you come to that conclusion?"

"I'm sorry to say there was no real detective work. I just remember a lot of the staff talking about a short, middle-aged man who was always wearing a fedora and was always asking very technical questions. Since you seem always to be wearing one it seemed logical you and the G8 coordinators are one and the same."

"Now that you are privy to our loosely kept secret I think it's time to fill you in on the grand scheme of things. As you have probably already guessed, I am both financially and politically deeply involved in both projects. What neither the clinic nor NSA knows is there is a third leg to my stool."

"The G8 Ministers gave me carte blanche to set up an arrangement with your Rosch Clinic to provide stem cell treatments for each of the eight secretaries. The fact that your patients needed to be close to the clinic for the entire six-month treatment created a logistics problem since these Secretaries are traveling more than they are home. It quickly became evident they could not receive the treatment and be gone for up to six months. With the help of your naïve NSA, I quickly devised a plan to select a group of trusted look-a-likes to fulfill many of the routine activities of the secretaries. The NSA then selected and vetted eight men who to fill the role. To increase the potential for success, we decided each of these men would receive carefully selected plastic surgery and, during their healing process, to have them learn as much as they could about the man they were about to replace. As soon as the first look-alike is ready, we will let him walk into his office and convince his staff he is truly who he is supposed to be, and if successful, the look-a-like will go out into the real world, and the Secretary would step into the treatment program. Our go-forward plan is to treat the Secretary to the United States Minister first since he has a special relationship with one of his staff that will require an elaborate integration program. If the first test works, he will take off a few days and will inform his staff by email that he will be gone for minor surgery to remove a polyp from his vocal cords and his voice will sound a little different for a while. If it does not go well, we will transfer some of the office staff and eliminate any troublesome staff. Sparing you the details, we will take them out of the picture."

Again Peter was astonished by how detached his new his boss was from the possible outcome of his various actions. *I think he means eliminate will be more permanent than just being fired or transferred. Just kick them out of the way like an annoying dog. I'm not sure how much longer I can keep a straight face.* "I am assuming you mean firing or relocation until the project was over."

"Dr. Hayes, it's not good for you to dwell on these petty things. You do the science and let me take care of the details."

"Not a problem sir, not a problem."

Chapter Thirty-three

S teff, do you have any idea what could be on this tablet? You knew Max the best."

"I'm not sure, but I remember Max telling me a while back she was switching from writing in her journal every day to a digital journal; this might be it. Steff turned on the tablet, and the screen lit up just long enough to indicate "low battery," and turned off. "Do you have a charger for an Apple tablet?"

"No, but remember the place we photocopied your stuff? They have a free charging station. I would assume with Apple's popularity we could charge or, at least, turn on the tablet there."

Steff thumbed through the papers. Showing Mike the top three sheets she asked, "What are these?"

"It looks to me like these are either originals or photocopies of the paperwork generated by the clinic for Max's entrance into the program. Looking at some of the short notes written on top of some sheets I'm going to guess we have Max's Journal. If my theory is correct, then that tablet should be an interesting journal. Let's get back to the store and see what Max has put in her tablet. You take the tablet, and I'll take the papers, just in case something happens - pardon my flair for the dramatic, but your friend Manny spooks me a bit."

"I agree. While we are there, let's get a couple of copies of all of these medical records. We can both keep one but let's send a copy to Manny for safe keeping - just in case. Before we go, let's go back up to Max's apartment. Now that we know we are looking for a tablet charger, maybe we can find one." After an additional fifteen minutes of searching, there was no evidence that Max even owned an Apple tablet. "Mike, I find it odd there is no evidence of any electronics in this apartment. No USB chargers, no cords, not even a cell phone charger, which is odd since I swear Max had one of those grafted to her ear. She was always talking to someone. Also, there was no cell phone with Max's personal belongings I received at the clinic. I do remember they asked her to leave her cell phone and Bluetooth in her dressing locker. Now that I think about it, I remember she had one of those curly-stretchy things around her wrist with a key attached."

"You're right; the standard protocol is for a patient's personal belongings to be kept in a numbered locker. If the patient loses their key, they are charged $125 for a locksmith to replace the lock. There are no duplicate keys and no master key. Was there a key in her personal effects?"

"I don't think so. All I got was a manila envelope with a friendship ring, a small gold chain with a cross, her sunglasses, and a small clutch purse. When I asked about her clothing, the secretary lady told me she would check into it and give me a call. She called later and informed me Max was cremated in her street clothes, per her health directive, which we both know are bogus."

"If necessary, I think I can find the security tapes for those patient lockers. But with what we have seen so far, I'm going to guess there was a camera malfunction or some other lame excuse. However, I will check."

"Mike, if I may be so bold, I think the fewer people who know we're looking into this, the better for both of us. We already have enough evidence to prove Max was in the clinic. One, she was part of your stem cell program. Two, She completed the first five treatments, even though the clinic's records stated she died in the ER and not in the treatment room. Three, her death is not related to the stem cell project. Come on; we are wasting time; we can talk in the car."

The drive back to the clinic and a short walk to the copy center was filled with all sorts of what-ifs and speculations. Both Mike and Steff soon agreed they needed a lot more information before they could even begin to figure out what's going on behind the scenes. It was also growing more evident to Steff that Mike's inquisitive mind was a match for her investigative skills. Steff made two copies of Max's clinic records while Mike went over to plug in Max's tablet. When he asked the assistant which charging station to use for an Apple tablet she indicated any of the USB's will work. Mike suddenly realized he had the same USB cable arrangement in his shoulder bag. Walking back over to Steff he suggested they go up to his office to look at the tablet and not do it out here in the open. Steff agreed. Like before Steff bundled up one set of the copies to send to Manny. The assistant placed the large Manila envelope on the scale and printed out the correct postage. Steff settled the bill with cash and decided the express mail drop box outside was safe enough and dispatched Manny's envelope. "Can we get something to eat? We've been so busy I don't remember when I last ate."

"Sure, the coffee shop in the clinic makes some pretty good sandwiches, and their coffee is actually drinkable. Come on it's on the way to my office. We can pick up something to go and eat while we look at the tablet." A quick stop produced two sandwiches, a bag of chips, two extra-large white chocolate macadamia nut cookies and two large coffees. Mike scanned his faculty ID card and charged their supper to his internal account. Steff was now familiar with the security routines to get to Mike's office. Mike quickly re-stacked the files on one corner of his desk and placed them on the floor. He then retrieved his USB adapter from his backpack and plugged it into the wall, then into the tablet.

Seeing the tablet screen light up, Steff forgot about how hungry she was and quickly began searching the file icons. It soon became evident these are large video files, each one attached to a date. Steff selected the earliest date and touched the active screen. A little "I am busy" circle spun for a few seconds before displaying a video file. Steff touched the play button, and Max's face appeared.

"Hi, this is Max; of course, you know that since you're looking at the very first entry in my new digital journal. Later on, I'll figure out how to use the password, but right now I am so excited about being accepted into this new stem cell program I can hardly stand still. They tell me the stem cells will be infused into my pancreas, where they will repair the stuff that makes my insulin. They also tell me I have at least a ninety percent chance of a diabetes cure. Wow – – Pinch me, I can hardly believe it. I will try to make an entry every day until I'm cured. I want to be able to share this with my friends and, in particular, Steff, who has volunteered to be with me as I walk this scary path. I know things will work out because my God is a good God … Bye, for now." The last image now frozen on the screen was of Max relaxed with glistening eyes and contagious smile.

"I can see why she is so special to you, and I would agree wholeheartedly that she did not change her health directives as the clinic is trying to make us believe." Mike turned toward Steff expecting her to say something. Instead, all he could see was the top of her head. Steff had buried her face in her hands to stop the tears. Instinctively Mike reached over and put his hand on her shoulder. Before he could say a word, Steff jumped up, threw her arms around his neck, and began sobbing uncontrollably. Mike figured it was best not to say anything just then, which proved to be valuable in his quest to gain Steff's confidence. His gentle rubbing of her back gave Steff permission to finish her cry without judgment. A couple of quick deep breaths and Steff lifted her head from the warm damp cleft between Mike's neck and shoulder.

"Sorry about that, just seeing and hearing Max's enthusiasm brought back an image I thought I had lost when she died. I guess I'm not as far along in the grieving process as I thought. I think I have been trapped in the denial stage for too long. If Max were alive now, I would give her a hug and thank her from the bottom of my being for making this video diary. Do you have a tissue hidden someplace in this mess?"

"Yes, but all I can offer is a lab tissue. They aren't as soft but are very absorbent. Sorry, you had to ask, I should've offered."

"Well, I guess it's not every day you have a hysterical crying woman in your office." Steff pulled a couple of tissues from the box and dried her eyes. Thank you for letting me get that out; I know I'll be able to think more clearly now. I have promised myself I am going to get to the bottom of this one way or another."

Mike's cell phone vibrated; then his recorded voice clearly enunciated, "3:30 PM, clinic staff meeting, second-floor lecture hall."

"Steff, I have to go to this meeting. We are reviewing our submission to FDA for an expanded clinical trial. I'll tell you what, let me take you to a real dinner after my meeting."

"I would love to, what time will you be through?"

"Why don't I meet you out front at six o'clock?" Mike reached into his pocket and tossed Steff the keys to his car. "You do have a driver's license, don't you? Why don't you take the time to glance through Max's tablet and see if anything stands out? I'll walk you out to the security desk and get you signed out."

Steff carefully put the tablet into her computer bag. Mike gathered up a half a dozen file folders off of his desk, put on his lab coat and locked the door. After signing Steff out, Mike started towards the elevators, but turned and yelled after Steff. "Be careful, I'll see you soon."

Mike waited for an answer. Steff just waved her hand without turning around and disappeared through the revolving door. As the elevator door closed, a feeling of excitement rejuvenated his tired frame. A sheepish grin spread across his face. *I still don't understand her, but she is definitely not a Ms. Stiff.* Mike's hand touched the neckband of his now slightly damp shirt. The events of the last hour sped through his brain, almost giving him goosebumps. The elevator door slowly moved back revealing an ever-widening slice of reality. Three steps and the hustle and bustle of the impending meeting quenched the lingering warmth.

The clinical director was waiting for him at the door. "I just checked, and I didn't see your PowerPoint presentation. Did I miss the file name?"

"No, I just ran out of time and didn't get it posted." Mike retrieved a thumb drive from his lab coat pocket. "The file's name is Clinical 3. My presentation should be about twenty-five minutes long. Am I still second on the program?"

"Yes, you will be following Dr. Hayes today. I haven't seen him yet. Do you know where he might be?"

The realization Peter would be speaking first troubled Mike. The information Manny had just shared would make it challenging to act normal during his presentation. Mike determined to carry out Manny's request to not share any of this information until he gave the all-clear. The clinical director picked up the microphone and began asking everyone to take a seat and quiet down. After a few minutes the auditorium was in order except for a couple of squeaking chairs, a sneeze, and then after a cleared throat, all was quiet.

"Thank you all for your quick assembly. We have a lot to cover today, and to make it easier for the staff to transcribe our notes we will be recording our proceedings. At any time if you have a question or comment, please face one of the cameras so we know who is speaking and can attribute your comments and questions properly. As you know from the meeting announcement, we are here to review the abstract of our draft application to the FDA. We will begin with two short presentations from our to research directors. We will first hear Dr. Hayes's summary of his Stage II clinical trials associated with his diabetic project. That will be followed by Dr. Lancaster's review of his Stage II clinical trials related to his hepatic regeneration project. Are there any questions? ... Then we will proceed with the first presentation. Dr. Hayes, you have the floor ... Dr. Hayes?"

The technician seated behind the video projector broke the silence. "I just received a text from Dr. Hayes indicating he will be unable to attend today and asked if the meeting could be rescheduled for next Tuesday. I sent a return text telling him we were all assembled and waiting for him, but it went to voicemail. I checked his phone number and redialed and got the same message."

The clinical director pulled out his cell phone, and speed-dialed Dr. Hayes and received the same message. Turning to Mike, he asked, "Do you want to give your half or wait until both of you are ready?"

Trying not to show his relief, Mike replied, "I think waiting would better,"

Again picking up the microphone the director announced, "I'm sorry we all have wasted this time. I will send out an e-mail rescheduling this meeting as soon as I hear from Dr. Hayes. Again thank you for coming and for your understanding."

Mike wasn't sure whether he was more concerned, or more relieved that Peter was a no-show. To find out just what Peter was doing he dialed Peter's private number. Both he and Mike had what they called backdoor numbers. With all the notoriety and the security at the clinic, they both subscribed to a call-forwarding service. With this particular service, they could call in and record a secure message. At the end of the message, they could key in a pin number and the service would send a one-word text which would let the other know there was a message waiting.

Mike dialed Peter's number and when prompted left a message. "Peter, what's up? Missed you at today's meeting. I hope you are feeling okay. Let me know if you need any help." Mike then keyed in his pin number, and the phone voice indicated his message was sent. A quick glance at his watch indicated Steff would not be by to pick him up for almost two hours. As Mike made his way back up to his office, he realized he was not living in the present. He completely ignored a colleague's inquiry into his health and uncharacteristically pushed his way past two technicians to get into the elevator. Mike closed his office door and fell into his chair. After placing the files he was carrying on the desk, he leaned back and closed his eyes.

Chapter Thirty-four

M ike soon realized he was playing back, scene by scene by scene, the events of the last forty-eight hours. His bewilderment over Peter's involvement in this other large stem cell project still did not process. Uncharacteristic anger welled up as it became evident that Peter had used his technology without even a word. Determined to find out as much as he could about Peter's apparent betrayal, Mike signed on to the clinic's mainframe and started searching for documents associated with Peter. His initial search yielded over twelve hundred documents Peter had either, signed, wrote, or sent since the project began. Narrowing the search to dates associated with Manny's timeline, the number of records quickly shrank to five hundred sixty-one. Restricting his search to documents related to his work reduced the number to one hundred twenty. A quick scan of titles turned up five which intrigued Mike. These documents were all associated with requests for stem cell samples for testing. The first one was for two samples for Johns Hopkins. The next two were for samples for the CDC. The next one gave Mike a chill. This request was for twenty-five production vials of Mike's stem cell line to be transferred to Peter's lead technician Reg Horn. Mike scanned down through the document. Nothing seemed to be out of place until Mike got to the section marked "proposed use." The usual detailed summary of proposed use was absent. Just a short note indicating a transfer to ongoing *in vitro* trials.

The last document was a request for fifty production vials of stem cells from Mike's FDA collection. These were the stem cells allocated for the current FDA trials. In this case, the proposed use section contained the innocuous words "transferred to the federal government for testing." *That's as many vials as I allocated for the whole next stage of FDA trials. I don't think Manny is going to have to convince me any further. Its obvious Peter has gone rogue, or, at least, he has some serious explaining to do.*

Mike spent the next hour and a half combing through more files. Except for a series of request for leave forms, Mike was unable to find anything which seemed to fit the situation Manny had described. The leave forms were spread out over the last eighteen months and were for medically approved leave. On each form just below the section detailing medical leave was a notation indicating Peter needed to rest for three to four hours each day as he recuperated from the after-effects of recent Bell's Palsy outbreaks. Scrolling down through the files Mike was able to ascertain during the last eighteen months Peter was out of the laboratory more than he was in the laboratory. Since he and Peter would meet for coffee around 7:30 am to discuss lab results, project progress, and shop talk in general, he would not have known Peter was absent for significant part or all of most afternoons. Peter's absence was also easily hidden from Mike since they worked on two different floors of the clinic's research facility. He would bump into Peter on some evenings, so it was natural to assume Peter had been there all day.

The William Tell Overture blaring from his lab coat pocket indicated a text message: "left apt cu in 20". *I had better get on the stick. I don't think Steff likes to be kept waiting.* Mike quickly printed off the two sample request documents, signed off, and headed out the door. About four steps down the hall, Mike remembered he was still wearing his lab coat. To conserve time Mike pulled off the lab coat, rolled it up into a ball, and pitched it into his office. "There's two for the home team."

Mike managed to beat Steff to the rendezvous point, but by only a minute or two. Steff opened the driver's side door and slid across into the passenger seat. As Mike buckled his seatbelt, he wanted to blurt out what he found out about Peter's requisitioning of stem cells but remembered what his father had always said, "Always give your date the chance to speak first. It's also helpful to ask a simple question first."

"Hi Steff, did you learn anything from Max's Journal?"

"Not a whole lot. Surprisingly, it felt like Max and I was talking over a cup of tea. Her entries were never very long, maybe a minute or two with just a quick overview of what the day had brought. She talked about almost making herself sick with the anticipation of her first treatment. She was glad the clinic provided a low dose of Xanax to calm her down. She laughed a lot about being a pill junkie. Since each entry was dated, I jumped ahead and listened to her entries about her fifth treatment. She said she couldn't put her finger on anything, but her response to the fifth treatment was very different than the first four. Several times between her fifth treatment and the one which killed her, she said she felt jumpy and hyped up like when she drank too much coffee. I don't know what it means, but she did mention it several times over a month."

"I don't recall any symptoms like those noted in the FDA follow-up files, but it will be easy enough to check when I get back to my office in the morning. Do you have any favorite place you like to eat?"

"I haven't been in Denver very long so why don't you suggest a place you think I might like. I'm not much for Asian food, and I've had way too much Chinese food last couple of weeks. Better to pick something else."

"Then it's off to the Spaghetti Factory. They have awesome pasta, superb seafood and salads to die for."

"Let's do it." As Mike eased out into traffic and headed towards his destination, Steff asked, "How was the meeting?"

"The meeting fizzled out because Peter was a no-show. Since I had a couple of hours, I started combing through the clinic's files. There were things Peter may have done which seem out of the ordinary. What I found troubles me greatly, and it does fit into what Manny has been telling us. Peter twice requisitioned, from the cell propagation laboratory, sizeable requests for test samples. One appeared to be for his research group and allocated to Reg, his chief tech. The second one is the most troubling. Peter asked for fifty cryogenic vials for the federal government. No indication to which agency or who. But that number of cells is equal to the amount we had grown out and allocated for the entire next round of FDA testing. I know one cryogenic vial doesn't mean anything to you, but there are enough cells in one vial to treat one or two patients."

"I think I see where you're going with this. If Peter is running this other shadow clinic for the G8 group and the NSA, he would need a lot of cells, would he not?"

"Yes, and with what he requisitioned, he could easily treat ten or twelve adults for the entire six-month protocol. But what I don't understand is why the large requisition to his chief tech. There were enough cells in his requisition to treat four or five adults."

Mike pulled into the restaurant parking lot and found a convenient parking place, turned off the motor and walked around the passenger side. He opened the door and extended his hand. "What do you say we not talk shop for the next two hours?"

Steff shook her head in agreement and took his hand. As they walked towards the restaurant, their clasped hands swung quietly. "It was your idea, now what should we talk about?"

"I would like to know more about how you became an investigative reporter. My Google searches the other day just hit the highlights, like where you graduated and stuff like that. I really would like to get to know you as a person rather than a statistic."

"So you think I am a statistic?"

"That wasn't what I meant. What I meant was I … ah-aaa I just don't know much about you as a person."

"So now I am a person? I will be happy to share something about me if you promise not to ask how I got my long name."

"I won't, Scout's honor." Mike held up the three-finger Scout sign. As they approached the door, a greeter stepped from the shadows, opened the door and welcome them to the Spaghetti Factory. They were seated in a booth overlooking downtown Denver. A small oil lamp flickered inside its small narrow chimney. The server indicated the specials for the day and asked if they would like anything to drink. Steff chose water with lemon and Mike ordered their signature wild raspberry lemonade. Their server indicated she would be back momentarily with their drinks and to take their order.

After a short awkward silence, as they both stared blankly at the menu, Mike repeated his question, "How then did you become an investigative reporter?"

"In one sense I think I was born with a question mark in my mouth. My grandfather was a Pinkerton detective, and my father worked for a small regional newspaper for almost his entire professional life. When I was twelve, he was nominated for a Pulitzer Prize for his work surrounding a group of merchants who were fixing the price of farm commodities. He didn't get the Pulitzer Prize but was on the list of honorable mentions. He also got a broken nose from one of the merchants who pounced on him in the courtroom after the jury found them all guilty. The doctor got it almost straight but he always joked about his crooked nose was how he was able to sniff out really juicy stories."

"Your father sounds like a neat guy. I would like to meet him someday."

"After we figure out what's going on with Max, oops, I remember, no shop talk. What I was going to say is that mom and dad are going to be in Denver in a couple of months. Dad has some writers' conference he wants to attend. He has been writing short story mysteries based loosely on some of his articles. He's had quite a few of them published, but he wants to write a book or, as he calls it, his tome."

"Now I want to meet your dad. I'm a sucker for a good mystery. Not the fast and flashy CSI mysteries on TV, but a superb book with several hundred pages to solve the mystery. That's what I like."

The server placed their drinks on little round coasters. "Are you ready to order, or do you need more time? Okay, what would you have, ma'am? "

Steff looked up. "I think I will have the coconut shrimp and a garden salad with ranch. Oh, could you please put the dressing on the side and no onions, thank you."

"And you, sir?"

"I'll take the same, except I would like a bowl of Manhattan clam chowder instead of the salad."

"Thank you, I'll be right out with your order."

"Where were we?"

"You were telling me how much you like mystery books."

"When I was a kid I read every one of the Hardy Boys' mysteries a couple of times. But enough about me. I want to know more about your dad. How does he know Manny?

"He and Manny went to college together, and both did a tour in the Air Force before settling down. Or at least, dad did. Manny applied to join the Secret Service but based on his aptitudes and work in the Air Force they asked if he would be interested in joining the NSA. He and my dad talked the pro's and con's for days until he finally accepted their offer and had been with the NSA ever since. When I was born, my parents asked Manny if he would be my Godfather, a role which I think he still enjoys immensely. Uncle Manny, as I call him, would stop by our house whenever he could. Sometimes for just for couple hours and sometimes a lot longer. He even went with us on a vacation trip out to Disneyland when I was eleven or twelve. I'm not sure who had the most fun. He took me on everything that moved."

"This question is not shop talk. Do you call Manny for help very often in your investigative work?"

"It started when I worked, if you call it worked, at the college newspaper. If I had some fact I needed to verify or some bit of information, I needed to dig up. He always came through and seemed to enjoy being able to help. Remember this was all before Google, so any help was much appreciated. He's always told me the information he gave me was part of the public record. However, there are times he gave me a bit of info or a reference which I am pretty sure was in a gray zone. All he ever asked was that I never print where I got the information or from whom. That's why when he told us about the G8 project I decided to take him very seriously and at his word. I am glad you were there, Mike. I'm not sure I could have been as productive by myself."

"I have a great deal more respect for him and investigative work of any type since I became involved in … oops, no shop talk."

"I think we should acknowledge the elephant sitting at our table and go-ahead and talk about what we found out today."

The arrival of their food provided a natural break in the growing tension. The rest of the meal and a calorie-laden dessert was filled with a mixture of small talk and rehashing the day's activities. After paying the check, they walked arm in arm back out to the car. On the way back to Steff's apartment, the discussion turned to what should they do next. Steff indicated she had a mandatory production meeting at the studio that would last until about eleven. "Then why don't I pick you up at the studio around noon? We can grab a bite to eat and find someplace where we can sort out our information."

"Sounds good to me. I'll bring the tablet with me tomorrow. By the way, last night, I went out and bought a 64 Gig thumb drive and backed up Max's entire Journal. I put the tablet inside of the instruction book for my flat screen TV and put it all inside of a zip-lock bag. So what I will bring tomorrow is a searchable copy. To listen to any particular day, we just click on the calendar day, and it will play automatically."

"Smart girl. I guess the short answer is to bring anything which might be even remotely related to Max. I will get what I can find out from the clinic's mainframe without making it look like I'm snooping." Mike pulled the car up to the front steps of Steff's apartment complex. Before he could get out and open the door, Steff leaned across the seat and kissed him on the cheek and said goodnight. Before Mike could say anything, Steff jumped out of the car and disappeared into her apartment building. *That sure felt good -- I'm glad I shaved.*

Chapter Thirty-five

M anny hung up the phone and fell back into his chair. *This is beginning to unravel. There's too much information in the wind. I need to get this Detective Foster off on a rabbit trail before he stumbles in where he doesn't belong.* Manny opened up his contacts list and secured Elizabeth Petersons' direct dial number. After the second ring a pleasant, almost husky voice filled Manny's ear, "Good afternoon this is Elizabeth Peterson, you have reached the enforcement division of the ATF. How may I help you?"

"Liz, this is Manny, I'm calling you today from my office in DC. I need to ask a special favor of you."

"Hmm - sounds mysterious, how can I help?"

"I have an asset in the Metro Denver area that I need to talk with on a secure line."

"Is this part of an ongoing NSA investigation? If so, what is the case number so I can log it into my system?"

"This is a new case, and I need to determine if the source is reliable before I go through the tedious paperwork to open a new case file. Can you still do this?

"Of course, I can silly boy. All you had to do was ask me to hand the guy the phone and go get a cup of coffee. Oh, I think I presumed your source was male."

"Yes, he is male. His name is EJ Foster, and he's a senior detective with the Metro Denver Violent Crimes Task Force. Just so you're not completely in the dark, he is investigating a murder there in Denver, which may be tied directly to an ongoing NSA program. I need a few minutes on a secure line to either thank him or open a new case file."

"Not a problem Manny. How should I get a hold of him?"

"He is on his way to your office. He should be there in about thirty minutes or so. I have asked him to go to your floor and identify himself and ask for you. That's all he knows, nothing else."

"Aren't you even a little bit presumptuous? You assumed I would be in the office and without even asking you send the guy over here. What if I had not been here? The receptionist wouldn't know what to do with him."

"I know you're not clairvoyant, and I do have a tiny bit of common courtesy left. I called your secretary to verify you would be in your office and asked when would be a good time to pop in and see you."

"Manny, you haven't changed a bit, you old rogue. You owe me dinner next time you're in Denver. And I don't mean a taco and a beer at some sports bar downtown."

"Liz, you're a doll, and as long as I don't have to cash my pension, you can pick the place. I should be back in Denver with enough time for dinner in about six weeks."

"I'm going to hold you to this dear boy. Just make sure you call me in advance so I can at least comb my hair."

"I miss you too. Tell you what; I'll spot you enough time to get your nails done, and I'll even bring flowers."

"I won't hold my breath, but I will get my nails done, on your dime."

"Fair enough. When Detective Foster gets to your office, just give me a quick call or text, and I'll call your office on my secure line. I am sorry for having to rush this, but..."

"I know. It's good to know you do think about me once in a while."

"You're welcome, and I do think of you a lot more than just once-in-a-while." Manny hung up the phone glanced at his watch ... *I have enough time to get a sandwich and get back up here before Foster gets to Liz's office.* A quick trip down to the snack bar was successful in acquiring a ham and cheese on black rye and a large cherry lemonade. Back in his office, Manny realized he was almost stuffing his sandwich down with large gulps of lemonade. *Settle down; this is not your first prom.* Making himself sit down helped.

As he was reaching for the last bite his cell phone buzzed in his pocket. Stuffing the last bite and a couple of gulps of lemonade brought Manny to a text message from Liz "ur guy here." Manny picked up his lemonade, his key card, and hurried down the hall to the secure line center. His key card opened the door, and the attendant behind the counter asked him to place his forefinger on the biometric pad and when the LED light turned green, to enter his passcode. A quiet four-note melody indicated he was successful. "I need to place a secure call to the enforcement division of the ATF office in Denver, Colorado."

"Reason for your call today?"

"To speak to a source concerning a possible leak in an ongoing NSA project." The attendant quickly typed in the pertinent information for the call and opened the NSA secure phone directory and scrolled down to ATF, then to Denver, then to Enforcement.

"I'll secure your number for you in room C."

Manny never did like to use these secure phone rooms. They made him feel like he was sitting in a bad dream. The rooms are narrow and furnished with only a gray government issued steel desk and a steel chair with no cushion. In the middle of the desk was a phone without a keypad, just a single button with the word 'hold' inscribed into its plastic face. These rooms were secure for more than one reason. No one in their right mind would steal anything out of them. Manny closed the door, pulled out the chair, and sat down, with its cold, uncompromising back against his thin shirt. Momentarily the only phone rang. It was more like a buzz than a ring. Manny spread out his file and picked up the phone. "This is Manny Alexander, badge number 94776."

Liz's familiar chuckle indicated Manny had reached the right number. "I'm going for coffee now -- I'll be back in a few minutes." Manny could hear the muffled sound of a door closing in the background.

After a moment, the silence was broken. "This is Detective Foster. You asked me to call. Well, I'm here. What's all this secrecy about?"

"I need you to tell me everything you know about Bradley Smith; then I promise I will tell you what this is all about." EJ relayed everything he had learned from the scene and Steff in as great detail as he could, often checking his notes. After a few minutes of Manny feverishly scribbling down EJ's recollection of events, the line became quiet.

"Is that all?" Manny asked.

"Yes Sir, that's all I can remember. You'll have to talk to a Ms. Stephanie Huffman if you need anything more than I've already told you. I would also like to get a hold of this Mr. Smith. Apparently he is the last person to have spoken in person to the victim. Again, like I already told you before I took Ms. Huffman's statement, I had never even heard of Bradley Smith. Agent Alexander, it's your turn."

"Detective Foster..."

"Please call me EJ."

"Will do. Now EJ what I'm about to tell you I would ask that you not write any of it down. Until we have definitive information about Bradley Smith and what he may be involved in I would rather not have information accidentally lost or misplaced. Do you understand?"

"Yes, Agent Alexander, your request is very clear."

"Please call me Manny. Only my boss calls me Agent Alexander. I'm going to give you a thumbnail sketch of what I know about Mr. Smith. I plan on being in Denver in a couple of days, and hopefully, I'll have more information to pass on to you at that time. I prefer face-to-face communication in situations which are aah ...shall we say, sensitive."

"I look forward to meeting you. You are welcome to stay in my mother-in-law apartment above my garage."

"Let me get back to you on that. Your Mr. Smith may be both real and fraud at the same time. There is a secret program in which the person who you think is Mr. Smith may be a well-placed double, who has memorized the real Mr. Smith's dossier. Its unfortunate Ms. Hamilton seems to have seen right through the ruse. I agree with your conclusion that Brad Smith is indirectly responsible for Ms. Hamilton's death. At this time we are also looking for Mr. Smith, and, like you, I believe we are being misdirected to believe he is out of the country on a secret assignment for some government agency. I have checked with my contacts both in and out of the NSA, and right now all we have is his name and two pretty good pictures. We have quietly distributed what information we do have to our agencies in and around Denver, including Homeland Security, who have now put him on a watch list. That's how your friend in the State Department knew to give me a call. At this time, I am the point agent in our search for Mr. Smith. We are pressing this search because we believe the real Mr. Smith is probably in a great deal of danger, and may already be dead."

"I knew something wasn't right when his secretary gave me the runaround about where he was the day after he was seen in the office building where he works for the US Minister to the G8 Economic Group. She insisted he was in Geneva and was out of communication; then she stonewalled the conversation and finally hung up. I had a detective stop by her office to bring her down to the station for questioning, but she had clocked out of the office and was not answering her cell phone. Right now we have no idea where she may be hiding, but I am sure she is hiding."

"Do you think she's involved?"

"I'm not sure but when I talked to her she was very agitated and the longer we talked, the higher pitched her voice became. If I had to take a guess right now, I would say she's more afraid than involved. Also, since she hasn't answered her phone, I'm going to guess she may be hiding. After all, I did tell her Ms. Hamilton had been murdered. As soon as we find her, I will pass on any information we get from her. Is there anything else?"

"Thank you for your call, EJ. I do appreciate your candor, and when I get to Denver, I will seriously consider your offer of a bunk. See you in a few days."

A distinctive click indicated EJ had hung up. Manny cradled his phone, gathered up his files, walked to the door of his gray cage, and waved at the attendant who then buzzed him out. After reentering his passcode, a small red LED on the biometric scanner turned on. After a couple of scans of his index finger, the LED light turned green. Manny threw a two finger salute to the attendant, as his key card opened the exit door. Manny then escaped into the hallway where the air seemed to smell fresher.

Chapter Thirty-six

I t was becoming more and more difficult for Peter to retain his composure. He felt he had to get out of Mr. Burke's presence before he screamed. "Mr. Burke, I've had an interesting and informative time but I think I am passed saturation, and if it's appropriate I would like to go home and rest. I'm beginning to feel a little bit nauseous from overeating."

"By all means Dr. Hayes, please understand you are not a prisoner here. Reg will make arrangements to get you back to your apartment." With a quick nod, Reg and the NFL-like guerrilla in the black suit both got up from the table, carefully folded their napkins, and placed them neatly on the left side of their plates.

Reg motioned to Peter. "Follow me, Dr. Hayes, let's get you home." The guerrilla in the form-fitting black suit led his small entourage back to the garage. Opening the Limo's back door, he motioned for Peter to get in, then handed him a black hood and closed the door. Reg slid in from the other side. "I had to wear it the first several times I came out here."

Peter reluctantly pulled the hood over his head, leaned back and prepared to endure the trip back to his apartment. He was pretty sure the guerrilla made a dozen or more random turns to make it difficult to memorize the way back to Burke's compound. After about an hour the car stopped.

"You can take off the hood now Dr. Hayes; we are back at your apartment. If you like, we can drop you off here or take you back to the clinic."

"Here will be okay. Thank you, Reg, I am assuming I will see you in the lab tomorrow?"

"Yes sir, it's important to both of us that things appear normal. Remember the staff around here are all very smart and are trained to be observant."

Peter handed the hood to Reg, opened his door and stepped out into the crisp air and took a deep breath and slowly exhaled. The longer Peter had worn the hood, the staler its contained air pocket became until Peter began to feel claustrophobic. *Another few minutes and I would've ripped it off.*

"Good night Reg, thanks for the ride." Peter felt Rag's "anytime" comment seemed to be cynical. Peter closed the car door and hurried up to his apartment.

Slamming the door shut, Peter ran to the bathroom where he threw up everything he had eaten all day. After flushing the toilet, he was able to reach the sink and retrieve a cold, wet washcloth. Leaning back against the wall Peter covered his face with the washcloth and for the first time since junior high school sobbed uncontrollably. *What have I done – – what have I done? I'm screwed... I'm totally screwed.* Peter pulled down a bath towel, folded it into a makeshift pillow and lay down on the rug next to the shower. Within a few minutes, pure exhaustion drew him into a profound and dreamless sleep.

Peter became conscious of the unrelenting buzz of his alarm clock. Glancing at his cell phone, Peter realized he had slept for almost twelve hours. Using the toilet as a lever, Peter stood up and walked to the bedroom and sat down on the bed, reached over and turned off the alarm and fell back asleep. Fortunately, he had pushed the snooze button and was promptly reawaken after fifteen minutes. *I have got to get it together. The last thing I need is for Reg to think I am soft or can't control myself ... he would rat me out to Burke in a second.* Peter made it back to the bathroom where he took a long warm shower and shaved. Clean clothes seem to lighten Peter's grim attitude. Two pieces of toast with butter and blackberry jelly settled his stomach. He skipped his usual mug of strong black coffee and opened the bottle of cold sweet raspberry tea instead. Peter was glad his laptop and the usual bundle of files were still in his office because he was sure he could not have carried them to the office today.

Even though it was nearly nine o'clock, Peter decided to take his time walking to the clinic, one of the advantages of living in one of downtown Denver's luxury apartment buildings. A couple of taps on his android connected him to his secretary's desk. "Ramona, I'm going to be a few minutes late this morning. I had a lousy night. ... Thank you for asking, yes; I'm okay but still a bit queasy. ... Yes, I'll take it easy. I'm going to walk and benefit from the fresh air. Oh, by the way, tell Reg I want to review our part of the new FDA stage III trials protocol. ... Yes, I am trying to catch up from missing the meeting yesterday. ... Yes, please have him prep in the small conference room across from my office. Thanks again, Bye."

Peter put his phone back in his jacket pocket and continued his leisurely walk to work. He had walked through the small flower garden east of his apartment building, at least, a hundred times during the last three years and never took any real notice. But today the flowers seemed intense. The landscape gardener in charge of the small plot used flowers and bushes to create a collage of colors and greens. The tranquility of the garden drew Peter to sit on one of the benches. While leaning back, he tried to fit the obscene knowledge he gained yesterday into the reality of his present world, but to no avail. Wittingly or unwittingly he realized he was now beholding to a sociopath who could have him killed on a whim.

A brown and white pigeon fluttered down and landed across the path from Peter's bench. Its arrival snapped him back to the present. *I suppose you expect me to feed you ... Well, good luck ... I wonder what it would be like to just fly off away from all of this ...* Peter remembered he had a single packet of soda crackers in his right-hand pocket. Retrieving it, he carefully crumbled the crackers and scattered crumbs in the no man's land between he and the pigeon. Peter had never taken the time to see how awkwardly pigeons walk. Sort of side to side and front to back all at the same time while scampering to pick up the cracker fragments. After a few minutes, it flew off without even a thank you nod to its benefactor.

Realizing it was way past nine o'clock, Peter decided he couldn't put off going back to the clinic any longer. There was a part of him which now began to despise the work he was doing for the NSA. *Eight innocent men ... are probably dead because of my project ... Can't do it ... Just can't keep going to their clinic every day knowing I'm treating criminals so they can live a longer and healthier life and accomplish whatever Burke's evil plan is in the meantime.* Peter took a deep breath, slowly exhaled, and pushed himself off the bench, squared his shoulders and with a quiet determination headed to the clinic at a quickened pace. He had no idea what he was going to do to figure out some way to stop the coming catastrophe and manage to stay alive at the same time. The time to rid himself of Burke was fast approaching.

Chapter Thirty-seven

After a fitful night, Mike decided to go to work early. He quickly fulfilled his essential morning activities and arrived at the clinic a bit before seven o'clock and went straight to his office. Quickly logging into his internal e-mail account was not as helpful as hoped. Nothing from Peter; however, he did receive good news from the clinic's IT department. His administrator status is reinstated, and a courier would deliver his new password today. His enthusiasm was tempered by a second IT e-mail indicating they were unable to determine how Mike was deleted from the clinic's administrator list. They did, however, provide the date it occurred. Initially, the date meant nothing to him until it dawned on him this was the day after Steff's friend Max died.

Acting on a hunch, Mike signed onto the resources' section of the clinic's mainframe and opened up the archives section and scrolled back to the day Max died and clicked on the timeline. The minute by minute activity of the clinic computer usage was displayed as a series of blue lines pointing above and red lines pointing below the weighted average CPU usage. The blue line upward indicated the amount of information in megabytes which entered the system at any given minute. The downward pointing red line demonstrated what was being removed from the system or moved from the system to the cloud at any given moment. It came as no surprise that for several hours after Max's death hundreds of megabytes of data was removed from the system. *I have to print this ... come on Lancaster; a screen print isn't that hard.*

After a couple of tries, Mike finally accomplished a screen print of the day before Max's death, the day of her death and the day after. After laying his printouts side-by-side, it was evident the day of Max's death was very different than the day before or after. It also indicated that the data in question was deleted from the system in the evening after the clinic closed for the day. Mike's lack of technical understanding of the clinic's computer system became evident as he tried to access the archive information which would indicate who had deleted the files. He knew it should be there but was afraid if he involved the IT group whoever was behind the deletions might find out. A knock on his door broke into his scattered thoughts. He looked up and waved the young man into his office at the same time he signed off the mainframe.

"May I help you?"

"Dr. Lancaster?"

"Yes."

"I have a secure letter from the IT department. May I see your ID Badge?

Mike pulled his badge from his shirt pocket and pointed it at the young man.

"Thank you. Please inspect the seal and sign my receipt book. ... Thank you."

Mike retrieved his letter opener and carefully opened the envelope and extracted its contents. Unfolding the letter revealed his new administrator password, with the notation to memorize the password or keep it in a secure location. *If Steff were here, I could let her memorize it ... yeah, that would be a safe place.* Mike opened his address book and transferred the password to a random page for safe keeping, then shredded the original. Mike had a thing for positional memory. He could remember where something was in relation to what was around it. He would be able to recall the new password by remembering where he wrote it down. This unusual gift was the reason the vertical filing system on and around his desk could work.

Mike then signed back into the mainframe as an administrator and began to search for documents accessed the day Max died. As

146

PHOENIX PROJECT: MURDER BY STEM CELLS

Mike expected, the entire series of files bearing Max's ID number was marked as "corrupted, data unavailable." After attempting to open each one of the records separately, Mike gave up and made a mental note that if he ever wanted any of his personal information removed he should try and find the person who scrubbed these files. After signing out, he pushed the autodial for Peter's office.

"Ramona, is Peter in yet? ... Sorry to hear he was sick yesterday ... What was it? ... Okay, I'll ask him.... Do you know when he will be in? ... The walk would do him good; please have him give me a buzz when he gets in ... Take care, bye." *Now maybe I can find out what's going on ...*

Mike busied himself with the routine of his research group, reviewing and approving reports, requisitions, and other details which in Mike's mind were becoming more and more mundane and less and less important. He managed to fight his way through his inbox by 9:45 AM, about the same time his phone rang. "Hello, this is Dr. Lancaster. ... Peter, I heard you were sick yesterday, what happened? ... Yes, those twenty-four-hour bugs can knock the wind out of your sails. ... Glad you're feeling better. When would you like to sit down for our next planning meeting? ... Two this afternoon would be great. ... The conference room across from your office will work; see you at two." Mike was a little bit embarrassed, knowing he was able to act normal about Peter's involvement in the NSA project. In the past, he would have just blurted out what he was thinking with no thought to the consequences. *So this is what suspicion does to you ... I don't like playing the game this way.*

Chapter Thirty-eight

Reg 's first update call to Burke after Peter's induction was, to say the least, tense. When he reported Peter had called in late because he was sick last night, Burke became agitated and demanded to know if Dr. Hayes was that easily upset. Reg tried to explain that yesterday's meeting and dinner had to be stressful because Peter was being torn from one lifestyle and pushed into another very different lifestyle.

"I don't give a damn about Dr. Hayes's lifestyle, what I want is for him to quickly finish what he started at the NSA clinic. From now on I want updates at least twice a day. Remind Dr. Hayes how important I think this project is and to behave accordingly, no more calling in sick."

"In Dr. Hayes's defense, he is recuperating from a bout with Bell's Palsy."

"I don't think you heard me Reg, no calling in sick, even if you have to go into his apartment and drag him to the NSA clinic. You will make it happen. Have I made myself clear?"

"Yes sir, crystal-clear. I will make sure Dr. Hayes is at the NSA clinic every afternoon, and yes I will give you an update at least twice a day."

"I also think it's time Dr. Hayes starts devoting more time to the NSA project."

"But what about his other research projects? They need his oversight too."

"Again, I don't give a damn about any project except the NSA project. You tell Dr. Hayes to start thinking about an eight-hour day at my clinic. I'll take care of getting his boss to agree to allocate more time, or so help me, I'll pull my considerable funding for Director Godfrey's precious Rosch Memorial Clinic. From now on there is only one game in town. All the rest of my doubles have to be ready and integrated before the G8 summit four months from now. I will not tolerate anything which will infringe or delay their integration. Make it happen! Call me after you talk to him this morning." The instantaneous silence indicated Burke must have slammed down the phone

Reg did not relish the thought of having to strong-arm Dr. Hayes. But he also knew the substantial consequences for even dragging his feet a single day. He finished laying out the Stage III FDA documents just as Ramona had asked him. *Dr. Hayes could not have picked a better gatekeeper for his projects. Ramona must've had military training; she barks orders and doesn't even blink. I need to make sure Dr. Hayes finds a way to keep her in her office and out of the way. The last thing I need is to try to stand in her way.* Reg noticed Dr. Hayes was in his office and walked over to tell him everything was ready for their planning session. As he started to open the door, Dr. Hayes's phone rang. After answering, Dr. Hayes held up his hand and motioned Reg back into the conference room. While he was waiting for Dr. Hayes to complete his call, his cell phone buzzed in his pocket. He picked it up, and to his surprise, the call was from the clinical director.

"This is Reg ... Yes sir, I have time to talk now. How can I help you? ... What? ... Yes sir, I heard what you said I just don't understand why. ... Yes sir, I know I don't have to understand. ... Yes sir. ... Eight-o-clock tomorrow morning, yes sir, thank you."

Reg just stood there a bit stunned. It was now obvious Burke is considerably more powerful than he first appeared. It took him less than fifteen minutes to get Reg transferred from the Rosch Clinic to the NSA shadow clinic, and the transfer was permanent, at least until the NSA project was complete. The director also approved two hours a day of overtime effective immediately, and his immediate supervisor was now a Mr. Clive Burke, the civilian oversight director of the NSA stem cell project who would bring him up to speed tomorrow morning. It was also apparent to Reg the Rosch Clinic's CEO, and Director was entirely in the dark about the true nature of the NSA project but was politically astute enough to realize the financial cost to the clinic had he not capitulated to Burke's demands.

Reg again went across the hall to Peter's office to deliver Burke's demand. But before he could say a word, Peter hung up the phone, grabbed his Apple tablet, and headed out the door, telling Reg he had an urgent meeting with Director Godfrey and that they could finish their work later. It didn't take Reg long to guess Dr. Hayes had just received the same troubling information he was still trying to process. Reg entertained a fleeting thought that maybe Dr. Hayes would have a modicum of success with Director Godfrey, but just as quickly, he dismissed the possibility. Reg had long ago realized Burke's considerable wealth gave him a very powerful hammer in any negotiations, except in Burke's world they were most often orders, not negotiations. Reg attached an "I'm in the lab" sticky note to Peter's door and slowly walked to his cubicle upstairs on the primary research floor by way of the stockroom where he picked up a cardboard file box to carry his belongings over to the NSA clinic. He sat down in his cubicle and began sorting out what he would need tomorrow from what can stay until later.

Patty, one of Peter's research technicians, stuck her head in the cubicle. "What's up?"

"They're running behind schedule over at the NSA project, so I'm being transferred over there to help get things back on track."

"How long is back on track going to be?"

"Don't know for sure, but I would guess at least a month."

"Don't be a stranger." Patty quickly disappeared into the lab.

Well, now that Patty knows I am being reassigned, I wouldn't be surprised if the whole lab and the president know before it gets dark. Reg finished packing his file box with his lab stuff and at the top two neatly folded lab coats and an extra pair of safety glasses. Replacing the lid, Reg slid it up against the wall and logged onto the human resources employee assignment tracking program. After typing in his employee ID number, he clicked on the box marked "authorized leave" and typed in "temporary off-site assignment as per Directors Godfrey's instructions," and in the field set aside for duration, he typed "indefinite," and logged off the mainframe. Reg then powered down his workstation and all of its peripherals. He cleaned off the top of his desk and locked it.

Reg's final administrative detail was to key in call forwarding to his cell phone. *This is going to be strange. After working here all, this time, I can find my way around almost blindfolded. Now I have to start all over again. Dr. Hayes told me both clinics had virtually identical equipment layouts. ... Time will tell, but I am sure it's not going to be a painless transition with Burke constantly on my back.*

Reg usually packed a delightful lunch, but after this disturbing turn of events, it tasted more like cardboard. After a few more minutes of picking through the contents of his Tupperware lunchbox, Reg realized eating was not at the forefront of his thoughts. Picking up one last strawberry, he snapped the box closed and stuffed it into his backpack. He would take care of it later.

Chapter Thirty-nine

Manny's first impressions of EJ Foster were very positive. *My gut tells me I can trust this man.* But since Manny always tried to err on the side of caution, he ran his Denver confidant through the NSA background program. Everything was pretty much as he expected no rap sheet or arrests. He did notice a couple of juvie notations for disorderly conduct, but from then on a clean record. *Hmm, top secret clearance ... honorable discharge with commendation ... full colonel in the Air Force Reserve. That explains how he maintained his clearance all these years. When I have more time, I'll dig in just to find out how he did it.* Manny spent the balance of the day getting caught up on his reports and other bureaucratic paperwork, a task he often times felt was a waste of time. *I believe the last tree on earth will be cut down and made into paper ... What a waste.*

After determining his calendar was empty for the rest of the day, Manny decided to pack up what he could and head to his apartment. He needed some serious quiet time to try to sort out what to do with the information now trapped inside his skull. A solitary thought kept running through his mind over and over. *The answer has to be in Denver ... the answer has to be in Denver.* On a whim he checked his calendar for anything he could not miss for the next few days. Only one meeting stood out as being a must-be-there meeting.

Throwing caution to the wind Manny called his supervisor and asked for administrative clearance to head back to Denver to follow-up on a possible serious information leak concerning an ongoing project. "Yes sir, I believe it is a credible event. ... It concerns the G8 project, the one we named the Phoenix Project. ... I think a recent murder in Denver has the possibility of compromising the project's secrecy. ... Yes, I have a local contact; his name is EJ Foster, a senior Denver police officer, who by the way has an active top-secret clearance. ... Yes sir. ... I'll report back if I find the threat credible. ... Also, could you call David's office and inform him I have to miss our next meeting? ... Thank you, sir. ... Thanks, I will. Goodbye."

Manny called the travel office and requested an open return ticket to Denver as soon as possible, indicating he had administrative clearance and that they would receive an e-mail confirmation shortly. Manny had hoped to leave that evening, but the first flight available was at 0600 tomorrow.

After printing out his boarding pass, Manny placed a call to Steff. "Stephanie, this is Uncle Manny. ... Yes, I'm all right, but before you say anything, I will be in Denver on routine government business tomorrow morning, and I would like to take you up on your offer for lunch. .. Yes, an excellent choice. Also, why don't you see if your boyfriend could join us. ... Okay, so he's just a friend who happens to be a boy. I get it. Take care yourself. See you tomorrow. Oh, by the way, I was able to find the DVD you wanted; I'll bring it. TTFN." Manny was sure Steff was able to interpret the true reason for his visit. He then placed a second call to EJ Foster and left word on his answering machine that he would take him up on his offer tomorrow night and would give him a call after landing at DIA.

Manny was glad he used the Metro because he had some extra time to try to think himself out of the box which now trapped him. He knew too much to quit and too little to finish. The thirty-minute trip to his apartment was without incident, and because of the early afternoon commute, his car was empty except for an older couple at the other end. Manny leaned back and ran various scenarios of how things might end after this trip to Denver. Shortly before his commute ended it became evident that if he pursued his current course, he would probably lose his job and stood a better than a fifty-fifty chance of being charged under the Secrecy Act. Now that he decided to go the course he felt oddly relaxed. He hadn't realized how much tension the last several days had produced. His mind ratcheted up a couple of notches as he now began to plan his strategy for the Denver trip. *This trip could well be my last as an NSA agent*

Chapter Forty

Steff's production meeting was a lot shorter than she had anticipated. She was back in her office a bit before ten and decided to do some research into what Manny had shared a couple of days ago. After logging onto Google, Steff keyed in Clive Burke and touched enter. She was surprised how many entries he had. Over the next hour, Steff systematically clicked on and read over fifty individual files. She was able to determine where he was born, which schools he attended and his current position as the coordinator of the G8 economic group.

She also learned he was very successful in a significant number of financial circles. There were a number of files concerning his involvement in hostile takeovers of banks both here in the US and overseas. Reading between the lines, Steff determined Clive was ruthless, very smart, and very rich.

Steff then turned her research eye toward Burke's current activities. Several linked searches came back with no new information. Steff then decided to see if she could find where he lived. A search of real estate transactions in the Metropolitan Denver area turned up two files. The first was for a twenty-acre parcel in the foothills near Evergreen. The second was a recorded lease. The only useful information in the second file was a document number from the County Clerk's office.

A call to the County Clerk's office indicated the document was a twenty-one-page lease for office space in downtown Denver. "Thank you, may I ask another question? ... Has this particular file been digitized? ... Great, can you e-mail me a copy of the lease? ... No, I'm not a real estate agent. I'm a reporter for Channel 7 news. ... No, I don't think there's anything wrong, I am doing some background checking for a possible story. ... Yes, I understand there is a fee for copying the document. Can I use a credit card over the phone? ... Good, here is my Visa." Steff quickly transferred the number, thanked the document technician and hung up. Steff opened her e-mail account and stared at the screen for what seemed like forever. After a few minutes, an e-mail from the County Clerk's office popped up. She right clicked on the small PDF icon and sent it directly to the high-speed printer located in the newsroom. Steff jumped from her chair and ran down the hall and into the newsroom just as her document finished printing. Steff started reading as she walked back to her office. After she had skimmed through the entire document, she retrieved a highlighter from her drawer and carefully highlighted three sections. The first was the name, address and telephone number of the leasing agent associated with Downtown Development LLC, the second was a physical address and description of the space leased, and the third was Burke's signature at the bottom of the lease.

Even though Mike had warned Steff to be careful about who knew about their search for information related to Max's death, her reporter impulse was to keep digging. Without weighing whether her actions would be helpful or not, Steff continued her headlong search for information. She opened up the city of Denver's GIS map program and typed in the address of the building Burke was leasing. Much to her surprise, the building is at the corner of the next block over from Mike's clinic.

Steff then called the leasing agent and under the guise of a potential tenant, she inquired when the fourth-floor lease would expire. She almost blurted out a sharp disbelief phrase in response to finding out there were still eight years left on a ten-year lease. Regaining her composure, she thanked the agent and told him she would pass the information on to her colleagues. Opening up the Channel 7's extensive reverse telephone directory she determined the phone number associated with the fourth floor was under the name of CB III Enterprises.

The receptionist at CB III Enterprises very carefully explained to Steff even though her friend may have told her there was a free clinic in this building she was misinformed. When Steff asked what did they really did if there was not a clinic, she was politely told it was a facility for diagnosing sleep disorders and then referred her to the free clinic over on West Colfax and hung up. As Steff begin to process what she just uncovered, a chill ran down her spine. She forgot all about caller ID. Manny's admonition to be careful began to haunt her. *I don't think the leasing agent will be a problem ... I just hope the receptionist blows me off as a crank. ... Steff just broke the number one rule of investigative journalism; don't let anybody know who you are until you spring the story.* Steff regained her composure and determined to be more careful. To make sure all of she covered her bases, Steff entered an inquiry about Downtown Development LLC into the Secretary of State website to determine ownership. Her search in the trade name section almost produced a panic attack. Right there in the middle of the screen under "agent responsible for filing" was the name: CB III Enterprises. Unknowingly Steff had called two of Clive Burke's Enterprises and the caller ID in each case would have read Channel 7 News.

Steff grabbed her burner cell phone and quickly dialed Mike. "... Mike, I may have screwed up royally. ... I'm not exaggerating. ... Yes, I know my voice is high pitched, but I'm not exaggerating. ... I may have unwittingly let Burke know we are looking into him and his activities. ... I know I shouldn't have, but I called the clinic, the one Manny told us about. ... No, I did not identify myself, but I did use the Channel 7 telephone, so they have my caller ID and number... Yes, I know that was not very smart, but there's more. I also called the leasing agent to find out more about the release. ... Yes, I know they just lease the space but what I didn't know was that Burke also owns the leasing agency. ... Yes, I know there are two sets of footprints back to my door. ... Yes, I'm through here; just come and pick me up now and I'll fill you in on the rest of what I know. Oh, by the way, Manny will be here in the morning, so we need to get all our ducks lined up this evening. ... Okay, I'll be at the side entrance. ... Yes, the one where the limo dropped you off. Watch your back."

Chapter Forty-one

Mike logged into the laboratory and spent the next couple of hours more or less bumping into things and asking his staff questions they already answered in last week's progress reports. Two of his key staff even asked what was wrong and why was he acting so strange. Mike assured them all was okay but was trying to solve a particularly difficult problem, and no they couldn't help. He assured his staff he would be back up to speed in the morning and returned to his corner of the lab. Mike glanced at his watch every five minutes or so until 1:50 PM.

He logged out of the laboratory and caught the elevator to Peter's research floor. As soon as the door opened, Mike made a beeline to Peter's office. Not surprisingly, Peter was not in his office, nor in the conference room across the hall. Mike decided to give Peter the benefit of the doubt and went into the conference room and sat down. Without thinking about what he was looking at, Mike picked up and put down several of Peter's files for the proposed Stage III FDA tests. He soon realized these files contained all the information Peter was to present at the recently postponed all staff meeting.

The conference room door swung open and in walked Peter. He looked a little pale and entered with his shoulders slumped. "Mike, sorry I'm late, I just had a very disturbing meeting with Director Godfrey. He seems to be in a rearranging frenzy. He is moving part of my research staff along with a couple of your technicians to an off-site project. When I confronted him with the importance of finishing our application for Stage III testing to the

FDA, he said the FDA could wait for a few weeks. I told him I thought that was a very foolish position to take, but he shot back with a comment about if we can't finish this off-site project on time we can all kiss our stem cell funding goodbye."

"What do you mean kiss it goodbye?"

"Apparently a sizable portion of the clinic's funding for our stem cell projects comes from discretionary funding managed by a nonprofit foundation. Godfrey said the foundation's director made it abundantly clear this off-site project is more important than everything else the clinic is doing."

Mike could feel his muscles tensing up and begin to feel like a tiger ready to pounce. He was finding it very difficult to maintain his composure but decided the air needed to be cleared right now. "Peter, what does he mean by the off-site project?"

"Don't you know?"

"What don't I know?"

"With the board's approval, Godfrey entered into a contract with the NSA to do some testing on our stem cells." Peter was beginning to feel uneasy about hedging his answers to Mike's questions. "Apparently the foundation which funds our research was also jointly supporting the NSA project. I thought you knew about what they call the Shadow Clinic."

Mike decided to broach the subject of Peter's involvement head-on. "I did not know about the project until a few days ago, and the more I hear about it, the more I distrust the NSA and our benefactor. I understand there are individuals associated with the project who have a different outcome planned for the project than was initially explained to Director Godfrey." Mike looked directly at Peter and asked. "What is your involvement in this project?"

"A little over a year and a half ago Director Godfrey and the Chairman of the Board of Directors approached me and asked if I would direct a testing project for the government. They went on to explain the NSA would like to test one of our stem cell lines for its ability to enhance the lifespan of critically important bureaucrats. At first, I wasn't too thrilled with the aspect of trying to play God with our stem cells, but as he explained the details, it seemed to be a next logical step to what we are doing here. At this point, Godfrey made a very strange request or rather a veiled demand. He said this off-site project would almost double our

159

clinic funding for the next five years, and that was not counting the overhead generated from the off-site research project. Godfrey told me the NSA had already provided me with top-secret clearance, and I would be given a great deal of latitude in how I would approach the project. When I asked what about my current work Godfrey explained "50% here and 50% there do the math."

"You still haven't explained what's going on. A friend told me this off-site project might have the potential of doing a great deal of harm."

"Mike, I had to sign a contract protected by the US Secrecy Act. I can't tell you without violating the contract. If they found out, I could go to jail for a long time."

Mike decided to tell Peter what he knew. After all, Peter had been his very best friend for over twenty years. "In a nutshell here's what I know. The NSA in conjunction with the G8 Economic Ministers entered into a joint venture to use our stem cells to prolong the life of the Secretaries to each of the eight G8 Ministers. The logic behind this is that it's very time onsuming to train new Secretaries every twelve to fifteen years. The G8 hopes to extend the useful life of these critical bureaucrats by additional ten or so years. But what you may not know is the guy who is in charge of the project wants a very different outcome than the one you were initially told about."

Peter turned ashen white and had to sit down. Mike thought he sat down because he was surprised, but in reality, Peter thought Mike knew his secret and if this were true Mike was now in a very dangerous position. "I'm sorry, but you really caught me off guard with that one. What do you mean a very different outcome? The contract I signed was for a project named Phoenix and the outcome was to finish the project with eight very healthy Secretaries." Peter decided it was in Mike's best interest that he not know about the Science Czar he had recently so painfully become entangled with. Peter did not want Mike to become aware of Burke. "Well so far everything you have told me is part of the project, but I still can't talk about some of the specific details."

"For what we are talking about to work, I think I already know most of the specific details. But what I don't know is why all the secrecy. You guys could've just told me. I would be glad to help." Mike decided not to put all of his cards on the table just yet.

Hoping to get more information from Peter, Mike continued, "How did you guys get the stem cells to do this project?"

"The first thing I did was to quietly ask two of your technicians to begin growing out additional quantities of our two best stem cell lines. To help keep things secret we would bring critical supplies in our backpacks or in small boxes. We knew your team would very quickly begin to miss large quantity of supplies. There were plenty of supplies being delivered to the other clinic daily. As soon as we had sufficient cells, we pulled them from inventory by marking them as requested samples and one large transfer to 'a governmental agency.' Just before your two techs supposedly left for their new jobs, they hand-carried all of the cells cryogenically to the other clinic. I didn't want to jeopardize the FDA stage III testing, so I made sure there were adequate supplies of pluripotent cells for your work. I would never do anything to harm your research."

"I'm glad to hear we have the cells in storage for the next FDA trial." Not wanting Peter to know how much information he really had Mike, decided not to reveal that he discovered the two cell propagation technicians forgot to adjust the inventory with new cells after Peter and Reg had sequestered them from inventory. Mike assumed Peter thought the inventory was in balance.

"So all those afternoons we thought you were recuperating from multiple bouts with Bell's Palsy you were really over at other clinic supervising the project?"

"Yes, and I'm very sorry for not being able to tell you. The NSA thought it would be a good cover to explain why I had to leave the clinic several afternoons a week. To be honest, I thought you would have figured it out a long time ago."

"No, it caught me by totally by surprise. I guess that's what I get for believing what my best friend tells me about his health. Peter, how much more can you not tell me about?"

"In reality, I think you know just about everything I know." Peter again chose to keep his sociopathic benefactor out of the picture. Peter did not want to give Burke or Reg even the smallest hint how much Mike knew about the Phoenix Project. Peter nervously looked at his watch for the fourth time in the last two minutes.

"You keep looking at your watch. Do you have someplace you need to be?"

"Yes, as a matter of fact, I am due at the other clinic for staff progress reports, but I didn't want to short our time."

"Get on over to it. We can finish this tomorrow. Thanks for trusting me ... Later." Peter picked up two files off of the conference room table and opened the door. As the door swung outward, Mike noticed Reg was standing right next to the door just out of sight. Peter turned to the right and glanced down the hall. Seeing Reg, he waved a come on and Reg followed him down the hall and out of sight. *I wonder how much Reg overheard? I need to find out ...*

Mike closed the conference room door and took the stairs down to the main floor to Director Godfrey's office.

Chapter Forty-two

M ike pushed open the tall glass door to the Clinic's Director's office suite, "Hi Karen, is the boss in? I need about five minutes."

"Just a second, I'll see if he is busy." Karen touched her Bluetooth earpiece. "Dr. Lancaster is here and would like a few minutes if you have time. ... Just a second I'll ask him."

"Dr. Godfrey would like to know what it's about to make sure he has enough time before his next meeting."

"Please tell him I have a question about Peter's clinic."

"Dr. Godfrey, he has a question about Dr. Hayes's clinic. ... Yes, thank you." She turned toward Mike. "Dr. Godfrey asked to give him about five minutes, and then he will come and get you. Would you like a cup of coffee or soft drink?"

"Yes, bottled water would be nice, thank you." Karen stepped across the office and retrieved a six-ounce bottle from the concealed refrigerator next to a large display case. Mike walked over and met Karen by the display case.

"Thank you very much." As Mike began sipping water, his eyes began a quick tour of the cases' contents. He had not realized how many public service plaques the clinic had received. He wandered over to the next case and, much to his surprise, found Peter's and his picture holding the check for their stem cell grant. Suddenly Mike felt old. It seemed like forever ago when this whole project began its march towards the Catch 22 situation which has now embroiled Mike. Darkening thoughts were interrupted by Dr. Godfrey's entrance into the room.

"Dr. Lancaster, do come on in. I always have time for you." Dr. Godfrey motioned Mike into his spacious office and pointed to a pair of rich maroon leather chair sitting across from a rectangular glass topped table "Make yourself comfortable, can I get you anything?"

"No thank you. Karen got me some water."

"What is so important it brings one of my favorite researchers to my office in the middle of the afternoon?"

"Dr. Godfrey, you know I hardly ever question any of your decisions, but one I just heard about is troubling. Not so much the decision itself but more about it being made without even asking me my opinion."

"And which recent decision concerned you?"

"I heard through the grapevine you have reassigned some key technicians from throughout the clinic to a project I was unaware of." Mike was struggling to find the right words to express his frustration without letting on how much he already knew about this project.

"I am assuming you are inquiring about a testing project we have with the government. This project began about eighteen months ago. When we entered into the contract, we knew it had a timeline for deliverables we were expected to meet. The reassignment which seems to be troubling you was the Board of Directors' response to a deliverable deadline which we determined had a high potential for being late. Our contract has a significant monetary penalty for missing any of the project deadlines. After discussing it with the project's technical staff, we determined the temporary assignment of ten or twelve staff would allow us to meet the deadline. I hope this has assuaged your concerns. You should have your technicians back in about a month or six weeks on the outside."

Mike decided to press gently the subject one question further. "What about our FDA Stage III application? Is this going to have an adverse effect?"

"We did alert the FDA we were going to delay our application for an additional sixty days so we may assimilate the larger than expected volume of critical data from our current Stage II trials. We waited to announce the reassignment until we received an e-mail from the FDA approving our request for additional time."

You don't anticipate any problems with the FDA. I've invested too much time to have our Phoenix Project rejected over some technicalities. I would like to see that FDA e-mail; I would bet a nickel Peter was reassigned before the FDA's approval. "Thank you sir, I think that about answers my questions. I need to get back to the lab. Again thank you, sir." Mike made sure his handshake with Dr. Godfrey was firm and not too long. Dr. Godfrey walked him to Karen's desk and retreated to his office closing the door behind him.

"Thank you, Karen. Take care of yourself." Mike made his way back to his office by way of the break room where he grabbed a small bag of popcorn. *It's obvious Godfrey knows a lot more than he wants to share. I would bet an another nickel he has no idea what's really going on with this project.* Mike gathered up all the files he had accumulated over the last couple of days and stuffed them in his backpack, clocked out, and headed off to pick up Steff at the studio. During the drive to Steff's, Mike had to keep refocusing on traffic. The last thing he needed now was to be distracted and cause an accident. Steff was already outside when Mike pulled up. He reached across and pushed the door open. "You look tired. How much sleep did you get?"

"I actually got more than I thought I would, but apparently not enough to think straight. Mike, I'm so sorry I never for a second thought about caller ID. I just hope … well, I just hope."

"Don't worry; it is what it is. What else did you find out?"

"The big thing is that we need to head out to DIA and pick up Manny. I received a text. He was able to get an earlier flight and should be on the ground in about an hour. He said he would meet us outside Terminal B and would text us when he was on the ground. We should be able to get out there about the same time."

Mike eased out into traffic and headed north to get onto southbound I 25. "Well, I sort of took the bull by the horns and confronted Peter."

"How did it go?"

"I think it went pretty well. He freely told me a lot about the project, but I sensed there was something he wasn't telling me. He acted a little bit like he did several years ago when he told me my favorite aunt was sick when in fact she was dying. Later on, he said he held back the truth so he could have time to get me a plane ticket since he knew I would be a basket case, which it turned out I was."

"Do you have any idea what he may be holding back?"

"Right now I'm going to guess it has something to do with the NSA project."

"What makes you think it's about the project?"

"Every time the project came up, Peter seemed to hesitate a bit before he answered. Also, I felt his words were very guarded. I am relatively positive Peter does not want me to know any more about the project than what he has already shared. He tried to act like it was just another day but could hardly wait to get out of the building. Which brings up another concern. Peter's chief tech, Reg may have overheard my confrontation with Peter."

"Do you know how much he heard?"

"I think we had best assume he heard everything. In retrospect, he may already know all of this since he and Peter have been virtually inseparable for quite a while. Late last year Peter told me Reg had suddenly become very interested in the project and quickly became more than just a pair of hands. Peter said he was able to give him more and more responsibility."

"How involved is he in the project?"

"That was one of the things I discovered while digging through some of the older files around the time Max died. Reg was enough in charge to be responsible for sequestering stem cell cultures from cryo-storage for what turned out to be the transfer of our two pluripotent stem cell lines over to the NSA project. Both Peter and Reg were very careful in their record-keeping, so I am pretty sure Reg knows, at the very least, a lot."

"Not to be too ignorant, but what are pluripotent stem cells?"

"I thought you would have figured out, after all, you are an investigative reporter are you not?"

"I'm serious; I don't know."

"Sorry, I sometimes can't pass up a chance to ... Well - be an idiot. Seriously pluripotent stem cells are what most people think about when you mention stem cells. These are cells which have the ability to become any other cell in the body. When we put them in the pancreas, they make cells which produce insulin. If we put them in the liver, they make new liver cells which have the ability to detoxify the blood, and so forth. Is that understandable?"

PHOENIX PROJECT: MURDER BY STEM CELLS

"This little key I wear around my neck has to count for something, yes, it was very clear thank you."

"I keep forgetting you have a Phi Beta Kappa key, and yes it counts for a lot."

"Did I hear you say two different cell lines?"

"Yes, when Peter and I began this project we tested several various sources of stem cells and came up with two which were particularly good for what we wanted them to do. One of them came from a prisoner directly, and the other line came from stem cells produced by a recipient of one of his donations. The cell line we call 01 is the parent strain directly from this prisoner's bone marrow. The 02 line came from a person who was a recipient of his bone marrow. About a year after this female recipient received the bone marrow transplant, she was killed in an accident. Because she was an organ donor, she was kept breathing for several days for organ viability testing. As scientists, we have very little data on the viability of organs obtained from a donor who received radiation treatments to kill all of her white blood cells before receiving her bone marrow transplant."

"How did it work out?"

"For us, it was very well. After the harvesting team had removed her usable organs, they extracted significant amounts of stem cells from bone marrow and other potential harvesting sites."

"I thought bone marrow was the only place you could get stem cells."

"Over the last few years, we have been able to extract stem cells from all sorts of odd places like salivary glands and fat tissue, to reference a few. It's important to remember some of the stem cells are not pluripotent stem cells. These cells have received a prior signal of some sort to start becoming a particular cell. For example, stem cells which we can isolate from heart muscle can grow into new heart muscle tissue but not liver, and so forth."

"So how close are you guys to being able to build the Six Million Dollar Man from a bunch of different stem cells?"

"We are nowhere near that. And if we were, I think it would cost a lot more than six million."

"How are you and Peter's stem cells being used to treat these G8 secretaries? Can you use one of your fancy pluripotent lines or do you have to use a bunch of different ones?"

"It's both simple and complicated at the same time. The key to what's happening to the G8 Secretaries and our volunteers in our FDA Stage II testing is that we use a mixture of both the 01 and the 02 pluripotent cell lines. Early on we found out the 01 line would not work individuals with normal to high levels of testosterone, so basically most men would not be good candidates for the treatment. However we found the second-generation stem cells, the ones we call the 02 line, had somehow been changed by spending a year in a woman who, because of her cancer, had her ovaries removed and subsequently did not produce significant amounts of testosterone. For reasons Peter and I are just beginning to understand, it takes both cell lines to reverse tissue damage in multiple organs. We found that works best is to treat first with only the 02 cell line. The next three treatments are a mixture of 01 and 02, and the last one or two treatments are just the 01 stem cells. Does that make any sense?"

"I'll take your word for it." Before Steff could form her next question, her cell phone signaled the receipt of a text message. "Manny has just landed and should be at the United Airlines' passenger pickup gate in about thirty minutes. How far are we from DIA?"

"If I slow down a bit, we should be there right on time. Let's not talk shop. I've had to absorb so much during the last couple days I feel like my head is going to explode. "

"Well we sure don't want that, or at least, I would hate to be sitting next to you when it happened."

"Good let's talk about where you would like to go if you won an all-expenses paid vacation anywhere in the world. You first, then I promise I will tell you my ideal vacation unless you talk the whole the whole thirty minutes." Which did happen.

Chapter Forty-three

Reg, this is Clive. ... It's time for an update. ... Peter did what? ... Did you hear the whole conversation? ... How much does Lancaster know? ... So you're telling me you are sure Lancaster only knows about the NSA story and not ours..... Yes, I think trying to find out for sure would be wise. How do you propose to do that? ... I didn't ask you to think about it; I asked you how are you going to get it done. It's imperative no one gets in the way.... You keep your eye on Lancaster; I'll talk to Dr. Hayes. He's not your concern.... Yes, I would like to know why by tomorrow morning." Then Burke slammed the phone down. *This is beginning to be troubling. I thought Hayes had enough sense to leave well enough alone.*

"Dr. Hayes please.... Yes, he's expecting my call.... Thank you.... Dr. Hayes, this is Clive. I understand you had a long talk with Dr. Lancaster. ... I would consider ten minutes a long conversation, particularly when it concerned our project. I need to know how much Dr. Lancaster knows about the project. ... You have any idea how he may have found out about our project? Your clinic assured me no one outside of the approved group would learn about this.... Yes, I think it's important not to tell him any more than he apparently knows. ... I'm not interested in what he doesn't know. I am interested in what he does know. ... Don't apologize; it's a sign of weakness. Just find out how much your friend really knows.... For his well-being, I hope he is functionally ignorant of our involvement.... No, it's not a threat; it's a fact of life. Find out how much he knows immediately." This time, Burke deliberately placed the phone quietly in its cradle, turned and walked slowly out of his office, slamming the door as he left.

Clive decided to sit in the sunroom and think out his next move to prevent his project from unraveling. After a few quiet minutes the NFL guerrilla, now wearing a black spandex T-shirt so tight you could see the seams stretching entered the sunroom. "Mr. Burke, I just received a call from the clinic's front desk. They received a call from what first appeared to be some bimbo thinking we ran a free clinic. Nancy was ready to let it go when the caller began to pry into what was really going on."

"What did she do. Did she stay on script?

"Yes, she told the caller we did sleep testing and told her to go to the free clinic on Wadsworth."

"And ... "

"Nancy said she hung up and started back doing her transcription work."

"Is that all?"

"No, after a few minutes she kept thinking about how the caller sounded when she asked questions. Nancy said the first part of her conversation seemed like a bimbo who had the wrong kind information, but the way she asked her second questions made Nancy think she was disguising her voice. So she got up and checked the caller ID."

"And ..."

"The caller ID was from Channel 7 News. So she used the burner phone you gave her and called the number. The person answering said, 'Channel 7 News, Stephanie Huffman's desk.' Nancy said she had the wrong number, apologized and hung up. Nancy looked at Channel 7's website and found out our caller is an investigative reporter with the evening news team. Nancy felt it was significant and wanted you to know. She also sent you an e-mail with the link to Ms. Huffman's bio."

"Call her back and thank her for her thoughtful and prompt actions and ask her to speak to no one about the call."

"Yes sir. Will there be anything else?"

"No, I'll be in my office. I'm going to do a bit of poking around to see what I can find out about this Ms. Huffman. I don't like news people; they always seem to misunderstand every word I

PHOENIX PROJECT: MURDER BY STEM CELLS

say." Clive made his way back to his private office, not the one he kept in pristine condition to entertain visitors. The room is small but comfortable. The smell of dark chocolate permeated the stale air. Clive signed on and spent the next forty-five minutes looking at Stephanie's web page, the Channel 7 News website, and several links. Clive slowly begins to resent Stephanie without ever meeting her. Her academic credentials far surpassed his. She seemed to have received numerous regional awards for her news stories, all of which pointed towards someone Clive did not want looking over his shoulder, much less poking into his business.

Clive downloaded Stephanie's picture from the Channel 7 website and sent it to his Android. Clive then used his Android to call another of his minions, Adrian, instructing him to go over to Channel 7 news and follow Ms. Huffman, take pictures, and send them back with text every time she moved. To make sure Adrian was following the right person, he attached Stephanie's photograph. Clive then e-mailed both Reg and Peter with instructions to be on the lookout for Stephanie. He included a short note explaining she might be investigating the clinic and under no circumstances were they to talk to her about the clinic or any of its activities. He had no sooner leaned back in his chair when his phone rang; caller ID identified Reg.

"This is Clive. What do you have for me Reg?"

"I think I saw this reporter gal at the Rosch Clinic."

"When?"

"A couple of days ago I think I saw her in Doc Lancaster's office."

"Could you see what they were doing?"

"Not really, it seemed like they were looking for something on the computer. The gal, I mean Ms. Huffman, was holding open a file for Doc. Lancaster while he was pecking away at his keyboard. At the time, I just thought she was one of the Doc's new technicians. The Rosch clinic did just hired two more to replace the ones we stole."

"Could you hear anything, or see anything on the screen?"

"Not really, but when I was almost past his office, Ms. Huffman jumped up, pointed at the screen, and I think she yelled something about a Max or something that sounded like Max. I couldn't make it out, but Ms. Huffman was pretty animated."

"Did that seem strange to you?"

"Not really, when you're doing research and some experiment works out the way you hoped, there's almost always some high-fives and yelling about it, so I just walked on by."

"Do you still have your friend in security, the one you call Pug. The one you caught smoking Mary Jane several times, inside the clinic?

"Yes, I think he still works here, why?

"See if he can get you a look at the security tapes for a couple of days before and after you saw Ms. Huffman in Dr. Lancaster's office."

"That's a lot of video. Help me narrow it down."

"Just look at the ones which show Dr. Lancaster's office and the entrance to his lab suite. They should give us an idea if she's been there more than once."

"I'll remind Pug he still owes me. I'll get back to you as soon as I can."

"Good boy, thank you for the call and, if you see her anywhere in the clinic again let me know immediately. I want to know where she's going and with whom she's talking. Oh, by the way, if you see Adrian, pretend you don't see him; he's also following Ms. Huffman." Clive was trying to decide whether to slam the phone down on his desk or throw it against the wall. Realizing how much trouble it would be to reprogram his Android, he simply touched it off and placed it on his desk. *Troubling news, indeed very troubling. I now have an investigative reporter in the same room with the man who developed my stem cell line ... Yes, troubling indeed.*

Chapter Forty-four

O n Mike's second pass by the United passenger gate, he saw Manny waving. He was unable to pull his car into the curbside lane, so he just stopped opposite Manny. Steff jumped out, opened the trunk, grabbed Manny's carry-on bag, and tossed it in.

"Good to see you, Uncle Manny. Jump in the front seat, you have longer legs." Mike was able to pull back into the main flow traffic before one of the ever-present terminal cops made a fuss over him stopping in a traffic lane.

"How are you two kids doing? Maybe I asked the wrong question. You both look like I just sent you to the principal's office. What's up? -- Don't everyone speak up it once. You first Steff, Mike needs to concentrate on driving." Before Steff could start telling Manny about her faux pax, he leaned forward and keyed an address into the Volt's GPS. "Now Steff."

"I think I've done something which may have jeopardized what we are trying to do."

"And what might that be?

"I think I may have tipped off Burke we're looking into his project."

"What do you mean, tipped off?"

Manny leaned back as Steff relayed how she called the NSA clinic and the leasing office in search of information but forgot all about caller ID. "Steff, that little mistake may actually work to our advantage. I will fill you in after we get to where we are going. Anything else?"

173

Steff then relayed how she discovered the leasing office for the NSA clinic is owned by Burke.

"Uncle Manny, is there any way we can find out if Burke knows about my two calls?"

"I think there might be a way, but let's cross that bridge a little later today. If you don't mind, I need to spend a few minutes on my laptop before we get to our destination. Since I am easily distracted, would you guys please hold the chatter down -- thanks." Manny opened up his laptop and began reading files, composed a couple of e-mails, transferred them to his cell phone, and then went back to reading. After about twenty minutes a pleasant voice from the GPS unit told Mike he had arrived at his destination. Manny closed his laptop.

"Where should I park, asked Mike?"

"Go around back and park in Number 17."

Steff's curiosity got the best of her. "Where are we? Why are we here? Why ..."

"I think Detective Foster may be able to answer that question better than I can."

"Do you mean the Foster who is investigating Anne's murder?"

"Yes, he's one and the same. In fact, he's standing in the door of unit 17. Don't worry about my carry-on, just grab your laptops and your file bundles and let's have a sit down with one of Denver's finest. "

"Why here?"

"Mostly because this is a safe house used by the Denver police for off-the-record meetings with informants. And also, because their IT guys sweep the apartment on a regular basis for bugs. EJ told me this apartment was swept yesterday so that we can have some electronic privacy." Manny led his small entourage into the apartment and EJ closed the door behind them.

"Dr. Lancaster, I'm Detective EJ Foster with the Major Crimes Taskforce of the Denver Police Department. Remember me from our brief meeting at Anne Hamilton's apartment?"

"Yes." Mike extended his hand and asked to be called Mike.

EJ turned to Stephanie, "You I already know, and Manny has told me you prefer to go by Steff. I would prefer EJ."

After a short chuckle, Manny piped in. "Looks like the whole lot of us prefer not to use our real names. I'll be the first to admit my parents made a mistake. When I changed schools in the second grade, I made it amply clear to my new teacher I would only answer to Manny. Took a few days for her to realize how stubborn I am, and I have been Manny ever since."

"I use Steff because it takes the rest of the alphabet to get my full name down on paper. Enough of this chit chat. Now that we are all here I'm hoping someone has a plan?"

EJ motioned to the kitchen. "The chairs in there are almost comfortable. At least, they were the last time I met with one of my CI's." After a small amount of scooting backward and forward, everyone looked at Manny.

"After all, of my years with the NSA, I'm going off the reservation because of this project. My direct supervisor in DC thinks I'm here to follow up on a possible security breach of the Phoenix Project. What he doesn't know and can't ever know is how true that really is. I think all of us to one degree, or another have serious doubts about the NSA's involvement in the Phoenix Project. Mike, because they're using his stem cells in a project he knew nothing about, Steff, because one of her very best friends died taking this treatment, and EJ, because of the connection between the Phoenix Project and the murder of Anne Hamilton on his watch. And for me, primarily because I don't like to see some smartass hijack an NSA project.

All four of our concerns point either directly or indirectly to one Clive Alexander Burke III and his involvement through the G8 economic ministers. Three of us, Steff, EJ and myself, have a connection to one Bradley Smith, who is supposed to be the Secretary to the US G8 minister. It now appears likely the person walking around claiming to be Bradley Smith may not be him at all. This Mr. Smith may have already undergone Mike's full stem cell treatment."

"If it's true, this Mr. Smith's treatment had to be outside of our approved FDA protocol."

"That appears to be what has happened." Manny quickly opened a file on his laptop, turned it around and pushed it across the table so Mike could see clearly. Steff and EJ quickly became bookends. "As you read this file, realize I am now in violation of the US Secrecies' Act. This executive summary came from an NSA file marked Top Secret – Eyes Only." As the new Three

Musketeers read Manny's summary, it became evident to Mike it sounded more like science fiction and less like his adult stem cell research.

Steff looked up, a bit perplexed. "I know what Top-Secret means, but I'm not sure what Eyes Only means."

"Eyes only simply means the file is not to be copied. Say, for example; you are handed an Eyes Only document, you could look at the entire document, read it and reread it, but you are not to copy any words down, make a photocopy or scan it into an e-mail. I'm not sure, but I think it's mainly so the owner/guardian of the document can have plausible deniability."

Mike opened up one of his file folders and pulled out the copies of Peter's requisition for stem cells from cryogenic storage. "Manny this may be important. On the second requisition, Peter wanted equal amounts of both our 01 and our 02 stem cell lines. Our preliminary studies suggested the use of both cell lines was more efficient than either cell line by itself. This synergism became a quantum leap forward in being able to treat multiple organ failures effectively."

EJ looked up. "Are you telling me this may be the Holy Grail of eternal life?"

"No, not at all. We know stem cells could fix a lot of things, but I doubt very much if we'll ever be able to repair nerve damage in Alzheimer's disease or other forms of dementia or other complex organ systems like the pituitary or the adrenal gland. These are just too complex for Peter's and my simplistic mixture of two different stem cell lines. That being said, I have to agree with Manny's Eyes Only document. It appears the NSA is in cahoots with at least the coordinator of the G8 economic group. Also, when I confronted Peter with his involvement in what I'm going to call the shadow clinic, he fessed up, but I could tell he was holding something back. Something about the project didn't set right with him."

The Detective in EJ came out. "How'd you know? I mean do you know Peter well?"

"Peter and I have been virtually inseparable since the third grade. I know how he thinks and acts. I know when he tells a lie. It's kind of like we have this brainwave attachment. If you guys are so connected, how come he didn't figure you out?"

"Peter was so upset I don't think he had a clue that I was also holding something back. The fact he could hardly wait to get away from me also tells me he was thinking only of Peter."

Manny took back the laptop and deleted the file using an app which wrote over the file several hundred times, ensuring it was no longer readable from his laptop's memory. "I'm deleting every file we look at so in a worst-case scenario we don't get caught with a laptop full of Top Secret documents. Now, Steff, it's your turn to tell EJ how you got your foot caught in your mouth."

Steff briefly filled in EJ with her faux pas as she was doing research into the shadow clinic. EJ shook his head side to side several times during Steff's trip to the confessional. When she finished her sad tale, EJ slowly scratched his chin. He soon looked up. "I know half the time you must have felt very terrible. However, I think we may be able to use this to our advantage, since one way or another we have to flush Burke out into the open. If he does know about your two calls, then he is going to try to find out what you know. Since I think we know more than Burke, we will be able to follow the breadcrumbs back to the witch's gingerbread house. What do you say Manny?"

"Point well taken. I see where you are going with this."

"You have lost the investigative reporter; I haven't a clue what you're talking about."

"What EJ is suggesting is we leave misleading clues for Burke or his cronies to find. They have to be subtle, so he has to think about them. The Hansel and Gretel routine works best when the person being led along thinks they have discovered something new and unique, which is known only to them."

"Uncle Manny you are indeed a scoundrel and one of the best Godfathers a girl could ever ask for. So if I get this straight, Mike and I have to go out in the woods with a basket of breadcrumbs and come back alive."

"Something like that, but we try very hard not not to put Hansel and Gretel in harm's way."

"I'm not so sure I want to play the part of Hansel. This is not a fairytale, and I am a terrible actor. I couldn't even get a role in a high school play. Just how dangerous do you think this Burke character really is? Tell me honestly, on a scale of one to ten."

"I'm not going to lie to you. From what I have been able to find out so far is he may be an eleven or twelve. What do you think EJ?"

"The fact that he apparently moved very swiftly to kill Anne makes me say he may well be a sociopath. Also, since Anne is dead I think it's safe to assume the real Bradley Smith is no longer with us, and if that's true, then the possibility exists the other seven secretaries are in danger or are also dead. I can't think of a scenario other than perhaps a massive international kidnapping for ransom were Burke would let them live. Just to be clear, I don't believe they were kidnapped."

EJ opened up his notepad and flipped back a few pages. "If you remember Steff, you gave me a pretty detailed account of your last meeting with Anne. When the medical examiner ruled her death a murder, I got to thinking about what you said. I then called Mr. Smith's office and got a royal runaround about him being overseas in Geneva at a conference and was unavailable for at least a month. I then remembered you told me Anne had talked to Bradley's secretary a couple of hours after her encounter in the elevator. At that time she said Anne Brad wasn't feeling well and went home for the rest of the day. It became apparent to me at this point someone was lying and in my line of work whoever lies most is often guilty of something. So I had an officer go to her office and ask her to come down to the station and give us her statement. When the he arrived, he was told Bradley's secretary was no longer an employee and had left the building. When asked why he was informed she abruptly gave her notice, packed up her desk, and left in the middle of the day. We have been unable to find her. Her apartment looks like she just left for work, a couple of dishes in the sink and things like that. I checked with the doorman who indicated he had not seen her since the morning I called."

Mike's somewhat blank stare moved from Steff to EJ. "Do you think she's okay. I mean - aaah - I guess I'm really asking; do you think she's dead?"

"Based on how things have been going the last couple of days, she is either dead, has left town, or has gone into hiding without returning to her apartment. We ran a quick check on her bank account and found no action since a debit card charge the night before she disappeared. I'm beginning to think this Burke character has an annoying habit of tying up loose ends before I can find them. I am waiting on a subpoena for her cell phone."

"If you have trouble getting a subpoena, let me know, and I'll call my office in DC. I can get a federal subpoena practically over the telephone. Is there anything else we found out we need to put on the table? -- None? Okay, now let's go a little bit deeper into the rabbit hole."

Manny then opened up another file marked Top Secret-Eyes Only and turned the screen toward Steff." This may be hard for you to look at, but I think it's important to get this information out so we can use it."

Steff pulled the laptop closer and began reading, this time with Mike and EJ looking over her shoulder. After a few minutes, Steff exhaled and fell back against her chair. "Is this true?"

"I'm afraid so, but I'm not sure what it all means yet. I was hoping you could help me out. This information came through a routine wiretap we had placed on a security guard at Mike's clinic. At the time, we were trying to tie him to a mid-level marijuana ring. We dropped our investigation recently after voters in Colorado legalized marijuana for recreational use. The part which is troubling me is the transcript of a call he made to his girlfriend the day your friend Max died. As you can see, he called her to let her know he would not be able to pick her up at work. When she asked why he said he had to help clean up after this gal died during treatment. When she asked how long he would be, his reply was as soon as I can get her down to the clinic's morgue, the sooner I can pick you up.' This suggests to me someone needed to do an autopsy before she was cremated."

Steff put her hand to her mouth. "Then there's a real possibility Max was not immediately cremated as I was told over the telephone. Since I didn't come to the clinic until hours later, they would have had plenty of time to do all sorts of things. And to be honest, when I stopped by to pick up Max's personal effects they just pointed at this urn, then told me Max's ashes were waiting for her parents. Now, when I think about things which have been going on, I have no way to verify that Max was cremated at all." With that, Steff pulled out a large manila envelope from her backpack and spread its contents on the table. A quick shuffle and she pulled out an official looking legal sized document and spread it down on the table and turned to the last page. She pointed to the bottom of the page where it clearly stated the time of Max's cremation and the disposition of her ashes.

Mike did some quick math his head. "If the security officer is telling the truth, then Max could not have been cremated when this certificate said she was. The timestamp on the wiretap was almost six hours after certifiecatin of her cremation. I think we need to have a chat with the guy who signed this certificate."

EJ held up his hand. "I'll put him on my list for later today or first thing tomorrow."

"Steff you still have the business cards those two lawyers gave you when they told you how Max changed all of her health directives?"

"As a matter of fact, I do." Steff quickly retrieved the two cards and handed them to Manny. "At the time, I met with the lawyers I did not know what to think. How they told me about Max was not very convincing. As I remember, we only talked for maybe five minutes and then they left. Manny, can you check out these lawyers?

"Can do. Is there anyone else we should do a background check on?"

"I think the gal who gave me Max's personal effects and a copy of her new health directives needs looked at for any connection to the lawyers. Her concern for my loss seemed mechanical -- like she had done this before. Come to think of it; I have her card here also." Steff secured the brightly colored business card and read its contents to the group. "Marianne Sylvester, MS, Grief Counselor Shenandoah Funeral Services, and a local address and telephone number."

Manny inquired, "Steff you have your burner phone handy?"

"Ya, let me get it. Do you want me to call the number?"

"Please."

Steff turned on the speaker and punched in the number. After two rings a pleasant recorded voice clearly spoke *The number you have dialed is no longer a working number. If you think you have reached this message in error, please check the number and dial again.* "Why does this not surprise me? EJ hand me back the lawyer's business card. As long as I have the burner phone warmed up, let's try calling them. If someone answers, I will apologize for the wrong number, and we'll know if they are real." Again it was no surprise when the proprietor of a barbershop in Evergreen answered the phone. "I feel like I have been the victim of a sting operation."

EJ asked if anyone would like to bet ten dollars the man who signed Steff's cremation certificate was also a figment of someone's imagination.

Mike reached into his pocket and placed a dime on the table and asked EJ what odds he would take for a dime.

"Save your money; but I'm still going to follow-up and see if he is real. Mike, are you at all familiar with that part of the clinic? I mean the morgue and its crematorium?"

"As a matter fact, I am. As part of the clinic's safety team, I had to spend time in every one of the major areas which present themselves as a potential safety hazard. I spent a half of a day in the morgue a couple of years ago. That was enough to last me the rest of my life. Why?"

"I was hoping you had a contact down there who could shed some light on the activities the day Max died."

"I don't have a contact as such, but the Diener played on my volleyball team the last two years."

Steff wrinkled her nose. "Isn't the Diener the guy who takes care of all the dead bodies in the morgue?"

"Yes that's part of what he does, but he also is responsible for record-keeping, getting everything set up for autopsies, cleaning up, and, in general, is in charge of the morgue, and by default, its residents."

Steff leaned into Mike's face. "Why does your clinic need a morgue in the first place, much less a crematorium?"

"In the first place, Peter's and my research clinic does not need a morgue. The Rosch's hundred and twenty-five bed clinic is associated with several regional medical schools. There are many programs were terminally ill patients receive free treatment using experimental drug protocols. In many cases, the experimental procedure does not work, and the volunteers die here in the clinic. When that happens, their remains are subjected to a very detailed forensic autopsy."

"What about the crematorium?"

"Many patients have chosen cremation, which the clinic provides at no charge. In many cases, this relieves financial hardship. Sometimes the family has to transport the deceased hundreds of miles for burial, which is a significant cost. So when you first told me Max was cremated it did not seem out of place.

Manny looked up from his notes and asked Mike. "Would you feel comfortable in talking your Diener friend to see if he has any recollection of the activities which happened that day?"

"Not at all. In fact, I can give him a call right now if you'd like. I have his number in my contacts."

"Go ahead, but use your burner phone."

Mike opened up his iPhone to retrieve the number and dialed it on the burner phone. After a couple of rings, Dan answered the phone. ... Hi Dan, this is Mike, got a minute? ... Good, I need a favor. ... Thanks, a friend of mine lost a loved one several weeks ago and was wondering if she was able to donate her organs before her cremation. She's pretty sure she died here in the clinic. Is there any way you can find out? It means a lot to her.... You can? Good, what do you need from me? ... Her patient number? I don't have it, but I do have the day she passed. Will that help?" Mike read the date of Max's death, the fact she was a twenty-six-year-old female and a registered organ donor. Mike put the phone on speaker and they all leaned towards the phone. All they could hear was Dan humming off-key. "Anything Dan?"

"Yes, it appears the board was pretty busy that day we had four deaths. One was an elderly gentleman, and the other three were younger women. It looks like two of the gals were organ donors, and the other is listed as a provisional Jane Doe. Can you tell me anything more about her?"

"She was blonde, and ..." Steff quickly jotted a note and passed it to Mike. "She had a tattoo of a small blue Maltese cross on her left shoulder. Does this match any of your records?"

"Let me take a look. Yes, do you happen to know her name because the girl with the Maltese tattoo is listed here as a provisional Jane Doe."

"Dan, what's a provisional Jane Doe?"

"Someone whose records are in conflict. For example, their driver's license might say 5'2" and they're actually almost six feet tall, or the index fingerprint taken at admission doesn't match the deceased and things like that. They are held in our records as a Jane or John Doe until we have confirmation of identity. This one is a bit odd since these conflicts are usually cleared up in a day or two after death. Someone in the clinic's medical staff must have known this patient and something unusual must have happened to her because why else would they have called in an outside contract pathologist to perform the autopsy? This one stuck in my mind because I usually help out in the autopsies, you know getting instruments ready and catching someone if they faint, but I was asked to stay out and not let anyone else in. Four of them to do one procedure seemed odd at the time. One was the pathologist. Then there was this short guy with a strong British accent. There was another guy in a white lab coat and your friend Peter. I don't recall having seen any of them down here before. When I asked how I should log in this autopsy, the short guy said it was a forensic autopsy to establish a cause of death, as per FDA protocol. At the time, I thought the short guy was from the FDA since he was obviously in charge. That's about all I can remember Mike; I hope it is enough."

Thanks Dan. I'll tell you what, why don't you take a picture of her autopsy photograph and send it to this phone and I'll ask my friend if your Jane Doe is the one she's looking for."

"Coming at ya; take care."

"Thanks again, how I owe you one more. Bye." Almost as soon as Mike closed his phone it rang again. Flipping the phone open its screen indicated a text message. When Mike opened it, a headshot of a young blonde woman appeared on the screen. Mike pointed it at Steff. "Is this Max?"

"Yes." Steff could hardly hold back the tears.

Mike reached over and put his hand on her shoulder. "At least now you know what happened to Max after she died. I know it's no consolation for how you feel right now, but it does give us a more accurate timeline of what happened after you left her at the clinic. I can tell you the use of an outside pathologist is very unusual since the clinic has two top notch pathologists on staff.

Manny closed his laptop and put it back in his briefcase. What Dan just told us is troubling. It appears Burke has his fingers in more pies than even I realized. "Mike, do you have any idea why Peter would have been at this autopsy?"

"Peter was the lead investigator on the diabetes' side of our project. If any of our volunteer patients die during any clinical trials, our FDA's guidelines are very specific: a detailed autopsy is required. It's essential to determine if the volunteer's death was due to, in this case, Peter's stem cells, or perhaps from some outside factor such as a stroke or kidney failure. If Peter were at this autopsy, it would be a first. He has a pretty weak stomach for that kind of thing."

"Is there any way you can get a copy of the autopsy?"

"I'm not sure. Usually, one of the staff pathologists prepares a very detailed report using an FDA template to answer a whole myriad of questions. If an outside pathologist performed the autopsy, I'm not sure. Also, since Dan indicated Max was listed as a provisional Jane Doe it tells me her autopsy probably does not exist in the clinic's files. The FDA protocol requires over fifty different samples of tissue, blood and bone marrow, to name a few. When Steff and I tried to find out more about Max we found all documentation other than pre-admit files attached to her Minnesota driver's license was purged from the system or were listed as corrupted data. Three of the FDA required tests would have provided Max's identity."

Steff now stood up. "What are they?"

"The FDA requires a full set of fingerprints, a confirmatory DNA analysis, and a certification from the clinic of her Social Security number."

"What are you suggesting Mike?"

"It would be difficult to purge that much information from our system without the IT guys knowing about it. Just think about how many tests would need to be performed on fifty samples. In the Rosch clinic, those fifty different samples would be spread across at least six different laboratories and probably a dozen of those tests would have been farmed out to contract laboratories. So I guess what I'm suggesting is the samples left with the pathologist, and if Burke is behind this then it may be nearly impossible to get a copy of the autopsy and its laboratory results. We don't even know who this pathologist is. Even if we did know, we don't have any leverage to get a copy of his report. We should do some background checking on the Clinic's IT guys to see if anyone stands out as a possible data stripper."

Manny glanced at his watch. "I have to be across town so I can report to my boss; otherwise, he'll pull me back to DC. EJ will get me to my meeting. Steff, Mike, give me your burner phones for a minute." Manny quickly entered two additional numbers and handed them back. "You now have a speed dial number to both my and EJ's burner phones. Remember, don't call or text any of us using your regular phone. Steff, do you still have keys to Max's apartment?"

"Yes, do you need them?"

"No, but I think it would be a good place for us to meet, say around 6:30. EJ and I will pick up pizza and soda. Speak now or we will have pepperoni and black olive and in Anne's memory Canadian bacon and pineapple. I'm assuming shaking your heads means okay. Let's go around the table and review who is going to try and find out what."

EJ indicated he was to find out if the person who signed Max's cremation certificate was real. He would inquire from the medical examiner's office if any of them knew a pathologist who might do work on the side and lastly obtain a copy of Max's death certificate.

Although a bit hesitant, Mike said he would stop by and talk with Dan and see if he had any data links or ideas about Max's clandestine autopsy. He also vowed to find out what Peter's involvement was in Max's diabetes treatment. He also would do a database search on which specific vials of cryogenically frozen stem cells were used in each of Max's treatments.

Steff, although still shaken from seeing Max's autopsy photograph, indicated she would go back through all of Max's video diary entries and the paperwork they found at her apartment. She felt there must be something she overlooked when she quickly skimmed her first time through.

Manny would make additional phone calls to his internal NSA contacts and determine what was known about Burke and his associates. He also had an appointment with the NSA lead agent in charge at the shadow clinic to get his impressions, and hopefully what was not in the official reports. "Remember to be careful; we are entering into Burke's territory to find out information. Do not leave a trail. Steff, please do not jump ahead of us on this. No impulsive telephone calls, no face-to-face confrontation. Just stop being yourself until we are ready to set up Burke for our Hansel and Gretel trap, understand?"

"I don't often make the same mistake twice. If you weren't my godfather, I would consider scratching your eyes out." She smiled and gently poked Manny's ribs. "Now let's get out of here, we have a murderer to catch."

Chapter Forty-five

P eter felt a bit of relief being able to stop talking to Mike. He was very reluctant to talk about his involvement in the NSA project. Peter's innate curiosity made him wonder how did Mike find out about the project, and in such detail. The NSA guys are paranoid about secrecy, not to mention Burke's maniacal single-mindedness. *I think I better call Mr. Burke and give him more information about what Mike told me. During his last call, I bought some time, but I think I'd better take Burke's veiled threats seriously and tell him more about my conversation with Mike. I'll just tell him I had another short talk with Mike. Burke doesn't have to have all of the information. I got myself into this mess. I sure don't want to drag Mike into my problems. He sometimes goes off half-cocked and usually gets himself into a royal mess. -- Well enough stalling, I'd better get with it.*

Peter dutifully pushed Burke's speed dial number and hoped it would go to voicemail. "Hello, this is Peter ... Do you have time for a short report?" Peter's hope was again to no avail. "You do? Aha – good. I had another interesting talk with Dr. Lancaster. ... He came by the office again and wanted to talk to me more about the other clinic. You know the NSA one we are working on together. ... No sir I still do not know how he found out about the clinic... No, I still don't think he knows much about it, but he did know it involved stem cells. ... Yes sir, I understand. But I still don't know how he found out; he didn't say.... Yes, I should have asked him but the agreement I signed with the NSA gave me strict instructions about not talking to anyone about the project. ... Yes sir, I understand you are in charge, but I could go to jail.... Yes, I know there are things worse than going to jail; however, I felt it was important not to let Dr. Lancaster keep asking questions, so as soon as I could I excused myself and left. ... I told him I had a meeting at the other clinic. ... You are right; perhaps I should not have mentioned the other clinic, but he already knew about it, and I needed to get out of the Rosch building. ... No sir, I believe all he knows is that it exists. ... Yes, I think he will keep looking, and knowing Dr. Lancaster he will soon discover its location, and will try to visit. ... How do I know he is going to find out? I know because he's the golden boy of the Rosch Clinic. People practically worship him. To be honest, I'm surprised he hasn't found out before. ... Yes sir, I know we have had excellent security, and if it wasn't for my Bell's Palsy, I think he would have become suspicious of my leaving the clinic most afternoons long ago. ... Yes sir, if I think Dr. Lancaster is getting close to the clinic I will call you immediately. ... Yes sir, it is unnecessary to remind me of my contract, and yes, I do remember its unwritten second page. ... Goodbye." *Why did he repeatedly warn me about my obligations to his so-called contract? I got the feeling ... Well, I guess I wouldn't trust me either.*

Peter busied himself getting ready for his full-time temporary assignment at the other clinic. *Boy am I glad I confided in Ramona about the other clinic. She has done a yeoman's job of keeping people at bay all those afternoons I was gone.* Peter walked down to his clinic's main office and closed the door. "Ramona, I want to thank you again for watching my back these last many months. I now need to ask you to double up some of your activities. Director Godfrey is moving me, Reg, and a couple of other techs over to the NSA project."

"How come? I thought things were pretty much on track."

"Apparently the Board of Directors is worried about a financial penalty if we don't finish the project on time."

"Yes, I know we made the first deliverables on time, but now they're worried about the next. Why."

"I didn't know the financial penalty was significant until Dr. Godfrey hinted the entire stem cell project would lose its funding if the Rosch Clinic defaulted on the next deliverable."

"I thought this was a government project. You hardly ever hear about any penalties for federal projects getting behind or for that part defaulting."

"Apparently it's much more complicated. Some of the financial backings for our stem cell project come from some endowment fund and after that things just get too complicated. Suffice it to say if we don't deliver; we could both lose our jobs."

"What can I do to help?"

"I need some beliveable cover story which will allow me to be gone but still run my stem cell program. Any ideas?"

Ramona's brow wrinkled as she mulled Peter's request. "Humm ... I think it may be best just to tell your staff you are going to be working on a new adult stem cell line with a private research company, and you will be in and out of the office for the next six to eight weeks while you finish the project. Anybody asks I'll just tell them its proprietary research, and that's all they're going to find out."

"You're a genius, excellent idea. Draft a memo to the staff indicating we will have a group planning meeting at four tomorrow afternoon in the small lecture hall downstairs. Have them bring all of their notebooks and any suggestions for experiments they would like to see accomplished during the next two months. Have the cafeteria send over our usual goodies tray. Be sure not to tell anyone, and, in particular, don't let Patty know about my temporary assignment, or it will be all over town. I would like to tell the crew myself tomorrow. Thanks again for all you've done, and if I don't have the time or forget to say thanks during the next few weeks, know I'm thinking it."

"Glad I can help. If you need anything else, just let me know." After a moment of awkward silence, Peter opened the office door and headed to his laboratory. Much like Mike, Peter also found solace working in the laboratory. Peter admired Ramona but often felt uncomfortable being around her alone because she seemed to stand too close. Peter always tried to have a chair or desk between them when they were alone. Glancing at his watch, Peter sadly realized he didn't have time to check in with his lab staff so he headed over to the other clinic for a long afternoon of unrelenting stress.

Chapter Forty-six

When Steff got back to her apartment, she found Harry had tried calling her four times. She realized she hadn't explained to him about her blowup with Mike. Steff reluctantly picked up the phone and called Harry's office. "Harry, this is Steff. Before you start yelling, please let me explain. ... Yes, I know I should've come to your office immediately, but I felt it was important to meet with Mike umm...aah, I mean Dr. Lancaster and apologize for my actions. He was very understanding and would like to reschedule the interview. ... I don't know. I forgot to ask. I would guess it would be best if we ... Yes, I know I shouldn't guess. I will check with production and offer Dr. Lancaster a choice of times so we can reschedule.... Yes, I know I trashed the set. I'll be happy to pay for my damage. ... Yes, I'm glad to know all I broke was that hideous bunch of yellow flowers and its vase. ... Yes sir, when I reschedule I will bring an appropriate bouquet."

Steff spent the next few minutes explaining to Harry more about what happened to Max and without realizing it she inadvertently gave Harry too much information. Not knowing just what to do, she asked Harry to hold what she had just told him in confidence. Much to her surprise, Harry asked if she would be interested in documentary. Steff was able to regain her composure and told Harry she would have to verify a lot more information with a confidential informant before she could commit to doing the story for 7 News. It was a relief when Harry confirmed he would hold what was said in confidence, but only until the 15th of next month. Harry explained to Steff what she had shared was much too important to ignore but would give her until the fifteenth to decide on the documentary or he would assign another reporter. After Harry had hung up, Manny's words of warning haunted her.

Steff decided she needed to let Harry see her at work and slowly walked back to her office. *Stephanie, you dummy, you have got to learn to engage your brain before turning your mouth loose. I know I can trust Harry, but the fifteenth is not very far from now.... Oh pot! Now I have to confess to Mike and Manny again.*

Once in her office, Steff called down to Sue's office. "Sue, please sign me out to research and let Harry know I checked in, and I'm working on the project." Which in reality was true, but not honest.

Sue asked, "When do we expect you back?

"Why don't you put down tomorrow after three and please no calls. ... Thanks kiddo, bye."

Steff gathered up a few files, her notebook, and laptop and headed back to her apartment. She took her time walking. Part of the time she fretted about what to tell Manny about her second faux pas with Harry and the rest of the time the thinking about Max and Anne, knowing in her mind Burke was behind both of their deaths. She stopped by the mailbox and retrieved a plethora of junk mail interlaced with the real. She dropped the pile and her keys next to the TV and went right to the kitchen table and cleared off its contents. She then made a neat pile of file folders on one corner, her laptop in the middle and her notebooks on the other corner.

She retrieved Max's tablet from its hiding place and opened it up ready to begin sifting through Max's diary entries. A small flashing icon indicated "low battery". Steff retrieved the USB charging cable Mike gave her and plugged in the tablet. Taking advantage of the parenthesis in her activities, Steff microwaved leftover lasagna and green beans, which were delicious with a cold glass of milk. After clearing everything into the dishwasher, she turned on Max's tablet.

Steff began to watch Max's e-journal entries in their daily sequence. She turned the tablet slightly to make it visible while she made a pot of Earl Grey tea. Steff alternately watched a journal entry and sipped tea until she had watched all entries up to the day of Max's fourth treatment.

Steff had watched this particular set of journal entries twice before. The third time she noticed a change in Max's face and demeanor. It was subtle but a few days after her fourth treatment Max making comments about being tired all the time. At the same time Max noted she had to increase her insulin dose slightly. Max observed this more than once. Recording during the first three treatments her insulin requirement had been steadily dropping. The clinic staff assured her that her need for insulin would decrease throughout her treatments. Max's Journal entry on the twenty-first day after her fourth treatment noted a call to the clinic about her need for insulin and her becoming discouraged. The clinic's Outpatient Coordinator assured her this was normal in some individuals and not to be concerned, but please check back with her in a week.

Max's entry on the twenty-fifth day was much brighter. She reported her need for insulin dropped dramatically during the last three days, and her light-headedness and bouts of dizziness were also subsiding. Steff grabbed her notebook and made a note to ask Mike whether this was normal because Max went in for her last treatment on the thirty-second day after her fourth treatment. *I need to make sure Mike understands Max only told the clinic nurse what happened during the last week before the treatment which killed her. I wish I had known this before her last treatment. I'm not sure the clinic knew anything about her problems after her fourth treatment.* Steff was lost in thought as she watched Max's last entry, the morning she died. Something Max said did not sound quite right, so Steff clicked back to the beginning. About halfway through her journal entry, Max went from the euphoria of anticipating a complete cure of her diabetes to an almost a manic dread of what might happen if the stem cells didn't do their job. It wasn't the words which bothered Steff; it was Max's uncharacteristic high and low mood swing. For all the time Steff had known Max she was always level headed and never showed any signs of any mental problems much less being manic. The second question for Mike was to determine if other patients exhibited this manic-depressive behavior. After a couple of minutes of depressing ramblings, Max suddenly was bubbling with enthusiasm again.

When I met Max at the clinic for her last treatment, I attributed her excited state to her understanding her diabetes may be completely cured. But now I think about the way she talked; it was almost like she was high on something. She could hardly sit still, giggling all the time and talking a hundred miles an hour. Steff jotted, in her notebook, recalling that the nurse had to give Max some Xanax to quiet her down so she could set the delivery system and begin the treatment. *That's strange, as many times as I told everyone what happened that day, I had apparently forgotten about the Xanax and the effect it had on Max.*

Steff turned off the tablet and wrote in her notebook all she could remember about Xanax's effect on Max. Steff remembered the nurse telling her it was a small dose, about the same amount they give someone who's taking an MRI and having trouble with the confined space. A couple of minutes after Max dissolved it under her tongue, she almost became a zombie, laying on her bed and stared blankly at the wall. About half way through the prescribed ninety minutes infusion cycle Max became her old self. She asked the nurse how things were going and asked a lot of questions about how long it would be before she was completely cured. The infusion nurse explained the new FDA protocol required the sixth infusion to provide the body with additional stem cells for normal wear and repair functions in the body. Also, many of the volunteers had reduced their insulin requirements to almost zero, and in most cases, they no longer needed to use insulin a couple of weeks after their fifth treatment.

A quick check of the time almost panicked Steff. She realized Mike was going to pick her up in a few minutes and drive them to Max's apartment for their meeting with Manny and EJ. She quickly gathered up her files, put the tablet back in its hiding place, gathered up all of her assorted electronic cables and stuffed them in her backpack along with her files and notebooks. Steff just had enough time to change into clean clothes and primp a bit. The doorbell chime broke into her warm collection of thoughts. A last quick smile to check her teeth and Steff headed down to the lobby to meet Mike, eager to share what she found out from Max's tablet.

Chapter Forty-seven

Burke was unable to sleep. The thought of not reaching his goal after all of his planning was now plaguing him day and night. Like Dickens' Scrooge, Burke tried to blame his lack of sleep on a myriad of incidental things including something he had eaten. Finally accepting the fact that his lack of sleep was a byproduct of not being completely in control of his destiny, he slid out of bed, donned his slippers and his best Persian silk robe. Pausing to look in the mirror and straighten his tussled, but thinning hair, Burke plodded down to his inner office. Clearing the miscellaneous clutter from his desk, he pulled out a legal pad and began making notes. On the left side of the page, he listed the goals he had set for his project months ago and on the other listed the goals which had already come to fruition. Burke was troubled by the apparent fact that the right-hand side of the page was shorter than the left. He drew lines from goals listed on the left to goals which had been accomplished on the right. He then tore off the top page and set it aside and transferred his unfulfilled goals down the left-hand side of a new sheet. For the next hour, Burke made notes along the right-hand side opposite each of the unmet goals of obstacles he perceived was blocking fulfillment of the remaining goals. Carefully removing this sheet, he sat it aside, and then arranged his list of perceived obstacles on a third sheet in a sequence he thought could be systematically accomplished.

Burke then went to the kitchen and prepared a pot of Oolong tea. After a few minutes, he poured a cup, stirred in two heaping spoons of natural sugar and walked to one of the tall windows overlooking the back of his property and sat down in one of the plush chairs. The moonlit vista slowly relaxed him. As he sipped his tea, he began to put slowly together a dangerous plan to overcome the obstacles plaguing his grand scheme.

As he reached the halfway point in his cup of tea, Burke had decided to accelerate the release of his G8 look-alikes into the banking world. For that to happen, he needed the expertise of both Drs. Hayes and Lancaster. After all, Dr. Hayes was using Dr. Lancaster's methods. His clinic had to have Dr. Lancaster's knowledge base if there was any hope of accelerating his plan. Taking the last sip of his now cold tea, Burke headed back to his office. A quick click on his keyboard brought up the extensive background search he had been performing on Dr. Lancaster. Now, turning to the fourth sheet of paper, he listed any person or activity he might be able to use for leverage to convince Dr. Lancaster to help him reach his goal.

I don't see a lot of leverage in this search. Both of his parents are dead. He has no brothers or sisters. It seems he's a regular Boy Scout. Other than Dr. Hayes he doesn't appear to have any close friends, but wait a minute. He seems to be spending a lot of time with that reporter. – Hum, this may be my leverage ... Ahaa - - Yes, it is. Burke then printed Stephanie on his yellow pad and with his pen drew several circles around her name. The next two hours were spent in first developing then rejecting some scenarios for using Stephanie as leverage. His final plan was the direct approach. Now that he had decided what to do, Burke headed back to his bedroom for some sleep, but discovered the sun was already up, and he'd spent most of the night developing his nefarious plan. *I'm famished. It's time for an old-fashioned English breakfast.*

After calling the kitchen, Burke took an unusually long shower, shaved and changed into some uncharacteristically casual clothes. Humming the tune of a long forgotten English lullaby, Burke entered his walk-in hat museum and retrieved a bright white box resting on an upper shelf. After carefully lifting the lid Burke moved aside two layers of crisp red tissue paper revealing its contents. Burke gazed at its contents. After a long steady inhale and a quick exhale Burke lifted out a brand-new black fedora with a lime green band sporting a short, angular, clipped red feather. Turning around and facing the full-length mirror he carefully placed the hat on his head and quickly adjusted its position atop his thinning pate. Tipping his head from side to side Burke relished his new prize. This was the hat he would now wear until the achievement of this final goal, after which it would be immortalized in his fedora collection. Turning on his heel, he went down to breakfast. Alex, his Spandex-clad NFL guerrilla, stood up as he entered the breakfast room. "Sporting a new hat today?"

"Yes, thank you for noticing."

"What's on the agenda today, Mr. Burke? I heard you up stirring around last night. Is everything okay?"

"Yes Alex, I think everything will be fine today. Please sit down -- let's eat; I'm famished." They finished breakfast with hardly a word spoken. It was Burke who broke the silence. "Come, let's take our coffee in the great room, I have some things which you need to accomplish today." Burke led the way and was soon seated facing the expansive lawn. Alex joined him. The server, dressed in a crisp white uniform, poured, coffee and left the room. Burke outlined a short list of items he wanted to see finished by the end of the day. "I want you to reach out to both Reg and Adrian. Have them find out where Ms. Huffman and Dr. Lancaster are going to be around noon today. I want you also to reach out to Dr. Hayes and have him wait for me in the secure room at the clinic."

"What time do you want Dr. Hayes to meet you in the secure room?"

"Let's say around one."

"Do you want Reg and Adrian just to report in, or ...?"

"Yes, but as soon as they can tell me where Huffman and Lancaster are going to be, I will have further instructions for them. Please make it very clear to both Reg and Adrian that losing track of these people this morning is unacceptable."

"Yes sir, I understand. Is there anything else?"

"Yes, I need you to reach out to our transport team. Please tell them I will need a pickup and delivery of two items shortly after lunch today. Make sure they understand these are fragile, and I will not tolerate any damage."

"Yes sir. How will we get the address for the transport team?"

"Tell them I will forward photographs of the two items along with GPS coordinates and hopefully an accurate address. Also, have them stand by in the downtown area."

"Yes sir. Do we have an address where they will be taking these two items?"

"I'm not sure yet, but have our security men at the clinic on standby in case they're needed to help with the delivery."

"Consider it done. Is that all?"

"For now. Now let's enjoy our coffee. It's a new blend from Hawaii."

Chapter Forty-eight

Reg was finding it more and more difficult to keep tabs on Dr. Lancaster and keep Burke's clinic staff on track at the same time. He was hopeful Dr. Hayes's temporary full-time assignment would allow him more time to keep track of Dr. Lancaster. Today was one of those days he wished he had a clone. Sleeping in his car outside of Dr. Lancaster's apartment was not what Reg signed on to do. He was thankful he could shower and change into clean clothes at the clinic. He figured he had enough clean clothes for two more days before he had to surrender his clothing to the local Laundromat.

Since the clinic provided housing for the look-alikes during their stem cell treatments, Reg was able to eat a good breakfast before tackling the day's responsibilities. His promise to Patty of three tickets to an upcoming Red Rock's concert provided him a pair of eyes in the Rosch clinic. She and two of her friends were keeping constant eyes on Dr. Lancaster's whereabouts. Reg had led her to believe Dr. Hayes wanted to keep track of his friend while he was on temporary assignment. He wasn't sure whether Patty bought the cover story, but three hundred dollars' worth of tickets, at least, purchased her cooperation.

Reg retreated into his office. Keeping track of Dr. Lancaster had allowed him to fall behind on his paperwork. Reg had barely dug into his backlog when his cell phone rang.

"Hello, this is Reg. May I help you? ... Oh, it's you Alex. ... What? ... Yes, I understand this request is from Mr. Burke, but I'm so far behind on paperwork ... Okay, I understand, I can catch up tonight. ... Soon as I know for sure I'll give you a callback. What happens if he wants to leave the clinic? ... Yes, I understand I am to keep him in the clinic until at least noon, then what? ... Don't get hostile; I was just curious. I know when it is none of my business. Please tell Mr. Burke I understand the importance of Dr. Lancaster being in the clinic at noon. ... Thank you, goodbye." *I'm not sure I like where all this is going. Up to now it's just been bits of information, now I have to hold a grown man against his will ... I just don't like it.*

Reg's cell phone vibrated in his pocket. A quick look revealed a text from Patty. "Dr. L lving lab, in park lot now." Reg panicked; his car was two blocks away, and Dr. Lancaster was in the wind. Remembering Dr. Lancaster had recently been using the Colorado Boulevard exit from the parking lot, Reg dashed across the lab to Marco's cubicle. "Marco, I need to borrow your motorcycle right now! It's very important, and I'll make it worth your while."

Marco tossed Reg the keys. "You scratch it, and you're dead, man."

Reg ran down the back stairs like a man possessed. He jumped on Marco's Suzuki and exited the underground parking, made a quick left, then a sharp right just in time for Mike to drive past on his way to Colorado Boulevard. Reg pulled in behind Mike and followed him discreetly until he turned into a parking lot. Reg turned off the cycle and quickly called Burke.

"This is Reg; I just followed Dr. Lancaster to an apartment complex. ... He's alone, and he just went into the lobby. ... Yes, I understand. I'll wait until he comes out. ... Yes, as a matter of fact there is a white van parked in front. ... Yes sir, I understand Adrian will take over. I'll head back to the lab. Let me know if you need me. Goodbye. Reg drove back to the lab with a short detour to pick up a burrito. He parked the motorcycle and headed back to the lab. On the way back to his cubicle he stopped and thanked Marco. "Thanks, you are a lifesaver. Here're your keys. Your baby has no scratches, and for your troubles here is a green chili steak burrito."

"Thanks, but the burrito is just a down payment. You still owe me."

"I do Marco, I do." Reg headed back to his cubicle and dove into the mountain of paperwork waiting for his return. *I don't think I want to know why Adrian was already at the apartment, but I'm glad I don't have to keep track of Dr. Lancaster.*

Chapter Forty-nine

So far following Ms. Huffman was a piece of cake. Adrian waited outside her apartment, and then followed her to the Channel 7 studio, then back to her apartment. Adrian didn't like twenty-four-hour stakeouts. He usually gained weight from constantly eating junk food and drinking soda. Now, as he approached his fiftieth birthday, he had to watch how much soda he drank during a stakeout. Potty breaks were now part of his schedule. He was about halfway through a Dick Francis mystery when his cell phone rang.

"Hello, Adrian's Detective Agency, how may I help you? ... Oh, it's you. ... Yes, I still have her. She's in her apartment and has been there for a couple of hours. ... Around noon? ... What does Mr. Burke want me to do if she's on the move at noon? ... And how am I supposed to detain her? ... Don't get all huffy, I understand. ... Yes sir, I do very much understand how important this is to Mr. Burke. Please assure him he will know where Ms. Huffman is at noon today. ... Goodbye." *This is one of those days I wish I'd kicked my gambling habit before I had to sell my soul to Burke. I just hope I don't have to try to detain the young lady.*

Adrian had been in Mr. Burke's so-called employment for almost five years it would be safe to say he did not enjoy a single day working for Mr. Burke. His specialty had now become part Peeping Tom and part detective, but mostly Peeping Tom. His activities in support of Mr. Burke's grand plan were to find dirt on various people so he could control them. The pay was excellent. In fact, he was able to set money aside for his two grandkids in a blind trust for their college. Because of his past gambling he lost his wife and his house, and he could honestly say without Mr. Burke's bailing him out, he would probably be dead. He had little contact with his family but was able to convince his only daughter to allow him to set up the trust for his grandkids. Adrian was very careful to make sure those funds could not be traced back to his nefarious activities. He told his daughter, through his attorney, the money for his grandchildren's trust came from a lucky Colorado Lottery scratch ticket. He was never sure she completely believed him since growing up all she knew of her father was every time he got some money he gambled it away, and if it wasn't for her mom's second job they probably would not have been able to survive. The longer he worked for Mr. Burke, the greater his dislike for the man. If asked in private Adrian would say he despised Mr. Burke and his work. Four and a half years of Gamblers Anonymous has changed Adrian and how he thought about the world around him. He was no longer cynical and was able to see the good in some people which made it much harder for him to dig into their pasts to find something for Mr. Burke to use against them. Recently Adrian even considered moving away from Denver and beginning a new life somewhere else, but realized Mr. Burke had resources and felt in keeping with the unwritten half of his contract he could leave Denver but in so doing would become a dead man walking.

Before Adrian could think of yet another way to escape Mr. Burke, his charge emerged from the apartment building arm in arm with a young man who appeared to be Dr. Lancaster. Adrian quickly called Mr. Burke's office. "Mr. Burke, this is Adrian. Ms. Huffman is leaving her apartment as we speak. She's being accompanied by a man who I think is Dr. Lancaster. ... Yes sir, I have his photograph. Just a second, let me get my binoculars for a closer look. ... Yes sir, I can confirm the young man with her is Dr. Lancaster. ... I have no idea where they are going, but as soon as they clear the parking lot I will follow them. ... I can't make out the license plate, but he's driving a cobalt blue Chevrolet Volt, you know that new all-electric car. ... Yes, I'll put my phone on speaker, and I'll call out the route they are taking."

Mike and Steff turned out into traffic and were unaware Adrian was following them. With Adrian calling out each time they turned, Mr. Burke was able to forward this information to his package pickup team which was now only a few blocks behind. After a few more turns they pulled into the parking lot of Max's apartment complex. Adrian grabbed the newspaper off of his seat, folded it, tucked it under his arm and quickly fell in behind Mike and Steff as they entered the apartment complex. Their first stop was in front of the bank of mailboxes where Steff unknowingly revealed Max's apartment number to Adrian when she retrieved what little mail there was from Max's mailbox. Adrian moved quickly to the elevator just as Mike and Steff approached. In a gesture which Mike and Steff interpreted as graciousness, Adrian held the elevator door while they quickly stepped inside. Continuing his helpful façade, he inquired which floor and pushed the button for their floor. He smiled and pushed the button for the floor above theirs and stepped to the back of the elevator. After a few bits of small talk about the weather, the remaining time before the door opened was quiet. At Max's floor, Mike and Steff stepped out and started down the hall. Unknown to them Adrian held the elevator door open and then quickly stepped out and waited for them to turn the corner. He then follows them to the corner.

Adrian then pulled out his small video camera and turned it on. He tilted the screen until he was able to see around the corner and verify which apartment Mike and Steff entered. When he heard the door close, he quickly confirmed the apartment number and retrieved his still active cell phone. "Mr. Burke, they are in apartment number forty-nine. ... Yes sir, I will wait in the parking lot and let you know the minute they get back to their car. ... Yes sir, I am not blocked in, and I'm far enough away they should not recognize me from the brief encounter in the elevator. ... Yes, I will wait for the package delivery service. What are they driving? ... A white van? ... Yes, they just pulled in. ... How many? Just a second let me get my binoculars. It appears there is a woman who is a driver and two delivery men, wearing caps, who are now entering the apartment complex each carrying a rolled-up carpet. ... I'll sign off now, but I'll wait here until I can verify the disposition of their package. Goodbye."

Adrian did not like what he knew was happening. He had provided this watchdog service for Mr. Burke more than once. He had determined long ago he was safer if he had plausible deniability in Mr. Burke's actions. He was pretty sure, but not positive; at least, one of the people he followed in the past was no longer part of the living. But since he had no proof, all he could do was to use one of his burner phones to call into 911 a disturbance call to at least let the police know someone had disappeared.

Chapter Fifty

D etective Foster determined to find out more about the paperwork surrounding Max's cremation. Armed with a record's search warrant and two officers, EJ arrived at the Rosch clinic and presented the search warrant to Dr. Godfrey. "This warrant allows us access to any and all records associated with the remains of one Maxine Rice. Also, it allows us to access information for one year from either side the date listed on the search warrant. Please have someone escort me to your morgue and this patrolman to your crematorium."

"By all means Detective Foster, we have nothing to hide. A Security guard will escort you to the morgue. All I ask is for you to stop at the front desk and pick up an all areas visitors' badge which will keep people from asking you if you belong in the clinic. I will call ahead and inform Daniel Granger you have full access to the morgue and its records."

"I would rather you did not since Mr. Granger could have time to destroy records. To assure you don't call Mr. Granger or the crematorium, this officer will remain with you until I get to the morgue. I am sorry if this is an inconvenience to you but in my line of work we have cause to be paranoid. On behalf of the Metro Denver Police Department, I thank you for your cooperation in this ongoing investigation."

"Am I allowed to ask which case you're looking into?"

"I am sorry Dr. Godfrey, but I'm not authorized to discuss details of an ongoing investigation. However, when we finish our investigation I'll be happy to provide you with details as necessary. "Detective Foster extended his hand and gave Dr. Godfrey a firm, but brief, handshake. "Thank you, sir, but before I go, I would like you to make one telephone call to the security desk."

"I understand sir." Dr. Godfrey called security and handed the phone to EJ who inquired who answered and then passed it back to Dr. Godfrey. They then left Dr. Godfrey's office, leaving a patrolman to watch the telephone. As EJ passed Karen's desk, he asked if she would walk them to the security desk. What Karen did not know was this was EJ's way of making sure she could not call the morgue just in case she overheard too much. After obtaining the passes, EJ asked if Karen would show him to the morgue and crematorium.

"I would be happy to show you the way, but I need to get back to my office in case the telephone rings, or someone stops by."

"Don't worry about your office. Dr. Godfrey will be busy for the next fifteen or twenty minutes. The officer I left there has just put a sign up on your door saying you will be back in thirty minutes."

"What's this all about? We have never been served with a search warrant before."   "I would love to tell you, but that's a question best answered by Dr. Godfrey. I think he will be happy to tell you what's going on. By the way, it would be most helpful if you could give me your direct dial extension in case I have some more questions for Dr. Godfrey?"

"It's not a problem sir. Just dial the clinic's main number and at the prompt enter 7399."

"Thank you, now please tell me about your job. It must be fascinating to work at a world-renowned clinic and then in the office of its Director and CEO."

As Karen took them on the fifteen-minute walk to the morgue, she and EJ exchanged funny stories about the clinic and the Denver Police Department while the patrolman followed a few steps back. At the morgue's main door, EJ thanked Karen for the company and asked if she would take the officer to the crematorium. As soon as they had turned the corner, he opened the door and went in.

At the main desk sat a very tall young man dressed in a white lab coat with stains around its pockets, asked. "May I help you?"

"I am Detective Foster of the Denver Metropolitan Police Department, and I am looking for Daniel Granger."

"You have found him, sir. I am Daniel Granger."

"If you have time I would like to ask you a few questions concerning the disposition of the remains of one Maxine Rice." He then handed Daniel a copy of the search warrant.

To EJ's surprise, Daniel slowly read the entire document. "It looks legit to me. How can I help? But before you ask any questions I think it's important you know you are the second person in twenty-four hours who has expressed an interest in the disposition of someone's body on that date."

"Who else is interested in this case?"

"It's one of the docs here at the clinic. I won't get him any trouble, will I?"

"Not if he hasn't done anything wrong. Who is it?"

"It's Dr. Michael Lancaster the co-director of our stem cell project. He called and asked if I had any records about organ donation. Dr. Lancaster said a friend of his wanted to know if a deceased patient's organs were taken. He indicated she was an organ donor."

"And what did you tell him?"

"First of all, he didn't have the patient's ID number, so all I could go on was our daily records. So he told me she was a Caucasian female about twenty-six years old. After talking to him a couple of minutes, he seems to be interested in one case, in particular, the one we listed as a provisional Jane Doe."

EJ pretended he had not already heard Daniel's conversation with Mike in full. "I'm not familiar with the term "provisional Jane Doe" where I come from you either are or are not a Jane Doe."

"Well, here in the land of the dead, if there is insufficient information on the identity of the deceased, their identity is listed as a provisional John Doe or Jane Doe until we have verification of cause of death and their identity by Social Security number, fingerprints, and a DNA profile. Until all four of these criteria are complete, and the information put in the patient's file, they are shielded as provisional."

"So let's say if someone transposed a number, then until it was straightened out the patient would be listed in your system as a Jane or John Doe, right?"

"Yes. But in this case, Dr. Lancaster had some additional information which helped us narrow the list down to one Jane Doe."

"And what might that additional information be?"

"Dr. Lancaster said she had a small Maltese cross tattoo, and, sure enough, the provisional Jane Doe had a tattoo just where he said it would be."

"Then what happened?"

"Dr. Lancaster asked me to text a picture of this particular Jane Doe, which I did and that's the last I've heard from him."

"May I see the file of the person you and Dr. Lancaster were speaking about?"

Daniel indexed the date listed on the search warrant and pulled up the activity report which listed four deaths. Daniel moved his cursor down until he came to provisional Jane Doe number one and double-clicked. He turned the screen towards EJ. "There should be several files in this folder, but as you can see the only one I can access contains two pictures and a physical description of the deceased. No cause of death, no next of kin, no nothing. The picture in the upper left-hand corner is the one I sent Dr. Lancaster. As you can see the other picture is of her tattoo, a beautiful blue Maltese cross."

"Is that all of her file has or is there more in a different file?"

"Detective Foster, I swear to you this is all I know about this person. All the detailed clinic records which usually come down with the deceased are not here. Also, as I told Dr. Lancaster, the autopsy on this patient was not performed by one of our staff pathologists. Her autopsy was conducted by a contract pathologist."

"You sound like this is not the way things are usually done, am I correct?"

"Yes sir, at the time of this autopsy, I was told because of new FDA regulations a detailed autopsy was to be performed by a non-staff pathologist. This autopsy was witnessed by two clinic staff members and one guy who I thought was with the FDA. Apparently, our Jane Doe was a test volunteer. The government dude refused me access to the autopsy. As the clinic's Diener, I always help out with the autopsies, but this time, I was unceremoniously excused. I would have liked to have seen this one because they spent almost four hours. Must've been a doozy. When they left, I asked if I could help process the tissue samples they collected and again they told me, no thank you. 'They would be dealt with by an outside laboratory.' When I asked about the deceased's remains, they told me to transfer her to a new body bag and put her in cold storage. When I asked how long, they said, at least, a week. Her body would be picked up by a local funeral home for transport to her hometown for burial as soon as her paperwork cleared the clinic."

"In situations like this, how long does it usually take for the paperwork?"

"Once in a while it may take a week and hardly ever more than two weeks. As you can see from the files, she is still listed as a provisional Jane Doe. The odd part about all of this is one day about six weeks ago I came in, and her remains were gone and on my desk was a certification from a local funeral home of her cremation. The odd part was instead of the usual patient name; the cremation certificate listed her as a Jane Doe. The way those guys were talking during the autopsy I got the impression they knew exactly who she was, and to see Jane Doe as her listed name gave me pause to think."

"To think about what?"

"Why all this shroud of secrecy? Because this is a research facility, practically everybody who comes into the morgue is autopsied according to FDA guidelines. The researchers need to know why a particular volunteer passed. In all my years here, I've never seen an autopsy take that long. To make things more macabre, when I bagged her I noticed how carefully she was sewn up. They did not want anyone taking a quick peek inside her body."

"Does your receipt of remains notebook have the names of those four individuals?"

"No sir, but I know two of them I can describe the other two. One was Dr. Peter Hayes, co-director of the Stem Cell Institute. The guy with them was one of his research techs. I think I heard one of them call him Reg. The government guy was short and stocky. He acted like he was in charge. There was one strange thing. When I offered them our usual Tyvek Suits, they all readily accepted except the government guy who refused to take off his hat but chose instead to cover his hat with a head cover. I was told the pathologist was a contractor from outside. He seemed to know what he was doing. I could pick him out of the crowd any day of the week. He was a tall, thin but muscular man about 6'5" or 6'6" with sort of wavy white hair. He had the oddest thick black Boris Karloff eyebrows and a bulbous nose like you see in long-term alcoholics. Now you know everything I know about this provisional Jane Doe. Is there anything else I can help you with?"

"What do you know about the funeral home who performed the cremation?"

"Not a lot. I can give you a photocopy of the certification. We keep those in a locked filing cabinet. Just a minute, I'll get you a copy." Daniel walked into the attached supply room, followed by EJ. After a few moments, Daniel produced the photocopy in question. EJ thanked him and put the copy in his file.

"Can you do me a quick favor? Please call Dr. Godfrey's office and inform the officer waiting for me to meet me at the patrol car. Also, will you call the crematorium and tell my officer he can return to his regular duty schedule. Thank you for your time, Daniel. You have been most helpful. In case, I need to call you in the future what is your direct-dial extension?"

"5512 or 5513 both ring into this office."

EJ walked briskly to the front lobby, returned his visitor pass and signed out. As he left the building, EJ called the number listed on the cremation certificate. After identifying himself, he asked if they could verify if they had the cremated remains of a young woman. EJ then answered a series of brief questions just to hear the funeral home director say they had not received any remains similar to EJ's description. Not only had they not received remains matching Max's description, but they were also shut down for two weeks for repair and their annual inspection. EJ then asked if they could check for a particular certification number. EJ read the six-digit number proceeded by the letter J and waited a moment while the director checked his records.

"Detective Foster, I am unable to verify receipt of any remains for contract cremation with that certificate number in our records.

We are a relatively new crematorium, so our certificate numbers are still in the five-digit range. I think the certificate you are asking about is probably a forgery. I am sorry to say with insurance fraud and all; we hear about this a lot. If I can be of any assistance in the future, please do not hesitate to call."

"Sorry to have wasted your time but knowing this certificate is a forgery is vital to our case. Again thank you for your time. Goodbye." On the way back to the station EJ typed up his notes on his laptop in preparation for his meeting with Manny, Steff, and Mike later on. Back in his office, EJ pulled out his burner phone and called Manny. "Manny, this is EJ. ... Thank you, I am well. In fact, after today's activities, I am very well.... First, we were right; the cremation certificate is a forgery, and since all we have is a photocopy, there is no easy way to tell how it was first printed. ... Yes, there is good news. First, Mike's friend Dan collaborated everything we heard the other day. ... Yes, that is good news, but there's more. Dan was able to describe all four of the individuals who performed the autopsy on Max. Dr. Hayes and his research tech Reg were easy to verify. The government guy is a dead ringer for Burke even to his hat fetish. The really good news is I think I know the ID of our contract pathologist. ... No, I'm not clairvoyant is just that Dan's description matches one of the best forensic pathologists in Colorado. Several years ago he was dismissed as the head of the state Medical Examiner's Office because of unspecified substance abuse, but we all knew it was booze. ... He salvaged his practice by voluntarily committing himself to a rehab center. As far as I am aware he's been clean for several years. ... He has privileges at almost every major hospital in Colorado. He makes his living as a contract forensic pathologist mostly working for various big-name attorney firms. ... He must be good since he has busted wide open some high-profile cases over the years. The police don't use him unless absolutely necessary. We think he may have ties to a few crime bosses. He doesn't defend any of them, but he provides their expert witnesses with a lot of ammunition. ... Yes, I think I can get a judge to give me a court order to seize the autopsy report. ... I'll start the paperwork tonight and have a heart-to-heart chat with the good Doctor in the morning. ... Who's bringing the pizza for our meeting? ... What do you mean it's my turn? I think because

I'm driving you should pay for the pizza. ... That's better. Give me a call when you're ready and I will pick you up on the way over to Max's apartment. Later."

EJ then busied himself with the technical requirements for obtaining a court order and e-mailed it over to the judge he felt would be sympathetic to his request. About forty-five minutes later a PDF file from the judge arrived with a valid electronic signature. EJ printed off the court order and gave it to a patrolman to serve.

EJ had no sooner settled back into the afternoon's routine when his cell phone vibrated, signaling the arrival of a one-word text from Manny. EJ chuckled at the brevity of the word "now", knowing it heralded the beginning of what EJ hoped would be a very fruitful exchange of information and hopefully being able to set the Hensel and Gretel trap for Burke. In keeping with the spirit of brevity, EJ texted back "OK."

EJ called down to the motor pool and requested an unmarked car for a meeting with an informant. Within a few minutes, EJ eased out into traffic on his way to pick up Manny, hoping he would have enough sense to call ahead because ordering pizza this time of the day could be a slow process.

Chapter Fifty-one

Steff opened the drapes in Max's apartment hoping the light would chase the emptiness of her absence. Mike regretted the sealed windows on such a beautiful day. Steff filled the tea kettle and put it on the stove. The dishwasher yielded a teapot and the four cups clean from their last visit. Sorting through the teabags Steff found two of the same kind and put them in the teapot.

Mike busied himself with arranging their files on the table along with their laptops. "How are things going? Is the tea about ready?"

"Almost, it'll be about ten minutes. Why don't you give Manny a call and see how they're doing? Don't forget to use the burner phone."

As Mike was rummaging around in his backpack for the burner phone, it rang. A text read "have pizza on our way."

"It looks like they're on their way." Mike looked at his burner phone and decided he needed to find a better place than in his backpack to keep it. After several seconds, he remembered those tough guy movies as a teenager. One was where the tough guy carried an extra pack of cigarettes inside of his sock. Mike thought that might work so he tucked the burner phone under his sock in the cleft between his ankle bone and his Achilles' Tendon. *Ow – the corner is a bit sharp, but I'll give it a try?* His journey into hiding cell phones was interrupted by the tea kettle whistling from the kitchen.

Steff yelled from the bedroom. "Can you get that? Just pour the pot full and replace its lid."

"Will do." Mike went into the kitchen and poured the teapot full of hot water. He was about to remove the sharp cornered cell phone, which was beginning to irritate, out of his sock when the front doorbell rang. *Manny and EJ must've made good time; they're early.*

Mike opened the door. Before he could say a word two men pushed their way into the room. The first one through the door pushed the biggest pistol Mike had ever seen in the middle of his chest and whispered. "Not a word or you are dead." In almost total shock Mike obliged and weakly nodded his head. The second man came around and made a quick sweep of the kitchen and headed to the bedroom. He emerged with Steff walking in front of him. As they turned Mike could see the second man also carried the very same large gun. "Is there anyone else here? Be quick and truthful. If I have to find them, they are dead."

Mike was amazed how calm and collected Steff looked as she quietly told the gunmen. "We are the only ones here, and we are just waiting for a pizza delivery. What do you want?"

"You'll find out soon enough. Now I want you both to stand facing the wall." It was hard not to obey, especially with a large gun pressed against the spine. "Now there, put your hands on the wall above your heads and spread your legs."

The shorter of the two gunmen began to pat down Steff in search of a concealed weapon. "Sorry ma'am, but we need to make sure you don't have a weapon because the last thing we want is to hurt you." The gunman removed Steff's burner phone from her back pocket and tossed it on the table next to her computer. He then kneeled down behind Steff and finished patting down her legs." She's clean." Without getting up, he moved over and began frisking Mike, one leg, then the other, then finally his body and arms. "He's clean."

For a moment, Mike couldn't believe what had just happened. The gunman had found Steff's burner phone, but when he began to frisk Mike, he started an inch above where he had previously secreted his burner phone. *I'm sure not going to tell him he missed mine.* Mike even felt a bit cocky but quickly realized he retained his burner phone by sheer luck and the fact that he had pushed it so far down it was hurting his ankle. Mike decided to ignore the sharp pain and be thankful that it was off.

The larger gunmen spoke next." We don't want any trouble; we just have a couple of questions. First, are you Michael Lancaster and Stephanie Huffman? Just shake your head yes or no." Mike and Steff both shook their heads in the affirmative. "Thank you. You can relax now, but I want you to keep your hands on the wall." The larger gunmen stood behind Mike while, the smaller of the two positioned himself behind Steff. "We are going to blindfold you now. If you close your eyes, the blindfold will be more comfortable." Mike and Steff both closed their eyes and waited for the blindfold, but unexpectedly both felt a sharp prick on the side of their neck and then everything went black.

The gunmen caught both before they fell to the floor and lay them down carefully on the carpet. The short gunman took out a walkie-talkie and relayed to the driver they needed help cleaning up the apartment. Then both went outside to the hallway and retrieved the two small area rugs they brought with them as part of their disguise. As they unrolled carpets next to Mike and Steff, the driver entered the room carrying a large white laundry bag. The larger gunman pointed at the table. "Get all their stuff and check around for anything else that might look like what Burke wants, and be quick about it. This drug will wear off in an hour. Burke wants them in the clinic's security room before they wake up."

She moved quickly to the table and closed both laptops. She gathered up the files into Mike's backpack and Steff's into her shoulder bag. She was glad they were situated on opposite sides the table since Burke had instructed them not to mix the files. She quickly transferred backpack and shoulder bag into her laundry bag. A quick trip through the apartment revealed nothing else to include in the laundry bag. By the time she got back to the table, both Steff and Mike had been carefully rolled into the carpets. As the men shouldered their hidden burdens, the driver opened the apartment door and quickly determined the hallway was empty. She stepped back and motioned to the two men to go and then followed them out into the hall, leaving the door slightly ajar. Their trip down the elevator, through the lobby and out into the parking lot was observed by only one person, a gardener, who glanced up, and after determining they looked like what they were supposed to be he returned to his flowerbed.

With sighs of relief, the two white-clad mules gently deposited their loads in the back of the memory foam lined van. The smaller man jumped in the back and unwrapped their precious cargo to verify they were still breathing. The larger gunman occupied the front seat as they slowly exited the parking lot.

Their exit was not altogether unnoticed. Adrian set down his binoculars and picked up his cell phone. Two clicks and Burke's number rang through. "This is Adrian. ... Yes, Mr. Burke I can verify your packages were picked up and are in the delivery van as we speak. ... No, I don't think anyone saw what was going on. The only person around was a gardener, and he's still tending his flowers. ... Yes sir, I will follow the van at a discreet distance. ... No, I won't lose them. My tracking device from their last job is still active. ... Yes, I will let you know when we arrive at the clinic. ... Goodbye"

Adrian then activated the tracking device and moved into traffic about a block behind the van. The trip to the shadow clinic was without incident. They arrived at the freight dock where the van backed into the loading zone. Shortly the freight elevator door rolled up, and two men pushing gurneys moved to the back of the van. Mike and Steff were carefully loaded, covered with clean white sheets, and rolled into the elevator. Across the parking lot, Adrian observed the package exchange through his binoculars.

As promised, Adrian gave Burke a call. "This is Adrian again; your packages arrived safely. ... As far as I can tell no one saw anything. Your security guards were on both sides of the loading dock and followed your packages into the elevator. One of them picked up a large laundry bag and followed. ... Yes, that's all I have to report. The van has left the parking area and unless you need me, I have another client who wants to know what his wife is doing while he's out of town. ... Goodbye."

It was all Adrian could do not to scream at Burke. His dislike for the man had gone from a general dislike and distrust to a loathing bordering on rage. Every time he did one of these projects for Burke it was taking longer and longer to settle his anger down. More than once Adrian would wake up in a cold sweat at night having just horrifically dispatched Burke to his just reward. But today Adrian would have to settle for an obscene gesture and supper at his favorite Mexican restaurant.

Chapter Fifty-two

EJ pulled into the parking lot a bit too quickly, almost sideswiping a white van on its way out. "You drive like my boss. He sometimes drives by the noise aversion method."
"I've not heard of that method, Manny. What is it?"
"It's very simple. You drive until you hear a noise and then turn away from its source and then keep going."
"At least, I didn't knock the pizzas off your lap, but we better be careful opening those soda bottles." EJ pulled into a vacant parking place, and they headed up to Max's apartment to share their pizzas and information with the kids whom Manny now calls them. As they approached the apartment, EJ's police training kicked in when he noticed the door was ajar. He signaled Manny to wait, and after drawing his service weapon, proceeded to the door, pausing briefly to look through the crack between the door sill and the back of the door to verify nobody was waiting. He then slowly pushed the door open with his left hand while scanning the room from right to left using his weapon as a point of reference. With cat-like steps, EJ moved to the kitchen and quickly determined it was empty. He continued his systematic search of the bedroom, walk-in closet, and bathroom. Only then did he re-holster his weapon. "Manny, its okay. There is no one here."

"Where are they? Steff sent me a text saying they were here and don't even think about bringing a pizza with anchovies. Manny pulled out his cell phone and checked the timestamp on

Steff's text. "According to the timestamp, she sent that message less than fifteen minutes ago."

"Everything seems to be as it was when we left it last time, except the teapot is next to the stove." EJ walked over and put his hand on the teapot, pulling it back very quickly. "This teapot is still hot. They could not have gone very far." Manny dropped the pizza and soda on the table, and they both ran from the apartment and down to the parking lot.

Manny quickly pointed. "There's Mike's car." Manny and EJ both scanned the parking lot looking for anything out of the ordinary or would give them a clue about what's going on.

EJ spotted the gardener. "Maybe he saw something." As EJ ran towards the gardener he held up his badge and yelled, "Police, I need to ask you a question."

They frightened gardener backed up and held his hands up and yelled, "No English - no English!"

Manny caught up with EJ. "Do you speak Spanish?"

"Just enough to get in trouble, how about you?"

"It's been a while." Between Manny's broken Spanish and the gardener's broken English, he determined all the gardener saw was two men taking out and putting in rolled up carpets in the back of a white van, and the carpets that came out of the building were much bigger than the ones that went in.

The gardener, now more relaxed pointed at EJ and said the van was the same one he almost hit as it was leaving the parking lot. "EJ, can you put out a BOLO on the van? It can't be more than a mile or two from here."

EJ quickly called in a description of the van and indicated it might contain two kidnapped adults, one male, and one female. Manny looked back and thanked the gardener for his help as they ran to EJ's cruiser.

Manny was becoming uncharacteristically distraught. His years of the ice-cold-water-for-blood did not prepare him for the loss of his Goddaughter. It took him several minutes to manage some control over his emotions. "EJ, I'm sorry I am not much help right now, but this is not just some missing person, this is my Goddaughter! Give me a couple more minutes to get my head on straight."

"Don't beat yourself up. I can't imagine what it's like inside your head but Mike and Steff have become my friends and, like you, I want to see them safe. While we are heading back to the clinic, why don't you call the TV station and Mike's office and see if they may know their whereabouts? Just in case call Mike and Steff's cell phones, using your burner, and see if it rings through? Even if they don't answer, we may be able to track their cell phone's GPS locators.

"Thanks that will help me get my head back into the game." Manny's calls to the clinic and the station provided no information other than the fact they both were out until tomorrow. Unfortunately, when Manny called their burner phones, all he got was a computer-generated voice indicating they were unable to answer and please press one to leave a message. "No luck on all counts. I'm not very helpful."

"Manny, it's important to look at the information we have and how it could help us now. Thinking about the information we don't have is counterproductive at a time like this. Right now I believe that it would be helpful if we could have a good talk with Dr. Hayes and maybe his research tech, that Reg somebody. You have the magic NSA eyes and ears. What do you think?

"I think a talk with Dr. Hayes would be very helpful." The information I have been able to digest so far indicates he has known about this G8 project almost from its inception. I would really like to talk to Mr. Burke, but since he has diplomatic immunity I would need to have some serious charges and proof to even bring him in for questioning. What little bit I have been able to find out about Burke so far, tells me he would be less than helpful at this time. The NSA file didn't have very much on Reg Horn, other than he has been working with Dr. Hayes since the beginning of the Phoenix Project."

"Is there anything specific you know about Dr. Hayes that we can use for leverage? If he is involved, I can get all sorts of search warrants."

"Not a whole lot. There were some passing references to gambling, but a recent credit check indicated he has several thousand dollars in his local accounts and a couple of $25,000 CDs, not what you'd expect from someone with a gambling problem. Oh, by the way, have we heard anything about your search warrant for Max's autopsy report?"

"In all of the excitement I forgot to check." EJ picked up the radio and called his sergeant and inquired if the good Doctor had turned over Ms. Rice's autopsy report.

The radio crackled back in an affirmative.

EJ asked if the sergeant would e-mail him the cause of death. After a few more blocks, EJ's phone buzzed, and he handed it to Manny. "You take this. I can't drive and concentrate on e-mail."

"Will do." Manny opened the e-mail and then its attachment. After studying it for a minute, Manny looked up." Wow! Didn't see that coming."

"Just don't sit there. What did we miss?"

"Remember how we always assumed Max's death was something to do with the treatment?"

"Yes, but you still haven't told me anything."

"The official cause of death was listed as complications associated with ingrowth of non-compatible stem cells."

"What does that mean in short words?"

"Just a second I'm reading the pathologist narrative. ... It says here Ms. Rice would have died within a day or two of her last stem cell treatment one way or the other. It goes on to say an earlier introduction of non-compatible stem cells into her system caused tumor-like growths to start in areas where the stem cells attached to her organs. He says the patient had literally hundreds of one to three cm tumor-like growths throughout her body. DNA analysis of these tumors indicated they were donor-induced tumors, not spontaneous tumors derived from the patient's own cells. The DNA analysis indicated these tumors grew from a variant of the stem cells she was scheduled to receive. DNA analysis of a reference sample of stem cells provided at the time of the autopsy indicated this was a variant of the 01 stem cell line used in the current FDA trials at the Rosch clinic. The final comment indicates the Xanax she received suppressed her central nervous system. Although the dose was within recommended levels, it became a tipping point, causing an irreversible shutdown of her major organs. Because her heart also stopped beating, her death would have been painless, and would have occurred within a few minutes."

"I see what you mean. I thought stem cells were supposed to help you, not kill you. I wish Mike were here now. Maybe he could explain this. Hmm, this may be the leverage we need for Dr. Hayes. After all, he was at the autopsy."

EJ's thoughts were interrupted by a scratchy message from his cruiser's radio. "Adam-44, this is central, please be advised a white van matching your description has been located. Its location has been sent to your cell phone. Approach with caution. The vehicle is reportedly on fire. Local fire is on the scene and reports no occupants - Central out."

"Manny, I'm going to let the uniforms take care of call. We need to pressure Dr. Hayes. I think he may be the key to finding our kids.

Chapter Fifty-three

Mike's eyes begin to perceive light with red streaks. Soon he realized he was looking at the light through his eyelids. Opening them was a little painful. Inching his hand up to shield his eyes from the light took an enormous amount of concentration. His arm seemed to weigh a ton. Within the next few minutes, his body seemed to grow lighter, and his mind began to clear, but he still couldn't seem to move his head. Examining his neck, Mike realized he was wearing a foam neck brace. Afraid to move it, Mike squirmed a bit and managed to sit a bit upright. With some difficulty, he was able to focus on a figure wearing a white coat about ten feet in front of him.

Mike tried to form a question but discovered his tongue would not respond. Instead, he managed to wave weakly at the figure in the chair. Mike was surprised when the figure stood up and began walking towards him. The closer it got the more in focus it became. "Dr. Lancaster, good morning. You are okay but were drugged for your protection. You may remove the neck brace. It was simply a precaution to keep your head from flopping around while you were being transported. You are sitting in a recovery chair. Next to your right hand is a small keypad. You may adjust the chair for your comfort. I would not recommend trying to stand up for at least another half an hour. You will fall, and I'll have to put you back in the chair until you fully recover from the drug after effects. If you are thirsty, there is a glass of water on the table to your right. Sipping it will help you shake off the drug's effects."

Mike managed to slur out a question. "Where is Steff?" He hoped the person standing in front of him was able to understand.

"Your girlfriend is in the next room with her nurse. Like you, she is slowly recovering." Anticipating Mike's next question his nurse replied, "You will be able to see her in about an hour. We want to make sure you are both were unharmed by your recent ordeal.

Mike's mind had now cleared enough to realize they were kidnapped, but not by a bunch of hooligans. Mike wondered if there were jobs listed on Craig's List for professional kidnappers. If so they must be highly paid. Mike was unable to determine if his benefactor was a helpful nurse or a sophisticated guard. His yet un-named nurse moved a rolling cart of medical electronics close to Mike's head and began to hook wires to him. One to his chest to monitor his breathing and then reached over and put an oxygen sensor/heart rate monitor on his right index finger. He then wrapped a cuff around his left arm. "Every few minutes you'll feel this cuff tightening; all I'm doing is checking your blood pressure."

Mike was able to turn his head and look at the monitor at the back of the cart. He could see his heart rate was fifty-two, and his oxygen saturation was only eighty-nine percent. As Mike turned back his head, he realized he had an oxygen cannula in his nose and reached up to remove it. His nurse reached out his hand and gently pushed Mike's hand away from the tubing. "This is giving you oxygen, and you need to keep it on until your saturation is above ninety-two percent. It will help clear the fog you feel. Since you can't move for a while, I would suggest you take advantage of the opportunity and take a short nap."

Mike's eyelids were still leaden. Soon after letting his eyelids relax, Mike floated off into another dreamless sleep. As his nurse began to remove the electronic paraphernalia from Mike, he slowly woke up.

"How long have I been asleep?" Mike was surprised he was able to form the question so effortlessly.

"Almost an hour. If you're careful, I would like you to sit up on the side of your chair and slowly stand up. I'll be here in case you get dizzy." Mike slowly set up and instinctively felt a small welt on his neck.

"That will go away in a couple of days. It's where we gave you your drug injection."

Mike now realized this nurse is a guard and not the guarding angel he had hoped. *I better play along until I can figure out what's going on and is Steff safe. I sure wouldn't like another shot.*

Now here, take my hands and stand up and walk towards me slowly. Good, now turn loose of one of your hands. I want you to follow me."

Mike realized he was still pretty shaky but surprised how well he could walk a few steps. The nurse then led him over to the small desk tucked into one corner of his new prison and motioned to sit. The nurse set down opposite Mike and laid a thick manila file folder on the desk. "I'm going to guess the first question you want to ask me is why I am here?"

"Yes, I would very much like to have that question answered but first why did you have to use such extreme measures to get Stephanie and I here?"

Chapter Fifty-four

Steff's first conscious thought after the sharp pain in her neck was a sense of almost floating. But she knew she wasn't floating because her arms and legs would hardly work. They felt like logs. As her eyes begin to focus, the figure leaning over her transformed from a whitish blob to a middle-aged brunette woman dressed in white. "Good morning sweetie, glad to see you're coming around. You've been out cold for quite a while. Don't try and move just yet. I'm trying to take your blood pressure."

Steff could feel the cuff squeezing around her arm. Her attempt to get up and run became futile when an unforgiving assortment of restraints pulled her back on a pale green recliner-like chair. "I can't move. Why am I tied down?"

"We didn't want you to fall off and hurt yourself, sweetie. I'll unhook you in a few minutes. Just lay still while I finish getting your vitals. We don't want you to stand up and pass out.

"What happened? Where am I? Why am I here? Why..."

"Patience sweetie. Let me finish taking your vitals then I'll answer your questions. There, I am done. Now to answer your first question, you got a good shot of milk of amnesia. You've been out cold for about two hours, and I'm sorry sweetie I can't tell you where you're at, other than you are in the recovery room of a modern medical clinic and, no we didn't take anything out of you, and you're still who you were. And to answer your last question, sweetie, I can't tell you why you're here either."

"My name is not sweetie, dear, it's Stephanie. What's yours

dear?

"Who am I is of no consequence. You can call me anything you want, but until my boss says you can leave, you're stuck with me. See the door over there. It's the only way in or out and right now is locked from the outside, so don't get any ideas about getting up and trying to run. Now if you mind yourself, I'll start unhooking you from this chair, but you got to promise to behave yourself."

"Okay, I won't run."

"Good, now relax." Steff's nurse slowly released her restraints and removed her cervical collar. Steff then set up on the side of the couch. Staff still felt like she weighed a thousand pounds, but it felt good to rub her wrists. "Now Ms. Stephanie, let me help you into the bathroom where you can freshen up a bit, but I'm afraid you will have to keep the door open. I don't want you to fall and hurt yourself." Steff slowly walked into the bathroom and washed her face and neck with warm water.

"There's a small brush in the cabinet, but it's all you're going to find in there."

Steff brushed her hair the best she could and made her way back out of the bathroom.

"Here sweetie, I mean Stephanie. Sit over there; it is a lot more comfortable than the green chair." Steff's nurse-guard then walked over to the door and set down in a chair which looked a lot more comfortable than Steff's. In a few minutes, the doorkeeper was absorbed in reading a magazine.

"Ma'am - Where is the man who was with me?"

"He's okay. In fact, he's in the next room and, no you can't see him. He's busy working on a report for my boss he should be through in a couple of hours. So, unless you're dying or something like that, I'd rather not chat with you."

Being locked up is an entirely new experience for Steff. In fact, Steff was unable to remember an incident or time when she had to sit quietly against her will, except maybe one or two trps to the principal's office during junior high school and a couple of dentist visits. Steff looked around her pastel orange prison in a vain effort to find a way of escape. There were no windows, just two small air vents in the ceiling. Her furnishings consisted of a small rolling table containing an oxygen monitor, blood pressure cuff, a box of tissues and one of those small kidney bean shaped stainless steel pans.

Steff slowly got up and walked toward the bathroom. "Ma'am, I need to use the toilet."

"No problem, just don't close the door. Pretend it's a drug test. I promise I won't stare."

"Thank you, for that." When Steff finished, she quickly took a survey of contents of the bathroom. Her guard was correct, all she could find other than the inadequate hairbrush was a small toothbrush hermetically sealed in a clear plastic bag. *Maybe if I tore off this cabinet door, I could use it for a ... Forget it. It would be like beating an elephant with a broomstick, and I doubt I could choke anybody with strips of toilet paper or one of those folded paper towels.*

Steff continued the perimeter search of her cell. Other than the metal frame chair next to the recovery couch and the heavy duty rolling cart, there was nothing light enough for her to pick up and nothing substantial enough to be used as a club.

Chapter Fifty-five

Mike's keeper seemed a bit too full of himself. "My employer is a very thorough individual and felt this method would get you into your chair with the least damage to you as a person. Your girlfriend is here because she was in the same room and we couldn't afford to have her alerting the authorities, could we?"

"You still haven't answered my question."

"My employer would like you to examine carefully an autopsy report from a person who recently died during a stem cell treatment similar to what you and Dr. Hayes are doing at the Rosch Clinic."

"Why didn't he just call me? I would've been happy to help out. That's what I do."

"My employer needs you to concentrate and to do that he felt the distractions of the clinic needed to be eliminated."

"I've been kidnapped. What if I don't do what you ask? It seems I have already seen too much for you to allow me just to walk out of here."

"My employer will deposit $100,000 in your checking account as soon as you provide the scientific basis for what went wrong with this woman's treatment. He will also deliver you and your friend back to the apartment you were taken from, as soon as you complete this request."

"What will keep me from giving the police detailed descriptions of you?"

"You may freely do that, but my employer is also making arrangements for us to disappear into a country without US extradition, and, I for one am perfectly willing to spend the rest of my life where it's warm. We have already earned enough to live there quite well, so giving the police descriptions will be of no avail because we will have already left the country before your release."

"What happens if I choose not to cooperate?"

"My employer is also prepared to drop you and your girlfriend in the middle of the jungle with nothing but the clothes on your back. And believe me, my employer is a man of his word."

"Okay, but I want to talk to Steff first, alone, for five minutes I need to make sure she's okay, deal?"

"Okay, I will take you to her room, and you can have five minutes, then you keep your half of the bargain."

The nurse-jailer got up. "Follow me and don't try anything fancy. You are inside of a secure facility." They then left the room and walked a few steps down a short hallway. Stopping by the next door, he tapped. The nurse inside slid back a little window, like you see in jails. Her face looked pleasant. After a minute or two of conversation, the window closed, and the door swung open, and she came out.

"Go on in; you have five minutes."

Mike stepped through the door and there in an uncomfortable chair sat Steff. As soon as the door closed, he ran across the room, to a now standing Steff. "Are you okay? Did they hurt you?"

"Yes, I'm okay. My nurse has been quite friendly. You look a little stressed."

"And you don't?" Mike could constrain himself no longer. He stepped forward and threw his arms around Steff and held her very close. He realized his cheeks were wet with tears of joy knowing at least for the time being Steff was okay.

Like Mike, Steff was very glad to be held even for a minute. "It took me a long time to get my legs underneath me."

Steff found herself patting Mike on the back and whispering in his ear "Are you sure you're okay? Do you have any idea why we are here?"

Mike returned the whisper. "Yes, for sure I am okay. I was told they kidnapped us so I could read a file on a botched stem cell project by another laboratory. Apparently, they want to know what went wrong. They promised we would be let go unharmed when I finish. I'm not sure I can trust them, but I can, at least, buy us some time. When they searched me at Max's apartment, they missed my burner phone I had hidden in my sock, almost inside my shoe. Don't ask; it's a long story. I'll be happy to share later. Right now I will try to call Manny while I'm working on the file. I'm afraid to call him now. The place may be bugged. I know he is number one on my phone's speed dial."

"Just tell me everything will be all right. It's okay to lie. I just know if you say it, I will feel better.

"Everything will be all right, I promise, and I hope I'm not lying."

The door popped open, and Mike's nurse-jailer announced. "Times up lovebirds. Dr. Lancaster has some work to do."

As Mike reluctantly let Steff go, she surprised him yet again. She quickly put her soft hands on both of his unshaven cheeks and gave him a quick kiss. "Be careful I want to be around to give you another one of those."

Chapter Fifty-six

Mike followed his benevolent jailer back to his room. *Why did she have to kiss me? The stakes are higher now.* "I need a desk with better light if I am to spend hours going over your autopsy report. Also, since I don't have my laptop it would be helpful if I had a medical dictionary." Mike guessed if they could quickly produce a medical dictionary quickly then they must be held in or very near a medical facility.

"I'll see what I can do. Is there anything else you are going you need? I would like just to make one trip."

"I guess it would be helpful if I had a two legal pads and a couple of pens. If I have a choice, I would prefer rollerball pens, one red and one black."

"You can stay here and begin reading the autopsy report. I'll be back in a few minutes. Until then there'll be a guard outside this door. He is not armed but does have a Taser." Mike took the thick file folder from his keeper, positioning himself so he could see outside the door when it opened. Sure enough, as the door opened, Mike could clearly see there was a guard outside his door. In the brief moment, the guard was visible; Mike was able to determine the guard was probably a rent-a-cop because he was in full uniform, much like the ones who patrol the Rosch Clinic. They only carried Tasers.

Mike reasoned he and Steff were probably at a large hospital or a regional clinic. The fact he woke up on an expensive recovery couch reinforced this conviction. While Mike was thinking about how wonderful Steff's gentle kiss was, he felt sorry she had to touch his unshaven cheek. Mike rubbed his beard up and down a couple of times and made a guess they could only have been out cold for no more than two hours, including the hour he slept during his recovery. His beard felt like it did after a full day at the lab. Backtracking from the time they arrived at Max's apartment and how much beard he could feel he felt his two-hour guess was pretty good. This meant they were somewhere within an hour's drive from Max's apartment. Mike then began a mental inventory of all of the clinics or hospitals he knew about within his one-hour circle. The returning nurse cut short the inventory list.

"You're in luck. I was able to find an older medical dictionary, your pens, paper and a fluorescent desk lamp. Help me move this desk closer to one of those wall plugs." Mike quickly chose a plug closest to the back wall.

"After today's events, I would like to keep my back to the wall, if you don't mind."

"Not at all, there's only one door out, and I will be sitting next to it."

Mike begins arranging the top of his desk in such a way to obscure the right-hand side from his jailer. He placed one of the notepads and the two extra pins on left inside. He set the desk lamp towards the right side to further obscure his attempt to retrieve and use his burner phone. His jailer pulled his chair back next to the door, pulled out a John Grisham novel, opened it at a bookmark and began to read.

Mike now reluctantly realized he had to begin working on this autopsy just in case his jailer came to check and make sure he was not wasting time. To prevent this Mike started a two column checklist on the top page of a white legal pad to be sure he had a lot of details written out. The first two pages were just a bureaucratic formality. The first contained the name of the deceased, now redacted by a black marker. Also, the pathologist's name and the location of the autopsy were also unreadable. Michael thought they could have just left that page out of the file, for how little information it contained.

The second page contained a black square where a photograph of the deceased, should be attached. An attempt to redact the date of the autopsy was only partially successful since the marker only blacked out the bottom half of the date. *When I have some more time I think, I will be able to determine the date by the process of elimination.* The next section began the physical description of the deceased. White Caucasian female approximately twenty-five years of age having no visible markings, scars or tattoos except a small blue Maltese cross approximately one inch high on her upper right shoulder just above a smallpox vaccination scar. At this point, Mike gasped so loudly he was afraid his jailer may have overheard, but a quick glance revealed he never even looked up from his book.

Chapter Fifty-seven

Manny opened his laptop and accessed an aerial map of Metro Denver. He keyed in Max's apartment and pinned it. A few clicks later Manny drew a circle around the pin. "I've estimated about how far the van could have driven from Max's without attracting attention to itself by driving too slowly or too fast and ending up where it is now. Since we know what time the van left Max's and what time the dispatcher reported the van fire, we have a maximum distance they could have traveled in any direction. I am assuming they unloaded the van and then moved it a discreet distance away before they torched it.

How far away do you think the suspect abandoned his vehicle?" he asked EJ.

"My guess is less than ten minutes, and based on the traffic in the area I think your circle is, this should be about right. What I would do now is to draw a fifteen-minute circle around the location of the van."

Manny quickly drew the second circle and then expanded it to fill the entire screen and showed it to EJ. "Mike and Steff are most likely located inside this circle. Now we have to be smart and figure out a likely place to stash them."

EJ turned his cruiser into the front parking lot of the Rosch Clinic and parked. "Let me see the screen." EJ slowly moved his finger in and around the circle

"Manny do you realize this clinic is inside your magic circle."
"No."

"I didn't either, not until I could take a closer look. I'm going to play a hunch." EJ then transferred the image to his Android and e-mailed it back to his office with instructions to find out how many medical facilities of any type were found within the circle and e-mail the list back ASAP. "Now let's go have our talk with Dr. Hayes."

EJ and Manny made their way up the front steps into the lobby, secured visitor passes, signed in and asked for directions to Dr. Hayes's Office. The security guard picked up the phone and punched in a couple of numbers.

"Hello Ramona, this is security in the main lobby. I have two gentlemen from law enforcement here to talk with Dr. Hayes. Can someone come down to escort them? ... You will, thank you." The security guard then pointed to several chairs along the wall. "Gentlemen, you're welcome to wait over there. Dr. Hayes's secretary will be down shortly to escort you to his office. If I can be of further assistance, please let me know. You can reach Security by dialing *99 from any phone in the building, twenty-four hours a day.

EJ and Manny made themselves comfortable, as requested. "EJ, as a police officer how good are the rent-a-cops in this building? I mean are they mostly ex-policeman or ex-military?"

"A mixture mostly, I would guess. The company who provides security for this building is one of the very best in Colorado. They specialize in providing security for hospitals and office buildings. You won't see any of these guys walking around in a shopping mall. Why do you ask?"

"I was just thinking about Steff and Mike. I am no expert, but it looks to me like whoever took them was well trained in logistics, so I thought they were snatched by someone military trained."

Before EJ could answer, a pleasant young lady with light brown hair approached them. "Are you the gentlemen wanting to meet with Dr. Hayes?"

Manny stood and extended his hand. "Yes, we are."

"May I ask the nature of your business with Dr. Hayes?"

"My name is Manny Alexander; I am with the NSA. This is Detective Foster, with the Denver Police Department." Manny opened his ID and let Ramona take a look at it. EJ also presented his badge and identification. "We have a couple of questions concerning ongoing investigation of a young lady who was once a patient here at the Rosch Clinic. Our questions won't take long."

"Dr. Hayes is not here in the clinic, but if you can stand a little exercise we could walk over to an adjacent building where he's involved in a special project for the clinic. In fact, Agent Alexander, I believe the NSA is also involved in the project."

Manny was a bit surprised she readily revealed NSA's involvement in the project. To keep the advantage in their court, Manny chose to play ignorant. "NSA is a vast agency, and I only know about the activities in my division. But if there happens to be an NSA agent on-site I would be delighted to meet him. We agents never know when our paths may cross with each other."

"I understand. I was instructed to be forthright with anyone from NSA, who came to visit. You are the first agent who has come."

"May I inquire as to who provided you with these instructions?"

"Not at all, Dr. Godfrey, the Director of our clinic."

"Thank you, we will follow you." Manny made a mental note to speak with Dr. Godfrey.

Ramona led her small entourage to the back elevators and then down to the garage level. From there they walked along the street and through a little park into a nearby office building. Ramona led them past a large bank of lobby elevators to a steel door bearing a sign "restricted access - authorized personnel only", where she placed her magnetic ID card against a small black pad. With a buzz and click the door popped open. She pulled it open further and ushered them into a small blind hallway which housed a single elevator. Her ID card gave them instant access. Ramona stepped in and pressed the up button. Manny and EJ stepped inside as the door closed behind them, without the usual warning sound required on passenger elevators. "The NSA clinic is on the third floor and is accessible only through this passenger elevator and a secure freight elevator at the back of the building explained Ramona."

The door opened, and they stepped out into a hospital like setting. Ramona walked him over to a central desk opposite the elevator. "Nancy, this is Agent Alexander and Detective Foster to visit Dr. Hayes. Agent Alexander is with the NSA, and Detective

Foster is with the Denver Police Department. They have some questions concerning a former patient at the Rosch Clinic. I will let you take it from here. Gentlemen, when you're ready to leave, Nancy will have someone escort you back to the Rosch Clinic so you can log out through the security desk."

After bidding Ramona goodbye, Nancy turned her full attention to her two imposing visitors. "Gentlemen, I will need to see your IDs. Agent Alexander, may I examine yours first? Please open it up and lay it on the desk facing me so I can see your identification number. I am familiar with NSA regulations. I will not touch your ID, and you may retain it in your possession at all times. After a brief examination, she turned to Detective Foster. I will need to see your badge number and proof of identity."

"Here is my badge and police ID card."

"Detective Foster, this is a secure facility, and I will have to call my supervisor for approval to let you enter."

EJ then reached into the side pocket of his ID badge and retrieved a very official looking laminated card. "This may help when you talk to your supervisor." EJ then let Nancy look at his Air Force identification which noted a top-secret clearance.

"This is helpful. Please give me a moment." Nancy stepped back into her office, closing the door behind her. She picked up the telephone and dialed Burke's number. Hello, Mr. Burke, I have two gentlemen who are here to see Dr. Hayes. ... Yes, they have valid IDs, one is an Agent Alexander with the NSA, and the other is Detective Foster with the Denver Police Department who also a colonel in the Air Force with a top-secret clearance. What shall I do? ... I believe they have some questions about a former patient at the Rosch clinic. ... I'm assuming Ramona brought them over here because Dr. Hayes is now assigned to this clinic. ... I can probably stall them for five minutes without any suspicion but after ...? Yes sir, I understand. I will put them in the small conference room and tell them Dr. Hayes will be with them in about five minutes. I shall alert Reg that you will be here in less than ten minutes ... Okay, goodbye." Nancy then returned to the reception desk. "Gentlemen, thank you for your patience. If you will please wait in the small conference room to my left, I will have someone bring Dr. Hayes to you."

EJ extended his hand, "Thank you, Nancy; we will make ourselves comfortable. May I ask where is the closest restroom?"

"There is one two doors down to your left past the conference room." Nancy remained at her post until Manny entered the conference room and EJ into the restroom. Nancy appeared to be busy for about five minutes. She then walked down and knocked on conference room door and pushed it open. "Dr. Hayes will be no more than ten minutes. If I can get you anything, coffee or soda, please let me know."

Nancy then returned to her office where she called Reg, alerting him Burke would be in the building in a few minutes. She then called Dr. Hayes's Office. "Dr. Hayes, this is Nancy from the front desk. There are two gentlemen her to speak with you. ... They are in the small conference room. ... Agent Alexander is from the NSA, and Detective Foster is from the Denver Police Department. Both have top-secret clearance. ... They want to talk to you about a former patient from the Rosch clinic. ... I'm sorry, that's all I know. I told them you would be about ten minutes. I alerted Mr. Burke. He should be here in less than ten minutes, so I am assuming he will join you. Wear a clean lab coat and bring a notebook. Also, bring a small timer set for ten seconds in your lab coat pocket. That way if you have to cut the visit short or to put it on hold for a few minutes, just push the timer and when it goes off excuse yourself. ... It's a trick my father used when he would get cornered by a professor retelling the same stories. ... You're welcome. Glad I could help, bye."

EJ used his bathroom break for a chance to download the list of clinics inside of Manny's magic circle. It was a little hard to see everything on his Android's screen, but he was able to determine there were only two clinics inside the circle. The one is he was standing in right now was listed as a sleep clinic. The other was the Rosch Clinic up the street. Everything else listed was small veterinary offices, a few MD's and dentists along with a myriad of herbalists and chiropractors.

EJ called back to his office. "Sargent, your list was very helpful, thank you. What I need now is to get a digitally signed search warrant sent to my laptop for this building. Make it for the entire third floor of the Merchants Office Suites building at this address. Tell the judge we have credible information one or more individuals working on the third floor have had hidden information vital to solving a suspicious death of one Maxine Rice. I have all of the backup information in the precinct's computer. ... Yes, the case number is H, as in Howard, 1799-A. The file you need is titled Max-one. ... You are correct, the digit 1. I can be reached on my departmental cell phone if the judge has a question. Thanks, the next donuts are on me."

EJ flushed the toilet, in case somebody was listening. EJ wet his hands a bit and walked back to the conference room. "Your turn next."

"Thanks, I'm good. Have I ever shown you a picture of my new colt? She was born about three weeks ago." Manny opened up his briefcase and took out a thin black case. EJ was a bit confused by the whole thing since Manny had once mentioned he was allergic to most animal fur. "Here is one the day she was born; look at those knobby knees." Manny then moved shoulder to shoulder with EJ and hunched over slightly. He opened the black case revealing a small notepad and pencil. Manny then took the pencil and printed "bug and camera".

EJ got the message. "Is she a thoroughbred?"

"No, she is just a regular horse, but I do like the markings on her left shoulder." Manny made a gesture across his chest and up towards the left corner of the conference room.

"I don't know much about horses. Does she have any other markings?"

"Not that you can see just those Appaloosa spots on her upper left withers. Oh, there is one sort of a diamond shaped spot on her belly, but you have to get down on your hands and knees to see it." Here, sit over here where the light is better and look through the pictures. I think I'll take advantage of the head while I can." Manny closed the little black case and while handing it to EJ deliberately dropped it. "I'm sorry, here let me get it."

"That's okay; I'll get it. You use the facilities. If Nancy is correct, Dr. Hayes will be here in a minute or two." As Manny turned to leave, EJ knelt down to pick up the black case. As he reached, a quick look under the table revealed two wireless microphone systems, each with small green blinking LEDs. EJ put one hand on the table to help him stand up and at the same time was able to see the camera where Manny pointed. It also had a blinking green LED. It was now obvious to both EJ and Manny they were not alone in the conference room. EJ sat with his back towards the camera and slowly turned pages in the notebook, even laughing at one of the blank pages. He then closed the notebook loudly, carefully replaced it in Manny's briefcase, returned to his chair, put his feet on the table and leaned back until Manny returned.

"Well, what did you think of my young filly? "

"I'm still not much of a horse peron, but I liked what I saw. You're a pretty good photographer." EJ pointed to the door. "I think that might be Dr. Hayes coming down the hall. Why don't you say we ask him for a tour of his lab before we sit down for our talk?"

"Good idea, I don't often get to see this kind of technology." Manny and EJ gathered up their stuff and left to meet Dr. Hayes. "Dr. Hayes, I am Special Agent Alexander from the NSA this is my colleague Detective Foster from the Denver Police Department."

"May I see your credentials? It's a formality." Dr. Hayes quickly glanced at the two badges. "It's my understanding you are instigating the death of a patient from the Rosch clinic. How can I help you?"

"We are trying to fill in some blanks in the death of one Maxine Rice. It is our understanding you were present during her autopsy. Correct?"

Peter had steeled himself months ago for this day. A few days ago he would've lied through his teeth but had recently decided getting in trouble with the police would be an order of magnitude safer than dealing with Burke. "Yes sir, that is true."

"We have several more questions, but I'm curious about the setup here. The NSA files don't have a lot of technical details. I'm a techno-geek. I would love a brief tour of the facility. Detective Foster and I both have adequate security to at least look at the equipment. If you don't mind, we can ask you our questions during our tour." Manny did not leave any time for Dr. Hayes to think. He stepped forward, lightly brushing against Dr. Hayes's crisp white lab coat as he passed. "Come on, let's go."

Chapter Fifty-eight

Clive Andrew Burke III rushed into the clinic reception area, paused in front of the conference room, and stared blankly at the door for a few seconds, then scurried over to Nancy's desk. "Where are they? They were in the conference room a few minutes ago. I could hear them talking about some damn horse."

"I'm sorry Mr. Burke; they sort of took Dr. Hayes and headed towards the laboratory."

"What do you mean sort of took?"

"When Dr. Hayes came around the corner, they met him at the door. I couldn't hear what they were saying, but I think the NSA Agent asked him a question and then after Dr. Hayes answered they headed back down the hall towards the laboratories and out of sight. I'm sorry I couldn't stop them."

"Where's that stupid tech Reg? He's never around when I need him. I told him to make sure these guys did not talk to Dr. Hayes until I was in the room.

Reg appeared around the corner at a dead run, "Sorry I got hung up."

"Can't you follow one simple instruction? Don't answer, just circle back to Dr. Hayes's side of the clinic. I want to be in a place where I could accidentally bump into them. I need to know what's going on. I knew we should've put up more cameras and microphones. I'm blind as a bat. Just don't stand there, find me Dr. Hayes, now."

Reg hurried off to make his way around the perimeter of the clinic to the research area. "Nancy, is our NSA buffoon in the building?" asked Burke.

"I don't know. Just a minute I will page his cell phone."

"I want him here in front of me in five minutes and tell them not to run. The last time he fell. Never mind, I'll do it." Clive pushed Nancy aside and picked up the telephone. "What's his extension number? Do I push * before or after I dial the damn number?" Nancy very gingerly reached past him and keyed in the number. "What's his name again, Granite?"

"His name is Garnet, as the gemstone, Garnet Hathaway." Nancy realized she was providing too much information and quickly backed out of the room the whole while being saturated with Burke's menacing glare.

"Garnet, this is Clive Burke, you got a minute? ... Good. I have a troubling situation on my hands which needs your expert attention. ... Now don't go modest on me. Are you aware there is an NSA special agent in the building as we speak? I thought you guys always knew what was going on but yet here he is with a Denver police officer asking about some patient who died. ... I know you have no idea. Otherwise, I know you would have told me. ... It's my understanding he is in Dr. Hayes's office or the research laboratory. Why don't you be a good boy and find out what the hell they're doing here? ... Thank you, I would appreciate it. Call me on my cell phone as soon as you find out." Clive dispensed with the formality of saying goodbye and slammed the phone down, knocking the whole assembly off the edge of the desk and across the floor.

Nancy waited until Burke had left her office before she gingerly replaced the telephone back on the corner of your desk. *One of these days he's going to need to use the phone, and it will be broken. I just hope I'm not here when it happens.*

Her contemplations were interrupter as Garnet, a shorter man in his late forties, muscular, much like a weight lifter whose has no neck, just muscle from his ear to his shoulder, burst into her office.

"Is he here? I mean is Mr. Burke here?"

"No, he's down the hall waiting for Reg to report back. I would suggest the straightforward approach. Just go down to Dr. Hayes's laboratory and introduce yourself to your fellow NSA agent, then find out why he's here, simple enough."

"If Burke asks about me, tell him I'm on the way to the laboratory and will get back to him as soon as I can." Garnet then disappeared around the corner. Nancy could hear his hurried footsteps fade as he entered the laboratory complex.

Chapter Fifty-nine

D r. Hayes pushed open the door to the research laboratory and ushered Manny and EJ into his Sanctus Santorum. Manny's first impression was there was no check in and out measures for the laboratory, unlke those ued at the Rosch Clinic. "Dr. Hayes, how come this laboratory has no security measures for protecting your research?"

"There is security everywhere; it's just hard to see. Practically every inch of this floor is under twenty-four-hour video monitoring. The project manager felt it was more important to spend money on research rather than on dozens of security doors. I understand cameras are significantly cheaper. There's not much to see in this laboratory since we have completed much of the project. We are in what Mr. Burke terms the hurry up and wait part of the project. As you can see, a lot of the equipment is being prepared for its return to a leasing company. Since its only short-term project, the outright purchase would have been a waste of taxpayer dollars."

Ej's eyes narrowed, "Taxpayer dollars? I was under the impression grant dollars funded this projec."

"They funded a significant portion, but the NSA is the bigger player. They paid for the complete remodel of this 45,000 square-foot laboratory-clinic and secured all of the major equipment. The G-8 group provided funding for the personnel, most of who are on loan from the Rosch clinic. Several private grants also provided for staff costs and ongoing research."

Just then Garnet entered the laboratory. He extended his hand towards Manny. "My name is Garnet Hathaway. I am the NSA liaison officer for this project. How may I be of service?"

"Glad to meet you. I am special agent Manny Alexander with the NSA, and this is Detective Foster of the Denver Police Department. This is quite a project you guys have here. I would like to hear more about it, but right now we have some questions to ask Dr. Hayes."

"Is there anything I should know?"

"No, we just need to clear up a few bits of information concerning the death of a patient over at the Rosch clinic. Nothing to do with your activities here. Usually, we would talk with Dr. Hayes at Rosch, but since he's assigned here, we can save everybody time by coming over here. Now if you'll excuse us, we'll get on with our business and get out of Dr. Hayes's hair."

Manny shook Garnet's hand again and walked him to the laboratory door. "Glad to have met you, Garnet. I will be in town for a few days. I'll call you. I look forward to hearing all about your project over lunch; again, thank you." Manny then walked back to where EJ and Dr. Hayes were chatting about an inverted microscope. "Dr. Hayes, is there any place here in the laboratory not under constant surveillance?"

"Yes sir, over here were our large walk-in incubator used to be. It was dismantled a few days ago and sent back to our leasing company."

"Thank you, Dr. Hayes. If you don't mind, EJ and I will take a closer look just to make sure some security nut did not add more cameras." EJ and Manny's detailed search came up empty-handed. But as an extra precaution, they conducted Dr. Hayes's interview next to a cinderblock wall which housed the elevator shaft to the upper floors.

"Dr. Hayes would you please, in your own words, tell us what happened during the autopsy in question."

"My most vivid memory is I don't ever want to see another autopsy. That being said, all hell broke loose when Ms. Rice suddenly died during her stem cell treatment. Since she was being treated for her diabetic condition in my clinic, I felt responsible. When I reported her death to our director, Dr. Godfrey, he said he would contact FDA and ask which protocol they would prefer we follow. A few minutes later he called and told me to contact a Mr. Clive Burke and alert him about our pending follow-up to Ms. Rice's death."

EJ looked a little puzzled. "Why did your boss contact Mr. Burke? It's my understanding Mr. Burke is in charge of this clinic, not the Rosch clinic. Why call Burke at all?"

"Mr. Burke's involvement is complicated. You are correct; he is in charge of this clinic. This clinic is tied to the Rosch clinic because we both are using stem cell technologies developed by myself and Dr. Michael Lancaster. To make a long story short, the G8 contracted with the Rosch clinic to provide viable stem cells for an ongoing project. In essence, this project was to treat each of the eight G8 Secretaries, who coordinate all of the activities of their respective ministers, so they would be able to serve longer terms. This was to maintain continuity and reduce retraining. Shortly after the NSA built this clinic, I was asked to oversee the scientific part of these treatments. Since these secretaries had to be in close contact with the clinic during their treatments, the NSA sequestered eight look-a-likes about ten months before the treatment was scheduled to begin. These look-a-likes underwent some pretty sophisticated plastic surgery along with extensive coaching about the background of the Secretary they were chosen to replace. Let me back up just a bit. About two years ago Dr. Lancaster and I discovered that treatment with two biologically related stem cell lines was much more successful than treatment with one or the other individually. We received limited FDA approval for a small group human trial. We officially named the program the Phoenix Project, after the mythical bird who rose from its ashes to fly again. After the initial success of our small group trial, we were contacted by Mr. Burke. The Rosch clinic's Board of Directors, at first, refused to take on the G-8 group's request to treat the secretaries. However, a very large donation from a nonprofit foundation persuaded the Board to allow Rosch clinic personnel, along with carefully vetted technical and medical professionals, to apply our Phoenix process to the Secretaries under a veil of deep secrecy."

Manny decided to play his hand and not hold anything back. "Thank you, Dr. Hayes. What you have told us verifies what I have been able to glean from NSA files. What you may not know is that Rosch clinic's benefactor is your Mr. Burke, not a nonprofit foundation. We also know from our NSA contact how rapidly the project is being pushed forward by Mr. Burke. Garnet Hathaway may appear to be a bit of a buffoon whose every action are guided by Mr. Burke. Don't let that fool you. Not only is Garnet a gifted Ph.D. biochemist, but he is also one of our best undercover agents specializing in biotech and pharmaceutical investigations. A few months back he reported someone here in this laboratory had done a bit of tinkering with the cell line you call 02. This piece of engineering was supposed to speed up the generation of replacement tissue. Dr. Hayes, are you familiar with this set of experiments?"

"Yes sir, I am. The initial cell culture studies were very encouraging. Using recent improvements to CRISPR technology, we were able to splice into the stem cell genome an active DNA fragment which coded for initiating cell growth. We hoped by splicing the active gene damaged tissues could start the regeneration process even before the stem cells fully finished their transformation into new active cells. Our enthusiasm was tempered by the nagging observation that some cells grew significantly faster than their neighbors. Our chief worry was whether we saw a retrograde transformation into tumor-like growths."

"Am I hearing you right. The gene splice was unpredictable?"

"Yes sir, so I set the project aside and assigned one of my research staff to follow-up on what I considered a dead end. But much to my surprise, he was able to get around the problem and show consistent prediction across several different cell cultures. I told him to write up the data, and we would present it to the FDA for a test on a terminally ill volunteer. But since we were falling behind on the G-8 project, we dropped all side projects and concentrated on meeting our timeline objectives."

"Garnet indicated you shared these findings with the entire staff. He noted Mr. Burke was very interested and kept asking well founded technical questions. Garnet thought this was odd since in the past Mr. Burke barely tolerated these mandatory weekly meetings. Is this correct?"

"Yes sir, Mr. Burke kept asking where these findings applicable to the G-8 project. I told him perhaps. We didn't have enough data to think even about it then. Now I think about it; his next question was strange. He asked if I would allow him to talk with the technician who figured out the predictability problem. At the time, I thought it was just raw curiosity on his part and said no problem and didn't think any more about it. The strange part was Mr. Burke met with my chief tech, Reg several times over the next week. Usually, all Mr. Burke was interested in discussing was why we were behind."

Manny's cell phone buzzed. He nodded at EJ, indicating you take over while I answer this phone, and stepped around the corner. "Is this Reg the same one who was reported to be at the autopsy?"

"Yes officer, his name is Reginald Jonathan Horn or Reg for short. Mr. Burke asked him to be present at the autopsy. At the time, I thought it was a bit odd, but he indicated we needed a second witness. I took his word for it because, to be honest, I have no knowledge of the required protocols, other than any volunteer who dies is given a full autopsy to determine if one of the clinic's treatments was involved in the cause of death. It is unfortunate, but many times we learn more from our mistakes than from our successes."

"What you know about the pathologist who performed the autopsy?"

"Just that Mr. Burke said he was the best in the entire region and since he was a consulting pathologist he had no ties to the clinic and could render an unbiased report. During the autopsy, he seemed to know what he was doing."

"Without going into a lot of detail, what were the pathologist findings?"

"He indicated the patient died from secondary effects of a pervasive, non-differentiated encapsulated tumor. When I asked what that meant, he pointed to several small round tumors about as big as my thumbnail. We had noticed these tumors just about everywhere in her body, but specifically, he pointed to a group which was growing between the pericardium and her heart. These tumors put pressure on her heart until it stopped beating. He said this particular patient was in the process of dying when she received her last stem cell treatment. In other words, the clinic was not responsible for her death since she would have died with or without her stem cell treatment and her heart was so damaged she probably would not have lived even a few more hours or a day or two at most. That's about all I remember."

"Did either Mr. Burke or Reg have any comments during the autopsy?

"Like me, they were pretty quiet. The pathologist was constantly talking to his digital recorder. Reg did say something to Mr. Burke after the autopsy I thought seemed a bit odd, but at the time, all I could think about was not throwing up."

"You recall what he said?"

"I don't remember his exact words, but as I was leaving, I thought he said something like, 'I guess that's one less thing we have to try,' or something like that. Before you ask, I have absolutely no idea what they were talking about."

Manny motioned to EJ. "Dr. Hayes, please excuse me for a moment. I'll be right back."

"EJ, I'm not sure what is going on, but that call was from Mike's burner phone. What is even weirder is as soon as I answered it all I could hear was a tapping-like tone then the phone went dead. Before I could redial Mike's number he called me again, and again the same monotone tapping just like before. This time, I was able to dial his number before my phone rang again, but it went straight to voicemail."

"What did it sound like?"

"It sounded something like when you pick up the phone, and someone else is dialing a number at the same time but in this case just one tone. I haven't got a clue what it might mean."

"Let me try something." EJ retrieved his burner phone and dialed Manny's number. "As soon as your phone rings just answer and listen." EJ then pushed the number one on his cell phone. "Is that the sound?"

Manny shook his head no. EJ then pushed the number two. "How about that?"

Manny's head shook in the affirmative.

"I'm going to push some buttons, and you tell me if what I'm doing sounds like what you heard on Mike's phone." Using the number two button, EJ pushed the button nine times.

Manny heard three beeps rapidly spaced then three beeps with short pauses, then three more rapidly spaced beeps.

"Did it sound anything like this?"

"EJ, you're a genius. That's exactly what I heard. Now I know Mike was sending an SOS. How on earth did you figure it out?"

"As part of my police training, we would practice talking to someone and tapping out two or three letters using Morris Code at the same time. I never had to use it, but it was good training since we could pass on important bits of information like how many hostages, how many hostiles."

"Now I think we can safely assume Mike and Steff are still alive, and they are being held against their will. It's probably also safe to assume they are still inside our magic circle. You keep talking to Dr. Hayes. I'm going to pull in a couple of NSA favors and see if I can get a location on Mike's phone. I lied a little bit to the kids; both of their phones contain a modified GPS chip which can only be tracked using NSA satellite methods. Press Dr. Hayes, I want to know what is his real connection with Mr. Burke. I have the feeling he is filtering the truth for us. Remember this Doc is very smart."

Chapter Sixty

M ike was now trapped on the horns of ambivalence. On the one hand, he desperately wanted to find out how Max died and on the other he wanted to try to contact Manny. To maintain his façade of cooperation Mike begin making cryptic notes on one side of his notepad along with a physical description of the patient and other short, bland comments about the patient's age being in the right range. After noting half a dozen bits of unrelated information, he turned over the top sheet and tucked under the pad and reproduced his two columns on page two. Mike mentally drew an imaginary line from behind the medical dictionary to his occupied keeper to assure he would be unable to see the burner phone.

Mike then opened up the medical dictionary hoping to find a name somewhere on the front piece, but to no avail. He then slowly thumbed through the dictionary's pages, hoping to find some scribbled note, but struck gold instead. There in the crease of page 145 was a receipt for a coffee and a bagel. Top of the receipt read "Durango Joe's Coffee Store # 125." The date was less than two weeks old. Mike quickly scanned down the receipt looking for an address. Unfortunately, the bottom of the receipt had been torn off at an angle, leaving much of the address behind at the store. All that was readable was "ulorado Blvd". Mike was soon able to reconstruct 'Colorado Blvd' using the "u" as an "o" with its top torn off. After racking his brain, Mike was able to remember at least four Durango Joe's Coffee Shops along Colorado Boulevard. Mike quickly turned several pages in his notepad and drew a single line from top to bottom representing Colorado Boulevard. Mike then wrote down the major streets which intersected Colorado Boulevard and could be within an hour's drive of Max's apartment. He then put an "X" where he recalled a Durango Joe's location and an "O" where he could remember a hospital or clinic. Much to his surprise, the Rosch clinic was less than two blocks from a Durango Joe's in one direction on Colorado Boulevard and roughly 20 blocks in the other direction. The only other hospital was nowhere near Colorado Boulevard. Mike was now able to construct a rough location where they might be.

Mike stood up and walked slowly towards his keeper. "May I ask a favor, please?"

"I guess so, as long as is reasonable. What do you want?"

"I'm starving, and because I'm a bit hypoglycemic I don't think very well when my blood sugar is low. If possible, I would like a cup of coffee and a bagel. I'm pretty sure my girlfriend is also hungry."

"You're not pulling my leg about your hypoglycemic thing, are you?"

"I am not going anywhere so being a bit civil about it would be nice."

"I'll see what I can do." Mike again positioned himself so he could see through the half-open door when his keeper talked to the guard just outside the door. The guard nodded his head, and Mike could see him turn and start down the hall to the left before the door closed. When Mike was back at his desk, he glanced at his watch and noted the time. The keeper was soon absorbed in his novel.

Mike very carefully reached down and extracted his burner phone from inside his sock. He carefully laid the phone on the corner of his notepad. Mike realized how uncomfortable the placement is of his phone had been when he saw one corner was bloody from constant rubbing. He quickly wiped off the phone and then wiped his finger on the side of his sock. Mike carefully turned down both sound and vibration settings. The last thing he wanted was for his phone to alert his keeper. Mike quickly glanced up to make sure the man was busy. Seeing he was intensely reading, Mike took a deep breath pushed Manny's speed dial number then he positioned his index finger over the number two key. As soon as Mike could hear Manny's barely audible voice, he quickly tapped out in Morse Code S O S and then hung up. Mike then wrapped his hand around the phone and placed it under his arm to conceal any ring noise. Momentarily Mike could discern a slight vibration. As soon as he pushed the answer button, he quickly tapped out the same S O S and immediately hung up, turned off the phone, and returned it to its hiding place, but in his other sock. *I hope Manny is as smart as I think he is, or Steff and I may be stuck here, or worse.*

Mike decided he had better make some progress on his reading assignment. Reading the pathologist's narrative sent chills down his spine. On his notepad, he noted the near universal presence of the small tumor-like nodules. Opposite he noted a similar observation in a patient treated with embryonic stem cells published several years ago. Mike then turned his attention to the various lab tests run on the samples taken at Max's autopsy. Mike's pen was poised to make a note about the extremely high white blood cell count when he was interrupted by a knock on his prison door. When his keeper opened the door, the guard handed in a small white sack and whispered something to the keeper. After nodding his head and closing the door, he brought the small sack to Mike's desk. "Here it is. I hope you like cinnamon raisin?"

"That will be fine, thank you. Did my girlfriend get something to eat also?"

"Yes she did, and like you I hope she likes cinnamon raisin."

"I'm sure she does and thank you for your kindness." Mike quickly checked his watch and determined it took about twenty minutes for the guard to get his coffee and bagel. Mike reached in and retrieved his cup of coffee and searched for a receipt, but was unable to find one. Then he looked at his cup of coffee and to his delight saw the bright red Durango Joe's logo embossed across the cup. Mike was now even more certain he and Steff were being held someplace near the Rosch clinic, but not in the Rosch clinic because the Rosch clinic did not have any recovery rooms outfitted like this one. *I'll bet a nickel we are at the shadow clinic. Manny told us it was only a couple of blocks from the Rosch clinic.*

Mike's glee was abruptly cut short when the door burst open and in walked a short somewhat stocky man wearing an oddly colored fedora hat. "Dr. Lancaster, my name is Clive Burke. You may not know me, but I am the benefactor supporting your stem cell research. I would like first to apologize for the crude manner in which you arrived here, but stealth and speed were necessary. I am involved with a government agency who is conducting some very strategic tests involving your liver cell regeneration project. The folder you have before you is an autopsy report of one of our volunteers who unexpectedly died in the middle of her treatment. I don't think my colleagues conveyed the urgency associated with your professional comments about the cause of her death."

"No sir, I was just asked to review the autopsy and write a short report on why I think the patient may have died." Burke's intensity and aggressive manner prompted Mike to realize he and Steff may well be in deep trouble. *I've got to figure out a way to stall and give Manny and EJ a chance find us.* "Mr. Burke, I do have a good start, but I haven't had an opportunity to review the lab data. I also need to have a look at the histology." Mike then flipped to the last page of the report and pointed to a translucent envelope containing a DVD. "I need to have a computer so I can look at the histology photos on this disc."

"I think we can arrange that, but be forewarned I am not a very patient person so please do not try to stall. Do you understand?"

"Yes. I will continue working on the laboratory data until you can secure me a computer." Mike then broke eye contact and returned to the report pages spread out on the desk. Burke turned and nodded at the nurse who quickly left the room. At this point, Mike decided he should pay serious attention to the report and try to extract some meaningful information so he would be able to tell Steff how Max actually died. *Hmm ... The RBC count is less than half of the expected value for a healthy young female. Wow, her serum iron and Bilirubin are through the roof, must be a lot of cellular lysis occurring. That's odd; her electrolytes are all pretty much in balance, so cell lysis was not caused by osmotic shock.* Mike continued pouring over the laboratory data until the nurse returned carrying a small laptop. The nurse spoke briefly with Burke and handed it over. Burke then opened it and gave it to Mike.

"Dr. Lancaster, let me make myself perfectly clear. The program to open your CD is the only one not locked on this computer. You may use the mouse to navigate through the pictures, but I do not want to hear a single keystroke. If you try to use the computer for anything other than looking at pictures, my colleague next door will Taser your girlfriend, do you understand?"

"Loud and clear." *Well so much for stalling. I must get us out of this because the way it's going it's not going to end well.* Mike gingerly extracted the DVD from its storage envelope and inserted it in the D drive of the laptop and closed the drive. A couple of mouse clicks opened a short table of contents, containing twelve JPEG files. Mike clicked on the first file labeled "Normal Hepatic Tissue Distal to Bile Duct." A brief scan indicated a thin section of normal liver tissue. Mike enlarged a couple of individual cells. *They look like normal liver tissue to me.* The second slide titled "Typical Nodule Adjacent to Proximal Hepatic Vein." This slide was extremely different from normal hepatic tissue. Mike noted on his pad that the cells looked like liver cells except they were packed tightly together to form tight roundish bundles of liver cells centered around a normal arterial. That*'s an odd way for liver cells to grow . . . hmm.* Slides three, four, five and six were all slides of nodules taken from other parts of the liver.

Slide seven captured Mike's attention. "Atypical Lymphatic Nodule distal to the pulmonary aorta." This wide-field cross-section indicated that large numbers of mobile liver cells had invaded the lymphatic system. *I don't get it. What could have caused migration of liver cells?* Slides 8, 9 and 10 were slides of these same atypical nodules from other parts of the body. *I still don't get it. These slides indicate liver cells growing in the lymphatic system, inside the lung, on top of the kidneys near the adrenal gland, and inside the bladder. How in the world can liver cells even migrate, much less this far?*

Slide 11 also demonstrated liver cells growing on the outside of the thyroid gland. *This could explain Max's extremely low TSH and her hyperactivity.* The last slide "Cross Section of Evasive Mass Demonstrating Destruction of the Pericardium" had Mike shaking his head. *Now I understand why the pathologist said Max would've died respective of any treatment the Rosch clinic had given her the day she died.* "I don't believe it ... It's a medical impossibility!"

Burke, who was on the far side of the room quietly talking on his cell phone suddenly spring into action – dashing towards Mike in a penguin-like gate. "What's impossible?"

"For Max, aah, I mean, this patient, to have liver cells growing literally everywhere inside her body is a medical impossibility."

"What do you mean, Max?"

Mike in a desperate attempt to camouflage his slip up stood up and began waving his hand in a circular motion. "What I was trying to say is facts don't lie. It has to be a medical impossibility. For a moment I was beginning to think these slides were made up by some Hollywood producer, then I realized ..."

"Realized what?"

"There is no reason for anyone to kidnap us and threaten us with bodily harm just for some sick practical joke. And I can tell you are not the kind of person to waste time on a practical joke."

"You are absolutely correct. Now tell me, how did this patient die?"

Mike sensed this might be an opportune time to gain a few more minutes for Manny to figure out where they were. "I have a couple of ideas. Please let me finish reading the autopsy report and I'll let you know what I think. Fair enough?"

"I would think fifteen more minutes is adequate but any more than that will not be particularly pleasant."

Mike nodded his head and retreated quickly to his desk, sat down and appeared to be intently reading the rest of the autopsy report. He had already seen enough of the autopsy report to make an educated guess. *The only thing that makes any sense is Max's fourth stem cell treatment went horribly wrong, which I don't believe, or Max received some pharmaceutical or chemical which cause her liver cells to become mobile. Hmm... That's odd; the pathologist ordered DNA testing on some of the samples.* Mike quickly thumbed through the last few pages of the report to an attachment from a California DNA testing lab. The report indicated each of the four tissue samples submitted was first processed to remove blood cells and interstitial fluids from the samples. Each sample was tested in quadruplet for DNA markers.

The first sample was labeled "# 1 Normal Liver Tissue". The second was labeled "# 2 New Growth Pancreatic Tissue". The third as "#3 Atypical hepatic Nodule" and the last "# 4 Lymphatic Nodule." The DNA marker data was presented in a Technicolor format with similar markers in neat vertical rows along with referenced data from Mike and Peter's 01 and 02 stem cell lines. What nearly knocked Mike from his chair was the summary at the bottom of the table:

- All samples received in excellent condition
- #1-markers indicative of a female [patient]
- #2-markers indicative of male with one atypical marker [similar to stem cell line 01]
- #3-sample contains markers consistent with a blend of #1 and #2 above
- #4-markers indicative of a combination of # 2 above and an unrelated female donor [similar to cell line 02]

It looks like Max received both cell line 01 and 02. Humm - Max was not approved as a cell line 02 recipient. We have not received FDA approval for cell line 02 for female volunteers... How did she get ... Oh, no! Peter's lab is responsible for the formulation of all treatments for diabetic volunteers. I hope I'm wrong. Either Peter or someone in his group murdered Max.

Chapter Sixty-one

Ma'am, sorry to bother you again. Is there anything else to read?"

"Sorry Ms. Stephanie, and no, I am not going to find you anything to read. Just sit yourself down and stop bugging me."

Steff quietly returned to her chair. *For all the freedom I have, I might as well be tied down to my bed. Even in the prisons I visited the inmates had something to read. I don't think I'll look at having a good book to read as a citizen's right, rather as a privilege.* After a few minutes of sitting quietly, Steff was surprised her thinking manifested itself as cosmic bursts of intertwined threads of barely discernible words, rather than her usual orderly thinking.

As she relaxed some, or more accurately became resigned to her current condition, Steff decided to make a mental list of the positive things she had encountered in the last year. To her surprise, the kaleidoscope of recent events seemed to be all centered on Mike. If someone was to ask her yesterday what she thought about Mike, her answer would've been about friendship, but now she discovered her feelings were much deeper than mere friendship. Her thoughts about Michael became a warm shroud, dulling the reality of her current situation. The genesis of this beautiful shroud was interrupted by a loud banging on the door.

Her nurse guard lumbered up, and opened the door a crack, and whispered to someone in the hallway. Steff was unable to see anything outside the door. After closing the door, her keeper walked over and handed her a tall white bag. "Here something your boyfriend sent over. I hope you like cinnamon raisin and coffee with cream and sugar, enjoy."

"Thank you." Steff opened the bag and extracted a tall white cup of coffee and a cinnamon raisin bagel. Steff chuckled as she turned the cup exposing the large red logo of the Durango Joe's Internet Cafés embossed on the heat sleeve. She and Max used to meet at one of those and talk a couple of times a week. Steff mentally thanked Mike for the treat and the warm memories. About half way through nursing coffee and bagel her guard closed her magazine. "Ma'am, it's been more than a couple of hours. When can I see my friend?"

"Your boyfriend must be a slow reader. You're still not going to see him until he is done, so just hold your horses." She then tossed her magazine across the floor toward Steff. "Here sweetie, I didn't read all the words."

Steff reached over and picked up the magazine. "Thank you." Steff turned the magazine over and chuckled when she saw its name. *I don't think I will learn very much from reading this copy of the American Dairyman, but it beats trying to keep my thoughts under control.* Steff settled back and turned to the first article. "Software Programs for Calculating Protein Requirements of Lactating Cows." *This is going to be a fun read.* Steff fitfully paged through the magazine mostly reading the titles and an occasional sidebar. *When I get out of here, I am going to ask Harry if we can do a piece on the American dairy farmer. I did not know getting a gallon of milk was that difficult.*

Just then the door swung open, and a very tall and large middle-aged man lumbered into the room. The top of his head was only an inch or so below the doorframe. Steff's first impression was of a professional football player, probably an offensive tackle. His tight black polo shirt did little to hide bulging biceps and rippling abs. A large pulsing blood vessel protruded from the left side of his neck and disappeared behind the shirt.

"Ms. Hoffman, I am Mr. Burke's Personal Assistant."

Steff thought it odd a person of this stature projected such a quiet voice.

"Please come with me. I'm going to take you next door so you can see your boyfriend."

"It's about time. I've been locked in here for no apparent reason for hours." It took all of Steff's resolve to stand up to her new escort. "Perhaps you would be so kind as to provide me more information about why am I being held here against my will?"

"No can do, Miss. Please just follow me." He then stepped through the door and motioned Steff down the hall. "Your boyfriend is behind the first door on your left."

Chapter Sixty-two

After pacing the entire room several times Burke stopped and with arms crossed asked, "Dr. Lancaster, would you be so kind as to give me, at least, an estimate of how much longer you need to read a simple autopsy report."

"Mr. Burke, this is nowhere near a simple autopsy report. There are pages and pages of laboratory reports and transcribed narration from the pathologist. There's a lot of information to process quickly, particularly under duress."

"Dr. Lancaster, I will give you a few more minutes to provide me with a biochemical understanding of how this patient died, or I will begin to teach you what real duress is. Do you understand?"

Sensing Mr. Burke was starting to lose it; Mike decided he'd better stop stalling and, at least, give him something to mull over. "Yes sir, I do understand. In fifteen minutes I think I'll be able to... "

"Dr. Lancaster, I don't want you to think you'll be able to, I want your expert opinion of why this patient died, or I will carry out my threat against your girlfriend. Have I made myself particularly clear on this subject?"

"Yes." Mr. Burke then turned on his heel and began walking back towards the door. Mike decided he would probably only have one chance to communicate to Manny a hint about his location. Mike quickly retrieved the phone and picked up a small bit of his partially eaten bagel and pressed it tightly into the cell phone's speaker to muffle it. He then powered turned it up, and speed dialed Manny's number. Mike then placed the cell phone face up on the crash cart, behind the blood pressure cuff. *I don't think Burke or my gatekeeper can see this. I just hope Manny listens.*

As Burke approached the door, the nurse-gatekeeper quickly offered up his chair and stepped away from the door. Mike counted to fifty to give his cell phone time to ring through and for Manny to answer. Mike then stood up, glanced down at the partially hidden phone. The phone's small screen indicated Manny had answered. *Good, I hope he can hear.* "Mr. Burke, may I ask a couple of questions?"

"You don't have to shout. Are they germane to your interpretation of the autopsy report?"

"Yes, it would be helpful to know if this patient is being treated for cancer or was treated in the recent past."

"No, she was not."

"At the time of her death, was she a patient in a hospital or specialized clinic?"

"Give me a valid reason why I should answer that question."

"Since you indicated this is part of some government project, and you are using my stem cells, I suspect the patient was being treated at some specialty clinic, rather than a hospital. Also, since my stem cells have been shown to be user-friendly, I suspect she was being treated for an exotic disease or condition after she received the stem cells. If this is the case, then I can rule out a whole myriad of possible causes of death."

"Your question is fair. It's my understanding she was at a specialty clinic, but I don't know anything else about the clinic. It's your job to tell me if she had some exotic disease which caused her death."

"Thank you, now that I know she died at some ghost clinic where she received her stem cell treatment I can quickly narrow down the underlying biochemistry of her death. Before I tell you what I think killed your patient, I want to take another look at two of the histology slides and a couple of the lab reports to verify my suspicion." *Manny, now it's your turn. Please remember you are the one who gave this place its nickname, the ghost clinic.* Mike busied himself by glancing through the laboratory reports and writing down some numbers on his pad. He then carefully indexed two of the tissue slides, again making notes. His concentration was broken when Mr. Burke motioned to his gatekeeper. After whispering something in his ear Mike's nurse-guard then left the room. While Mike was reviewing the last of the two slides, the door swung open, and Steff walked in.

Chapter Sixty-three

Manny turned on his heel and walked back to where they left Dr. Hayes. "Dr. Hayes, you've been very helpful. We will get back to you if we have any additional questions." Manny pointed his finger down the hall. "Is this the fastest way back to the reception area so we can check out?"

"Yes, if you like I can walk you out. Sometimes these hallways are a little tricky."

"Thanks for the offer, but we can find our way out again. Thank you for your cooperation." With that Manny and EJ left the laboratory and started down the hallway.

As soon as they were out of sight, Manny dialed tech support in Washington, DC. "Hi, this is special agent Alexander. I have a priority request for location verification. ... Target is a generation six stealth cell phone chip. ... Yes, code Lincoln Lincoln alpha 77. ... Search codename Howard Jenkins. ... Thank you - - please send GPS location to this phone." Manny picked up the pace as they headed towards the reception area.

"Slow down. I can hardly keep up. By the way, what was all of the mumbo-jumbo you just relayed over the telephone?"

"The only thing important right now is the codename 'Howard Jenkins.' That is an NSA internal reference code to a specific GPS chip and in this case, the one I installed in Mike's burner phone. With a little bit of luck, we should have a general location in a few minutes."

"What you mean by a general location?"

"The system can give us a fast-track location within a quarter-mile circle. The downside is it will take fifteen to twenty minutes to be able to refine it down to a couple of meters."

"What are we going to do until we get the first general location?"

"I want to get out of this building, and away from all of these security and surveillance cameras just in case somebody in this ghost clinic is up to no good."

As they rounded the corner they discovered a security guard standing near the receptionist's desk, his arms folded tightly across his chest, and his feet planted firmly on the tile floor about eighteen inches apart. Except for his short stature, one might guess his second job was a bouncer at a cheap bar.

"Gentlemen, if you are ready to leave, Mr. Burke asked me to escort you out since Nancy is indisposed at this time." Without waiting for an answer, he took a step towards the elevator. "This way gentlemen."

The trip back out through the ghost clinic's security was both silent and without incident. As they exited through the final steel door and into the main lobby, their exit host pointed towards the main lobby doors and sent them on their way. The steel entrance door had no sooner clicked shut when the unmistakable sound of a closing deadbolt indicated the pathway back had now become more difficult.

"EJ, I get the feeling Mr. Burke doesn't want us to bother Dr. Hayes again."

"I think there's more hidden behind that locked door than Mr. Burke would like us to know. How soon do you believe that we'll get a location for Mike's phone?"

Before Manny could answer, his cell beeped indicating a text message had arrived. Manny tapped the screen and read the text. "I'm not surprised. The quarter-mile quick location circle is centered on Colorado Boulevard about halfway between here and the Rosch clinic." Manny turned the screen so EJ could see.

"What are we going to do while we wait for your gizmo to give us a better location?"

"I'm not sure, but I feel useless just standing here." Before Manny could finish, his burner phone rang. "EJ, get over here, the call is from Mike's phone." Manny pushed the speaker button and then the answer button. They both leaned in towards the phone hoping to hear something. The first discernible sound was a muffled click, followed quickly by Mike's voice. The words were clear, but it was obvious Mike was not close to the phone:

"Mr. Burke, may I ask you a couple of questions?"

Mr. Burke's English accent conveyed the next bit of information. "You don't have to shout. Are they germane to your interpretation of the autopsy report?"

Manny and EJ intently listened as the somewhat muffled exchange between Mike and Burke continued until Manny placed his thumb over the microphone and hoarsely whispered. "Did you hear?"

"Hear what?"

"She died at some ghost clinic."

"Yes, I heard. What does it mean?"

"Remember when we met with Mike and Steff at Max's apartment? I kept referring to the other clinic, the one we just left, as the ghost clinic. Mike is telling us he's being held somewhere in the ghost clinic on the third floor. Quick, give me your phone. You keep listening. Now that Mike's phone is active, we can get a location in just a couple of minutes."

After swapping phones, Manny stepped away and called NSA Tech services to request a priority mobile phone trace. "This is Lincoln Lincoln Alpha 77; I have a kidnapping in progress. One of the victim's cell phone is active. Search GPS code Howard Jenkins and text me the address on this phone. ... Yes, I'm aware this phone belongs to the Denver Police Department. This is a joint operation. Thank you."

Manny turned to EJ. "Anything helpful?"

"Nothing, all I can hear now is shuffling paper and Mike humming the first part of *Ode to Joy* over and over. Once in a while, I can hear muffled voices in the background. Just a minute ago I thought I heard a door open and close. At least, Mike stopped trying to hum."

All was quiet for about a half a minute when the unmistakable sound of a door opening broke the silence. "Steff! Are you okay?" Mike's voice trailed off. Whatever was said between he and Steff was not loud enough for the burner phone to transmit.

The next voice concerned Manny. "That's enough! You guys can play kissy face later. Now sit in the chair."

"EJ, do you recognize the voice?"

"No, I'm sorry I don't. I'm going to guess male, and he sounds military."

Before Manny could respond the distinctive British accent, Mr. Burke came through loud and clear, indicating he was close to Mike's burner phone. "Dr. Lancaster, your time is up. If you would be so kind, I would like your technical assessment of this autopsy report, Now. Remember my promise concerning a Taser and your girlfriend's health? In case you didn't ..."

All was quiet for what seemed an eternity; then a tortured scream exploded from Manny's phone followed by muffled sounds of metal careening into concrete walls.

Chapter Sixty-four

Mike could hardly believe his eyes when Steff first entered the room. Tossing aside his notepad, he jumped up and ran to the center of the room and held Steff close. "Are you okay?"

Steff turned her head towards Mike's ear and quietly reassured him she was okay. "Be careful of the guerrilla. Don't trust him for a second and I think he has a pistol tucked into his shirt. I saw it when he turned to escort me in to see you."

Mike whispered, so as not to attract undue attention from either Mr. Burke or, as Steff so aptly described, the guerrilla, "I've managed to use my burner phone to contact Manny. I plugged the earpiece, so the conversation is only one direction. I hope he caught my hint about being held in the ghost clinic."

"How do you know he can even hear?"

"I'll tell you the whole story later, but right now we have to keep our wits about us." Before Mike could say anything else, the guerrilla grabbed Steff's arm and pulled her across the room and motioned for her to sit in the straight-backed cold, metal chair which had now been moved from next to the exit door to the center of the room with its back towards Mike's work area. Steff tried to turn and look at Mike, but the guerrilla man roughly straightened her head and told her not to look around again.

Mr. Burke now turned his full attention to Mike. "Dr. Lancaster, your time is up. If you would be so kind, I need your technical assessment of this autopsy report. Remember my promise concerning a Taser and your girlfriend's health? In case you didn't ..."

What happened next almost tore Mike's heart out of his chest. The guerrilla reached into his pocket and in one motion retrieved a black small rectangular box and pressed it to Steff's right shoulder. Mike's first inkling of things going all wrong was a slight electrical crackle, sort of like the discharge spark after walking across a carpet. In the same split second, Steff screamed. Her head jerked back violently. Her arms thrashed as her wrenching body threw her from the chair. As Steff went down, one of her flaying feet slammed the now vacant chair, careening it off the wall. The spinning chair finally landed upside down near the exit door.

Mike catapulted across the room. His singular thought was to comfort and protect Steff. His trajectory stopped when Burke's cohort grabbed him, a single step short of Steff's now crumpled form. His huge hand grabbed Mike mid-stride and tucked him under his right arm like some large carnival teddy bear. Mike was then carried indignantly back to his desk. His short-lived attempt to reach Steff terminated as he was roughly returned to his chair. Mike tried to stand again but was pushed down. "Sit still, or I will zap your girlfriend again."

"Don't do that again. Have you no compassion?"

"No, Dr. Lancaster, I don't get paid to have compassion. Now I think you had better give Mr. Burke what he asked you for a few minutes ago." He then stepped back and signaled Burke with a quick two finger salute.

"Dr. Lancaster, I would rather not resort to the use of unpleasant methods to elicit the answer to a straightforward question. In case you have forgotten, I will ask you one last time. What killed the patient, and don't tell me it was just stem cells. I am not an idiot, and I ask you to be very forthcoming with your answer. Choose your words carefully and truthfully for your girlfriend's sake."

"Yes Sir." The stabbing pain in Mike's stomach was almost more than he could bear. *Come on Mike, now is not the time to throw up.* Mike inhaled deeply, waited five seconds and slowly exhaled. "Mr. Burke, not to be flippant, but would you prefer the short answer or would you like me to explain my answer?"

"Please do both, first the short answer, then help me to

understand what went wrong. A lot is riding on my understanding of this problem."

"Again, not to be flippant, but the short answer is her death was caused by stem cells. Not the stem cells this patient received early in her treatment but an infusion of what can best be described as stem cells on crack, that is, stem cells dividing several times faster than they should. How much detail would you like me to continue with?"

"Please don't drown me in science, just the Cliff's Notes version."

"I promise I will give you all the information I have, but may I check and make sure Steff is okay?"

"We'll make sure she's okay." Burke then nodded to Mike's nurse-gatekeeper who had been standing idly by the door. He quickly went over and retrieved Steff's chair, then carefully helped her sit up, again with her back to Mike.

"Steff, if you are all right, please wave your hand." Much to Mike's relief, Steff turned her head slightly towards Mike and weakly waved her right hand. Mike's relief quickly turned to concern when the nurse came across the room and pushed the rolling cart and its complement of medical monitoring equipment toward Steff's chair. As he passed in front of Mike he would see his burner phone still partially hidden by the blood pressure cuff. *If he takes Steff's blood pressure, there's no way he's not going to discover my phone, and if he does we are dead in the water.*

Mike was grateful that Burke seemed to be as interested in what the nurse was doing as he. The nurse quickly unwound a few wires and placed the oxygen monitor clip on Steff's left index finger and pushed a couple of buttons. A beep and a chirp later a bright red digital dial displayed 96%.

Burke now turned his full attention back to Mike. "Her oxygen saturation tells me she's back to normal." Burke turned to the nurse. "You can turn all that stuff off; she's okay."

Mike breathed a short sigh of relief as the nurse turned off the equipment and pushed the cart over against the wall without discovering its precious cargo hidden a few inches from his hand.

Burke's eyes narrowed, "Now Dr. Lancaster if you please, let's finish our discussion."

Mike had calmed down enough to realize the chances of his

and Steff getting out of this alive were rapidly approaching zero unless the status quo could be changed dramatically in their favor. "According to my understanding of the autopsy report, this patient had received the first three treatments of my stem cells." *Come on Mike it's just like your dissertation defense. Remember Dr. C's admonition: Measure each word as it could be your last. A major screw up and you flunk.* "The pathology suggests something went awry either with or after her fourth treatment since the pathologist indicated she would've died with or without her fifth treatment." Mike quickly weighed the pros and cons of telling Burke how much he knew about the fourth treatment. This time, the scales tipped toward the pros. *I can gain more time if I tell him how much I already know about the fourth treatment. At this stage, it can't hurt either way.*

"Mr. Burke, based on this autopsy report and the histology, which has presented itself, I believe this patient received an experimental strain of modified stem cells which was developed this past year in the Rosch Clinic by Dr. Peter Hayes and his associates. Early *in vitro* studies indicated these cells grew uncontrollably. After several months of intensive investigation, Dr. Hayes turned the project over to his colleague Reg Horn with instructions to wind up the project and put it to bed. However, without Dr. Hayes's knowledge, Mr. Horn continued working on this project. After a few months, he appeared to have solved the control loop problem. At that time, Dr. Hayes directed Mr. Horn to write up a test protocol for submission to FDA for possible *in vivo* testing and to write up a rough draft of his findings for possible publication."

Burke, trying to appear circumspect and to hide his involvement, acknowledged a casual knowledge of Peter's project. "I believe I remember something about a cell line like that during a seminar presented by the Clinic last year. Wasn't the project the one where they inserted some kind of DNA or something like that into a stem cell?"

"You have a good memory. What else do you remember?" *Must not jump ahead; the more he talks, the more time Manny has to find us.*

"That's about all I remember."

Chapter Sixty-five

L ines of concern began to form on Manny's forehead, "EJ, we have to get back to the third-floor clinic, any ideas?"
"I can give Dr. Hayes's secretary a call and have her hustle down here and lead us back through the security maze. I need my phone back."

Manny handed back the Android.

EJ then retrieved Ramona's business card and dialed her number. After the first ring, EJ pushed the speaker button. After the fourth ring, Ramona's quiet voice indicated she was out of the office until morning.

"Well, that's not going to work. You have another idea?"

"As a matter fact, I do. We just left Dr. Hayes in his laboratory upstairs. I am assuming it would be easy for him to come down and let us in."

"Excellent." EJ reached into his coat pocket and retrieved an assembly of business cards. After a quick shuffle, he dialed Dr. Hayes's number.

"This is Dr. Hayes. How may I help you?"

Manny leaned closer to the phone." Dr. Hayes this is Manny Alexander. We just spoke with you a few minutes ago in your laboratory."

"Agent Alexander, yes I remember. Do you have some additional questions?"

"Dr. Hayes, I have no time to explain, but I believe your friend Dr. Lancaster is in serious trouble and needs your help immediately."

"What's wrong? Is he's okay? He's not hurt, is he? ..."

"He was okay five minutes ago, but we believe he's being held against his will by Mr. Burke someplace in your third-floor clinic. We're in the first-floor lobby next to the entrance door can you please come down and let us in? Speed is of the essence. We are locked out."

"I'll be right down."

"Leave your cell phone on speaker, so we'll know you're okay. I think Burke had the downstairs door locked with a key. Is that going to be a problem?"

"No, I have a master key with me." In less than five minutes the door into the downstairs lobby burst open.

Peter frantically waved towards the open door, "Come in ... come in! Tell me what's going on with Mike. If Burke is involved, well, suffice it to say, I don't trust him for a second." A few steps down the hall and they were in the elevator.

As the door began to close Manny held out his hand, "Thank you, Dr. Hayes. We don't know what's going on, but we are sure Mike is being held someplace on the third floor. You have any idea where he might be?"

"I'm sure it's not on the laboratory side. That would leave the sleeping quarters, classrooms, and the clinic. We could probably rule out the classrooms as they have large glass windows. You have any other information?"

EJ added, "We thought we heard what sounded like thin metal, maybe a folding chair hitting against a solid wall, maybe a cinderblock or concrete wall. I know it's not much."

"That's very helpful. The only areas sharing a solid wall are those which surround the elevators which would rule out the sleeping quarters, the clinic itself, and two exam rooms. The only rooms I know of which have cinderblock walls are on the other side of the building.

Manny gestured towards the now open elevator doorway, "Lead on."

As they rounded the first turn on the way to the other side of the building, Peter said, "I think there are only four rooms, a couple of small storage rooms and the two recovery rooms. Each one backs up against the elevators. I'd guess it's the recovery rooms. We haven't used them since last month. I think my master key will still get us into that part of the clinic. Now tell me about Mike. What's going on?"

"I wish we knew, Dr. Hayes, but at this point, EJ and I are guessing it has something to do with one of the clinic's test volunteers who apparently died. Dr. Lancaster has rigged his cell phone so we can listen, but not talk to him. EJ has been keeping track of what's going on. Currently Mr. Burke and Dr. Lancaster discussing an autopsy report. EJ, anything new?"

"Dr. Lancaster just asked Mr. Burke if the patient who died is Maxine Rice. The question seems to have upset Mr. Burke. We better get on the stick. I don't know what Dr. Lancaster's game is, but he appears to be trying to infuriate Mr. Burke, and from what I just hear, he is succeeding."

The trio arrived at a set of double doors bearing a large red and black sign "Authorized Personnel Only." Peter already had his magnetic key out and waved it in front of the nondescript blue box next to the doors. A metallic click indicated the door was unlocked. As Peter moved to open the door, Manny touched him on the arm and whispered: "Let us take it from here."

As Manny opened the door, EJ handed Peter the active cell phone. "You can listen to what's going on with Mike. As soon as you hear me say its all clear, you can join us, but stay out here and let us do our job."

"Whatever you say. The two recovery rooms are the third and fourth doors on your right." Peter watched as Manny and EJ disappeared around the corner. He pulled the door fully open until it locked tightly against the wall. Peter's concern for Mike's safety was increasing. *I don't care what Burke's so-called contract says; I'm done being his stooge.*

Manny and EJ crept down the hall keeping their backs against the wall. After passing two doors, they encountered a sharp right turn in the hallway. Manny gave EJ a quiet sign. After a quick look around the corner, Manny stepped back. "There appears to be a single guard standing beside the next door. Cover me; I'm going to use the direct approach. "Manny stepped around the corner and casually walked toward the guard. "Perhaps you could help me; I'm lost. I'm trying to find Dr. Hayes's Office, but I think I took a wrong turn."

"Yes, you did. You need to turn around and go back the way

you came. After you pass the receptionist's desk, you should see the doors to the laboratory on your left."

"Thank you." Manny put his finger to his lips and retrieved his Glock 44 from its resting place inside his jacket and whispered. "Not a word and you will live to have supper tonight." A short wave of Manny's weapon and the surprised guard stepped back towards where EJ was waiting around the corner. Manny placed the cold muzzle of his Glock against the guard's neck. "Quickly now, how many are in that room and what's going on behind the door?"

A small bead of sweat slid down the face of the slightly overweight guard. "Don't shoot. I have a family."

"Answer my question, and you will see your family tonight."

"There are four men and one woman.

"Do you know any of them, and what are they doing?

"I recognize the girl from Channel 7 news, but I don't remember her name. There's Thomas, one of the male nurses who has been around here for months. There is a young guy in there working on some papers and then Mr. Burke and his bodyguard; I think his name is Alex. That's all I know, I swear. I'm just a rent-a-cop. My assignment was to keep people out of this hallway. There, now can I go now?"

"Not yet. Is the door locked?"

"I think they want the young guy and the news gal to think it's locked."

"If I wanted to get into this room, how would I do it?"

"Just knock on the door, and Thomas will open it."

"Before I let you go home, there's one thing you need to do. I want you to knock on the door and get Thomas to step out into the hallway and close the door behind him. Do you think you can do that?"

"Yeah. Thomas' girlfriend works over in the lab. I can tell him she needs to see him and is waiting around the corner."

"Tell me why you think that will work."

"Mr. Burke said nobody was to see inside the room. A couple of hours ago she went and got some coffee and bagels. She waited around the corner till I came and got them and passed them on inside to Thomas."

"Then do it, but if I hear anything that sounds screwy there will be a hole in the side of your head before you can blink, understand? Stay by the door until Thomas gets around the corner, then head to the nearest telephone and call 911. Tell them badge number 1734 needs assistance. Then get downstairs and open the door. Are those instructions clear? Now get going; remember badge number 1734."

"Yes Sir, 1734." The guard retrieved a large red bandanna from his back pocket and wiped the sweat from his face and headed for the door. A crisp knock followed. Manny and EJ could clearly hear the guard telling Thomas his girlfriend was around the corner and had an important message.

Manny breathed a slight sigh of relief as the distinct click of a closing door echoed down the hall. A few steps brought their quarry around the corner and into the cold muzzle of Manny's Glock 44. "Not a word. This detective has a few questions for you. Please go with him quietly."

EJ turned Thomas around and headed back towards where Peter was waiting. EJ kept the pace swift, encouraging Thomas along with a firm grip on his left shoulder. They unexpectedly met Peter, who by now had made his way to within a few feet of the third door. "Peter, didn't we ask you to stay back until we gave you the all clear?"

"Yes Sir, but Mike is my very best friend. Thomas? Are you mixed up in this mess?"

Before he could answer, EJ interrupted. "Dr. Hayes, is there a place where I can safely handcuff this man until backup arrives?"

"Yes Sir, there's a standpipe, around the corner next to the staircase, which should hold him until your backup arrives." EJ then disappeared around the corner with his charge in tow. Peter returned to listening on Manny's cell phone. Most of what he could hear was muffled voices until two words in Mike's unmistakable voice pierced the electronic darkness.

"Steff, run!"

Chapter Sixty-six

Burke soon tired of Mike's scientific chitchat. "Come on, Dr. Lancaster, you can finish the science stuff at a later time, but right now in simple English, what killed this patient?"

"As I said, this patient received a virulent strain of stem cells which populated hundreds of non-hepatic sites, including her pericardium, which had dozens of these tumor-like growths. As these cells rapidly grew, they put pressure on the heart until she finally died of heart failure."

Before Mike could finish, there was a crisp knock on the door. Burke nodded at Thomas, who then stepped over, opened the door, and stepped outside to hear what the guard had to say. Thomas ducked back in. "Mr. Burke, I apologize. I need to go tell my girlfriend to go home without me."

"How long will take?"

"Just a couple of minutes. She's just down the hall."

"Whatever, just be quick about it. Dr. Lancaster is just finishing." Thomas turned and stepped through the door, closing it behind him. "Dr. Lancaster, please finish. My patience is at an end, and we need to get you and your girlfriend out of here before rush hour."

Mike was now entirely convinced he and Steff would not leave this room alive. *It's now or never. If I can get Burke's bodyguard to come after me, Steff will have a fighting chance to get out of the room.* Mike glanced across the room and saw that Steff was leaning over rubbing her legs. He hoped she has sufficiently recovered to sprint the short distance to the door and escape. A quick breath bolstered his confidence. "Mr. Burke, may I show you slide number six on the laptop? I believe it holds the answer to your question about how your patient died."

Burke's single-mindedness about his replacement plan uncharacteristically blinded him to possible danger. The pale glow of the laptop seemed to hypnotic, "Yes, please show me." As Burke walked around Mike's desk, his bodyguard also stepped closer, leaving Steff's side. This new arrangement now gave Steff a straight line from her chair to the door.

"Mr. Burke, this slide will unequivocally show you that Maxine Rice was a victim of premeditated murder." Mike then turned the laptop a quarter turn, inviting Burke to take yet another step closer to the laptop.

"What do you mean premeditated murder?" Mike's bold declaration that he knew the victim's name caught Burke so off guard he instantly stepped to the side of the table and into Mike's mousetrap.

Don't choke; Steff is worth it all. Mike then pointed his finger towards the laptop and looked Burke square in the eye. "I believe she was used as a guinea pig to further your evil plan." Burke jerked back, not realizing his back was now against the wall. Mike grabbed the laptop and slammed it shut. "Steff, run!" Mike shoved the desk, pinning Burke against the wall. Using the laptop like an ax Mike crashed down on Burke's prized Fedora, knocking it from his head and opening a gash above his left eyebrow.

Alex sprang into action with the firm intent of protecting his employer. This desire was cut short when a metal chair ricocheted off the back of his head and thick neck and crashed into the medical instrument cart spilling its contents all over the floor and destroying Mike's phone. In his haste to protect Burke Alex had forgotten about Steff. He had never considered an indignant Channel 7 News reporter as a possible threat.

"That's for the Taser!" Steff's blow brought him to his knees and dislodged the Taser from his pocket. He quickly regained his composure as his Navy Seal training kicked in. He completely ignored Steff, knowing in his mind he could take her out at any moment. Even with the ringing in his head, he turned his entire attention to assisting his boss. Three quick steps brought him to the edge of the desk. His huge hand jerked aside the desk and sent it careening across the shiny tile floor.

Now fully standing he turned and reached for Mike's neck. He could almost hear it snap sending Mike on a quick and painless trip to the next life. For the second time in nearly as many seconds, his desire was thwarted. Instead of the anticipated joy of feeling Mike's neck in his hand, all feeling left his body as Steff discharged the military grade Taser into the back of his neck.

His complete disregard of any potential threat from Steff became Alex's downfall. The now motionless hulk lay motionless on the floor next to Burke, who was holding his hand tightly against his forehead to staunch back a tiny rivulet of bright red blood which had partially blinded his left eye.

This moment in time became surreal. Mike stared blankly at Steff, trying to assimilate the magnitude of what he had just seen. Steff, on the other hand, began to shiver as she came crashing down from her adrenaline high. Burke appeared to be in shock, moaning and shaking his head. After a small bit of eternity had passed, Mike regained his composure.

"Way to go Steff!" Before he could move a single step towards her, she leaned over her motionless prey and quickly extracted his snub-nosed revolver from its compromised hiding place. Waving it at Burke brought his focus back to the present.

"Move over there next to the wall."

Burke gingerly stepped around his useless bodyguard who was now beginning to move a bit. Steff backed up in case Alex tried to get up. "Mike, why don't you come over here and take this gun? My hand is beginning to shake."

Mike had to inch around the half-conscious bodyguard to reach Steff. In one of those moments you'd like to take back, Steff's concentration lapsed for a moment as she turned toward Mike to hand him the gun. In that split second, Burke reached out and wrenched the weapon from Steff, knocking her down in the process.

He then pointed it at Mike. "You so much as blink an eye, Dr. Lancaster, and I will blow your head off."

Mike quickly stepped back instinctively, raising his hands over his head.

Burke then turned his attention to Steff. "Get over there next to your boyfriend and don't make a sound. I've had enough of your antics." As Mike and Steff stepped back, Burke turned his attention to his bodyguard. "Alex, are you okay?"

"Yes, I think so, but I am having trouble focusing, and my arms and legs still feel a lot like jelly. I'll be okay in a minute or two."

"Good, as soon as you're able, I want you to go down to the van and bring back a roll of duct tape and two body bags. As soon as you get back you can have the privilege of sanitizing our situation, but not here. Take them out to the house, put them in the composting pit, and cover them with fresh straw."

Chapter Sixty-seven

D etective, come here. Hurry; I think Mike is in serious trouble." Peter could hear EJ running towards him from the elevator and Manny from down the hallway. Both arrived at Peter's location at the same time. "Guys, I think Mike is taking things into his own hands. I heard him yell for Steff to run; then total chaos. I could hear yelling and metal hitting the floor; then the phone went dead."

Manny chimed in. What do you mean, went dead?"

"I mean the phone went dead like somebody hung up. Lots of chaos and then nothing. We have got to get in there. Mike is a Boy Scout and impulsively tries to help people with little regard for his safety." Peter tossed Manny his cell phone and sprinted down the hallway, inadvertently knocking EJ down.

"Come on EJ; we've got to stop him before he does something rash." Manny had always prided himself in his physical shape but was amazed at how fast Dr. Hayes made it to the door. "Wait for us."

Chapter Sixty-eight

Alex was now standing with his hands on his knees and his head still drooping. As he put his hands on his thighs and started to straighten up, the door burst open. Peter was the first person through the door followed by Manny with his Glock 44 at the ready and EJ a couple of steps back. Without regard for his safety, Peter yelled at the top of his lungs and, with his eyes firmly fixed on Burke, ran screaming like a banshee. For a moment, Burke froze then turned his attention from Mike to face Peter, who was swiftly closing the distance between them with each stride.

In Peter's mind his plan was straightforward; use his speed as a collegiate sprinter to catch Burke off guard and disarm him before he could hurt Mike.

His plan almost worked. With his outstretched fist aimed straight at Burke's face, Peter's last adrenaline driven step put his fist on its target the same moment the revolver discharged. Peter's fist struck Burke's cheek just below his left eye. His momentum drove Burke back against the wall where they both fell into a crumpled pile.

Seeing Burke on the floor, Manny's attention turned to Alex, who was now standing erect. "Down on your knees and put your hands behind your head with your fingers interlaced. You know the drill."

The Taser hit and taken all the fight out of him. He quietly obeyed without a word.

"EJ take care of our friend." EJ retrieved a zip tie from its convenient storage space around his waist and cuffed Alex.

Manny then turned his attention to Burke and Dr. Hayes. Out of the corner of his eye, he saw Mike grab Steff's hand and start toward the now disheveled desk. "Stay back until I secure the area."

Steff instinctively put her hand over her mouth to partially muffle her gasp of disbelief. Mike turned toward Manny. "I can't. Peter's hurt."

"I can see that, but Burke still has a weapon." Manny took a step towards Burke. "Mr. Burke, please show me your hands." Burke pushed aside Peter's motionless right arm and with his left hand gripped the corner of Mike's desk and pulled himself up, keeping his right side hidden from Manny's view. Burke was hardly recognizable. The cut on his forehead had covered most of his face and neck with a crimson blanket. The force of Peter's fist striking his face broke Burke's cheekbone, nose and his jaw, which now hung slightly outward at an awkward angle. Burke pointed his bloody finger at Mike. A guttural sound emerged from his disfigured mouth, now too damaged to form words.

Taking a step toward Burke Manny renewed his request, "Put your hand up and show me your other hand. I'm not going to ask you again."

Burke uttered another unrecognizable sound and raised his right hand, which still held Alex's revolver. As he swung the weapon towards Mike, Manny's Glock 44 filled the room with a shockwave. Its fiery projectile struck Burke's shoulder about six inches below his right earlobe and spun him into the gap between the wall and Mike's desk. Manny stepped forward and trained his Glock at Burke, hoping there was no need for a second firing.

"Don't move. I don't want to shoot you again." He motioned for EJ, who leaned over the desk and relieved Burke's now useless hand of its deadly cargo.

EJ quickly removed the cartridges and put them in his left pocket and the revolver in his right and declared, "We're clear. Manny, you take care of Dr. Hayes, and I'll get Burke out from behind this desk and check him for other weapons." Manny holstered his gun and turned toward Peter. "How are you doing there Dr. Hayes? That was quite a display."

"I'm not sure. It feels like an elephant is sitting on my chest."

Peter had been able to push himself up to a semi-sitting position with his left hand, so his back was against the cool wall. "Hey Mike, I think I could use a little bit of help over here. I seem to have gotten myself shot."

Mike and Steff were at his side in a couple of seconds. Mike scooped up Peter's right hand and leaned forward.

"Oh - oo, be careful. I think I broke my hand." Mike carefully laid Peter's hand across his lap.

At that moment, four uniformed police officers entered the room with weapons drawn, followed by the rent-a-cop. Manny immediately took charge of the scene. Pointing at the first two he ordered, "You guys help Detective Foster with our injured perp. He's behind the desk." Manny then turned his attention to the other two and pointed at Alex. "Why don't you two read the big guy his rights and get him down to central booking?" Manny then made eye contact with the rent-a-cop. "You did good. Now get us a couple of ambulances."

"I can do better than that; I just alerted the clinics' two EMTs who should be here any second now. The clinic's ambulance is parked just outside the third-floor freight elevator. If you guys don't need me right now, I'm going to run down to the ambulance and secure us a gurney. A second ambulance should be here momentarily. The 911 operator told me officers and an ambulance was in route."

"Well done. You're a credit to your profession. I owe you lunch when this is all over." Manny now turned his full attention to Peter as the two EMTs entered the room pushing a gurney and a crash cart.

The taller of the two asked, "What do we have here?"

Manny, stepping towards Peter answered, "Two with GSW. The one over there by the desk, with the broken face, has a single GSW to his upper right chest. The other has an undetermined GSW to the upper torso."

"You take the bloody face, and I'll take the guy in the lab coat."

EJ had managed to get Burke out from behind the desk and was putting pressure on his wound. The shorter EMT was now kneeling at Burke's side with this trauma case open. With no wasted motion, he secured Burke's vital signs and radioed the information to his ER contact. Deft scissors removed clothing, exposing a smooth round hole slowly oozing blood. "You're lucky; it seems to have missed your major blood vessels."

Clattering wheels heralded the return of the rent-a-cop, pushing a gurney, "How can I help?"

EJ waved him over to Burke' location. Without missing a beat, the EMT handed him a plastic bag of Ringers Lactate. "Hold this about 4 feet above his head while I get his IV started. This task was soon complete. He then popped the cap on a morphine syringe and injected it into the IV. Burke noticeably relaxed.

The EMT then turned his attention to Burke's mangled face. He quickly broke out a large 8 x 8 square gauze pack and a roll of two-inch gauze. He gingerly placed the gauze pack under Burke's drooping chin and slowly eased it back to more normal position. Even with his morphine in full effect, Burke still tried to push the EMTs hand aside, but to no avail. With the gauze pad properly positioned, it was secured with multiple passes of the two-inch gauze until it covered the left side of his face. In spite of Burke's protesting, the EMT placed a red cervical collar around his neck, immobilizing his head. With EJ's help, Burke was transferred and secured to a backboard and put on the gurney. EJ experienced a moment of morbid pleasure as he tightly secured Burke to the stretcher. A quick check of Burke's shoulder wound determined normal clotting had stopped the flow of blood. The EMT gathered up the remainder of his trauma bag and placed it between Burke's feet next to the oxygen cylinder and secured an oxygen cannula. Turning to the rent-a-cop, "Sir, I need your help to get this guy down to the ambulance. Would you ride in back with our patient while I drive to the ER?"

"Not a problem."

"Let's go. It's only a few blocks away. The EMT pushed the gurney through the door, down the hall and around to the elevator with the Rent-a-Cop walking beside holding the IV bag above his head.

As the second EMT team ran through the door, the remaining EMT pointed toward Peter. With a fresh trauma kit, the trio worked almost as a singularity. Each part seems to know what to do and when to do it. Peter's vitals were deteriorating by the minute. Even with two IVs, his blood pressure was not stabilizing. A quick radio call requesting a lifeline helicopter for direct transfer to the regional trauma unit brought another gasp to Steff's lips. She was now gripping Mike's hand so tightly his fingertips became red.

Mike now pushed in closer to Peter's head. "How's he doing guys?"

One of the EMTs stood up; concern was written all over his face. "Step over here for a second." After a few steps away, "It's not well. I think the bullet may have shattered a rib and scattered sharp pieces of bone into his heart. He's bleeding internally, and even with shock bags on his legs to force blood back to his heart; we're falling behind. All we can do now is to keep pumping fluids into him until the trauma chopper gets here. They have plasma and whole blood on board. If you have anything you'd like to say, now is the time to say it. I don't know how much longer he will be conscious."

Mike kneeled down next to Peter. "Hey Bud, they're doing all they can do. We just need you to hang in there."

"Sorry Mike, this isn't going to end the way I planned."

"Don't talk like that Peter. Things are going to be okay."

"I don't think so, but just in case, I want you to know how sorry I am. I messed up big time."

"Don't worry about that now. We will straighten things later."

"From where I sit, I don't think things are not going to get any better. I can almost feel the bleeding inside. My heart is doing weird things. Mike, please don't interrupt. I want to finish this before I pass out. I figured out Reg was the one who prepared the altered stem cells. Burke ordered the two nurses to deviate from the protocol. That's why he wanted me at the autopsy, to show me how much trouble I would be in if I said anything. I'm ashamed to say I got caught up in Burke's paranoia. Ask Reg; he will tell you what I mean. I'm really sorry I had a part in that young ladies death just to satisfy Burke's ambition. Promise me you will tell her parents and friends she was killed by an evil animal, and he will be punished."

Peter's breathing was now becoming more labored, as he began to slur words. "Mike, you're the closest thing I have to a brother. In case I don't wake up on this side of glory, all my papers, Will, and wishes are in the grubby green lock box under my bed. ... (a cough) ... The combination is the same as our eighth-grade gym locker; you know the one I mean."

"Yeah, I understand. I think you're getting a little ahead of yourself. you'll come through this okay."

"That's my prayer, but if its not answered in the affirmative, please make sure my manuscripts about inserting multiple genomes are published." The EMTs lifted Peter onto the gurney and began strapping him down for transport. His voice became a whisper. Mike leaned real close to hear Peter's parting words. "I love you brother ... (a cough) ... see you on the other side ... (labored breath) ... remember God is good - all the time."

The EMT's radio broke into the growing silence. "This is Lifeline Four. We are touching down on your Hilo pad. Ready to transport." Three EMTs, Peter, and their paraphernalia loaded gurney disappeared through the door at a full run, leaving Mike, Steff, Manny, and EJ to their thoughts.

Mike glanced around the room, still dazed by what just happened. "I'm totally amazed by how much stuff EMTs leave behind." His gaze stopped at the red-streaked arc on the wall where Peter had been sitting. Bandage wrappers, strips of Peter's shirt, plastic trays, were strewn across the floor. One of Peter's shoes and a horrendous amount of blood, so fresh it still reflected light was mingled into the macabre scene.

EJ's cell phone broke the silence. "This is Detective Foster ... Yes, I understand, thank you for calling. I'll get back to you." EJ stepped back towards the group. "That was central dispatch; Burke is in surgery. I'm not sure whether it is good news or bad news, but his gunshot wound was superficial and not life-threatening. The injuries to his face will be dealt with in a separate surgery. Dr. Hayes's chopper just landed, but not in time. Your friend died on route. Mike, I am truly sorry for your loss."

EJ's message seemed to bounce off Mike as he walked over and straightened up the chair he had been sitting in this past couple of hours and sat down facing the blood-marked wall. Mike's countenance was serene, out of place in the midst of the recent carnage. Mike seemed to melt slowly as he leaned forward and buried his face in his blood-stained hands. His back heaved upward, remained motionless for a few seconds, and then collapsed as a muffled cry of utter anguish escaped between his fingers. It had been a long time since Mike had cried this deeply.

The last time Peter was consoling him after the notification of his mother's death started to sink in. Now his tears were for Peter. Mike's thoughts and feelings were so intense he did not realize Steff

Manny was entirely unaccustomed to this kind of emotions and was at a loss for what to say or do. His structured training soon won out. "EJ, before he gets out of the building, I want you to run over and arrest Mr. Horn."

"On what charge?"

"I don't care. I just don't want him to skip town."

"How about an accessory to murder? We can keep him locked up for at least twenty-four hours."

"Sounds good to me. Let's get him to central booking. That way we can question the big guy at the same time."

EJ called dispatch requesting backup for prisoner transport. Before leaving, EJ walked over and gently squeezed Mike's shoulder. "Hang in there." Mike acknowledged EJ's concern by patting his hand. EJ turned around and headed for the door. He was careful to clean off the blood on the back of his hand after he left the room.

As Mike slowly regained his composure, he was somewhat embarrassed to realize Steff was holding him tightly. Her arms relaxed as Mike straightened up to secure his handkerchief from his back pocket. Mike's reddened eyes were soon dry. "I'm okay. I'm sorry I lost it there for a few minutes. Peter's last words were to let me know he knew he was dying, and his conscience was clean, and he was okay with the outcome. I know it may sound corny, but during the past several minutes it felt like I was in a chapel with all its personal comfort."

"I don't think that's corny at all. You just lost your best friend, and you took solace in the knowledge he was at peace with his passing."

"It will probably be a long time before I come to terms with the knowledge that Peter died saving me. To be honest, for a second I thought I was dead. When Burke pulled back the hammer on his revolver, I closed my eyes. The next thing I felt was a shock wave. In that fraction of a second of silence following the shot's concussion, my brain tricked me into thinking I was dead. When I opened my eyes and saw Peter all bloody and tangled up with

Burke. I wished it had been me who was shot instead of Peter. I just can't get the picture out of my head of Peter strapped to his gurney with all those tubes sticking out of his arms, and blood everywhere, Peter's blood."

Manny intervened by waving towards Mike and Steff. "Let's get out of here. This is an active crime scene, and the police will want our statements while things are still fresh in our minds. Let's look at it this way, Mike, you now know Peter was not responsible for Max's death, and Steff, you now know how Max death was murder and was not caused by Mike's stem cells."

Mike and Steff grudgingly agreed, but both still had numerous questions. At this moment in time, Mike was satisfied knowing his growing attraction to Steff was reciprocated. As they left the room and started down the hallway, Steff was tightly gripping Mike's arm with both hands and leaning her head against his shoulder.

As they rounded the corner next to the reception area, they met EJ, who noted, "I finally figured out how to turn off the security cameras and microphones so we can use the rooms along this hallway for a command center without worrying that we are being recorded somewhere by these wireless snoopers. Before we give our statements, let's clean up a bit" Mike, and Steff quickly agreed and disappeared into the restrooms across the hall.

Mike began washing his hands, turning the sink into a bright red cauldron swirling around a sucking drain. *This is part of Peter I am washing down the drain.* In a macabre moment, Mike thought if he could capture one of Peter's stem cells he could clone him and have his friend back. *Stop thinking like that; it's not going to happen. Peter is gone.* Mike finished his sad task and met EJ in the hall just as Steff joined them.

EJ pointed at the smaller of two adjoining conference rooms. "Let's wait in there until the chaos dies down a bit." The closed-door muffled the growing cacophony of radios and loud talking as teams of police and FBI dispersed throughout the shadow clinic setting up all sorts of equipment. Mike and Steff stared blankly at several handcuffed men with bandaged faces as they were escorted past the conference room on the way to the elevator. Manny looked over at the kids. "I am assuming those were the look-a-likes. Too bad we taxpayers will have to fund the rest of their medical bills."

After what seemed like an hour or two, an officer tapped on the window. EJ opened the door and listened to the officer's brief message, then turned toward the beleaguered trio. EJ pointed toward the small conference room next to the reception area. "Mike, across the hall there's a detective who will take your statement. Steff, your detective, is around the corner in the receptionist's office. Manny, you and I are to be debriefed by a couple of FBI agents in the first office around the corner. When we're all done, let's meet back here. I've made arrangements for transportation to take us back to our cars. Let's all try to get some rest. I would like for us all to meet tomorrow afternoon at Max's apartment. Hopefully, by that time Manny and I, along with the FBI, will have this bizarre situation sorted out."

Mike's next comment brought a round of light laughter as they dispersed to their assigned rooms. "I sure hope you guys bring fresh pizza. I'm not sure today's will be any good."

Chapter Sixty-nine

No one got much sleep that night. Mike and Steff decided to grab some take-out. After much discussion, they decided to crash at Steff's place since Mike had not touched his pad for several days. They spent the evening sharing anecdotes and meaningful events in Peter's and Max's short lives. The first warm rays of sunrise found Mike sound asleep and curled awkwardly on Steff's apartment size futon, where he had fallen asleep little after 2 AM. Steff had retrieved an Afghan from her closet and carefully covered Mike. Before she retired to her bedroom, she leaned down and gently kissed the side of his forehead and whispered, "Good night Michael Lancaster. Sleep well."

While Mike and Steff begin their recovery from the evil which touched their lives, Manny and EJ were busy the entire night. First, EJ had everyone at Burke's clinic brought in for questioning. He would sort out the wheat from the chaff later.

Time slowly passed, assisted by less than acceptable coffee and yesterday's donuts. Manny and EJ double-teamed the interview with Alex. Their effort proved extremely fruitful. Before the first question was asked, Alex waved his right to an attorney and indicated he was ready to testify against Burke if the death penalty was off the table. Over the next two hours, Alex unpacked the practical details of Burke's plan to subvert the G8 economic group. The end game was to control its monetary decisions with his hand-picked stem cell treated look-alikes. Alex indicated Burke had used threats of exposure and monetary bribes against dozens of individuals over the last several years. He stated Burke kept a safe full of illegal contracts, which he used to control individuals. Alex was disgusted by Burke's constant bragging how they were untouchable since his house off the Evergreen Highway was part of the British Consulate in Denver.

After a break to retrieve new cups of old coffee, Alex continued his confessional. In all, Alex confessed to and provided details of eleven murderers which he committed at Burke's behest. The first was Adrian Bowman's brother, who was killed as leverage to make Adrian's one-man private detective agency available 24/7 for Burke's beck and call. Alex's next notches were the eight NSA vetted look-a-likes who were poisoned *in masse* by delicious dark English chocolates which he had prepared using a cyanide glaze. "Burke assembled them at his home for an initial briefing before beginning their training, sort of like a guy's night out. The NSA's vetted agents came, and Burke's vetted look-alikes left the dinner. All they had to do was to walk into the new clinic facility, and no one was the wiser.   Burke used another well-placed tech geek to substitute his team's fingerprints, biometric data, and DNA into the appropriate NSA files.

A few months later I took out Bradley Smith, the first of the true G8 sectaries to die. I broke his neck the day his look-a-like entered Smith's real life. We had to dispatch his friend Anne Hamilton the very same day when she blew his cover." Alex indicated he later dispatched the British G8 Sectary when his look-alike entered into the real world. Alex assured Manny there were only two of Burke's hand-picked cronies in the G8. Alex assured them that the death of the assistant to the Roach's IT Director was a fortuitous accident, and he had no part in his death. Burke pressured the Clinic to hire his geek as his replacement. It was he who stripped all of the data from the clinic's computers. At this time, they took another break while Manny alerted the NSA about the two G8 rogues and the geek.

After warming up their now cold coffee, they started again. Alex admitted the next two bothered him a lot, but not enough to spare their lives. These were the two nurses who witnessed the forged papers about Maxine Rice's death. These were also the same two nurses who administered the malignant stem cells which were provided by Reg Horn at Burke's insistence. Burke produced a cover story about working at a research clinic in Mexico. When pressed, Alex revealed Burke was planning to kill Dr. Lancaster and Ms. Huffman along with the two nurses and the rent-a-cop as soon as he got what he wanted from Dr. Lancaster. When asked about the kidnapping of the kids, Alex indicated he would tell them where to find Burke's little black book which contained the names and addresses of his helpers.

Alex's final grizzly revelation was that all the bodies were buried in a sizeable composting pit at the back of Burke's house. Burke planned to grind them all up come spring to fertilize his flowers and landscaping. Alex said Burke had one bizarre characteristic he was unable to understand. Every time someone was killed, or when Burke was able to put someone out of business or when he had an apparent success, he would go to a particular haberdashery on Denver's Sixteenth Street Mall, or if the event was in England, a similar haberdashery in Piccadilly Square. He would spend a couple of hours to pick out a new Fedora. Each hat was unique, different in color or headband design. He had a special room built off his master bedroom where the hats were on display, each with its cubicle complete with a small gold engraved plate describing the event. Alex indicated there were more than a hundred hats on display. "Burke really gave me the creeps when he told me he had arranged with a private crime museum in London to display his collection after he died." Manny and EJ agreed it did sound a little bit creepy.

EJ gave Alex a brand-new yellow pad and a couple of ballpoint pens. "We need you to write down everything you have told us. Use as much detail as you think necessary. This officer here will keep your company. Please let him know if you need anything. We will continue this conversation tomorrow afternoon after your arraignment on murder charges. By the way, how did Burke turn you to the dark side?"

"Like most of the rest of his minions. He bailed me out of a very dark hole I had climbed into while gambling. I could have taken getting killed for what I did, but my IOU holders said my Mom, Dad, and sister would meet with an accident if the debt were not paid on time. It turned out Burke was behind it all, and he reminded me of my operational loyalty from time to time by showing me recent photos of my parents and my sister's family."

"You can rest easy. Your former boss will never see the outside of a prison."

Chapter Seventy

Manny and EJ took a well-deserved break. An officer had brought in a couple of fresh sandwiches, cans of soda, and chips, which they consumed in almost total silence since both, were approaching exhaustion. The restful quiet and food seemed to revive their enthusiasm. After a few minutes of planning, they began their questioning of Reg Horn. Like Alex Reg waived his right to have an attorney present and also asked if they could make a deal.

Since EJ had arrested Reg, he took the lead and began the interrogation. "We appreciate your willingness to help us in our investigation. The type of deal we can make for you depends on just how good and truthful your information turns out to be. Why don't you start at the beginning so we can understand how you got here?"

Rag's part in the story began on a positive note with a chance meeting with Dr. Hayes which led to his employment at the Rosch Clinic as part of Peter's research group. Reg rose quickly to become the head tech in the diabetic stem cell research program. His downfall began when he thought he had won an all-expenses-paid ten-day trip to Mexico. The nail in Reg's coffin, so to speak, came when he checked in at the resort hotel. Part of his package was a player's card for $1000 at a local casino. At the time, Reg was unaware of the trap Burke had set for him. After a couple of days of gambling and winning almost $80,000, he ended up at a high-stakes poker game. The next morning Reg woke up on his bed entirely dressed and with a roaring headache. After he cleaned up and went down to get breakfast, he was approached by two men requesting him to pay up on three IOUs he was supposed to have signed the night before. The two men made it abundantly clear to Reg that his $125,000 marks were due in full within ten days or bad things would happen to him and his family.

Shortly after he returned to Denver, Alex approached him as he left the clinic. In short, a benefactor would pay off his IOU in exchange for technical information about the stem cell program at the Rosch Clinic. Also, he would receive an additional $5,000 per month deposited in an offshore bank account. Alex assured him his benefactor was only interested in the technical progress of the program, and the doctors would still be able to publish and receive credit for all their work. He had no interest in publications, just results. In the time since then, Reg had also learned he was also set up by Burke and that Burke was his so-called benefactor. He also discovered he was not the only one to sign one of those infamous contracts.

Other than furnishing Burke useful technical information about the stem cell program, things went along relatively smoothly until he learned about the look-alike's switch Burke had been planning. Reg's next revelation was that he had crossed his moral barrier when he secured for Burke stem cells which had been genetically modified to include multiple initiator genes. Rag's choice passed from simple felony to accessory before the fact to second-degree murder. When Burke intimidated two clinic nurses to give Maxine Rice the modified stem cells without her knowledge, Reg became an accomplice to murder. An act which cost the nurses and Ms. Rice their lives when things went all wrong.

When Manny broached the subject of Dr. Hayes's involvement, Reg became less responsive and only answered direct questions with short answers. After an hour of give and take, Manny was able to ascertain Dr. Hayes had been sequestered into Burke's sphere of influence by the same Mexican press-gang. In Dr. Hayes' case, his downfall came with his annual outbreak of Bell's Palsy. Each year about the same time Dr. Hayes would visit a Mexican Clinic, which specialized in the treatment of Bell's Palsy. Reg indicated he was to call Burke as soon as Dr. Hayes began making arrangements for his leave of absence. Burke worked his evil magic and, like Reg, Dr. Hayes woke up deeply in debt with no knowledge of how he got there. Reg surmised Burke used spiked drinks to set up his marks. Reg indicated Burke forced him to approach Dr. Hayes and offer him a "get out of debt free card." Taking Burke's payoff was by far the lesser of two evils. Dr. Hayes's new job description was to provide Burke with leading-edge information in the field of adult stem cell research.

When asked how information was passed, Reg indicated he was the go-between for almost a year. But when his look-a-like project with the NSA began to fall behind, Burke came out of the shadows and spoke with Dr. Hayes virtually every day. More than once Dr. Hayes expressed his disdain with Burke's tactics and bemoaned his stupidity for allowing himself to be entrapped in Burke's never-ending story. When Dr. Hayes was forced out of his research lab into Burke's look-alike lab, he indicated this was the last straw. Reg said a few days ago Dr. Hayes began talking about trying to find a way out of his so-called contract. He even suggested going to jail was better than being a prisoner in his own laboratory, unable to make even the smallest decisions without Burke's approval.

Manny broke in. "Was Mr. Burke aware of this?"

"Not that I know. I was supposed to report anything out of the ordinary, but I decided after Dr. Hayes, and I were forced to attend Ms. Rice's autopsy I would selectively omit any reference to Dr. Hayes's growing displeasure with the whole situation. Also, Burke was becoming paranoid about not being able to finish the stem cell treatments of his look-alike cronies in time for the next G8 economic summit."

Questioning shifted back to EJ. "How much did Dr. Hayes know about Burke's look-a-like project?"

"From our conversations in the laboratory, I think all Dr. Hayes knew was that he and Dr. Lancaster's stem cells were being used to treat Secretaries to the G8 Ministers to make them more productive for a longer period. I think if Dr. Hayes would have known that two of the real Secretaries had been replaced he would have gone straight to the police, that's just the kind of guy he was."

"What became of the real secretaries?"

"One thing I learned early on was not to ask questions, but I know Burke had one of them killed, and if I had to guess, I would guess Alex did the deed."

"What makes you believe Alex was responsible?"

"When Burke made me sign my so-called contract he nodded towards Alex and in so many words let me know what would happen to me if I tried to bail on the contract. Alex just looked at me, smiled, and then cracked his knuckles. Later on, he told me that's what it sounds like when someone's neck breaks. The analogy was not lost on me."

"Do you know of anyone else who may be involved in the look-alike project?"

"Two nurses were part of the treatment team."

"What was their involvement?"

"They were the ones who administered the altered stem cells to Ms. Rice."

"How do you know?"

"Detective, there are some things you just know. They were the only ones who were authorized to remove stem cells from pretreatment storage. A couple of days after Ms. Rice's fourth treatment I was doing our FDA required audit and discovered two ampules of Dr. Hayes's altered stem cells were missing from our primary inventory. It doesn't take a math genius to figure out who removed the cells, and after Ms. Rice died during her fifth treatment, I knew these two gals must've been forced by Burke to substitute the altered cells. A day later we got a memo from HR indicating they were reassigned to an off-campus project in Mexico. I didn't believe it for a minute, and I guess that Alex snuffed them."

Again, Manny chimed in. "Why do you think they gave Ms. Rice the altered cells?"

"Like I said before, Burke was becoming more and more paranoid about not being able to have all the look-alikes through the treatment process in time for the next G8 summit. It started when he asked me what was so unique about the altered cells. He had heard Dr. Hayes's in-house seminar on insertion of protein specific initiator genomes into stem cells. I told him the idea was the possibility of having a stem cell which would make more than one copy of a specific protein. In Dr. Hayes's case, he was trying to produce viable stem cells which could synthesize more insulin using fewer donor cells. The idea being it would take fewer stem cells to cure diabetes."

EJ broke in, "Why is that so important that a girl had to die testing it?"

Reg held up his hands "Whoa, that was not what I was doing. Burke was becoming more and more infatuated with the possibility of speeding up his look-alike project. To that end, he had Dr. Godfrey authorize additional resources for me to insert Dr. Hayes's initiator genome into Dr. Lancaster's stem cells. My initial trials seemed to work. I grew more stem cells for a larger *in vitro* test."

"What happened then? Please skip the hard science and give me the short version."

"To make it short, it took a lot of failures to get secure a positive result on three sequential tests. When I told Burke, he got all excited and asked me to grow enough cells for a single FDA approved volunteer human test. When I suggested the test needed to repeat, at least, two more times, he said okay, but at the same time he wanted me to grow enough cells for the test so if and when my research trials validated the protocol, the cells would be ready."

Manny became more interested and asked, "Is that the way things are always done? It seems it's a cart-before-the-horse method."

"Not at all. It takes so long to grow these cells that we often produce more cells than we need and freeze the unused ones. What I didn't know until it was too late was Burke was making arrangements to test these modified cells in a patient without her knowledge.

Manny continued, "How did that happen? Don't you guys have safety protocols to prevent cutting off the wrong leg?"

"Yes, we do. But let me finish and I will try to answer your question." Reg continued, "When I set up the first set of validation protocols, twenty tests were positive, and one was negative. Basic science demands the validation needed to be repeated at least two more times."

"Is it normal to do that many tests?"

"Yes, the FDA suggests when we submit data we provide two consecutive sets of positive data. When I told Burke we had a single failure, he asked what failed. When I said to him in the failed test cell division sort of went berserk, forming tight colonies growing on top of each other. The generation time was much faster, indicating growth out of control. His suggestion surprised me."

"And why is that?"

"Usually, he tries to jump ahead. But this time, he seemed concerned that I repeat the tests until I was satisfied we could predict how the modified stem cells would react. After about a week of successful trials, I thought it would be a good idea to test some of the original modified cells we grew up for a possible human test. When I went into cryogenic storage, the cells were gone.

EJ interrupted again, "What do you mean ... gone? Can't you guys keep track of anything over there?"

"I knew where they went. I checked the cell registry it looked like Dr. Hayes authorized the treatment team to remove the cells for the NSA project. Dr. Hayes had given me specific instructions to use those cells to develop an FDA protocol for possible human testing, so I asked the lead tech from the treatment team to show me the storage logs indicating where the cells were stored."

"Where are they now?"

"I was told the cells had been administered to an FDA-approved human protocol volunteer and that Dr. Hayes' team would be following the patient's progress. It wasn't until the autopsy of Ms. Rice I realized what Burke had done. When I went to confront the treatment team, I was told the two nurses had been transferred to our clinic in Mexico to continue the testing of Dr. Lancaster's modified stem cells on a group of volunteers from Mexico. I still tried to follow up on the nurses but hit a stone wall."

Manny asked, "What do you mean?"

"They just disappeared. I was even unable to find any record of our so-called sister clinic in Mexico. It was at this time I began to be frightened of Burke. His intensity and paranoia were going off scale. He would call and ask questions wanting information at all hours of the day and night. That answers your why question, and, no, I did not ever confront Burke on this matter."

"By the way, how did Burke purge all of the information about Maxine and her death?"

"He planned to use the same Mexico set up to ensnare the assistant to the clinic's IT Director, but when he died in an accident, Burke suggested a replacement and told Dr. Godfrey to hire him. I assumed Alex had a hand in the crash."

Manny closed his folder and stood up. "Thank you, we are through for now but will have more questions tomorrow. In the meantime, you are being held as a material witness."

EJ followed suit and nodded to the police officer who had patiently stood by the door all this time. "Officer, would you see that Mr. Horn gets some breakfast? Also, he is not to be housed with the general population." EJ then followed Manny out of the interrogation room and down the hall to the break room where they discovered fresh donuts and coffee all set up for the morning shift. "Manny, I think it's time to call it a day."

Manny rubbed his eyes and yawned. "It's almost 7 o'clock. I believe that it would be prudent for us to grab some shut-eye before we meet with the kids this evening."

"You're preaching to the choir. Let's get out of here. I think your suitcases are still in the back of my patrol car. Why don't you come home with me and crash on our extra bed? I can guarantee a good hot breakfast."

"No argument here. In case, I forget it in the morning, thanks for the offer." EJ then tucked his sheath of file folders into his desk drawer and headed for the parking lot with Manny in tow. "Well, what do you think?"

"I believe we pulled off a good piece of police work today."

"It would have been better if we hadn't lost Dr. Hayes, but still we tied up a lot of loose ends today."

Chapter Seventy-one

T he smell of freshly perked coffee and simmering bacon penetrated Mike's consciousness. The last thing he remembered was leaning back and thinking how comfortable a lumpy futon feels when you're exhausted. Sitting up returned Mike to the present. Intermingled with the wonderful smells of breakfast was a whisper of Jasmine. This intriguing scent came from the Afghan hanging loosely around his shoulders. *I don't remember this from last night, but it smells just like Steff.* Mike's enjoyment of the moment was cut short by Steff's cheerfulness.

"Good morning sunshine. I thought you would sleep all day. How do you like your eggs?"

"If that's bacon I smell I would like mine over easy, but just two eggs, please." Standing proved to be a little bit tricky after spending the night scrunched into the confines of the small futon. "What time is it?"

"A little past ten. You were asleep a solid eight hours. I laid out a couple of fresh towels. If you're quick about it, there is time for a shower before breakfast."

"Thanks." Mike hobbled down the short hallway and disappeared into the bathroom.

Breakfast seemed like a feast topped off with the last two slices of pepperoni pizza from the previous night. The silence of the morning's routine was broken from time to time with small talk. Neither Mike nor Steff wanted to broach the subject of yesterday's carnage, much less the specter of Peter's death and the discovery of Max's murder. This troika of events was the unassuming elephant occupying most of the apartment.

Steff soon decided it was incumbent on her to at least acknowledge the elephant. "Mike, how did you figure out Burke killed Max as part of his diabolic experiment? I don't need all the details; just give me the salient points."

"I guess it all started when I called and talked to Dan Granger about the mysterious autopsy Peter and Reg witnessed with Burke. After that disturbing call, I dug around a little bit in the clinic's records. It seemed odd to me that an outside pathologist would be called in to do what was purported to be a routine autopsy. A quick check of the Diener's online records listed three deaths on that day. Two were from the hospital's cancer wing, and one from the clinic. Remember how we were unable to find any information about Maxine from the clinic's records? Whoever purged those records was unfamiliar with how the hospital and its associated clinics process a patient's death. When Dan picked up Max's body, she was assigned a tracking number which he wrote on the bottom of her left foot, using a permanent marker. As part of the protocol, Dan takes a series of identification photographs of the decedent's face, unusual markings, like Max's Maltese Cross and the number on the bottom of her foot. These photos are sequentially numbered and downloaded to Dan's computer. The bad news is that whoever hacked the clinic's computer was able to remove the photographs from Dan's computer. The good news is that the master sequential number file is not stored in the cloud. With Dan's help, I was able to retrieve Max's tracking number and two accompanying photographs from Dan's tablet. The hacker missed these because Dan turns off his tablet every night. He's a bit paranoid about hackers, which worked well for us. You saw one of them; the other was of her tattoo."

"So are you telling me you had suspicions almost from the very beginning?"

"Yes, and I'm sorry I didn't tell you, but I wanted to be sure."

"What else are you not telling me?"

"Just the part about what I learned while we were kidnapped."

"And what might that be?"

"When Burke gave me the autopsy file and demanded I tell him why this patient died, I had no idea it was Max's autopsy report until I saw Dan's tracking number. While I was trying to slow things down to give Manny more time to find us, I read the report line by line, highlighting important points. It didn't take very long to realize. Max's stem cell treatment was not what Peter had recommended. It took a while to figure out why, after over a hundred successful stem cell treatments for diabetes, one went completely awry. Fortunately, Burke had chosen a very thorough pathologist; otherwise, there wouldn't have been any DNA marker tests performed on her tissue samples."

"Whoa, slow down. What you mean DNA marker tests?"

"Marker tests are used to identify specific stem cell lines and, in Peter's and my case, we had two non-convergent cell lines which we happened to name cell line 01 and cell line 02."

"It seems you guys lack imagination."

"Not really, just wanted to keep it simple. I think the question you want me to answer is, are these cell lines safe. The short answer is cell line 01 has been tested in volunteers over a hundred times with few or no side effects; however, cell line number two is still in what we call phase three testing."

"What does that mean?"

"The cells are available for very limited, well-documented human volunteer studies, usually ten or fewer individuals, and not approved for anyone who had or are to receive cell line 01. The FDA requires we test only one variable at a time."

"Makes sense, but why does it matter now?"

"Max's lab tests indicated she had received both cell line 01 and cell line 02. Also, the DNA test found an extra marker in cell line 02 which meant it was modified before it was given to Max or it mutated after Max received the cells. As soon as I read about these markers, the odd histology began to make sense. I remembered Peter had been doing a lot of work on modifications to cell line 02 about that time, and a lot of his tests were going haywire."

"I'm not sure what you're getting at."

"For most of yesterday afternoon, I was sure Peter was involved up to his neck since he was the only one in the world doing research on genetic augmentation of cell line 02."

"Wasn't Peter your very best friend?"

"Yes, and I still can't believe he had anything to do with Max's death. I sure hope Manny and EJ will have some answers to validate what Peter told us just before they took him to the helo pad."

"I'm sure if there's truth in what Peter said, Manny will be able to find it. It will be interesting to know if any of the guys they arrested yesterday can shed any light on your conundrum."

"There's a big part of me which knows Peter would not do anything evil. Couple that with the fact that he was the last person I expected to see come bursting through the door yesterday, and I'm pretty sure Peter was not involved. What puzzles me is how did those cells get from Peter's laboratory into Max. That's a question I hope Manny answers this afternoon.

Steff reached over and brushed back a tuft of Mike's unruly hair. "I'm with you. If Peter was even half the man you told me he is, then the truth will show him not to be a bad guy."

"Thank you. Your confidence means a lot to me." Before Mike could say anything else, Steff's cell phone rang.

"It's Manny. Hi, what's going on? ... Yes, we are looking forward to meeting this afternoon. ... What time? ... Okay, we'll meet at Max's apartment at two. TTFN."

"What on earth is TTFN?"

"Dear boy, did you ever read Winnie the Pooh?"

"I had almost forgotten. I think it means Ta Ta For Now?"

"I'm glad to see there's more stuff inside that big brain of yours than biochemistry."

"I hope you find more things to surprise you, but now I need to get my car and go back to my apartment to shave and get clean clothes. Shall I pick you up, say at 1:15? That should give us enough time in case the traffic's heavy."

"TTFN." Steff's warm smile and twinkling eyes escorted Mike out the door. In fact, they carried him for the next couple of hours. After a cab ride back to Max's apartment to pick up his car, Mike drove back to his apartment.

Chapter Seventy-two

For Mike, the next couple of hours seemed to whiz by as he busied himself with previously unattended domestic chores. While shaving, he spent an inordinate amount of time playing with the front part of his cowlick, flipping it up and down trying to remember how Steff just flipped it up and somehow made it stay put. *I still can't believe how someone so gentle could have dispatched Alex and made it look easy. I hope she feels the way I'm beginning to feel - oh come on Michael be realistic, she's way out of your league, but she does seem to like me - I guess time will tell. Oh – oh, I'd better get on the stick, or I will be late to pick her up.* Mike quickly finished shaving, jumped into clean clothes and headed to Steff's apartment.

"Well, all I can say is you scrub up pretty good," Steff smiled as she buckled her seat belt.

"Thank you. I wasn't sure you would remember how I looked yesterday. But honestly, I feel a lot better. You need to make any stops on the way to Max's apartment?"

"Nothing I can think of. Let's get on with it. My mind has been spinning the last several hours, and I need Manny and EJ to fill in a lot of blanks."

As Michael eased into the early afternoon traffic, he glanced over and saw Steff staring at him. "What are you looking at?"

"I don't know. You just look different - uh, I mean different, in a good way. You seem more confident than you did yesterday. That new look becomes you."

"Well, I guess in more than one way I am a very different

person today than I was yesterday. Yesterday my world hinged around stem cells, Peter, writing reports, and lots and lots of busy work. While I was cleaning up my apartment this morning, I realized there is a lot of stuff I need to clear out of my life. I now understand more about how you felt when you lost Max. If her death changed you as much as Peter's death has already changed me, then I think we're both different people. In some ways, we're probably better people, and before you say anything, I like who you are."

Steff's forehead wrinkled a bit, "There are times when I talk way too much. I think this is one of those times I should not talk but just agree with you. If you would've asked me a week ago if I could have had any feelings other than anger towards you and Peter I would've laughed you to scorn. It's amazing what a few days can do when you have a chance to see truth in operation. But now just a short week later I can say I very much like you."

The sirens of a passing fire truck broke up the growing intimacy of the conversation. Realizing they were both walking on unfamiliar ground, they retreated to the safety of stilted chit-chat. Periods of silence gave them time to digest what they had just exchanged.

The emotional agony of the short trip to Max's apartment soon ended as Mike pulled into the parking lot next to EJ's unmarked police car.

Manny and EJ had already settled into two somewhat uncomfortable chairs against the north wall of the apartment's minimalistic atrium. As Mike and Steff entered, EJ was the first to stand up and greet them.

"You kids are a sight for sore eyes. There was a time yesterday when I wasn't sure we were going to see you again. Pardon the apparent lack of concern for my partner, he drank too much police coffee last night and turned into a zombie." With an infectious grin, EJ extended his hand and pulled Manny up from the chair.

"Don't listen to him he's just jealous because I got an hour of sleep. Come on, let's go on up. I know you kids have a hundred questions. I just hope we have a hundred and one answers." Like a couple of junior high boys, Manny and EJ managed to make getting into the elevator a humorous task.

Before opening Max's apartment, Steff turned and handed

Mike the key. "Go ahead; I can't bring myself to open the door. The last time I did, I ended up strapped to a couch."

"No problem, I'll open it." Mike turned to Steff and with a mischievous grin retorted, "But I'll let Manny and EJ go in first; after all they have guns." Mike pushed open the door and followed the guys, with Steff close behind. "My memory is a bit fuzzy, but everything appears to be where it was just before I felt a needle-stick in my neck. No, wait a moment our computers and packs are gone. The kidnappers must have taken them. What about you, Steff?"

"I'm still a bit fuzzy and, unfortunately, short on details. How about I make some tea, and we sit down? I'm dying to hear what you guys found out."

Soon the four of them had settled down around Max's small dining room table. After few sips of sweetened Earl Grey, Before Manny began retelling the epic of the last few days, he told the kids their stuff was found in the clinic's office unharmed. "EJ has agreed to get each of you a copy of the police report and get your laptops and files back. That being said, I'm afraid I will not be able to give you anything in writing about the NSA's involvement in all of this. You may take all the notes you want with the following two stipulations: First, you cannot use me as a quotable source, and secondly, you can only use the information you can verify outside of the NSA's involvement. Steff, the stipulations are primarily for you, since I know you're going to run to Harry in the morning and pitch this as an exposé for Channel 7 News."

"Are you telling me this as an NSA agent, or as my Godfather?"

"I know you, and your father were both cut from the same cloth, so I guess I'm speaking as your Godfather. Just make sure anything you report is verified outside of this meeting. "

"You make it sound like you're going to reveal national secrets or something similar. Oh my goodness, we are going to hear some pretty heavy stuff, aren't we?"

"Not super heavy but nevertheless a genuine threat to national security, or more accurately the safety of the world banking system. Don't worry about not being able to publish any juicy details, EJ's police report will have everything you need, and I believe if you play your cards right you might even get a Pulitzer nomination."

Steff flipped open her notebook, "I doubt that will happen in my lifetime. Let's get on with it!"

"Before we begin I want to say that this was not the way our Hansel and Gretel sting was supposed to play out. But I have to say Mike left a clear trail of crumbs; otherwise, the wicked witch would have got you two. Well done Mike, well done!"

EJ and Steff chimed in with grins and a brief round of polite applause. Mike began to blush, "That's enough; let's get on with what you guys know, I'm dying to close the book on Burke."

Over the next two hours and two more pots of Earl Grey tea, Manny and EJ untangled the web so carefully laid by Burke. Apparently, Clive Burke, acting as the chief secretary and confidant to the British Minister to the G8 banking system, began planning a way to take over the system shortly after his appointment as head of the group of Secretaries. His greed and avarice were fueled by a long string of hostile bank takeovers, which made him part of the Nuevo-rich, and bank stockholders became poor. It should take the Brits, at least, a couple of years to sort it all out.

Manny, looking across the table at Mike, "You got pulled into this saga by being in the right place and at the right time to save the life of one of Burke's colleagues. Remember a couple of years ago when you and Peter used one of your stem cell lines to save that Brit who was brought to your clinic experiencing multi-organ failure?"

"So that's when it all began. Peter and I were both surprised how well he responded. To be honest, we thought he was a dead man walking, so infusing him with active antigen neutral stem cells might work, but if it didn't, well, you know, he would have died either way soon."

Steff leaned over, and while refilling Manny's cup, asked. How did the NSA get involved in all of this?"

"The real answer is that Burke was able to convince several high-ranking G8 officials the value of keeping their executive secretaries healthy and hopefully prolonging their lives was the smart thing to do. Remember, the actual power in the G8 banking system lies in the hands of the bureaucratic executive secretaries whose appointments transcend in some cases a dozen or more ministers. Burke's plan was simple enough: have all eight Secretaries processed through the clinic. The downside was the Secretaries had to be in public on a regular basis and, to keep the stem cell treatments secret the G8 leaders decided to ask the NSA for assistance. The NSA brain bust, I mean brain trust, came up with the idea of using look-alikes while the real Secretaries were taking the stem cell treatments. It was an excellent idea, but since the NSA is good at thinking of things to do, but not so good at following up on things. So they basically gave Burke a blank check. No thought or consideration of the possibility that anyone would hijack the real look-alikes and replace them with their cronies was never discussed. Well to make this long story short, Burke built the shadow clinic, sequestered and killed the NSA selected look-alikes, replaced them with his own, and almost pulled it off."

Steff looked up from her notes. "Almost?"

At this point, EJ began filling in the gaps in Burke's almost perfect plan. "Steff, it was the death of your two friends Max and Anne which started dominoes falling. Burke's desire to speed up the stem cell treatments led him to inject Max with unproven stem cells which we now know carry a lethal gene. Burke is apparently superb at planning when he has ample time but doesn't do too well on the fly. He rapidly set in motion an ill-conceived plan to cover-up Max's death. We now know how well that went. The second domino to fall was when your friend Anne shared her doubts about her friend Brad. Fortunately, Burke did not know she talked with you; otherwise, you would probably have also been killed."

"So Burke killed Anne?"

"Not Burke himself. You've already met the person who murdered her: Alex, the guy who used his Taser on you."

"Had I known then, I would have hit him at least twice more."

Mike jumped out of his chair, leaned over, and put his hand on EJ's arm. "You should have seen her! I didn't think Steff could even pick up one of those metal chairs much less cold cock the guerrilla with it."

Steff began blushing, "Don't get all mushy, it was pure adrenaline."

Looking Steff straight in the eye, Mike whispered softly, "I am confident he would have killed me had you not taken him down."

Again, standing upright and grinning ear to ear, he pointed his finger at Steff. "Remind me never to cross her, especially if she has a Taser in her purse." A round of laughter and head nodding broke the growing tension of reliving yesterday's brush with eternity.

EJ continued, "The moment I saw the crime scene I knew Anne did not fall down the stairs, but I will admit Mr. Alex did a professional job. We could find nothing which would have tied Alex or Burke to her death. And, had Alex not confessed, Anne's death would've ended up in Denver's cold case archives."

Steff looked up from her notepad. "When did he confess?"

"Last night between Manny and my first and second cups of coffee. So far he's copped to at least eleven, including both Amy and Brad. He still swears he had nothing to do with what happened to Max and is willing to testify against Burke."

Before EJ could continue, Mike took over the conversation. "Well, we know from the autopsy report Burke made me determine Max's death as from was genetically altered stem cells from Peter's lab. Have you guys been able to find anything which can corroborate what he told me yesterday before he died? Help me prove Peter was not a murderer?"

EJ looked across the table at Manny. "Your turn. You're the one's who has been tracking the stem cells and look-alikes."

"When we finished questioning Alex last night, we spent two more cups of terrible coffee talking with Reg Horn, who also was very helpful and forthright about his involvement. It seems Burke would select someone he felt would further his cause, and then arrange for them to win a free ten-day vacation in Mexico. As Reg explained, part of the vacation package included a thousand dollars of casino chips. To make a long story short, the casino would allow the mark to have a hot winning streak, followed by a devastating losing streak. A judicious sprinkling of the right drug greased the skids until one or more large IOUs were signed. In Reg's case, his IOUs were over $25,000. That's when Alex, the gorilla, approached Reg with an offer he couldn't refuse."

This time, Mike looked up from his notes. "And what couldn't he refuse?

"A benefactor was willing to pay off his IOUs, put $100,000 in an offshore bank account, and then pay him five grand a month."

"And what did Reg have to do to buy back his soul?"

"Here's where things get a little cagey. He was to prepare for his benefactor, who turned out to be Burke, a summary of everything which happened in Peter's laboratory every week. Alex explained the benefactor was not interested in stealing Peter's research for publication. All he wanted was to keep track of Peter's research. Reg said he wasn't sure he wanted to sell out Peter's research, but the alternative would require his parents to buy a tombstone.

Mike shook his head, "Never in the thousand years would I have guessed Reg was a bad guy. During his first two years, he moved from being a staff technician to basically running Peter's lab."

Manny continued, "According to Mr. Horn, the driving force behind his advancement was a continuous threat of bodily harm from Burke. Apparently, Mr. Burke is an expert in communication by innuendo. Reg indicated he never heard a direct threat from Burke or Alex, but each of his visits to Burke's enclave east of Denver ended with a carefully constructed veiled threat along with an admonition to get closer to Peter. Mr. Horn also became very wealthy during this time since Burke handsomely rewarded Reg for each advancement."

"Did Reg admit to any harm he may have predicated on Peter?"

"He did indicate, as soon as the shadow clinic began operation, he continuously siphoned off small batches of your Phoenix stem cells. Apparently, he was pretty sneaky about it because no one had any idea of what was going on. When I pressed Reg for how he pulled it off, he indicated it was just a small hiccup in the accounting system. When cells were harvested and cryogenically frozen, he simply shorted each vial one or two percent and logged the difference as transfer loss. His impeccable laboratory technique allowed him to maintain high cell counts during transfer, thereby camouflaging his pilferage."

"What was he doing with my cells?"

They were delivered to the shadow clinic. How did you think Burke and the NSA were able to maintain active and homogeneous cultures of your stem cells?"

Rubbing his chin, Mike mused, "I hadn't given it much thought. My assumption was Director Godfrey provided cells from critical storage. Samples of both my and Peter's stem cells were sent out on a regular basis to all sorts of research facilities."

"You're partially right; Director Godfrey did provide initial research samples to the NSA. But to maintain cell stocks Burke used Reg's weekly samples to bolster his inventory.

Mike made a note in the margin of his notebook to take a look at how the clinic handles inventory.

Manny glanced over at Mike, On a side note, apparently, your Director had full and unfettered knowledge of the NSA shadow clinic and was complicit in the considerable research grant you and Peter were awarded. The bad news is that your grant came from Burke's war chest. As soon as he got wind of the unexpected healing of one of the G8 Secretaries by your stem cells, he set his nefarious plan into motion. He knew from discussions with Director Godfrey you and Peter would not work for him directly, nor for that matter, the NSA. So what better way to get you boys on board than to give you a fifty million dollar grant to do research on the very same stem cells he wanted to use on his G8 doubles? He just set up a paper foundation to pass the money to your stem cell clinic."

"Are you telling me Peter and I were given this grant to further Burke's ambitions and not for our research accomplishments?"

"Yeah, I guess so. Why is it so important?"

"Peter and I thought we received the grant because of the importance of our research to the scientific community. Now you're telling me the whole grant thing was a sham."

"Mike, I want you to take a deep breath and think about the reality you have here. When I was doing background research on the clinic, I discovered that between you and Peter you guys were publishing, at least, eight peer-reviewed articles a year each along with a dozen or more abstracts. My friends in academia tell me your level of research is phenomenal. Remember; the grant gave you guys complete autonomy in the laboratory, so don't hand me any of that sham crap. Besides, I understand there is still a bit over thirty million left in the directed trust which funded your grant."

"Yeah, we did do a lot of good research, but…"

Steff broke in. "Don't give us any buts. You and Peter have done a phenomenal job, and you owe it to Peter to finish the job

317

you and he started. So don't even think about quitting."

"Okay, but ..."

"There you go again, no if and or buts."

"What I'm trying to say is there's a big void to fill. Peter and I were a real team. I don't think I can fill his shoes. In fact, I know I can't fill his shoes."

"There you go again, trying to get the cart before the horse." Steff placed her hand on Mike's arm and looked him in the eye. What you need to do is to look at this as one of your research projects. Assess your past accomplishments and see how they can lead to future achievements. Sure Peter will be missed, but I'll bet they're more than one or two sharp young scientists out there who would jump at the opportunity to pick up where he left off. You're not responsible for finishing Peter's research any more than he was responsible for completing your research. However, as Peter's friend and colleague, I think its well within your purview to guide a new team to carry out his research and to do so without shortchanging your Phoenix Project, which I personally think has a real chance to get the attention of the Nobel Prize people.

Chapter Seventy-three

Six months later . . .

M ike's mind was taken back to a similar setting when he and Peter received the considerable grant to continue their work on adult stem cells and, in particular, to continue their Phoenix Project by developing specialized stem cell to cure specific diseases. As before, the auditorium was full, with interns standing along the outside walls. A quick glance to his left assured him this was not a dream. "Well, Steff, today's the big day, or, as Peter used to say, today is today, there'll be none like it ever again."

"I think Peter would be pleased with what you're doing today. I can't think of a better tribute to Peter's memory than to name the clinic in his honor

"I'm not sure it would have been possible without your news stories about Peter's bravery and the clinic's research."

Steff retrieved a cream-colored business sized letter from her thin shoulder bag and started to turn towards Mike, when her phone vibrated. The text from Manny read 'Congrats on Mike's big show tonight. When things calm down have him give me a call, I need to ask him what he knows about a stem cell line known as *Ambrosia Serum. Hugs . . . M'.* Steff texted back 'Still all business with you - OK and tx.' Closing her bag she leaned towards Mike.

"I was going to save this for after the banquet tonight, but if I don't show you, I think I'll explode." Steff handed Mike the envelope. "Go ahead, open it."

Ignoring the humdrum of activity around him, Mike opened the envelope and unfolded the crisp linen letter. *Dear Ms. Steffen-Huffman, The Pulitzer committee is pleased to inform you your four-part investigative series titled "**The Murder of Max, A Conspiracy of Silence**" is the recipient of this year's Pulitzer Prize in the category of <u>Breaking News Reporting</u>. A member of our staff will be contacting you shortly with specific details concerning your award.* ... Mike almost tipped over his chair as he turned toward Steff. "You've got to be kidding me! The Pulitzer!"

"I picked up it up on the way over here. No one at the station knows about it yet. When I thought about all the people I should tell, I wanted you to be the first to know. I'll call Dad, Manny, and the others tonight."

Ignoring the fact he was on a stage in front of a huge crowd Mike jumped up and gave Steff a quick kiss and a gentle bear hug. "Thank you for letting me know first. Now we both have something special to remember this day by, your Pulitzer and the dedication of the Peter Franklin Hayes Research Center. Wow, who would've ever guessed? A Pulitzer!"

"Come on now, don't get all mushy on me. You need to concentrate on your speech and the next fifteen minutes."

Mike settled back in his chair, fidgeting with the half-dozen pages of his upcoming speech. *Peter, this is what you are good at, you know, public speaking. Wow, I must be losing it. I don't often talk to dead people, but I guess today's a good exception. Boy, I wish you were here today. By the way, in case you didn't know, Burke lost most of his fortune and was found guilty by the Brits for the murder of the Phoenix look-a-likes at their Consulate House. If he ever gets out of prison, he'll be sent back to the States to stand trial for your murder, and five US citizens.* The growing quietness pulled Mike back from his thoughts.

After a couple of minutes of platitudes and introductory remarks, Mike found himself standing in front of the microphone. A quick glance downward assured him page one of his speech was actually on top. "Ladies and gentlemen, colleagues and friends, today we gather to dedicate this state-of-the-art clinic to my colleague and lifelong friend Peter Franklin Hayes ...

Epilogue

B urke took his turn in the prison's commons area for his one-hour recess from solitary. The chair was utilitarian and a horrid shade of mauve. He chose this hour so he could watch the National BBC News Hour. The lead story broke the silence.

"Good evening. Let's go to a developing story from America, involving our Consulate Retreat Center near Denver, Colorado, We thank Channel 7 News of Denver for this tape."

"Good evening, this Dave Freeman, from News 7 with a developing story. Firefighters responded to a fire at an estate near Evergreen. For breaking details let's go to Connie Madison reporting from the scene. Connie, what have you learned?"

"About an hour ago local firefighters were able to quickly extinguish a fire located inside the main building of the British Consulate's retreat center outside of Evergreen. The blaze was discovered by Adrian Bowman, a local Private Investigator hired by the Consulate to check on the house and grounds. We were able to learn the previous resident of the Center was Clive Andrew Burke III, who was recently convicted of charges surrounding the Phoenix Conspiracy, a story, which was first reported by our own Stephanie Huffman. Now over to Jess, who has Mr. Bowman."

"Thank you, Connie. Mr. Bowman, tell us what you saw when you discovered the blaze."

"Thank you. I was making my daily inspection of the Consulate buildings when I smelled smoke. A quick search revealed a fire burning in a closet off the master bedroom. The small extinguisher by the door was ineffective, so I called 911."

"Were there any belongings in the closet?'

"Yes, there was a large collection of hats. I do not know my hats very well, but I think they were fedoras. This collection was the hobby of the former resident. I believe that, even though he remains in custody in the UK, his lawyers had made arrangements to move the entire collection back to Britain next week. I feel sorry for the guy. There must have been over a hundred hats in there. They must have been valuable since some were even in glass cases."

"Thank you, Mr. Bowman." Turning toward the camera, "A local fire official indicated the entire contents of the closet were destroyed. Now, back to you Connie."

THE END

ABOUT THE AUTHOR

Joe A Bowden and his wife Elaine lived in Southwest Colorado for forty years before moving to Montana, to be near much of their extended family. Dr B, as his students knew him, is a biochemist, former university professor, storyteller, poet, and technical writer. He is currently settling into semi-retirement by writing stories for all ages. He has produced hundreds of technical documents and reports, edited and published technical books. He has recently published in cookbooks, guidebooks, magazines, and anthologies. As a father and grandfather 'Papa Joe, Ph.D.'s keen sense of mystery and technical background make science-based fiction come alive.

For the past 25 years Dr B has written and served as editor for *The Southwest Scribe,* the newsletter of the Southwest Christian Writers Association

Dr B is a member of the American Christian Fiction Writers (ACFW); Southwest Christian Writers Association, ACFW-Colorado Western Slope Chapter, and the Society of Children's Book Writers and Illustrators, Montana Chapter.

Readers are welcomed to connect with Dr B at www.joebowden.com or http://www.southwestchristianwriters.com/joe-bowden

BOOK SERIES

Michael Lancaster – Stephanie Huffman Mysteries
Joe A Bowden PhD

Book One:
Joe Bowden PhD   *Murder by Stem Cells – The Phoenix Project – A Conspiracy of Silence*

Book Two:
Joe Bowden PhD   *An Unwitting Murder – The Ambrosia Serum – A Painful Truth*

SOCIAL MEDIA:

Facebook: Joe A. Bowden
Twitter: JoeBowd43343177.
Website: joebowden.com
Pinterest: Joe Bowden
Goodreads: via Facebook
Google+: papajoephd@gmail.com
Linked: cdsenviro@frontier.net

Made in the USA
Middletown, DE
28 August 2021